I0591500

THE
FAVORITE

THE
FAVORITE
THE DADIRRI SAGA 02

TY CARLSON

4 Horsemen
Publications, Inc.

The Favorite
The Dadirri Saga Book 2
Copyright © 2022 Ty Carlson. All rights reserved.

4 Horsemen
Publications, Inc.

4 Horsemen Publications, Inc.
1497 Main St. Suite 169
Dunedin, FL 34698
4horsemenpublications.com

info@4horsemenpublications.com

Cover and typesetting by 4 Horsemen Publications, Inc.
Editor Laura Mita

Library of Congress Control Number: 2022942211

Audio ISBN: 978-1-64450-678-3
Ebook ISBN: 978-1-64450-679-0
Print ISBN: 978-1-64450-680-6

DEDICATION:

To my mom—I always knew I really was your favorite. And to Finley, Asher, Ellis, and Kipton—you really are *my* favorites. But don't tell anyone.

TABLE OF CONTENTS

ACKNOWLEDGEMENTS:

First and foremost to my wife, who listened intently while I explained crazy theories about the characters in this book and hid her looks of disapproval when I went off the rails. Next, to my kids, who provide endless excitement that weaves its way into my stories. To my mom, who may not read my books but helped shape me into the father and husband I am today. Then, I'd be a terrible friend if I didn't acknowledge the members of my writing group Abby and Scott, both of whom are ingenious writers and gave invaluable feedback throughout this process. Thank you, Laura and Jen, for making this story even better with your edits and recommendations. And finally, thank you to you, the reader. Writing stories is all well and good, of course, but without someone to share them with, they're just words on a page.

CHAPTER 1

June sunlight danced across the sandy blonde hair of the five-year-old in the backseat who sat blissfully unaware of the dread weight that seized the two adults in the front. One of my hands clenched the steering wheel while the other was clasped tightly by the woman in the passenger seat. Her eyes were red, and her cheeks shone wet with the trails of recent tears.

My name is Grant Taldo, and at this point, I was driving my only son to school, while his mother—and my wife—worried herself sick in the passenger seat next to me.

Jackson, the sandy blond in the back, sat contentedly in his booster seat staring out the window with a whimsical smile gracing his round little face, still a little baby fat clinging to his cheeks. I couldn't help but glance in the rearview mirror every few seconds, which made watching the morning school traffic more than a little tedious.

With my mind distracted, I couldn't hear much of what he was saying, but I knew the last thing I wanted to do was give away that I was terrified. My heart was beating out of my chest, and my stomach felt like a twisting knot of eels. But I answered his questions—sometimes nonsensical—with a dutiful "Oh really?" or the other classic response, "Wow, that's crazy, buddy." Jackson didn't notice, surprisingly. His biggest concern was whether or not his kindergarten friend would bring an orange for lunch again. That was good. He didn't need to know that his parents had just received devastating news. Well, devastating for one of us. No, that wasn't fair. Both. It was devastating for us both.

I could feel my throat tighten as my mind wavered between the upcoming appointment and some other subject Jackson raised. I did my best to avoid it, but what's a dad to do but stare at his son and try to drink in every last detail? I was sentimental this morning.

I noticed Kathryn, my wife and best friend, wipe a tear from her eye as she sniffed and stared out the window. She had been so sweet when I got the call the previous evening from Northwest Regional Hospital. The kind nurse on the phone said that the tests had come back with some suspicious results, and Dr. Keller wanted to discuss them with us.

Suspicious results.

We knew what that meant. We knew what they were testing for. We knew what the results showed. The twinge I'd felt several weeks ago in my groin was something more than just a sore muscle or a random nerve misfiring. I didn't want to believe it; I was barely thirty.

When I pulled into the school parking lot, I glanced back once more. The sun landed on Jackson's smile just so. He turned his eyes to meet mine in the mirror, and I smiled to keep the tears at bay.

His smile faltered, but I winked at him, and he went back to looking out the window. Then, when he hopped out, I said, "I love you buddy. Mommy will pick you up from school today."

Kathryn turned to look at him over her shoulder and added, "Yep, I'll see you in a little while, baby."

He nodded and said, "Love you, Mommy and Daddy." Then he hesitated a second longer before closing the door and walking into the school.

He knew. Even with our colossal efforts to hide it from him, he knew something was off.

I took a deep breath as we pulled away from the school and pointed our way toward the hospital. Kathryn rubbed my hand with her thumb and used the other to wipe her tears away, finally releasing the pent-up emotion. Her sobs broke my heart.

I felt tears threaten to wrestle their way from my eyes, but I wanted to be strong. I wanted Kathryn to feel cared for. My mind reeled with the consequences of what was about to take place, what kind of decisions would need to be made and the life that now lay ahead of us all, no doubt shortened as it would be.

I don't really remember arriving, checking in, or waiting to be called back. I withdrew and began making plans. The next thing I remember, actually recall with clarity, was staring at the doctor across from me, stunned.

Cancer.

I felt Kathryn's hand cover mine, but it seemed distant to me. My body was buzzing. If there was a worst-case scenario, this was it. The little bit of preparation we'd had in the last twelve hours wasn't enough to prepare us for this.

"I understand this is not the news you wanted to hear, Grant." The doctor was—blessedly—sitting quietly, now. He wasn't one of those doctors that filled the silence after bad news with solutions in order to make up the difference.

Cancer.

I heard Kathryn sniff beside me, so I looked at her. I tried to paste a reassuring smile on my face, but all I managed to do was make my lip curl up. She was looking back at me, and unshed tears threatened to spill down her cheeks. She would cry. I would cry. But we were both being tough right now.

"What stage is it in?" I managed to croak out of my desert-dry throat.

"It's stage two, technically called a stage two-A Seminoma. It's not the worst case, but it's not the best."

I nodded and stared at the floor. The carpet was an unimaginative, uninteresting gray.

"Would you like to hear your options? We can always schedule a time when things might be easier for you to process."

Kathryn squeezed my hand gently and whispered, "Grant?"

I closed my eyes against the light sting that was growing behind them. The tightness in my throat, as unwelcome as it was, made it hard to swallow, but it gave me a moment to kick the gears in my mind that had ground to a halt. I tried again and held a finger up for him to wait.

"Take all the time you need," he said gently.

The seconds passed in a kind of hazy slowness. I worked my tongue back and forth across the roof of my mouth to try and work up some saliva, but it was no good. The sting in my nose was starting to fade, but that just meant it would come back later.

My first thought was for myself. Call me selfish, but it seemed like all my plans were shot to hell. All the work I'd done, my current projects, my plans for the future of my family. What's that saying? The best laid plans of mice and men—something.

My next thought was for Kathryn. She was now smack dab in the middle of something much larger and scarier than she'd signed up for. She was forced, now, to be a part of this nightmare, forced to see it through to the end. Well, that wasn't true, either. If she wanted to get out, I'd let her.

My final thought was for Jackson. What if all of this went awry? What if, after all the tests, surgeries, and whatever else they'd throw my way—what if after all of it, I ended up unable to recover? Jackson would be left without a father, without someone to teach him about all the things dads are supposed to teach their sons. Oh sure, there are millions of people who grew up without a father to become fully functioning adults. To think of the things I would miss was almost too much to bear. The weight of fatherhood had doubled. Now the time I had to accomplish it all had been, what, halved at best?

When I felt I had a grip on my emotions, I told him to go ahead with options.

"With all the wonders of medicine and technology, cancer treatment hasn't made many gains. There's one, but I'll give it to you last. All of these will depend on the marker levels after surgery to remove the testicle and spermatic cord. Once that is done, we'll run some tests to see what we need to do, but I'll lay them out for you, that way there are limited surprises.

"After surgery, if the marker levels are still high, we can utilize radiation targeted at lymph nodes at the back of the abdomen, called the retroperitoneal lymph nodes. Since this is stage two, generally a higher level of radiation is given.

"Another option is chemotherapy. This would consist of four cycles of something called etoposide and cisplatin, or 'EP.' Or, depending on what side effects you prefer, we can opt for three cycles of those two and bleomycin, or 'BEP.' After those cycles are finished, we would have regular checkups every couple of months. If no cancer returned after a year, we would move to appointments every six months for several years. Of course, that's all well into the future and might change.

"Of course another option—and one I don't recommend—is to do nothing. I will let you know that if we do nothing, the cancer will spread, and it will only get worse for you."

"I don't think we want that," said Kathryn quickly. "I mean, do we, Grant?"

It wasn't fair to her, but at that moment I wasn't sure. It sounded kind of nice to just go on with my life pretending that everything was fine and maybe eventually drop dead when going out for coffee. Living life under the haze of impending death sounded ... unpleasant, however. And there was Jackson to think about, too.

"No. No, I don't want that." I smiled weakly at her.

"There is one other option."

We waited until he continued.

"There's a relatively new treatment that's being rolled out in certain areas of the country. We received the go-ahead earlier this month to begin initiating human trials, and if you're interested, we could of course see if you qualify."

"What is it?" I asked, only mildly curious.

"As someone who deals with the infinite unknown, you might appreciate this a little more."

"Doc, if you're referring to my job, I'm not sure I follow."

He smiled tightly. "I was, yes. There's a new treatment called Bi-Directional Interruptive Anomalism. It's fairly complicated, but so far has had significant positive results in treating patients with the early stages of cancer."

"Still wondering how this works, Doc." My worrying was making me impatient.

"Right. Of course, I apologize. Without getting too deep into the science of it all, a small robot—I don't like the word 'nanobot' but that's what it is—is inserted into the region where the cancer is found. It releases a small gravitic anomaly into the

cancerous cell mass. The anomaly is controlled and monitored by a program here at the hospital. Essentially, a robot uses a minuscule amount of gravity to alter the composition of the cancer cells. What we've found is under this effect, the cancer cells can't continue to grow and eventually die. I'll say again that the explanation is very basic, but that's the gist of it all."

I looked at Kathryn and was sure that my expression reflected her own.

"So ... you're going to shoot a black hole into my balls? No, I don't think I want to do that."

The doctor spread his hands. "Then the decision becomes that much easier. The good news is that this cancer hasn't spread to your other lymph nodes. We can target these testicular spots aggressively and, I truly believe, work toward getting you cancer-free."

But *cancer*.

What a cruel joke. Kathryn and I had just started our family. Jackson was barely five.

I laughed bitterly to myself. Then, "You know, this might explain why we've been having trouble getting pregnant again."

Kathryn didn't laugh. The doctor didn't either, but he did smile in a kind of I'm-sorry-you're-going-through-this way.

"Maybe. But now that we're on the topic, it sounds like you are still wanting to have another child, is that right?"

Kathryn spoke up. Her earlier hesitation had been replaced with a kind of cold, factual voice. It was the one she used after telling her emotions to stay out of the way; the equivalent of "mommy's working" to a toddler.

"Yes. We've been trying for several months. With our first—he's five—we were able to get pregnant fairly quickly, several months or so of not using condoms. But this time, it's been nearly ten months and still nothing. We wanted to have more babies. Well ... one more, at least." A small bit of emotion crept back into her voice at the end, making it shudder unsteadily.

This time the doctor did smile. "Well, the good news is we do have some time. Even if we scheduled the surgery today, you would still have around ten weeks. I would advise you to try as much as you can in the coming weeks. I understand that removing the emotional aspect of a very emotional act can sometimes change our perception of it. But you have time. That's what I'm trying to say. And if we're still not there at the end of those ten weeks, you can always freeze sperm to be used in the future."

Kathryn was nodding, moving into her "planning" stage.

"So you remove my balls, right? That's got to be a lot of fun, just an empty sack hanging between my legs." Probably the wrong thing to be mad about, but I had a right to be angry at a lot of things, I figured.

The doctor smiled apologetically and humored me. "Well at first, yes. We'll only remove a single testicle. You currently have two based on what I've seen."

I nodded.

"Usually the removal of a single testicle doesn't affect fertility. There are cases where infertility occurs after a single testicle is removed, but it's unlikely. If we were removing both, or if you'd already had one removed and we were removing the other, then we'd be discussing infertility options." He waited a heartbeat before continuing. "If it would make you feel better, we can insert a silicone testicle during surgery, so your scrotum remains more or less the same as prior to the surgery."

I smiled coyly at Kathryn and whispered the word "sexy" a little more bitterly than I intended.

She smiled back, but the tears in her eyes echoed the pain I felt in my chest.

Cancer.

"So when do we schedule this thing?" I was already tired of being there. I was tired of the clean smell. I was tired of the unappealing carpet beneath my shoes and the comfortable cushioned seat beneath my ass. I was tired of feeling hope slip away, leaking like a crack in a fish tank. Like the fish in the tank, actually, swimming around a submerged porcelain castle while the water level gets lower and lower, wondering why but content with scraping my belly across the blue neon river stones at the bottom because the water level is so low. Soon, I won't be able to swim at all.

I felt like my belly was scraping the rocks.

"Actually, can we think about this, doc? Can we come back next week?"

My abrupt one-eighty probably surprised him. Probably Kathryn, too. But I had to get out of there.

He saved himself the embarrassment of sputtering a response and simply said, "Oh, by all means! Of course, we can. Just call my office and set it up when it's most convenient for you. I want you to be comfortable with this decision."

I shook his hand and smiled, told him "thank you," and made my way out of the office holding Kathryn's hand.

It would be fine.

I'd be fine.

Fake testicle and all. I'd be alright.

We'd be okay.

If only I knew then what I know now.

CHAPTER 2

The next ten weeks passed by slower than I thought possible. The sun rose, and I dreaded what the evening would bring. It was difficult to even enjoy the time playing with Jackson. He was such an easy kid that it's strange even looking back now and having only a hazy recollection of that time. We'd play, and I'd mourn how much time I had left. It cast a pall over every aspect of my life, and there was nothing I could do. When I wasn't working, I was spending time with my family. Luckily, I'd spoken with my employer and explained what was happening. They gave me plenty of slack in what I was supposed to be doing during this time. It was mostly busy work, anyway.

It didn't help that I imagined the cancer slowly taking over my body in those distant weeks. I knew it wasn't real, that it couldn't spread that fast even in stage four, but there were times when my head would ache or I'd have a sudden spasm in my leg, and I'd immediately think "Is that the *cancer*?" It was terrible. Kathryn was wonderful, of course. Understanding and doing more than was even necessary to ensure my comfort. Before my diagnosis, we had discussed at length what it would look like to continue growing our family. We knew we wanted another child, and cancer didn't change that. So we had a lot of sex. Teenage me would have thought that it was a dream, but over the weeks, it lost a bit of its glamour. It became a means to an end, which was fine. It all turned out fine in the end, I suppose.

There was only one point when we thought we had successfully gotten pregnant. Kat was just over a week late, and the excitement started to build. Kathryn's cycle was like clockwork ever since coming off birth control. Imagine our disappointment when she started her period the next morning. I had a rougher time of it than she did, if I'm being honest. I'd allowed myself to hope... to hope that we could stop working for it.

But nothing comes easy for the Taldos. The tenth week came, and we still weren't pregnant. After a very difficult discussion, we both agreed that maybe it just wasn't meant to be. We both cried that night and researched—briefly—how much it would cost to cryogenically freeze my sperm. Then we cried again. It was far too much.

The only thing left to do was to go in for the surgery that we'd booked the day following that fateful appointment. Besides, there was still a chance that we'd get pregnant after the surgery. A high chance, the doctor said.

We went in. They prepped me. And Kathryn walked alongside my bed until they stopped her from continuing at the large metal doors. She whimpered when they continued on without her.

"You'll be fine, babe. I'll see you when you wake up!" I heard the last bit through the doors just before they closed. My heart was hammering in my chest, and it felt like my legs were on fire. I just stared at the ceiling and the alternating tiles. A lighted panel, a gray panel, light panel, gray. Light. Gray.

Before I even entered the room, they began the IV drip that would knock me out. Just to be sure, they gave me a facemask with nitrous as well. They asked me to count down from ten, and the last thing I remember was saying the number seven.

When I woke up, it felt like I'd sucked on cotton for an hour. Kathryn was standing over me with tears in her eyes and relief palpable on her face.

I tried to speak, but with the cotton feeling, I winced. She reached for something out of my field of vision and then placed a small cup in my hand with both of hers.

"It's just ice, for now. The doctor said to just suck on it, and you'll feel better."

There was a joke in there, but my brain was too muddied to tease it out. I nodded, but it felt like the entire planet shook and I heard her call for the nurse. She wasn't frantic, but she told me later that she just wanted the all-clear.

The nurse came in and checked my vitals. She was a blurry form moving back and forth across the sunlit room. When she spoke, her voice sounded distant, and my medicine-addled mind couldn't hear everything she was saying. It sounded like instructions, then she told me that I'd be staying a day or two. Kathryn squeezed my hand after the nurse left and smiled down at me.

"The doctor said they removed the testicle, and after some initial scans, it appears they got all of it. You now have a real testicle and a fake one, down there. Congratulations!"

I tried to smile, but my face felt numb. I wasn't sure if there was even a muscle twitch.

She squeezed my hand again and continued. "I asked about fertility, and he said it didn't appear to have affected it in any medical way they can measure. You can come in and have your sperm checked for viability after a couple of weeks of recovery."

I could feel myself fading even while I looked at her. Kat must have noticed because she patted my hand and told me to get some rest. She'd be there when I woke up.

I drowsed myself awake an interminable amount of time later. Something was bothering me. The windows were dark, and the lights dim. Kat was asleep in one of the hospital chairs next to the bed, her head cocked at what looked to me like a terribly uncomfortable angle. My mouth was dry again. My head ached, and my whole body felt clammy and sticky. Before I could think about the throbbing dullness between my thighs, I twisted my hips to reach for the cup of ice I spied on a nearby tray.

The bolt of fire that raced through my groin made my vision go black for a moment. I groaned, and it woke Kathryn up. She looked at me, saw I was in pain, and jumped out of the chair.

"What is it, babe? Grant?" She was nearly frantic as she searched my face and bent her ear close to my mouth, yelling over her shoulder, "Nurse!"

I couldn't speak, but I moved my hand toward my crotch, trying to indicate the location of the pain.

I was squeezing my eyelids shut, but I heard shuffling feet coming in and the covers were pulled back. Kathryn's gasp made me look up at her. Through the tears of pain that stung my eyes, I could barely make her out, but the look on her face told me enough.

"Page Dr. Keller, now," I heard a female say nearby.

The pain in my groin should have faded, but as I lay there trying to keep my body as still as possible, I felt it grow. The blood pumping through my body felt like an electric current that carried it in ever-growing circles of frenzied pain. With each beat of my heart, it was amplified. I could feel myself teetering on the edge of consciousness. Black and orange dots coalesced behind my closed eyelids, and just as I heard heavier footfalls entering the room and man's voice ask, "What happened?" the pain reached an unparalleled crescendo, and I passed out.

When I came to, I don't remember much. I was in and out for a few hours, at least that's what Kathryn told me that later. Where usually a patient begins to heal quickly following surgery, that wasn't the case for me. The silicone insert that I'd been so staunch about had poisoned my body. I've never been allergic to silicone, so it was a surprise to everyone when instead of treating it like just another body part, my body instead began attacking it, creating an infection and lowering all kinds of medical levels within it. The doctors said that I had begun to show signs of approaching sepsis, and they were stumped that it happened in such a small amount of time. I didn't know any better before they did it, but they were forced to remove the silicone insert. I'd just have to be okay as the One Ball Wonder. Crude, I know. But like I said, nothing is easy for the Taldos. The foundation of my identity as a man was beginning to shake a little.

Our first question to the doctors after Kathryn and I were able to talk was whether or not the infection would affect my fertility, bearing in mind that the surgery I just left may have already taken care of that.

The doctor said that he'd have to run some tests, and there was no way to know without a sample, but he didn't want to do anything to upset the balance of my body at the moment. Any infection, however, can be dangerous in that regard. Just another thing we'd have to figure out together in a couple of weeks. Until then, I'd need to stay in the hospital for the next few days to ensure there were no lasting effects from the reaction.

All tests came back normal over the course of the next eight days. The highlight of my stay, however, was when Jackson came to visit. On days three through seven, Kat brought Jackson up to see me. He was anxious as soon as he stepped into my room. I could see his little mind begin to whir as he saw the tubes coming out of my body, the machines with their complicated rhythmic beeps and colored displays. To his five-year-old mind, I'm certain I looked very much like I was on death's door. When his eyes met mine, however, they lit up and he ran to me.

"Daddy!"

"Careful!" Kathryn warned.

I reached for him as best I could without yanking the IV out of my hand or the monitors from my arm. He leapt onto the bed, and I groaned playfully as Kathryn lifted him to sit at the edge of the bed.

"How are you, buddy?" I asked into his messy hair as he hugged my neck. "Have you been a big helper for Mommy?"

I felt him nod, and as I rubbed his back, he began to tremble.

"Jack? Are you okay?" I pulled him easily from my chest so that I could look at him.

His eyes were red and tears stained his cheeks. His lip trembled, and his shoulders began to shake.

"Jack, buddy, what's the matter?"

Kathryn stepped closer, a look of mixed concern and empathy complimenting her features.

He sniffed and wiped his nose on his sleeve. When he finally did talk, it was in a tremulous, breathy voice. "I just missed you, and it's scary seeing you so sick." He broke into sobs, and I brought him gently to my shoulder, hugging him close and telling him that it was okay. That I was okay.

Kathryn put a hand on his back and rubbed it alongside my own. Our eyes met and she stuck her lower lip out then mouthed, "He's so sweet." I nodded and smiled.

Jackson had always been a fairly emotional child. Even at five, he seemed more in tune with other's emotions than other kids his age. When the relative of a close friend passed away the previous summer, Kathryn cried as we sat at the kitchen table and talked about it. But by the time Jackson approached us, the only evidence was her red eyes. I'd had my hand over hers and was rubbing it with my thumb. Jackson immediately picked up on it. He stood up straighter and looked at each of our faces in turn, then burst into tears. It was as if he could feel it in the air around him. There were several instances just like that one. In instances where nothing was even discussed regarding the emotions—anger, sadness, excitement—he reacted as if we'd included him in the conversation.

Now, rubbing his back and making soothing sounds, he eventually calmed. Kat and I were able to distract him about all the fun he'd had at Grandma and Grandpa's, and he regaled me with adventures of pirates, dinosaurs, and exotic animal hunting on Poppy's farm.

Some of those thoughts I'd had at the beginning of this journey crept up, and I was able to mostly quiet them. He'd be okay. We'd be okay. I'd still be around when he needed me the most. I hoped then, at least.

Now that I was more than stable, Kathryn was spending most of her time at home with him. Both of them would visit me each day for the rest of the week, which helped the time pass. Those hours in between, however, were anything but exciting.

The nights were mostly restless, which was not surprising when taking into consideration that my balls—scratch that, *ball*—was on fire, and I needed meds frequently. On top of that, I was having a recurring dream. I was certain it had something to do with the cancer or the treatment. Maybe both.

In the dream, I was standing in the front yard of our home, our first home. It was a single-story house, probably built in 1970. The red brick was only broken by the four windows across the front, two to either side of the front door, like eye sockets. But as I watched, it looked as if the two sets of eyes began to cry. Only it wasn't water or tears coming from them, it was blood. It stained the rusty brick an even darker crimson and ran across the ground. I tried to scream, but no noise came out. The reflection in the glass of the front door was liquid and insubstantial, but it was me. Blood ran freely from the reflected nose and eyes, all the way down my legs to join the blood from the house in a puddle at my feet.

I woke up sweating and in pain when I had this dream, and it was always the same. It would eventually fade, but in the hospital and for some time after, I feared sleep.

I was able to get out of bed on day five, which was when they removed my catheter, and I could finally go to the bathroom on my own. I hoped to never take that for granted again.

When I could finally go home, I had strict instructions to take it easy. Lots of sitting and resting and several weeks of absolutely no lifting.

"I mean it, Mr. Taldo. We have patients—mostly men, I might add—who think that these instructions don't apply to them because they're built differently. Well, you aren't. No lifting. None whatsoever." I nodded a little sheepishly as he turned to Kathryn. "Mrs. Taldo, your instructions are to call me the moment you see him lift something so I can chew his ass to ribbons." She laughed. I did, too, when the corners of Dr. Keller's mouth began to turn into a smile.

"Thank you, Dr. Keller. I appreciate your help." I shook his hand from the wheelchair.

He pumped it once. "Absolutely. I would say it's been a pleasure, but we both know it hasn't. You let me know if you feel any pain in your groin or abdomen, and we'll get you in first thing." We agreed, and he turned to leave. "One more thing. I know you both might be itching to jump in the sack again. Unfortunately, you need plenty of healing. The body is amazing and can do much of it on its own. However," he met both of our eyes in turn before continuing, "if you two can restrain yourselves, I want you to wait two weeks from now before engaging in intercourse. Any questions?"

I looked at Kathryn whose cheeks had turned a very pretty red.

"Loud and clear, doc," I said with a boyish grin.

"Good deal. The nurse has your discharge papers, and I'll see you in a couple of weeks for your follow-up tests and subsequent radiation treatment, if needed. Have a great day." And he turned on his heel and was out the door.

CHAPTER 3

T he days passed slowly at home. I was able to work for a few hours a day, but the company understood that I was more or less immobile and wouldn't be making any grandiose progress until I was back to one hundred percent. To fill the time, I did a great deal of reading while lying on my back making notes here and there on my work computer when I ran across an interesting idea, or the germ of one, at least.

I worked for a company that dabbled in multiple areas of science. Many claimed we were merely grasping at straws on the fringe of the scientific community, riding the coattails of better science and claiming the result as our own.

My current project, and the one I'd been working on long before cancer kicked me in the dick, was finding sustainable energy sources. More specifically, being able to manipulate the rivers of energy that circulated the globe and to harvest them. There was plenty of evidence to suggest that the earth was full of untapped energy, but most of it was brushed off as nothing more than science fiction, The Paducah Principle notwithstanding. But if we follow the logic that the only sound science is the science we know, we wouldn't have the light bulb, or an understanding of gravity, or even the ability to detect emotional roots within behaviors. Scientists by nature need evidence to be convinced, but that evidence can't be shown until the hypothesis is proven. What Eastwind Energy worked to do was create a scientific community that encouraged diving into the fringe and seeing what you could come up with. Eastwind worked hard to garner support, and there were a surprising number of rich philanthropists who believed this was a legitimate branch of science. The general scientific community could snub their noses at us, but even if we stopped accepting investors, we wouldn't need more funding for over a decade. It was all part of human psychology, wasn't it? Everyone wanted their name on something that would last beyond their years on Earth. I was no different, it turned out.

The work itself was simple. It wasn't even really that I was trying to interact with new energy sources. Not really. The bulk of my work was simply *looking* for these Ley Lines using machines that measured different energy frequencies across the country. The real goal was to hijack the energy stream.

I put the book I was reading down. *The Waves That Make Us* by William Paducah was interesting and had given me an idea that I believed could be added to Gretchen. Gretchen was the name I gave the Frequency Accelerant Detector (FAD) that I was currently utilizing. Or would be as soon as I found a good place to set it up.

I placed my laptop gently on the pillow that covered my groin. I could feel the pressure, but it was bearable. The blueprints of Eastwind's Frequency Accelerant Detector spun in a three-dimensional interface on my computer, and I stared at it. Lines, curves, bulbs, and wires all made up a framework that looked like one of those plastic toys that could be expanded just by pulling it apart.

The FAD was a fairly new piece of science. It was a remarkable machine that stood about three feet high on a tripod: its base near the ground, and the top, what looked at first like a large egg, reached the middle of my torso. Upon closer inspection, a person could find a complicated network of gears, wires, and servos encased in a transparent dome. The dome itself was a mix of glass, plastic, and nylon fibers, which Eastwind trademarked glassteel. The FAD is capable of measuring the energy levels across differing altitudes and areas of Earth, then correlating them all into a map of a kind. The Earth was full of these energy concentrations, which had in the past earned the moniker "Ley Lines." Where the Ley Lines intersected is where the energy could be harvested most easily and most efficiently. The energy levels at these intersections would illicit a specific frequency on the FAD, and by placing several around the country at these crossing points, the FAD gave even clearer data for Eastwind to interpret. There hadn't been any breakthroughs yet, but we were close.

The nice thing about the gig was that I didn't *have* to understand the science. I was someone who worked in the field with a set of instructions. I left the science of it all up to the actual scientists back in California.

"How's it going?" Kathryn leaned over the couch and gave me a kiss on the cheek.

I closed my laptop and looked at her. "It's good. Trying to finish up a little research and plan on what to do with Gretchen when I'm back on my feet." Kathryn knew Gretchen and frequently called her my "work wife."

"How's Jack?" I asked.

"He's fine. Playing in his room with his dinosaurs right now."

I nodded, then smiled a cheeky smile. "Do you think he's gonna play for a little while?"

Kathryn smiled back at me but shook her head. "Doc said two weeks. It's been three days, Don Juan. You'll have to cool your jets." Then she leaned over and gave me a seductive kiss on the lips. "Besides," she whispered, her lips brushing mine as she spoke, "I'll have to call the doctor and tell on you if you don't behave."

I hesitated, nervous at what could happen if we fooled around. Then I leaned in and she pulled back. Her hands slid down my chest and rested just below my navel. I was only wearing basketball shorts, and I could feel myself getting more and more interested in where this could lead.

Kathryn glanced down below my beltline and smiled at me. "Mr. Taldo, you'd best be careful. I would *hate* for something to happen while you're in recovery." She moved her hand an inch lower.

My heart began picking up speed and a dull ache began in my groin, a slight pulling, but I ignored it. "Oh yeah, wouldn't that be terrible."

She nodded and moved her hand an inch lower. I could feel the pressure of her hand just above where I wanted it to be. The pulling had grown into more than just an ache, and I tried to ignore it.

I shifted my body, so her hand slid another inch lower. She didn't move it, and I didn't mind. She caressed me over my shorts. I shifted once more to give her better access and gasped as pain shot from my groin and up the side of my body.

Kathryn pulled her hand back as if she'd touched a hot stove. "Oh God, Grant, I'm sorry!"

I groaned and could feel the excitement draining out of me as sweat sprang from every pore. I tried to steady my breathing and ignore the burning barb wire in my groin. When it began to fade and I was able to speak, I tried to tell her it was okay.

"No, babe. It's no big deal. Turns out the doctor was right. We should definitely wait a little while longer." I could feel my cheeks throbbing with the flush of pain. Kathryn didn't know what to do with her hands. She wanted to help with the pain but didn't want to touch me anywhere, it seemed. "Really, Kat. It's okay," I said as I settled myself back in my original position. "Rain check, yeah?"

She nodded, her face a mask of guilty worry.

I swallowed hard and let out a sigh. "Seriously." I grabbed her hand. "It's okay. I'm good, now."

She nodded and looked up as Jackson walked into the room. His face was red, and he looked from face to face just as he had in the hospital.

Before he could say anything, I said, "Hey bud. Daddy's fine. Just had a little owie, but it's better now."

He nodded and walked cautiously up to the couch, resting his hand on my shoulder and studying my face. "Are you sure, Daddy?"

I nodded and gave him my best smile. "Definitely."

Kathryn and I tried again on day nine. While we weren't able to get as busy as we wanted, the pain wasn't as great. On day twelve, we had much greater success. We took it slow, but that wasn't all bad, either.

The time at home gave me the opportunity to get to know my son even better. He was, in a word, remarkable. The window through which he viewed the world wasn't rose-colored. It was a rainbow splash of all the best things. We'd play games together, and his almost constant laughter was contagious. I had to be careful, or I'd end up pulling something from all the laughing. But as the days wore on, I was able to move around much more easily and laugh more readily. I still felt a slight tugging in my groin, but overall it was bearable if I didn't move too fast. Jackson was quick to grab my cane—an insufferable necessity at this point—but the pleasure of walking in the sunshine with my five-year-old skipping beside me was the highlight of my time as a cripple.

I realized quickly something that was probably obvious to many others—Jackson was my absolute favorite.

The visit to the doctor was something Kat and I were both nervous about, but the scans came back faster than we'd thought, and the doctor was quick to call us back in to review them.

"It's not bad news," he began with a forced smile, "but it's not what we'd hoped for."

My stomach dropped to my toes, and I felt Kat grip my hand tighter.

"Is the cancer gone?" Her face was pale, and I hated that for her.

Dr. Keller nodded. "Yes. That at least is the best news so far. It looks like the removal of the testicle and spermatic cord removed the cancerous cells. Now, we just need to schedule a few follow-up appointments, and if those are clear, I'll be able to announce you're in remission. But let's not get ahead of ourselves."

We both sighed in relief, and Kathryn closed her eyes.

"So what's the problem, then?"

"Well, I won't bore you with specifics. But do you remember when we talked about treatment options and post-surgery radiation?"

We both nodded.

"Well, your levels are still elevated, and that means there could be some cancer in the nooks and crannies, specifically the lymph nodes in your abdomen. So what we'll do is a couple of rounds of radiation and then check your levels again."

Kat and I were speechless. It wasn't terrible news, but my guess was that it could turn terrible pretty quickly.

"When can we schedule that?" I wanted to get this nightmare over with as quickly as possible.

"We can schedule that for as soon as you're able. This week or next week, if that works for you. I'll have the nurse put it on the schedule."

We talked for a half-hour longer about side effects, which would be unpleasant on the best of days. We also talked about fertility issues that may arise. He asked if we'd been able to have intercourse and didn't balk when we relayed that we had, just slowly. I suppose when your job includes dealing with the reproductive organs of adults on a daily basis, sex may lose much of its mystery.

"Fertility may be affected. We won't know until after the radiation treatments are complete and your body feels well enough for a few more tests. With luck, we can be done with this in a couple of months, and all of this will be behind you."

It would all be fine. Yes, the radiation would make me sick. Sometimes, I'd lay in bed all day dry heaving and feeling like my blood was on fire. But in the end, the scans came out clear, and I was announced as "in remission."

Fertility was affected at first, but it also turned out fine in the end.

Our second and final pregnancy brought us our greatest mystery. Tests confirmed that my sperm count was a little lower—no surprise since I thought of myself as only working at half capacity—but they were still swimming. Keller was born in September, almost a full year after my final radiation treatment.

Kathryn's pregnancy with Keller was no walk in the park, though. It felt like the moment he was conceived, Kathryn's body changed. Well, I know that technically it did. But it was more than just the normal changes of being pregnant. Her hormones were all over the place. Many of the days in that first trimester were spent in bed. She was weak and nauseous, both of which weren't out of the ordinary and every doctor check-up confirmed it. Everything just felt strange.

Jackson, however, was enamored with the baby growing in her belly. He sang to her stomach every night after reading a book or two. His version of reading was mostly just repeating the memorized words or describing the pictures in more detail than the book even gave.

It was an immediate bond, though. There was no doubt in anyone's mind that Jackson would be the best big brother of all time. He asked Kathryn if he could make her tea, which meant that I would make her tea and he would bring it to her. He would bring her pillows for her head or to prop up her feet, all the while talking about the adventures they'd go on together.

There would be an adventure; that's for certain. But it wouldn't be one they'd enjoy. But I'll get to that.

For now, I'll start at the point where life was easy.

CHAPTER 4

The cab of the moving truck lurched violently in the late summer sun as the passenger-side tire ran up on the curb of a large two-story house on the corner of Creek Blossom Circle and Poplar Street. I winced, hunching my shoulders and sucking the air between my teeth. "Oops," I muttered under my breath. I was wearing my "RAD DAD" hat, and the sunlight washed the world with sanguine clarity. I loved the hat because I was, in fact, a Rad Dad. But it also worked to hide my balding scalp. And it looked good with my beard. At least, that's what I told myself.

Sighing with relief, I patted the steering wheel in a "good girl, Bessie" kind of way and turned to my passenger, a woman of striking beauty with dark hair cascading in lazy curls around her head and eyes that shone with a sly intelligence that I'd always found incredibly sexy.

"Do you think we broke something?" Her voice sounded confidently nonchalant, but her face showed genuine worry.

I pointed a thumb over my shoulder toward the trailer that housed every bit of the belongings that we'd accumulated in this life, including Gretchen. "You mean all that stuff back there? I doubt it. But you can blame me if I did." She smiled and smacked my arm playfully. "Oh," I said, feigning understanding, "you meant with the truck. Yeah, it's busted, I'm sure. Too bad, so sad."

She rolled her eyes and shook her head, but the smile spreading across her face reassured me. "Grant Taldo, you're a mess," she said, sighing.

As my wife stared out the front window of the truck looking at our new home, I couldn't help but stare at her. I'd met her in college, one of those cross-dorm functions that build relationships on a healthy foundation of alcohol and awkward conversation. Even then—fifteen years ago?—she had captured my heart. The intelligence she'd flaunted then had only expanded in the years since. She'd been a marketing major with the intention of brushing shoulders with some of the most well-known firms in some highbrow skyscraper in New York. She was going places, and I knew I wanted to tag along.

I had been a student in little more than name only. I went to class and did the work, but outside of that, I was either playing video games or sleeping. College, for me, was a time to finally break free of the Evangelical schedule that I'd been raised with. So I spent my time how I wanted. Until I met her... Kathryn Prince.

We'd talked for a good bit of the party, drinking enough to feel that pleasant buzz but not enough to forget that we had class in the morning. By the end of the night, we were both laughing and telling stories about our very similar upbringing. She was raised in Mankato, Minnesota. Her dad was a pastor and her mom was a dutiful homemaker. In a similar fashion, I was raised in Jonesboro, Arkansas, dad a pastor, and mom stayed home. It worked out, but both of us having experienced something similar, we were ready to live life on our own terms.

The night ended with nothing more than a hug. Though, I was so pleasantly intoxicated that I hoped more would happen.

The next time I saw her, however, I was glad that we didn't have to steer the conversation around it. We spent most of that year dating, and when we graduated, we got married.

She continued her upward trend, becoming a Senior Marketing Advocate with a very prestigious firm in Chicago. Not quite New York, but it did the trick. Working her way up from there, she became the VP of Marketing in a very short time but chose to take a step back to part-time when we started a family, a decade past today's moving day. In the early days of our relationship, she had said, "Grant, I know we've talked about it a little, but I want to make sure you know that I want to rock my babies to sleep. I don't want to miss it. I know a lot of women choose to work, and that's wonderful for them, but for me, I'll take any hit to my job so that I can be home with them at night. I want to work only part-time."

At the time, I had agreed without much thought. When the time came for it, the budget rework looked a little tighter and forced me to look at our spending. But in the end, it was workable. And watching the way she gazed at them rocking in the crook of her elbow, for me, it was all worth it. Plus, my job with Eastwind was paying the bills just fine, especially with the relocation bonuses.

Of course, when she did it, there was pushback, both professionally and familial. Despite plenty of her friends and relatives giving expert parenting advice to avoid rocking them to sleep, per her own Aunt Patty: "They'll never sleep on their own, and you'll be hooked to them as surely as a criminal in a chain gang," she did rock them. She rocked them when they were sad or when they were sleepy. Sometimes when they were grumpy and cried the whole time, kicking and flailing about, she sang a lullaby her gran sang to her when she was young, something about the "morrow wind."

She had long since forgotten the words of that childhood lullaby, but the tune stuck with her through her adolescent years and into adulthood. She often hummed it to herself when she was worried or sad, and she told me that it reminded her of the comfort of childhood—smells of fresh-baked cinnamon bread and foggy lakeside mornings.

She turned to me, breaking me free from my reverie and placed her hands on my cheeks. She pulled me close to her and planted a kiss firmly on my lips. "Grant, this place is beautiful. Are you ready to unload all this junk?"

"I am. How are you feeling?" I nodded toward her midsection. Her maternity pants stretched comfortably, and her red t-shirt bulging around it, too. It got my blood pumping.

"I feel fine." She rubbed her stomach affectionately. "Tired, like always. But I'm ready to get this little guy out here. And I'm ready to get all of our stuff out of here, too."

I smiled at her and pulled the garage door opener—our *new* garage door opener—from my pocket. While holding her hand with my right, I held the opener in my left, pointed it at the garage door—still don't know if that makes a difference or not—and pushed the button.

We waited for a few seconds.

I clicked it again.

Still nothing.

I shrugged and moved the pointer around the cab while clicking until I heard the distant rumble of the garage door moving. It opened to reveal a spacious garage—twice as big as the one at our last home—with shelves and space that I knew Kathryn was filling up in her mind's eye.

"Let's go," I said and opened the driver-side door. I heard her squeal in excitement as she opened the passenger door.

Unloading the truck wasn't fun, but it wasn't boring, either.

We were able to completely unload the truck in a matter of hours thanks to my parents. They'd invited Jackson to stay the weekend with them, which freed us up from worrying about squishing him with boxes we unloaded. The three of them would fly down on Sunday.

Of course, we didn't get everything in place, and that meant the garage was filled with stacks of boxes that we'd still have to sift through and organize, but we could return the moving truck on time.

One corner of the garage was stacked with cardboard boxes bearing the Eastwind Energy logo, an "E" that stretched over hills as if it were wind. Eastwind had found a Ley Line that needed monitoring and had asked their field researchers who wanted to move. Arkansas wasn't high on anyone's list, but Kathryn and I had talked about it and decided that we could do with the change. Growing up in the city was fine, but the freedom a house in the country offered its own attraction. Of course, the neighborhood we moved into wasn't "in the country" to the locals, but to us, we might as well have been on *Little House on the Prairie*.

After lugging several boxes marked "kitchen" into the house, I told Kathryn that I was going to return the truck and asked if she would follow me to the facility so that I wouldn't be stranded.

"It shouldn't take too long, maybe an hour. I know you're itching to get these cabinets filled, but I'd rather not pay a sixty-dollar late fee, if it's all the same to you."

She looked up from a box she was working on, silverware by the sounds of it. "Yeah, that's..." she blew a strand of hair out of her face, "that's fine. Like, right now?"

I smiled at her, and she returned it with a knowing, goofy grin. "When you're done with that box." She returned her attention to the forks and knives. The sound they made when they rubbed against each other made my teeth hurt. "I'm going to go make sure everything is ready. Meet you at the truck?"

She grunted, which I assumed meant "yes," and went outside where the air was free of the sound of cheap silverware grinding against itself. I busied myself with checking the moving truck's return policy instructions.

Are the straps placed in their holding receptacle? I checked the straps. Yep.

Is the moving truck empty of all personal effects? It better be, I thought to myself.

Kat came out when I was double checking that the roller door was locked and secure.

"You ready, babe?" She smacked my backside as I bent over to check the lock, and laughed, getting into her white four-door coupe. She flashed me a thumbs-up.

"Now I am," I said and hopped into the cab.

On the short fifteen-minute drive, I thought about all the things that come with new home ownership. The excitement of making it our own, the joy of finally having room to grow, and the fear of huge expenses like air conditioners and water leaks. It wasn't as fun thinking about those things.

After arriving and checking it in, I handed the keys over to the technician at the store, signed my name, and got into the passenger side of our car. The ride back was mostly me listening to Kat tell me about all the ideas she had for our home. She couldn't wait to build shelves in the living room, expand the countertops, and change the coat closet by the kitchen into a pantry. By the time we got home, my head was spinning, and she could tell.

"Oh, Grant, sorry. I'm just so excited about making it *ours*." She beamed at me. What was I gonna do, deny her?

I smiled and grabbed her hand, kissing it gently. "I know you are. And I am, too! It's going to be awesome. Thank you for going on this adventure with me, Kat."

She leaned over and kissed me, then. Her soft lips fit perfectly on mine. Warmth spread across my face, and I felt that old flame dance in my chest. I really loved her. Truly.

We spent the rest of that day unpacking boxes and sorting items into their new homes. A quick bite in the evening—supreme pizza—and we were back at it until we were too tired to continue.

"I think I've gone up and down those stairs a hundred times," she said, her head lying on my shoulder. In one hand she held a glass of deep red wine, a luxury she afforded herself once a week with permission from the doctor. Her other hand rested on the inside of my thigh. I was drinking a glass of wine, too. My other arm was draped across her shoulders, fingertips roving gently across her upper arm.

"Well, the good news is that we worked off that pizza, right? No need to count calories today." We toasted glasses together and laughed.

Kathryn grew somber, lips pursed in thought. "I've barely even thought about Jackson today. I know that sounds bad, but I mean we've just been so busy, and I know he's safe, so there hasn't really been a need to worry. But I miss him. He hasn't even seen his room, yet." She put a hand on her midsection. "Or the nursery."

I took a slow drink, enjoying the warm hum as it settled in my stomach. "He's gonna flip, you know."

"I know." I could hear the smile in her words. We'd decided early on to do his room in a kind of superhero theme. We also accepted that we'd need to paint over it when he grew out of it. But until then, he'd have Superman, Batman, Green Lantern, all of it. Being only six, it was tricky trying to get him into super-heroes without including all of the fighting and violence that goes along with it. Thankfully, there were enough companies that realized this and began making toys and shows centered around friendship and being a good person rather than just beating up the bad guys. But once he saw the superheroes as grinning, friendly people with powers, he was all in.

"I'm about to turn into a pumpkin." Kat's voice was low and gritty with exhaustion.

"I can tell," I said, kissing the top of her head. "Let's go to bed."

So we did. In our haste to unpack everything, we'd forgotten to build the new bed frame Kat had bought online. So we contented ourselves with sleeping on the mattress. We could rough it for one night, after all.

The next morning greeted us with bright sunlight and sore backs. But the show must go on. Kathryn focused on setting out the decorations since the boxes which held them numbered more than we both cared to admit. I built the bed frame and focused on organizing the tools in the garage. My parents would be arriving later in the afternoon with Jackson, and we wanted to be at a stopping point, if not quite finished.

Kathryn was putting the final touches on the living room, and I was in the middle of carting multiple boxes to the attic when our new doorbell rang. The lack of a pause between the *ding-dong* and creak of hinges told me it was either a robber or my parents. The cry of joy from Kathryn *could* have been construed as surprised terror if taken the right way, but not the accompanying voices of an older couple.

I arranged the boxes in something resembling order and made my way down the attic staircase. I checked my watch on the way down, surprised to find it displaying 3:23. It was

as good a stopping point as any, and after lifting the staircase back into the ceiling, I dusted my hands in a way that said, "that's that," and went down to join the rest of the family.

Dad was standing in the kitchen, hands in the pockets of his blue sleeveless vest. His cowboy hat—once gray but approaching the color of bone, now, with a dark gray sweat band running its way around the hat—sat on his head. It fit him just as well as the well-worn cowboy boots on his feet. He was taller than I was, gray stubble on the jawline that spoke of hard work and long days. His jeans were the blue ones he always wore on the farm, discolored with dirt, age, and god knows what else. His face was tanned and leathery, wrinkles and smile lines standing out clearly with each grin. Mom was sitting at the table, fawning over Kathryn's growing belly while Jackson did the same. She was shorter than everyone but Jackson, but her smile always lit up the room. Her hair was fixed in the same way it always had been, a short bob, curled under near her neck. She colored it, but not in a way that was gaudy. The light brown color was almost natural, but the gray roots gave it away.

"Hey, Pop," I said, wrapping him in a hug as I stepped from the final stair.

"Well, hi, Son!" His default greeting was no less welcome now than the other thousand times I'd heard it, and I was sure I'd miss it greatly.

I turned to mom. "Hey, Mama. How was the flight?" I hugged her sitting down, which was always awkward.

"It was just fine, honey."

"How's this rotten kid?" I hefted Jackson up onto my shoulders with squeals of laughter.

"He was wonderful, of course," said Mom, smiling. "How are you both? Looks like you're just clicking along unpacking.

Kathryn," she turned a little more serious, "you aren't over-doing it, are you?"

Kathryn smiled. "You remember what it was like, mom. Overdoing it is part of the job description."

They both laughed and nodded.

"Y'all are staying for dinner, right?" Jackson had picked up some of the twang I heard in Dad's voice.

"As long as your mom and dad say it's fine. Our flight leaves tomorrow morning, so we figured we'd either go eat something fancy or eat with you."

"Of course you can eat with us, Mom and Dad. We're just having casserole that a friend sent for us."

"That's perfect."

We showed Jackson his new room and talked about all the painting we wanted to do, and he was all smiles. Of course, it may have been hard for him to imagine, but he knew what superheroes were and that was enough.

We gave mom and dad the full tour while the casserole heated up in the oven. They gave the proper "oohs" and "ahhs" at all the right places. They were very impressed. It was only ruined slightly by Mom commenting on how she was surprised we could afford it. She was also curious what we'd do with all the extra space.

The frustrating thing about growing up an Evangelical is that it's frowned upon to have anything extra. Extra space, extra money, any of it. Because if it's extra, it should be used for God. Which is to say, not used by humans. Now that Kathryn and I had the extra space, Mom and Dad had a hard time seeing it as anything but a misuse of "God's blessings." Kathryn and I were in agreement, however, that maybe god was blessing us, anyway.

When the casserole was warm, we turned the oven off to let it warm while we took a walk around the neighborhood to show them that, too. They were impressed with how large the houses were—these were "large" only because they had a second story. Some were barely larger than our old house as far as square footage went. The first house to begin the tour was the house next to ours. The neighbors, the Shelbergs, were a kind older couple that tended a small garden in the small space that separated our houses. Patricia Shelberg was an avid birdwatcher and the multitude of bird baths and feeders that covered their yard were more than an eyesore. Buddy Shelberg—yes that's his name—was an airplane enthusiast. He flew commercially for years, he said, and when he retired, he just couldn't put them down. Models could be seen from every window in their home, and Mom commented on how tacky they looked. I hoped she knew how tacky it was to comment on his hobby like that, but I would never say it out loud.

Mom and Dad loved all the children riding bikes, and shortly after starting our walk, we were even greeted by a sweet couple pushing a stroller. The man had curly hair that touched his broad shoulders and kind eyes that smiled when he did. His wife had beautiful curly hair that framed her dark face and the body of a long-distance runner. Jackson was quick to take a peek inside the stroller, and they were very gracious.

Through conversation, we introduced ourselves. The other dad and I shook hands.

"Brandon Upton. This is my wife Jo. Nice to meet you, Grant. Just moving in?"

I pumped his hand twice with a firm enough grip to let him know that I, too, was a man. "Yep, just moved in. This is my wife, Kathryn, and these are my parents, Dale and Rita Taldo. They're visiting from the Northeast."

Each couple made another round of handshakes and polite small talk before we waved goodbye and continued through the neighborhood. Mom and Dad commented on how nice the Uptons were, and we agreed, but without much intent.

We made our way through the neighborhood without any rush. Truth be told, this was the first time Kathryn and I had a chance to walk the neighborhood, too, and it was just as illuminating to us as it was for my parents, I'm sure.

When our path brought us toward the outer edge of the neighborhood, we had our first glimpse of a run-down, decrepit old home. The house that would cause so many of our future problems. If only we had known it, then.

"Well, that's *something*," said Mom in a voice that approached disgust.

Dad stood staring at it, hands resting comfortably in his vest pockets, no doubt wondering if it had "good bones."

The more I looked at this husk of a home, my anxiety began to grow. Kathryn threaded her fingers through mine and leaned on me. I noticed Mom move closer to Dad, too, also grasping hands. It was as if the eerie structure commanded our attention, and we all wanted to look away but couldn't. As if at the sight of the old house, I'd remembered the times I had made a mistake or hurt someone. The feeling of wanting to crawl away in shame crept up my spine, and I realized it was a similar feeling you get when someone is watching you. Though, I doubted heavily that the house had seen any tenants in any less than a decade.

I don't know how else to describe it.

"That makes my tummy wiggle," said Jackson, and we all laughed. The temporary spell the house had cast over us disappeared in an instant. We joked about how it looked like a snaggle-tooth old crocodile and walked on, but the feeling that I was being watched made the hairs on my neck prickle. It didn't relent until I was back in our own home. The source of my unease and the house on the corner were forgotten by then.

Dinner wasn't anything exciting. Jackson was exhausted and had to be carted off to bed after falling asleep on the couch with a full tummy. To be honest, we didn't even notice he'd zonked out while we were talking over greasy plates and half-empty glasses.

After I put him in his bed, Kathryn and I invited Mom and Dad to play Rook, a card game that we played with them throughout the course of our relationship. The goal of the game was to bet the number of hands one can win not only with the hand dealt but also on the partner's hand. Boys versus girls was how we played, and while players weren't supposed to bet on the bonus hand, I couldn't help it. The bonus hand—five cards called "the kitty" that could be won with the highest bid—were dealt out separately from the players' hands. Once a player had "the kitty," they could replace any cards in-hand with those from it. I had a bad habit of betting on the kitty, but it was what I did. First to five hundred points won, and the games usually lasted thirty minutes, give or take.

Regardless of how the score came out, it was always fun, and I cherished the memories of playing that night, along with many others.

Dad and Mom said goodnight and left for their hotel after the girls reached a score of five-sixty. "We let them win," Dad joked before I could say the same, and we all laughed good-naturedly. Kathryn and I told them to visit anytime, and they said they were thinking maybe in a few weeks. I asked Dad to call me before booking flights so that we could work out the logistics. That close to Keller's birth could spell more than frustration for both parties.

Kathryn fell asleep almost as soon as her head hit the pillow. Tomorrow was Kat's birthday, but a long day of moving and a late night of games resulted in little more than exhaustion. Not to mention, with everything going on that week, we hadn't planned much of a birthday celebration for her. But being the wonderful husband I am, I'd bought her a couple of things the day before. I hung up the banner and put her presents on the table, then flipped off the lights and went to bed.

Much to my frustration, and despite exhaustion forcing my eyes closed, I lay in the dark listening to the new house sounds and the gentle breathing of Kathryn and *not* sleeping. My mind was restless with a multitude of things but eventually wandered to the overall subject of parenthood. It was equal parts fear and excitement, and it was a bizarre change when I transitioned from the relatively complex role of "adult man" to the role of "father." It was even stranger when it happened with Keller. Not only because it was so unexpected but also because it took lot of trying.

That moment felt so distant and so close. An odd mix of time dilation occurred as I lay in the dark remembering the time when Kathryn called my name from the bathroom one bright Saturday in February.

I smiled sleepily as I heard her voice echo through the ages of memory.

"Grant?" her voice had echoed through our small house and into the kitchen. My coffee cup had paused just as I was about to take a sip, and I put it back on the counter.

"Kat? What is it?" If she needed toilet paper, she sounded a little more hyped up for it than I thought possible. You never know. Could have been the sushi.

I limped my way there, winking at Jackson whose toes thumped rhythmically against the counter where he sat eating cereal. I grabbed my cane from beside the door and made the slow progress toward the hallway. It had been almost four months since the surgery and the radiation therapy were done, but I was weak and had sudden bouts of nausea. Other than that, I was feeling remarkably well at the time.

I'd knocked on the door lightly. "Kat, you need some TP?"

She answered by opening the door. Her eyes had been wide, and she was chewing on her thumbnail, something I hadn't seen her do in a long time.

Immediately, I was worried. "What is it? Are you okay?"

She'd nodded dismissively and pointed to the bathroom counter. A small white stick I hadn't originally noticed was lying there, its pink lid now clearly visible on the counter. It took a moment to register that it was a pregnancy test. "What's it say?" I'd asked the question before actually registering that I was going to ask the question. Using context clues, it didn't take a genius to figure out what was happening. "You're pregnant?"

She coughed a small laugh, and her eyes began to well with tears. She stopped smiling, then laughed again and nodded. "Yeah," she responded in a whisper.

I leaned the cane against the bathroom counter and picked up the stick. Sure enough, two pink lines were clearly visible in the viewing window.

"Well," I said, adopting a professorial tone, "looks like you got knocked up."

There was silence between us for several heartbeats before we both started laughing and hugging. I had to brace myself against the wall, so Kat didn't accidentally touch my abdomen or groin, but we embraced gently, and she was cry-laughing into my shoulder for several minutes.

Jackson's small footfalls could be heard from outside the door, and he quietly asked if everything was okay.

We separated from our light hug and turned to him, deciding to sit in the living room instead of standing in the small half-bath when we broke the news to him.

When everyone was seated comfortably on the couch, we asked him what he would think about having a brother. He thought pensively for a minute, tapping his chin and then said, "Would I stay the big brother?"

I nodded and said, "Well sure. You'll always be the big brother. What do you think about having a little brother—"

"Or sister," Kat interjected.

"Or sister, of course."

"I think it would be really fun." He shrugged his little shoulders and put his hands between his knees. "I really want to be a big brother."

Kat and I made eye contact and grinned.

"Well," she began, "that's great. Because you're going to be. Mommy is pregnant. That means there's a baby in my tummy!"

Jackson gasped and stood up, walking slowly toward us, his eyes glued to Kathryn's midsection. He reached out and gently put his hand on her. "In here?" he asked.

Kathryn nodded and placed her hands over his. "You can't feel it yet, but in a few weeks, you'll be able to."

Jackson didn't stop grinning, transfixed as he rubbed his hand back and forth gently across her belly. "I can't wait," he whispered.

CHAPTER 5

The following weeks were filled with plenty of family time. My mom and dad lived in Hartford, Connecticut. But as retirees with ample time and money to spend, they flew out every few weeks to say hello and spoil Jackson into oblivion. Kathryn, bless her heart, didn't mind at all. She didn't have the kind of relationship with her mom that I had with my parents. And while she encouraged me—sweetly—to ask several times that their next trip be planned in advance instead of surprising us, we usually enjoyed the change of pace.

In the days leading up to the transition to a family of four, Kathryn spent a good deal of her time waddling around the neighborhood. Her bulging belly moved back and forth across the path ahead of her while Jackson waltzed alongside her, pummeling her with questions. Being a part-time employee had its perks. No one expected much from her when she only had to be at the office for a portion of the week, and according to her, as long as the job got done, nobody cared. And with her belly growing, she was having less and less room to accomplish tasks that months earlier caused no issue. With each new day, it seemed that our miracle pregnancy was changing from a dream to a reality.

I was able to tag in on one such day when Kat would normally take Jackson with her on a walk. It happened to be an emergency meeting with the firm, and her boss said she could move her hours around to accommodate the extra time, but she had to be at this meeting. I currently had time to spare. My job required working remotely and much like Kathryn's, as long as the job got done, nobody cared. Besides, I could work with Gretchen and video call my team with any issues. I still hadn't found a good place to put her, but the Ley Line was huge, and I was busy running tests and gauging responses based on several days' worth of data. Overall tedious, but it more than paid the bills. I was doing pretty good for myself, and Kat was doing even better.

Jackson had been wanting to visit the neighborhood dogs that he and Kat met in the first few weeks of their walks, so I obliged, putting on a hat and grabbing his hand on our way out the door.

Jackson, however, quickly tired of the speed at which a middle-aged man can walk and ran ahead, weaving in and out of people's lawns and the sidewalk. I encouraged him to stay on the sidewalk, but kids, you know?

The first stop was at Beck and Caroline's house—two college girls that owned a Black Lab named Sully and a Pomeranian named Fritz. Sully was outside and eagerly greeted us with licks and excitedly frustrated yips as we walked on the other side of his fence. We could see Fritz sunning himself comfortably in the bay window on what appeared to be a feather pillow. He gazed out at us with quiet disregard as if to say in an English nobleman's voice, "Ah yes, I know that small child, but that other chap appears to be new. No bother to me. Carry on, old man."

But Jackson still waved and skipped past.

The sidewalk curved around a large clearing in the middle of the neighborhood nicknamed "The Green" where three large elm trees grew as points in a triangle, their shade darkened half The Green for most of the day year-round. Houses lined the street, their front doors and windows facing The Green as if to watch the goings-on. We made our way around the curve, saying hello to each animal we saw.

The next house, a sprawling white two-story with gaudy yellow shutters, was Mike and Ellen Godsen's. I met them once but only briefly while walking with Kat one quiet evening. They seemed alright, though a little dubious of "the new family in the neighborhood." Their house sat a comfortable distance from The Green, their yard immaculately manicured.

Mike and Ellen had a huge Saint Bernard named Bernie. Much like Fritz, it sat in the bay window of their front room. Unlike Fritz, however, Bernie didn't so much as *sit* in the front window as much as *dominate* it. His fuzzy, furry bulk took up the entire space, and as Jackson waved and danced on the sidewalk, Bernie's considerable feather-duster of a tail thumped against the massive panes of glass. His long pink jowls hung low, and his eyes were red rimmed as if he'd just woken up from a night of heavy drinking. Maybe he had. Who knows with the Godsens.

Jackson skipped the next home. The "FOR RENT" sign a clear indicator to me that no dog would be greeting us there, but the empty yard and long, unmown grass the indicators to Jackson. I followed promptly, feeling much like a little lost puppy. I was in awe of Jackson's ability to find joy in the mundane. The sunlight, the leaves, the wind that whipped them into a miniature tornado—all of those things were *wonders* to him, and he seemed so at peace with the world. I hoped then that he would never change in that regard. And still do.

We worked our way around The Green and eventually the rest of the neighborhood, saying hello and goodbye to half a dozen dogs and even a few cats—Muriel Anthony had a real bitch of a cat named Harriet or Helen that hissed at us through the window and then jumped at it as we walked past. Jackson's joy was undiminished by this, and at least from my perspective, he seemed to draw a sense of stoic duty from it. As if, at that very moment, he swore an oath to befriend that hissing terror. He even tried playing peek-a-boo with it around the tree in her front yard, but the cat put its tail in the air and stalked away.

Part of what made the move to this neighborhood so attractive was how quintessentially novel it felt. We'd lived in a small house on a busy street. Here, the houses were close, sure, but there were people walking their dogs and kids playing basketball in their driveways. Even when we'd visited this area to check out the house that we'd eventually buy, we saw clusters of kids riding their bikes around. It felt like a neighborhood should feel—full of neighbors. We wanted to raise our kids in a place where life happened outside the doors as well as inside, and so far, we weren't disappointed.

After winding his way through a few blood-red Japanese Maple trees that lined a tall wooden privacy fence, we approached the last house we wanted to visit. Jackson stopped at Alice and Greg McKahee's—pronounced "mi-KEE," I wouldn't be making that mistake again. But before having to cross the street and make our way the few blocks back to our own address, the McKahee's Yorkshire Terrier just *had* to be petted. The fence was literally a white picket one and a tiny black sniffling nose poked between the pickets, insisting on affection. A small pink tongue appeared between the fence pickets when Jackson bent low enough to pet it.

"Hello, Daisy," he said in a lilting, singsong-y voice. The sniffling went into overdrive, and I could just barely make out the brown and black curls of its body wriggling back and forth in excitement. Daisy, I learned later, was nine years old and probably the sweetest dog in existence. She literally jumped into Jackson's arms one day when he ran to meet them out on a stroll. They didn't mind, and neither did Jackson. Alice and Greg were about as old as my parents, and with no children of their own, Daisy took that role and took to it beautifully.

Today, I noticed Greg at the back window, coffee cup in hand smiling at us. I waved and said, "Morning, Greg." He waved back and said, "Morning, boys," which I knew because I could read his lips. He continued to smile at us in his light blue polo and pressed khaki pants, his gray wispy hair was styled in a way to hide his bald spots but didn't do a very good job.

After some fierce baby talk between Jackson and Daisy— well, from Jackson *to* Daisy—we made our way back home. We passed plenty of houses, some of which were empty. At these, Jackson had no interest in pausing and continued on as if they were invisible. Some others had human tenants only. And without pets, they might as well have been empty to Jackson.

Not certain of the route he usually took with Kat, I continued walking. I didn't realize it was an unusual path until he said, "Where are we going?"

I looked around and realized that we were farther than we normally would go. Now, we stood by the old house near the edge of the subdivision, right where the road ends in one of those "we'll connect this to the main road later" configurations. In its current state, it turned from blacktop to gravel and then dirt, straight into a field. It was the same house we'd seen when Mom and Dad had visited several weeks ago, I realized.

The grass was unkempt, long and dead. The shutters hung at odd angles, and the fence was loose and rickety, pelted by rain and snow without any care or upkeep. The railing on the front porch was bowed and spokes of it were missing. To be honest, it was creepy. Even on this second viewing, I felt my hackles rise and that same feeling of eerie unease settle over me like early-morning fog.

Jackson stopped in front of it, staring at it through one eye, the other clenched closed against the autumn sunlight. "Daddy?" His voice seemed doubtful I was still there.

"Yeah, bud?"

"What's wrong with this house?"

It was an odd question. He could have gone with "Why is this house ugly?" or "Why does no one live here?" but instead he went further. Interesting.

I took a breath, scrambling a little for an answer that would both satisfy him and help me avoid a further complicated explanation. I settled for a question of my own. "Well, why do you say that?"

He scraped his foot along the sidewalk and ran his fingers lightly over the scarred and scabby pickets. "Well, there aren't any ants on the sidewalk here, and I don't see any birds around it. Is it sick?"

I hadn't noticed either of those things. "Well, houses can't really get sick. But maybe it's just in a weird spot where animals can't live, you know? Maybe there's too much sunlight or not much access to water."

"The Parsons don't have any trees in their yard, but they have a bunch of ants. And at the other end of the neighborhood there's a road like this," he indicated the direction of the other dead end, "but there are still ants and all kinds of bugs

all around it. It just makes me think that this house has something wrong with it."

"Well, maybe you're right. I don't build houses, and I'm not a house expert, so you might be onto something there."

He gazed up at the two-story home, drinking in the sight. We stood there silent for several minutes. There was some kind of energy around this place, and I immediately thought of Gretchen. I decided to come by later and measure the energy frequency on this side of the neighborhood with a FAD-B device. The FAD-B was a sleek handheld device that measured broad-spectrum energy levels. A small touch screen located on the top of the device would reflect a user-friendly graph of resonant capacity detection with a mellow ping. I'd tried several other spots in and around the house, even on the other side of the street, but hadn't ventured this far to test it.

"Think I can have some juice when I get home? I'm really thirsty." Stretching the last word much longer than he would stretch his juice, Jackson's sudden left-turn in conversation brought me back.

"Of course, bud. Let's head home. Last one there is a rotten egg, yeah?" And like a flash, he was off. I was close enough to make him feel like it was a contest, but really it wasn't a contest at all; he would always win.

It wasn't too long after we moved into the new neighborhood that our tiny little miracle decided he was tired of the womb, and he was ready to join the real world.

"Grant, my back is hurting really bad," Kathryn said to me, wincing one morning in September and pressing her knuckles into her back.

I sat bolt upright, putting aside my coffee and FAD manual. "Is it labor? Are you in labor?"

She smiled wanly at me. "I don't know. Maybe. It doesn't feel like it did with Jackson, but you might call your mom and dad just in case."

I called them right then, knowing they'd hop the next flight for *any* reason to come stay with us and help take care of Jackson. When I explained the situation, they told me they were already packed and could pay the extra charge to bump up their already-planned departure date.

I tried not to roll my eyes and almost succeeded.

"Great, Mom. I'll see you soon," I said and hung up. "They're bumping up their departure date to today if they can. Tomorrow at the latest. Apparently, they have 'connections,' but I think they believe the standard website interface is their friend."

Kathryn laughed and winced again. "Babe, would you mind getting me an ice pack?"

I rushed to the kitchen and brought it back to her. When she put it on her back, she sucked in a breath and said, "Nope!" and tossed the bag onto the table.

"Heating pad?" I asked hopefully.

"Yes, get that."

When I placed it on the small of her back, she let out a sigh of relief.

"Much better," she said, sinking into it effortlessly.

Jackson entered our bedroom, bleary-eyed.

"Momma? You okay?"

She smiled at him as he clambered onto the bed holding a stuffed caterpillar.

"Yes, baby, I'm fine. I just think your little brother is ready to meet you." She booped his nose with a finger, and he giggled.

"Poppy and Granma are on their way, too."

His eyes lit up. "They are? Yay!" I had to stop him from jumping on the bed when Kathryn squeezed her eyes shut and put a hand on my forearm.

"Oh, right. Jackson, come here, buddy. Let's not jump on the bed where mommy is sitting."

Immediately, his face became serious, and he stared at her. "She's hurt. Isn't she?"

"Oh, buddy." His empathetic little mind was probably terrified. "No, bud. No. She's completely fine. It's just that when mommies have babies, their body goes through a lot, kind of like running a really long and hard race."

Kathryn glared good-naturedly at me, daring me to utter the joke aloud. I didn't, but it was hard.

"A race?"

I nodded to him. "Yep, it's like a big race and the prize is a baby."

"Oh okay." He turned to Kathryn. "Will it hurt?"

She hesitated and then nodded. "A little bit, honey. But that's okay. I knew it would when we decided to have another baby. It did with you, too."

"It did? I'm so sorry I hurt you, Mommy."

She held out her arms to him and he sank into her gently. "Jacky-boy, you didn't hurt me. My body wanted to push you into the world, and to do that, it cost a little bit of pain." She stroked his hair and kissed the top of his head. "And I'd do it over and over again. Really."

"And so," I continued for her, "that means we need to get you packed because, if I had to bet, I'd say Poppy and Granma are gonna take you to the hotel to stay with them! With a pool. And probably all the junk food you could eat."

His face grew more unbelieving and ecstatic with each word, and he leapt off the bed squealing toward the stairs and his room.

I leaned over and kissed Kathryn's head. "I love you. I'll get him packed."

"He's already packed; I did it last week. His blue dinosaur suitcase has everything he'll need except his caterpillar."

"You really are amazing," I said and meant it. She was an incredible mother and more than prepared for this. Meanwhile, I'd lose my head if it wasn't attached.

I went upstairs and gathered his suitcase, a coat, and his caterpillar, placing them all by the front door. Then I changed Jackson into something approaching an outfit while intermittently checking on Kathryn. She was doing "fine": her words, not mine.

Mom and Dad arrived late that night and chose to take Jackson to the hotel despite our—admittedly weak—protests. I called our doctor, and he said to keep track of the contractions. We did, and at eleven in the morning when they started getting more and more uncomfortable, we went to the hospital.

Our check-in was quick; they were expecting us and had a room prepared. The nurses gathered around, plugging Kathryn into the beeping and whirring machines, and I stood to the side watching them. I'd been through this once, but they say every birth is different. And this one... this one was a doozy.

When Kathryn started complaining about the pain, the doctors did something, and the nurses started scuttling around like tiny ants buzzing around an anthill. A few minutes later, Kathryn's machine beeped what sounded to me very much like a warning sound.

I walked to the bed, sidestepping a nurse carrying a tray of tools.

"Kat? Kat can you hear me?"

Her eyes moved slowly until they met mine, but they remained unfocused. She nodded weakly, and it scared me too much to ignore.

"Hey doc? Or nurse? Something's wrong with her."

The nurse moved close and looked into Kathryn's face, then took her pulse and looked at some of the printouts the machines were spitting out like long white tongues.

I don't know what happened next. All I know is that I found myself pulling on a blue smock and blue booties, following Kathryn into what looked like a surgery room.

Kathryn was pale, paler than I'd seen her before, and her breathing was uneven. Her chest wasn't rising as high as it should have been, I thought.

The next thing I knew, I was asked to stand behind a curtain the nurses erected. The room was a flurry of activity, and orders were being shouted all around us. The doctors pushed a massive needle into Kathryn's back, and then a few seconds later, they cut her open, hip to hip. I made the mistake of looking around the curtain and seeing my wife's insides, which required me to force back a gag.

When they took Keller out, he wasn't making a sound, and Kathryn wasn't awake. Her lips were blue, and they immediately wrapped him in a blanket while the nurses and doctors moved at a dizzying pace around us.

The words "rupture" and "hemorrhage" were tossed around, and I looked again past the sheet, avoiding the gaping wound that was my wife's stomach. Blood soaked the sheets in a way that seemed wrong. Very, very wrong.

While some worked on Kathryn, just as many—four or five—worked on Keller, warming him and doing all kinds of things to his mouth and nose. It couldn't have been twenty seconds since he'd come out, and he still wasn't crying or making noise.

"Is he okay?" I said to no one in particular, and no one in particular answered back. My pulse was racing, and my breath was hot inside the surgical mask I was made to wear.

"Excuse me, is he okay? Is my wife okay?" This time a nurse glanced back at me, and what I saw in her eyes made me step back. She didn't have to say anything, but she was pleading for me to stop asking. Pleading for me to stop so that she didn't have to answer.

I brought my hands to my face, and in the middle of all the chaos—dying wife on the left and dying baby on the right—I took in a deep breath to scream. When I opened my mouth to release it, a cry sounded instead from my right. Keller coughed, cried, coughed again, and then *wailed*.

The scream I'd prepared turned into a choking sob of relief, and I covered my eyes.

Whatever they were doing to Kathryn seemed to be working as well. She was still not awake, but she didn't look as pale. Perhaps her subconscious mind heard Keller calling for her, and it drew her in from whatever was pulling her away from us.

She was "stable" several minutes later after a few bags of blood had been emptied into her and she was sewn up, right as rain.

The whirlwind of the past several hours was almost too much, and I still can't remember much of it. I remember snapshots, though. A snippet of conversation here, an innocuous announcement from the PA system, and a host of feelings that I experienced at one point or another. When I put them all together, I got something of a narrative... or near enough.

That was how Keller entered the world, a whirlwind of blood and uncertainty. I should have known then that it would be an indicator for the rest of my time with him. I'd be lying if I said I hoped it would have been different. But it wasn't. Kathryn's story, my story, Jackson's—all of them were set in motion the moment Keller was born.

CHAPTER 6

Christmas came and went in our new neighborhood without any major events. Keller's first Christmas resulted in far too many toys for him. My parents bought lavish gifts for both of the boys, using any excuse to justify it. "It's his first Christmas!" for Keller and for Jackson "It's his first Christmas as a big brother!" They were wonderful grandparents.

Kathryn's did something similar, but she was close enough to bring them by on Christmas Eve. It was a special evening full of stories and happiness. The following year was what my dad would fall "fully lived." Keller was a sickly little thing, but what kid wasn't? Our year was filled with loving grandparents doting on my kids while Kathryn and I pretended to stop them. Spring blossomed and with it were plenty of adventures that continued on through summer and fall. We swam and fished and hiked and loved our new home. When Christmas came around again, Kathryn's parents joined mine as we celebrated the second Christmas on Creek Blossom Circle. It was a wonderful memory. For a while there, it felt like the *last* good memory we'd have.

Our neighbors began to learn Jackson's route, and their pets grew to love him even more. Kathryn and I were able to take turns going on walks with him. And despite the occasionally frigid temperatures, I got to know many of the neighbors and their daily routines, as well.

The Shelbergs had coffee on their porch every morning and tea in the afternoon, regardless of the temperature. They waved at us when we'd cross paths and always asked how the boys were doing.

The Godsens went to water aerobics together every morning at six, and if we were lucky, we'd catch them returning to the neighborhood, and Bernie would get a good head scratch from out of the back seat window.

The Brandhauers kept mostly to themselves, but on the rare morning that we saw them, Matt would greet us from his upstairs window. They didn't have a pet, so Jackson didn't usually notice, but I did. The man always gave me such an uncomfortable feeling, almost the same as when we passed the old rickety house at the end of the subdivision. It was unusual that I saw his wife out of the house, but I caught a brief glimpse of her in the kitchen that day.

We saw the Uptons on the very rare occasion. And, when they ventured from the house, we waved hello, made small talk while Jackson tugged on my arm, and promised vaguely to have dinner or drinks together. Our walks, especially during this season, could be a chatty kind of busy, or they'd be as quiet as the chill that had crept into the air. That was another strange thing about the Midwest. Or the South, I'm still not quite sure where Arkansas falls, but the weather can change from one day to the next in such extremes that we learned quickly to keep the summer shirts alongside the winter coats.

As far as my work with Eastwind was concerned, I was able to take some readings from the Corner House, and low and behold, they came back with the status of *High Relevance*. That meant that it was kicked up the chain to Gianna, my supervisor, and she'd put in the proper paperwork for an official request to be made.

The house on the corner never had anyone come or go. The old realty sign in the front had been there for years, perhaps even longer. Knowing I would need to spend more time at the site, I'd need to clear the red tape, first. So I made some calls to real estate agents, the city, even the neighborhood POA. In all three instances, I was given the run-around on who owned it. Turned out that it was part of some deed that was stuck in litigation purgatory, or it had been at the most recent census eight years ago. Since then, the owner had died, and the son or daughter, or whoever was supposed to inherit, didn't see the need for upkeep. I wondered aloud to the clerk I happened to be on the phone with why they didn't just sell it.

"I don't know, honey, and I'm not paid to know." Her voice had the tone of a practiced smoker, and it sounded like her vocal chords were scraping painfully together. "You can call the title company if you want to."

"Sure, that would be fine. Who might that be?"

I got the number from her for *Indigo Title and Land* and called them up, hoping they'd be amenable to someone requesting to do some work on the grounds. At least, that's what I'd tell them. I wouldn't detail what *kind* of work would be done, but I'm sure they'd dealt with someone local wanting to either tear it down or spruce it up, both of which would increase the property value of the surrounding houses.

The title company, unfortunately, wouldn't give permission, and there was too much red tape to even attempt to go the legal route. I asked when the last inspection was done on the home and if they planned on doing one soon.

"Listen," the woman on the line said without any affection, "that place has been more work than it's worth. The last

inspection was done almost twelve years ago in 2041. If there's an inspection scheduled, it's not listed here. I'm surprised the place is still standing, to be honest. The last person who left a note on it was several years ago, and it just says, 'Litigation ongoing.'"

I thanked her and hung up. It sounded like everyone was too busy to even keep up with the place. I was sure there would be legal ramifications if something *were* to happen, but I only planned on using the location and not the house itself. With that in mind, I made a plan to begin exploring the area and trying to find a location for Gretchen. At this point, I should tell you that time travel isn't real. Because if it were, I would travel back in time and stop myself. Hindsight twenty-twenty and all that.

The late January morning that I moved Gretchen to Corner House dawned clear with purple clouds on the horizon. They quickly moved in, and the day became overcast and foggy, the promise of rain told in the mist that wound its way across the chilly breeze. Kathryn would work for most of the week, citing a few new clients that needed the extra face time.

"Part-time will be relative this week," she said before jetting off to work.

"No worries, hon. Take your time. The boys and I will be fine, and we'll see you when you get home." She gave me a peck on the lips and then rushed into the chilly morning air.

I relished the idea of bringing Keller along to drop Jackson off at school, knowing I'd have plenty of time to work, even with a toddler in tow. He and I didn't get much one-on-one time, and I intended to make it count. I did, in a way. God help me, I did.

"Bye bubba," gibbered the snotty little monster strapped into the car seat, punctuating it with a cough.

Jackson reached over before getting out of the car and hugged him awkwardly. "Love you, Kel-Kel." I still wasn't sure of the nickname Jackson had given his sibling.

"Have a great day, buddy!" I tried to get it out before he closed the door, but he was already walking away. He gave me a half-hearted wave and then ran to the red front doors of the school.

As I pulled away from the school, I looked in the backseat. Keller watched the world go by, his eyes darting back and forth watching objects move beyond his field of vision. His very blond hair stood up in crazy ways as the static built up from the movement of his head, back and forth. His nose was still running, and his cheeks had a very feverish blush. Seeing that, I could feel my heart rate increase. I took a breath, hoping the anxiety would abate and I could just enjoy the time with him.

"You ready to work with daddy?" I said excitedly to no one in particular.

Keller sniffed, and I saw him nod in the rearview, not taking his eyes from the objects outside his window.

The windshield wipers squeaked across my view with a rhythmic *thump thunk*. I didn't relish the idea of carting Gretchen all the way to Corner House in this weather, but I suppose it could be worse. At least it wasn't an absolute downpour, yet.

I hadn't quite worked out *exactly* how I'd get into the house. It was locked from the inside, and I'm sure it wasn't rotted enough yet to just crack open. Maybe the door would be unlocked. That would be lucky. If I wasn't lucky—which I would never claim—I wouldn't even need to get inside at all. I hoped I could just set it up in the front yard and call it good. The only problem was that while the FAD didn't need to be in the *exact* place the Ley Lines crossed, it did help if it was as close to the center of the crossing energy lines. I'd brought the FAD-B out several times and did some resonant testing. The Ley Lines definitely crossed near Corner House. One seemed to run right down the middle of the street of our neighborhood and the other perpendicular to it. The initial readings I took while walking around the property all pointed to the house as being directly over the Lines. While the FAD-B was significantly better than nothing, it was still prone to some inaccuracies. I hoped that when I finally brought Gretchen out, she'd be able to give me an accurate reading and that I'd just need to put her on the porch or something.

I had a feeling, even then, that I was wrong.

Keller wasn't much help in loading Gretchen onto the dolly in the garage. He also wasn't helpful when he gagged from a cough that came a little too close to a choke. You'd think I'd be used to it by now, but I wasn't. I would never be used to it.

I put Keller on my shoulders and began to push the cart down the sidewalk. I'd bundled him up as if it were winter, but just put a jacket on myself. His mittened hands rested on my head, and he bobbed a little as I pushed. Most of the neighbors weren't out this early, but Greg McKahee gave me an inquisitive stare as we walked past his house. Daisy stared at us, her tiny head cocked to the side. I'm sure I looked strange pushing a large device down the sidewalk with a toddler swaying on my shoulders. I nodded at him and continued on.

We approached Corner House, and it may have just been me, but the more I think on that day, the more I seem to remember the sky darkening the moment the house came into view. It could have been that the streetlight wasn't lit and some of the others in the neighborhood were, but I didn't think so.

I parked Gretchen on the sidewalk and, holding onto one of Keller's legs, opened the rickety gate. The overgrown path led to several steps onto a wooden porch that ran across the front of the house, the front door in the center. I stepped up on the porch, careful of the rickety old stairs, but I put Keller down first and held his hand. The last thing I needed was for him to run off and fall through a rotten board or something.

The soffit above the door sagged several inches below the roofing timber. Several twigs and a few scraps of trash stuck out at odd angles, no doubt the haphazard nest of a grackle or squirrel when spring rolled around again. For now, however, it was just an empty eyesore.

In my mind's eye, I could see Gretchen sitting on the front porch, mentally measuring the dimensions to determine if there was enough room. It was longer than it was deep, running twenty yards in both directions and ending with a railing that I was certain wouldn't support even the slightest weight. A porch swing hung at one end of the porch, swinging lazily in the wind. One end grazed the ground, its broken chain dangling from the ceiling and making a staccato scratching sound against the wooden planks of the porch.

Certain now that my mental measurements would be fine, I walked back to the sidewalk and positioned Gretchen as best I could through the gate. She didn't fit, and I ended up cracking several wooden stakes off at knee-height. With the house in its current state, no one would be able to tell.

Once she was up the stairs—no small feat with a toddler, let me tell you—I opened the yellow control panel and wiped a few errant droplets of moisture away from the screen behind it. The touch panel prompted me for an access code, and I entered it from memory—0820. The panel changed to an interactive menu, and I started a preparatory scanning sequence. Gretchen wasn't the largest version of the FAD. In fact, they'd developed a massive one that could measure Ley Lines hundreds of miles away with relative accuracy. Gretchen could only detect Ley Lines within about ten miles, and the closer to the Ley Line Intersect, the more accurate the reading. It was kind of a game, trying to find the perfect spot for the FADs.

The lights around the two coaxial wheels in the middle lit up with a dull glow and began to pulse with a yellow glow and rotate around one another slowly on the skull-sized orbs within. I was used to this, but I wasn't sure Keller had ever seen the boot-up sequence. I held him up and watched him as his eyes grew wider and wider. Through the glassteel housing, much of the mechanism could be seen rotating, bobbing, and spinning. It protected us from any kind of debris that might be ejected in the event of a malfunction. But that hadn't ever happened that I knew of, so I wasn't worried.

After several seconds, Gretchen gave a series of beeps and musical tones, indicating the initial scan and prep work were complete. The panel displayed the energy readings, and I frowned. Her current position was close to the intersection of the Ley Lines Intersect, but it wasn't the *best* spot for her. It probably would have worked. It would have been fine.

I let Gretchen sit there, the lights glowing dimly, illuminating the geometric patterns of intersecting bars, gears, and cables. In the dimness of the mid-morning light, it cast an eerie glow across the dilapidated siding and porch planks.

I put Keller on my hip and tried the doorknob with my free hand. To my surprise, it turned easily, and the door swung open. I couldn't believe my luck. To this day, I wonder if it was luck or some other force that unlocked that door. I don't suppose I'll ever know.

"Hold onto Daddy, buddy." I had the sudden unease of being an intruder. I suppose I was, actually. But I felt sweat bead on my forehead and clasped Keller's hand even tighter as I took another step farther into the house, feeling all of the misdemeanors I'd just committed.

Dust covered the floor, undisturbed for what I assumed was over a decade, no doubt. It wasn't in complete disarray, I noticed looking around. The staircase looked unsturdy, and the two rooms to either side of the entryway had several sagging boxes stacked in their corners. Overall, I thought it would be fine. Even if I just borrowed this little entryway.

I told Keller to wait outside on the porch step, and I watched him toddle over with his green galoshes and put his little hand against a pillar to step down. He teetered on the verge of falling but simply plopped down on his bottom and put his hands in his lap.

"Thank you, buddy. Wait right there for Daddy, okay?"

"Tay, Daddy," he said. *Okay, Daddy.* Good enough for me, the little cutie.

I glanced at the darkening sky before grabbing Gretchen by the steel handles flanking either side, and I hefted her toward the front door. I could have used the dolly, but I was a man and didn't tend to think things through. Very on the nose, the process was graceless, and there may have been a multitude of expletives, but I was able to get her through the front door. And I only scraped a *tiny* bit of the doorframe. You couldn't even tell, really. *Like the gate*, I told myself.

I settled her evenly on the hardwood floors ten or fifteen feet inside the door. It wasn't much farther from where I'd run the diagnostic tool for the Ley Line location, but it was enough of a difference, apparently. When I engaged the panel again, it lit up with a happy green "initiate" button. This was the part that I really wasn't certain about, scientifically. Gretchen would send out a range of frequencies and measure the strongest return signal from the invisible lines that ran like rivers from horizon to horizon across the planet within the crust. Once she figured out what the most significant frequency match was, she'd begin the process of trying to match it exactly. I wasn't sure why or how, but the goal wasn't to harmonize with the Ley Line; it was to match it exactly and then move a hairsbreadth in dissonance. Eastwind's scientists believed that if the dissonant frequency could cause just the right amount of destabilization, Gretchen would act like an exit ramp. The lines could then be diverted toward Gretchen, and she would be able to capture the frequency of the diverted energy, match it in the inverse and create a kind of positive-negative attraction. That was the theory, at least. In this way, the energy would be attracted to the FAD and could then be harvested in an infinite amount of ever-present energy.

It didn't seem dangerous to me at the time. Maybe it was because I just didn't understand it at all. The instructions, the training, the machine itself—all of it felt safe behind the shield of ignorance I'd erected for myself.

I mentioned earlier how Eastwind was close to a break-through. Yeah, they were close. I was closer.

I tapped the green button, and Gretchen's machinery whirred to life once more. I walked outside to sit with Keller on the porch. The process would take a while, and there wasn't any reason for me to watch it; the sequence was automated, and I could hear the pleasant hum of Gretchen doing exactly what she was built to do.

Keller looked up at me as I approached. When I sat next to him, he smiled and leaned his head against my hip. I gently pinched his nose between my thumb and forefinger, squeezed out the snot that I saw clogging him up, and flicked it into the knee-high grass around us. I grimaced; he grimaced. It was a whole gross thing that came with being a parent. We didn't get to be grossed out by stuff, anymore.

Thunder rumbled in the distance.

We played patty-cake for a couple of minutes, and when he got distracted by the grass and hopped down from the steps, I let him. Knowing that Gretchen would be busy for a little longer, I didn't ever get to just watch him play.

He picked at the stalks of grass with his chubby little fingers. "Your fine motor skills need work, sir," I said to him. He looked up at me, gibbered something unintelligible, and bent to pick up a piece of paper, some kind of propaganda. I read the only visible words on it, "New Gods," and ignored the rest completely.

"Eh, let's not play with that," I said and reached out to take it from him.

He pulled it out of my reach with surprising quickness and grinned at me. He knew what he'd done, and it was, admittedly, pretty cute.

"Get back here, you," I said and screwed my face up into a monstrous scowl.

He squealed and began to high knee it through the grass. I pretended to chase, barking and growling at him as he ran away, clasping the trash like a trophy above his head.

I crouched low and waited for him to turn back to me, which he did a second later and jumped in surprise as I roared and leapt at him. He screamed excitedly and clambered up the steps of the porch. I pretended to fall at the same time and lay on my back in the moist grass, my eyes to the sky. The sky was making good on its earlier promise of rain as a fat drop landed on my cheek and then forehead.

I sat up, leaning on one elbow and looked at Keller who stood on the porch like a victorious gladiator, talking gibberish at me. The rain began, then. The initial drops turned into a downpour within seconds, and I hunched my shoulders against the sudden chilly wetness that soaked quickly through my jacket.

"Alright buddy, let's—" Movement had caught my eye behind my yellow-clad toddler. A sound that had been subtly irritating my ears. It suddenly ramped its way into the forefront of my mind as I connected it with its source. Gretchen was rocking back and forth in a way I'd never seen in all my years of working with FADs, and a steady buzz—more like the air was vibrating—was coming off of her in waves. The rocking wasn't matching the coaxial gyros I could see spinning out of sync within its glassteel globe, and it made me immediately uneasy. Terrified, if I'm being honest.

I stood up quickly. Too quickly. Keller thought it was part of the game and ran away in the only direction afforded to him: into the house toward Gretchen. No one would ever blame him, *could* ever blame him. He was a toddler, and life was a game. It was my fault, really.

"Keller!" I yelled at him, hoping he'd stop. Something terrified me, and maybe that same force that had unlocked the door for me also gifted me this new dread.

Gretchen rocked back and forth, more violently now. The feet that supported her visibly lifted off the ground several centimeters before clunking back to the floor. The buzz turned into a much less subtle keening whine, and it began rippling through the air in waves. It felt like nails on a chalkboard, or metal forks rubbing together, and I dipped my head against it.

I took a step, trying to reach for the railway, but my foot slipped in the long, wet grass, and I fell to the ground, my chin missed the first step by a hairsbreadth.

"Keller! Stop!" I screamed it at him as I stood back up, but even now I don't think he could have heard me. Between the sudden downpour, the rolling thunder, and the uproar of Gretchen's rocking, there was no way he could have heard me. And he was a toddler. What could I possibly have expected?

The keening that had begun as something annoying and mildly painful was now actively hurting my ears. Keller, who was now standing only a few feet from Gretchen inside the door, dropped the trash and stared fixedly at the rocking mechanism. He tried to cover his ears, but the coat wouldn't let him. I watched him turn, his face the mask of a toddler—little more than a baby, really—who had seen something scary and was looking for safety. Looking for me.

I yelled at him to come to Daddy, to come back, to get away. I tried to run to him, but I only made it to the top of the stairs before the air itself was rent in two. A shimmering ring passed through Keller, lifting him off the ground and throwing him out the door and across the porch like a ragdoll. The ring passed through me, but even a few yards away it had dissipated and felt like a light shove on my chest. The rain fell sideways as the ever-expanding ring crossed into the front yard. I didn't feel it, really. My eyes were locked on Keller as he tumbled through the air. I didn't have to dive for him, just take a step to my left to snatch him out of the air.

He was wide-eyed when I turned his head toward my face. He was terrified, maybe a little dazed, but when his eyes locked onto mine, he burst into the terrified tears of a wailing baby.

I hugged him to my chest and rocked him. "Oh buddy, it's okay. Daddy's here. It's okay buddy. You're alright. Everything is okay, Keller." Over and over and over.

I stared at Gretchen. White smoke slipped through cracks of the glassteel case in twirling, coalescing ribbons. A cog had embedded itself in the casing, and one half of the coaxial rig swung uselessly in the middle of it all, its lights blinking unevenly.

I didn't know what happened. Well, at the time I didn't. I know, now, but I'll get to that.

I was sitting on the steps and still hugging Keller to my chest, whose wails had quieted to whimpers, when my cell phone rang. It was Marco Riviera, my counterpart at Eastwind Headquarters in Santa Cruz, California.

"Hey, dude." His normal greeting made it sound like he'd just finished smoking a joint. "Just wanted to give you a shout. I got a crazy reading on your FAD, wanted to see if you were aware of any changes."

I sighed. "Hey, Marco. Yeah, I'm aware of the changes. Gretchen just blew up."

Silence.

"Who?"

Oh, right. Not everyone named their FAD. "Gretchen, my FAD. It just blew up."

"Oh shit, for real? You hurt?"

"No, I'm fine. I mean, I think. My toddler was nearby when it happened. He wasn't hurt. I don't think."

"Damn, bro. That's crazy. You want me to file the report?"

"Yeah, that would be great, thanks."

The report he mentioned was a Collateral Unit Event. It was a form that all employees were required to fill out when one of their machines malfunctioned in any way. Usually, a CUE was something completed when the touch panel wouldn't respond, or when a lightbulb burnt out in the gear housing. Now, I was filing one because Gretchen turned into a bomb.

"Alright, bro, I've got that going for you. Should come over in your email within a few minutes. You need anything else? You need me to send a message to Gianna?"

"Yeah, that would also be great. I've got to get my kiddo home to check him for any injuries. I'll file an Incident Report later tonight, probably after the kids go to bed."

"Right, yeah take your time. Rules say twenty-four hours. And I'll let Gianna know that it's in-process."

"Great. Thanks, Marco," and I hung up.

Gianna was our department head; she'd want to know what happened. She could also initiate a device requisition so that I could get a replacement for Gretchen, though I wasn't sure how long that would take. Gretchen might be useless at this point, but some part of me hoped that her readings could be salvaged. Whatever happened was different than any other FAD sequence I'd ever seen.

I loaded up the smoking machine onto the cart, surprised that none of it was hot to the touch. Keller wanted me to carry him, so I had to put him on my chest and supported his rump with my forearms as I pushed the cart. He wrapped his arms around my neck and buried his face in my jacket, closing his eyes against the light of the streetlamp as we passed beneath it, leaving Corner House behind for now.

By the time we got home, we were dripping.

"Wet, Daddy," he said as I changed him into fresh clean clothes, then myself.

"Yeah, buddy, we're all wet, aren't we?" His eyes were swollen and red from crying. He could probably use a nap. Hell, I could use one.

I gave him a sippy cup of milk and, after checking him for injuries and finding none, snuggled him in the rocking chair of his room. I kissed his cheek as we sat in the quiet and whispered into his hair, "You're my favorite." He was asleep before his milk was even gone, and I moved it after feeling it drip from his slack lips onto my own shirt. I was asleep shortly thereafter. The exhaustion you feel from fear is one hell of a sleep aid.

Kathryn came home later that afternoon before I'd left to pick Jackson up from school. I told her about the malfunction but absolutely *not* about our son being tossed through the air. That was something that was going to stay locked away in my own memory... or so I thought.

She responded much more level-headed than I would have.

"Well, are you okay?"

"Yeah, I'm fine. Just a little freaked, that's all."

She chewed on a carrot for a few seconds. "Well, are they going to replace Gretchen?"

"That's my understanding. I mean, I can't really work without her."

"Right, that makes sense. I wonder how much one of those things costs." She raised her eyes in a can-you-tell-me-that-secret kind of way, and I chuckled.

"I don't know exactly, but it's a lot. Probably as much as the house."

"Yikes. Well, I'm glad you're okay. Keller is good? He wasn't hurt?"

"Yep," I lied. "He's just fine, now. It scared him, too, but he's okay."

"Good." She checked her watch. "You want to go get Jack or should I?"

I shrugged. "You can if you want. You usually don't get to be the end-of-day hero."

"Yeah, I'll go get him." She smiled and kissed me. She tasted like carrots. "I'll be back soon."

"Okay, hon. I'll be here."

She kissed Keller's forehead and then walked to the door, keys in hand. "I think Kel's got a fever; you might check it."

"Will do, babe." I wouldn't have been worried if Keller hadn't been subject to some kind of energy pulse earlier in the day. Any other day Keller would be running a fever, I'd just brush it off as normal. I mean, I wasn't a first-time parent. Now, though, my heart picked up pace as I ran the temporal thermometer across his brow. Sure enough, one-hundred point nine.

I picked him up, gave him some anti-fever medication, and then sat with him on the couch to watch cartoons until Jackson and Kathryn came home, my laptop open next to me while I waited for a message from Eastwind.

Jackson came home, dropped his backpack by the door and made it three steps through the kitchen toward the living room before Kathryn hollered from the porch, "Shoes off!" Jackson's rainboots squeaked as he stopped in the kitchen and crept carefully back to the door.

"Dasson!" Despite Keller's fever and excitement from the day's events, he slid quickly from my lap and toddled over. Jackson lifted him up, and they began talking about all the exciting things they did today. Jackson's bright eyes and keen interest in the gibberish that Keller spouted made me smile in appreciation for the gracious attitude he would no doubt grow into as an adult.

Kathryn came in a moment later and began doling out orders for afternoon chores.

A chime sounded from beside me, and the icon for a "new message" blinked. I opened it up to a five-word message

> From: gScotelli@eastwindenergy.com
> To: gTaldo@eastwindenergy.com
> 3:48 pm CST
> (No Subject)
>
> Call me when you can.
>
> Sincerely,
> Gianna Scotelli
> VP of Field Research

I knew It was probably nothing, but when I get a message that simply said, "call me," it always kicked off my anxiety.

"How's everybody?" Kathryn asked as I walked into the kitchen with my laptop and phone out.

"We're good. He's got a fever like you thought," she bowed theatrically, "and I just got an email to call Gianna, so..."

She nodded. "Alright, babe. No worries, I'm sure she just wants to hear what happened and start that requisition-whatever form."

I smiled at her and kissed her cheek. "I'll be in our room."

When I was settled at the desk and the door was closed firmly behind me, I dialed Gianna's number.

It rang twice before a woman's voice answered in a light Mediterranean accent, "Hello?"

"Hey, Gianna. It's Grant Taldo. Midwest agent."

"Oh hello, Grant. Thanks for giving me a ring. Marco gave me a brief description of what happened, but you know Marco. I wanted to make sure everyone was okay."

"I appreciate that. Yes, everyone is okay. I think Keller, my toddler, and I were a little shaken up. But we're doing better."

"Yes, tell me about what happened. I looked at the data stream, and there was quite the spike in activity from your unit. Can you describe what was going on with it?"

"I set up," and remembering that she would have no idea if I called it by the moniker I'd given said, "my FAD just like I usually do. I had just run a test, and it indicated that a significant Intersect was present. The tests would have been fine, but it suggested that a stronger frequency could be attained by moving it just a few yards farther. I moved it, set up all the same diagnostics and sequences that I've done probably a thousand times before, and then I let it run."

"And when did you notice that something was wrong?"

I didn't want to say, "When it blew up in my toddler's face," so I settled for, "I noticed it rocking back and forth rapidly as if it was on uneven ground or some of the lifts had been seated incorrectly."

"And then?" she prompted.

"Well, and then it blew up."

"Was there anything else that happened?"

"Like what?"

"I don't know, Mr. Grant. Anything other than the explosion itself, I suppose."

I thought back to the explosion and the helpless fear that gripped me as I saw Keller standing feet away from a device that was obviously erratic and played the rest through my mind.

"Actually, yes. There was something."

"What was it?" Her mild curiosity sounded like it was winding up.

"It's kind of hard to explain, but I'll do my best." I inhaled slowly. "When the FAD blew up, there weren't any wayward pieces of the machine itself, everything was contained within the glassteel casing. But there was a... a pulse of some kind that expanded out from the FAD itself. It... well, it lifted my toddler off his feet. I caught him, and he was fine, but that pulse was a kind of shimmering ring."

"Did it continue on?"

"No, it dissipated shortly after I felt it pass through me, and I was maybe twenty yards away from it. Twenty-five at the most."

"Interesting. The data seems to support that there was a burst of some kind, something we haven't seen before, actually."

"Yes, that was what I'd call it. A burst. Was it energy?"

"That's something we don't know, yet. I would imagine it had to be a discharge of one kind or another. But rest assured, I've already got several teams combing through the data, and we'll let you know if we need anything else.

"Is there anything that you need, Grant?"

I could tell she was intrigued, but not as excited as I thought she'd be. She certainly didn't care about Keller or me, now that I told her we were fine.

"I think I need a new FAD, at least. Mine seems fried."

"Oh, of course, how could I have forgotten?"

It was silent for a moment aside from the taps from her keyboard in the background. "It looks like the closest site we have is a Repair office in Oklahoma City. Can you take the FAD there for repairs? It would mean overtime and a stipend for travel, of course."

I didn't relish the idea of driving to Oklahoma, but it would probably be faster than waiting for someone to come repair Gretchen. And a stipend may be small, but money's money.

"Sure, I think I can manage it."

"Great to hear, Grant. I'll get the details over to you and let Marco work out the rest with you."

"Okay, Gianna. Thanks."

"Absolutely. I'm glad to hear Kelly is okay."

"It's Kel—" *Nevermind,* I thought, "Yeah, me too." She wouldn't remember, anyway.

CHAPTER 7

The first time I remember Jackson waking up with a nose-bleed was the day following the FAD explosion at Corner House. I want to say he had them prior to then and I just didn't remember, but I just can't say. It was a mild one compared to others that would follow. I heard a commotion upstairs and went to check on him. He was washing his face in the jack-and-jill bathroom that connected his room to Keller's.

"Hey, buddy. You okay?"

He jumped in surprise and turned toward me. I hadn't seen it with his face turned away from me, but a streak of blood ran from his nose down the other side of his mouth. He wiped it away quickly, but immediately concerned, I stepped closer and knelt down.

"Jack, are you alright?"

He nodded as I opened the cabinet beneath the sink to retrieve a towel from the stack we kept there.

"What happened?"

His voice was muffled as I wiped away the water, then tilted his head into the light for a better look.

"I don't know, Daddy. I woke up because I felt my nose running, but when I wiped it, I saw it was blood, so I came in here to wash it off."

I remember that he wasn't upset. His voice was calm and even. I don't know if it was because it was—in his mind—a random occurrence that may or may not happen again, or if maybe he was still half asleep and didn't care. I think any parent should be concerned when they see their children bleeding, but I chalked it up to one of those quirks of kids and tucked him back in. I wish I'd known it was barely the beginning.

There wasn't another nosebleed for some time—several weeks later, maybe even a month. But I'm getting ahead of myself again.

Gretchen still wasn't fully repaired. The next appointment wouldn't be for another month, and I was spending much of my time running diagnostics and checking for Intersections nearby. The one that I'd originally picked up at Corner House seemed to have shrunk in both size and scope; it barely even registered, now—at least, according to the FAD-B. I'm not sure how it happened, but I attributed it to a faulty issue in the firmware that resulted in the explosion and moved on.

Between the explosion itself and the repair appointment in Oklahoma City, I'd be combing through the data and comparing it to other tests that have been run in the past. I had weekly meetings with Marco, Gianna, and a field team leader by the name of Josef Paschal out of Albany. Nothing could *really* be done about the Corner House readings until we were sure another test could duplicate the results—which couldn't happen before the repairs, anyway—or we were sure they *wouldn't* have the same results.

The weeks passed by slowly, working on the data each day at home, taking video calls with Marco and others, or taking the boys for a walk while Kathryn worked or went into the office. It was all a delicate and intricate dance that we were doing our best to perfect.

I'd gone to Corner House one chilly February day with a FAD-B to double check the results from Gretchen. Sure enough, the Intersect was still there, but it was still weaker. I logged the changes, deciding to call it a day a couple hours early and letting Marco know I'd be out of pocket.

After eating and cleaning the dinner dishes later that night, I bent low enough to allow Jackson to jump on my back. With his little arms wrapped securely around my neck and his legs locked around my waist, I stood up. For one fateful second, I felt his center of gravity change, and in my mind's eye, I saw myself teetering and falling, both of us crashing to the ground in a giggling mess of arms and elbows. Then I was up and as my knees cracked loudly, a relieved sigh escaped my lips.

"Holding tight?" I asked.

"Yep!" Jackson's bright voice was muffled into my back, and I grinned, galloping around the living room making animal noises while Kathryn pretended to shoo us away.

Laughing together, we started up the stairs. I took careful steps to avoid jostling Jackson, only because I could already barely breathe and didn't want a sudden movement to scare him into holding onto my neck even tighter.

"Good night, sweet boy. Remember we're watching a show tonight, so you need to stay in bed, okay?" Kathryn called from the couch below us, and Jackson turned and waved at her, his other hand clenching harder around my Adam's apple.

When I reached the upstairs hallway that led to both of my sons' rooms, I twisted Jackson off my back so that he could walk. The boy's blue robe billowed silently around his little feet as I lowered him to the ground.

My little son—well, not terribly little anymore—stopped and looked up at me. "Daddy, is it a monster movie you and Mommy are watching?"

I smiled. "Well, I don't think so. I think it's just a good guy and bad guy movie."

His little head nodded sagely, and we walked quietly to his room. Jackson's hand reached up to grasp my much larger hand, only releasing it when he crawled onto his bed. I sat on the edge and began tucking the covers around his form. He liked it when I made a "kid burrito." I kissed him on the forehead after he was snuggled in and wrapped tightly.

"Mommy and I are going to watch a movie downstairs," I reiterated. "You stay in bed, okay? I don't want you to come downstairs and see something that you won't like." My eldest had always been a curious child. We'd had to start handing out these warnings because of several near misses with shows that would have either scared him or intrigued him a little too much.

Jackson nodded quietly. "Okay, Daddy." He was silent and still for a moment while I looked down at him in the quiet darkness.

"Daddy?"

"Yeah, bud?"

"Is it a scary movie?"

I affected a smile of nonchalance. "No, it's not a scary movie. But I bet there'll be stuff in it that's a little too much for you. That's why I want you to stay up here."

Jackson nodded again. "Is it gonna be bloody?"

I acted as if I was thinking hard and then shrugged. "No, I don't think so. But I haven't seen it, so I can't be sure. And you know what we always say?"

"Yep. 'Better safe than sorry,'" Jackson answered in practiced unison with me. He remained silent for a minute more, but I could tell something was bothering him. He didn't want to appear anxious, certainly his mother's son, but he tended to wear his heart on his sleeve. In this case, there may as well

have been a neon sign above his head flashing the words "I AM ANXIOUS."

I felt for my son and wanted desperately for him to be comfortable talking about things that scared him or made him nervous. So I asked, "Whatcha thinking, bud?"

Jackson's fingers began entwining themselves together over the dinosaur comforter he lay beneath. He licked his lips, then said, "Daddy, do you believe in monsters?"

I breathed in deeply, debating in my own mind which direction to take in regard to the intricacies of what defines a "monster."

Part of me wanted to write it off as nothing. Say something along the lines of "No, I don't. There's no such thing as monsters." The problem was that I didn't want to lie to my son. I knew, in fact, that if I said that, my son would hear the lie and the unshakable faith in his father would become less reliable, less real.

A car's headlights reflected briefly off the windows of the house across the street and shined directly into Jackson's room. It was an odd occurrence, and each time it happened, I told myself that I'd try to figure out a way to block it. It was annoying, but probably wasn't even noticed by him.

The other part of me wished I could go into all of the intricacies that accompanied that word "monster." I wanted my son—now getting older and more accustomed to the hollow indifference the world held for the innocence of the young—to understand that the term "monster" held a multitude of meanings. To him, the word merely meant a beast of some kind, with razor sharp claws and needle-like teeth, its back lined with spines and its skin a sallow green from years spent scavenging beneath the surface of the earth.

My own understanding of the term, however, included the fantastic caricature of fear defined by my son as well as the more realistic—and sadly, the more familiar—version of it. Monsters could take the shape of an abusive father or mother, a bully on the playground, or a predatory stranger who wished ill on anyone they met. The term "monster" was, as unfortunate as it happened to be, much more realistic in my own definition than Jackson's. And at this very moment, I desperately wished it wasn't so.

Realizing he was still waiting for his answer, I sighed and smoothed a bit of the comforter. When I spoke, I affected a tone of leisurely academia, a teacher and a student. I hoped the tone would help put him at ease.

"That's a tricky question, bud. If you're asking me if I believe in a monster like Dracula or Godzilla or something like that, my answer is a pretty simple 'no.' But if you're asking me if I believe that monsters—in some form or another—exist, then my answer is 'yes.'"

Jackson cocked his head and squinted in that boyish way that meant nothing but clear confusion.

"Let me explain," I chuckled. "Monsters with spikes and claws and teeth are fun to think about, even scary if you think one is looking at you from your closet." I indicated the open door across the room, and he cut his eyes uneasily that direction. "But you know there's nothing there. Even when it *feels* like something is there, deep down you know there's nothing in your closet except for the clothes and hats, probably some legos you threw in there when Mommy asked you to tidy up." I tried to adjust my tone at the end from academic to playfully accusatory, and Jackson smiled in a "guilty-as-charged" manner.

"You look out your window or the door to the balcony, and you get that same feeling that something is out there. It's a much bigger world out there; maybe there could be. After all, the closet has walls, and out there," I hooked a thumb at the windows that now reflected the small reading lamp beside us, "has no walls at all."

I paused to let him digest what I said and cleared my throat before continuing.

"The problem is that your word 'monster' means a lot of different things. It doesn't just mean a scary beast. It can be, well, almost anything, actually. You have a bully at your school, right? That Jeffrey kid that likes to take the toys from the little kids and throw them in the middle of puddles or over the fence so they can't reach them?" Jackson nodded. "That kid is a monster to some of the smaller boys and girls because he's beastly to them. Bigger, meaner, uncontrolled. You understand?"

Again, Jackson nodded. His mouth opened and closed a couple of times before he could finally get the words out.

"But Daddy, do *you* believe in monsters? Do *you* have a monster?"

Well, shit. It looks like my son picked up on the fact that I'd left out my own definition of monster, or the part that mattered to him, at least.

I sighed in resignation. "Yeah, bud. I have monsters. Just like there are bullies for you there are bullies for adults, too. They do different—and worse things—than Jeffrey at your school. Usually, they try to hurt people because maybe they were hurt. Maybe they don't know anything *but* pain, so they believe that's how the world has to be. Inflict pain because it was inflicted upon them. But there's also *good* in the world. There are monsters, but like in those comic books you read or superhero movies, the monster has a nemesis, right? It has someone that knows how to fight it and how to beat it. In the end, even when it doesn't look like it, the good guy comes to the rescue and defeats it.

"A lot of times, that's how being an adult is. Sometimes there's a monster, and it takes a good guy to stand up and do something about it."

Jackson sat quietly for a moment before nodding, his fingers still twisting together like anxious little worms. "I think I understand. Is that what your movie is about? Good guys beating the monsters, the bad guys?"

Thankful that we'd circled back around to it, I nodded enthusiastically. "That's right! That's exactly right, buddy. You get it."

Jackson rolled onto his side and brought his knees up to his chest, snuggling further into his pillow and blankets.

I took his cue and kissed him on the cheek and whispered, "I love you. You're my favorite," then switched off the lamp and stood slowly to allow my knees to crack if they needed to.

The black windows of the balcony door stood as silent sentries, guarding against the darkness. It was hard to differentiate the reflective indoor lights and shapes with the outside lines of shingled gables and ghostly glowing streetlamps. It *was* a very big world, and while there was good in it, it also had its fair share of monsters.

I prayed silently that my sons would never have to face the kind of monsters I feared. I prayed until I could feel the corners of my eyes sting with unshed tears of desperation and until my fingernails began biting into my palms from clenching my fists. I prayed until the fear that had become a lump in my throat threatened to leap from between my pursed lips in one long, sobbing gasp, a desperate cry for a world without harm, where the sanctity of innocence was held in higher regard than the knowledge of the guilty.

With great effort, I released the tension and budding terror I felt. My shoulders sagged and instead of a raspy gasp, a deep sigh turned the starry sky before me into a muted, foggy pane of glass.

I stood a moment longer, steadying myself. The emotion that had crept into my chest so suddenly faded almost as quickly as it had come.

I made sure the balcony's deadbolt and doorknob were locked and then left the room, casting a final glance at my son's form beneath the covers. They moved silently with his even breathing, a steady movement that indicated peace and contentment. I feared for a moment during our talk that my definition of "monster" would scare him, but I was glad to see that Jackson took it in stride. I underestimated him, sometimes.

I peeked into Keller's room where he, too, lay still. His fever had come and gone, and now his sleepy breaths held only slightly less of a scummy rattle.

I made my way downstairs where the movie had been paused and a bowl of popcorn sat on the coffee table before Kathryn. She smiled up at me and patted the cushion next to her. I sat, and she wriggled closer until our hips touched. She threw a blanket across our laps and started the movie.

The show, in the end, was like any other. A problem arose for the main characters, they tried to solve it, someone tried to stop them, and just when it seemed like they'd succeed, the heroes were able to right the wrong and everything ended in happiness. Boring, but a pleasant deviation from the unknowns of real life.

After cleaning up the popcorn, I told Kathryn I was going to check on the boys and then come back down for bed. She kissed me on the lips. "I'll read until you're done," she said and then rested her head on the pillows and closed her eyes. By "reading" she must have meant "sleep on the couch," and I smiled and patted her exposed thigh.

I sat for a moment before moving. The house once again was blessedly silent.

The new stairs—our stairs—led to the second-floor landing, where I made my way picking up crayons and noisy toys that I was certain would wake the whole neighborhood along the way. I turned and walked the four steps up to the second-floor hallway. The hall was long, twice as long as our first house had been, and it passed both the boys' rooms before ending in another turn to the playroom. The hallway was lit by three small sconces along the wall, but the far end was lit by the playroom light, and like every dutiful husband, I could feel the pennies leaving my pockets as unused lights lit unused corners with unnecessary light.

I walked toward the playroom, stepping over the pair of shoes Jackson had tossed there, and I peeked quickly into Keller's room. He was sound asleep, his mobile light creating shadows that danced and changed across the uneven surfaces in his walls and ceiling.

Smiling with the contentment of sleeping children, I continued on to the end of the hallway.

While Kathryn and I had both agreed that the new house was perfect, I'd begun to realize that this small little end of the house always left me unsettled, as if when I turned the corner to the playroom, I'd come face-to-face with someone—or something—standing there in the hall. A bit too eerie for my liking.

It was no different this time. And while there wasn't any outward clue as to my inner misgivings, I swallowed and

walked around the corner with a rapidly thumping heart into the empty playroom beyond, breathing a small sigh of relief when, like always, I found myself alone in the room.

I hit the light, plunging the room into darkness except for a muted glow that came from the window at the opposite end of the room. I walked toward it, Keller's stuffed hippo under my arm and a rubber car clutched loosely in my right hand.

The blanket of night that covered the neighborhood past the glass in front of me was a velvety blue full of stars and stillness. I stood solemnly at the window and looked down upon the driveway and several houses across and down the street, their windows dark this late in the night. I tried to ignore the sudden tingle in my spine. A kind of lighthearted dread brought on by the thought of actually seeing someone standing in the driveway looking up at me.

The conversation with Jackson had made me uneasy, if I was being honest. All that talk of monsters had allowed my imagination to run with carnival-like freedom. My heart was beating a little faster than normal, and I couldn't shake that troubled discomfort.

My breath stopped short.

The tingle in my spine wasn't that feeling of watching an unwitting stranger below, it was the feeling of *being* watched.

I had the sudden urge to whip my head around. To double check that I was, in fact, alone. But I imagined turning and instead of an empty room behind me, the monster Jackson and I had discussed would be standing there, its claws and spikes ready to tear into me.

Realizing how incredibly childish I was acting and brushing the nightmarish discomfort from my mind, I gave the ground outside and below me one last glance. Before I turned, my eyes focused briefly on a reflection in the glass.

A scream tried to tear itself from my throat as my eyes lit on a shadowy figure standing silently in the doorway, silhouetted by the sconce-lit hallway behind it.

It stood in the doorway of the playroom, watching me silently and rocking slowly back and forth. The creature's head was listless, topped with ridges and cruel spines along its cranial ridge. Its arms hung loosely at its sides, and they were tipped with the same claws I'd just imagined tearing me apart. Adrenaline told me to turn and fight—

"Daddy?"

The little voice that came from the shadow pulled me from the distant terror and back into reality, and I blinked.

The terrible creature my mind had created was replaced with the familiar figure of my son. The cranial ridges were his robe's hood, which was a blue dinosaur. It did, in fact, have cloth spikes that ran the length of the hood from forehead to lower back. The claw-tipped fingers were my own son's curled hands, the light and shadow playing a nasty trick upon my already anxious imagination.

Jackson repeated himself. "Daddy?" and I turned to face him with a grin that hid a hammering heart.

"Hey bud," I said, "what's wrong?"

I walked across the playroom to my young son and knelt in front of him, taking his small hands into my own. "Is it another nosebleed?" I asked, checking the pajama top and his face for any sign. At this point, he had had several.

Jackson shook his head in the way that only a child can, that one that conveys nonchalant impatience.

"No, not a nosebleed." Jackson pulled his hands out of my gentle grasp and began twining his fingers together in that nervous habit he had that had always been a precursor to a sensitive question.

My heartbeat had slowed, but I could feel myself brace for a new question. Perhaps our talk of monsters had scared my little boy, as well.

"Daddy, am I going to die?"

I was momentarily taken aback. *Die?*

I thought I would have more time than this. Nine years wasn't a long enough time on earth to begin questioning one's mortality, but here we were.

Trying my best to put on a face of that same nonchalant impatience, I shook my head with a wide smile. It was the kind of movement that I hoped said, "That's the silliest thing in the world."

"Not any time soon, I think. I mean, you know that everyone dies *sometime*, but most people die when they're very old after they've had a very long life and enjoyed a great many things. I have a feeling that you will have a very long life and enjoy a great many things before it's your time to go." I swallowed hard. "Why do you ask, buddy?"

Jackson looked down at his writhing fingers and shifted his weight from one foot to the other.

"Is it because of your nosebleed?" I didn't want to lead him toward that, but I had the sneaking suspicion that they were the cause of his sudden mortal concern.

His eyes began to glisten before a tear rolled resolutely down his freckled cheek.

I felt my throat tighten, and I pulled my son into a tight embrace. Jackson didn't reach his arms around me at first; he only laid his head on my shoulder in a kind of resigned way and began to sob into my neck.

I could feel the warm wetness of his tears pressing into my skin and dampening my shirt, but I didn't care.

It wasn't until I stood and lifted him off the ground that Jackson put his arms around my neck in a hug. It was firm and his hands grasped one another between my shoulder blades; it felt like he was holding on for dear life.

Jackson continued to sob, but where they had begun in defeat, the tears were now fading into exhaustion. I'm not a betting man, but in this instance, I would have bet that this had been bothering Jackson for some time and he'd just now mustered the courage to ask the question. Maybe we had fostered the kind of relationship where he could bring his fears and concerns to me, after all.

I carried him out of the gloomy playroom and into the cheery light of the hallway, taking care to avoid jostling him too much on the way to the bedroom.

When I laid him back down on his bed, he was calm. His cheeks still bore the remnants of his tears, and his face was a little flushed, but he wasn't actively crying. Now it was just the hitching that followed. I kissed him on his forehead and covered him up.

"You okay?"

He nodded and smiled, not opening his eyes.

Maybe he needed just that small measure of reassurance. Maybe his fears were rooted in the unknowns. Or, more likely, they were rooted in the unintentional understanding that his brain was beginning to change. His concerns were no longer those of a little boy like what toys were important or what superhero underwear he wanted to wear. Perhaps he was coming to understand how big the world was and how much of it is unknown to him. A terrifying thought for anyone at any age.

I was kicking myself for not hedging some of the scarier parts of the earlier conversation a bit better, but the cat was out of the bag.

Kat was still asleep on the couch. I was still ruminating on the past few minutes when I made my way over to her. I woke her up gently, and we went to bed together, hoping that the house would remain quiet, and we'd get some sleep, but Jackson woke up that night with another nosebleed.

Kathryn helped get Jackson back in bed while I checked in on Keller. I was surprised to see him awake but barely. He was on his back and turned to me when I bent over the crib. I cupped his warm cheek and smiled at him. He returned the smile, took a deep breath, and let his drowsy eyes close contentedly before I walked Jackson's bloody pajamas downstairs. Kathryn came to bed a few minutes later, and we were asleep in no time, which was good, because the boys would be awake at six, I was sure.

Chapter 8

I woke up one morning, a Sunday, with a headache. It happened on those rare occasions when I happened to get a good night's sleep. In this instance, however, I remembered having a dream where blood poured from the windows in our home. It was eerily similar to the dreams I had in the months following my cancer treatment, but for some reason, this one felt far more visceral.

I groaned and stood up, the pressure in my abdomen prompting me to get to the bathroom soon. I relieved myself, shivered, and then washed my hands. The man staring back at me from the mirror seemed a stranger. I'd never been terribly concerned with my looks, but one thing I dreaded was adopting the physical features of an aging dad, complete with the pouch for a tummy and saggy muscles. I was pleased to see that body structure was more or less the same since the last time I cared to notice. My hair was a bit longer, and I could see a bit of gray creeping in at the edges of hair on my chin and cheeks. My blue eyes—greener to me, but what did it matter—were still bright. There might be a few more creases around them when I smiled, but it wasn't so bad, this aging thing.

"Did you fall in?" my wife asked, still lounging in bed. This was one of the prompts we shared for decades together. It was our way of saying "hurry up" without actually saying it.

"Yep, coming." I crawled under the bed covers again, covering my eyes with a palm. Kathryn rolled over to face me and put her hand on my chest.

"You okay?" she asked.

I nodded and said, "Just a headache from getting more than five hours of sleep."

I felt her smile, and she patted my chest. "I'll get some coffee going; that should help."

I lay in bed, drowsing until she brought me a steaming cup. Most adults I've met say that they like their coffee black, a boasting display of their supremacy over the normal man. Not ashamed of who I am, I boast that I like cream and sugar in mine because I don't like to drink muddy water.

Kat sat on the bed next to me, and we made small talk about the day and sipped our bean water while we waited for the caffeine to kick in.

"You still want to go to dinner tonight?" I asked.

Her eyes met mine over the coffee, and her eyebrows rose in surprise.

"Yes, I do. Actually, I thought you'd forgotten."

I made a "who, me?" face, putting a hand to my chest, and we both chuckled. "No," I said, "I haven't forgotten. We planned this a while back and while yes, things have been a little crazy, I'd still like to take you out."

Kathryn grinned and wriggled her shoulders in delighted anticipation.

"We have reservations for six o'clock tonight. I should be home before five, and we can change and go. I've already tapped Lily Carlisle to watch the boys tonight—"

"You did?" Kathryn interrupted as her excitement reached full swing, and she punched me on the shoulder playfully.

"Ow, and yes," I continued laughing. "She'll be here at 5:15, so we can have plenty of time to get to the restaurant."

Kathryn set her coffee down, and she crawled toward me suggestively, her t-shirt giving me an eyeful of cleavage. "Well, Mr. Taldo, maybe we can get dessert, too."

I kissed her and said, "Oh, yes. I'll take two."

She kissed me, letting her lips linger on mine for just a moment, then said, "Maybe I won't wear anything underneath my dress. What do you think about that?"

I felt my heart flutter and said, "I'm definitely into that."

She laughed, and I hugged her.

"What are you guys doing?" The little voice from the doorway startled me, but I laughed and beckoned Jackson over.

"We're just loving on each other, buddy. Come here."

He climbed up on the bed with us and snuggled into the crook of my elbow. Despite his age, he still somehow fit perfectly there. My headache had disappeared; the prospect of dinner and a show had me excited for the day.

I confirmed with Lily later that day while waiting for some readings off the FAD-B at Corner House. She was a local kid attending the community college, and she babysat for a few extra bucks here and there. I could appreciate the hustle. Finding reliable sitters had proven difficult since we hadn't really established a circle of friends and trustworthy people. But Kathryn and I agreed that using the same sitter would be beneficial down the road for several reasons. First, the boys would be used to the sitter and wouldn't feel like they were being left with a stranger, and Kathryn and I wouldn't feel like we were leaving them with one. That alone was worth the fifteen bucks an hour we'd pay her. Second, it would be nice to have someone around in case of emergency that knew the boys well enough to care for them until one of our parents could come take the reins.

After the readouts of the device at Corner House gave me the "success" message, I packed up my things. Around four o'clock, I left for home. The day consisted of taking samples of the soil, readings on the FAD-B with alternate scenarios and input variables, and other tests measuring atmospheric pressure, barometric pressure, and a few other things. I felt good as I walked home, content with the work I'd accomplished.

The neighborhood on this chilly afternoon struck me as incredibly pleasant. The afternoon sun, even diminished as it was in the late winter months, shone down on houses that lined the streets in tidy little rows. All the lawns had that sickly brown grass sprouting the occasional green shoot in a smattering of emerald. Several couples were bundled up walking hand-in-hand, some with dogs in tow, tails wagging happily and breaths coming out in puffs of white. I waved to the Godsens, who were walking Bernie. Well, maybe they were just following him. Either way, they waved back with cordial smiles.

"You'll like us, just you wait," I said to no one in particular as I walked into our driveway. As the Godsens left my field of vision, they were replaced by Matt Brandhauer several houses away cleaning his gutters. Matt wasn't a particularly friendly neighbor, and much like the rest of the homeowners, he hadn't warmed up to the new family, yet. Kathryn and I were intent on making friends with as many people as we could, so I threw him a casual wave and smile. He nodded in return without smiling and went back to grabbing handfuls of brown sodden muck and tossing it to the ground below.

He was weird, I decided.

By the time I'd showered, Kathryn was dressed in a beautiful coral-colored dinner dress, her hair falling around her face in beautiful semi-curls, and she was chatting with Lily, giving her the rundown on the routine.

"The boys are fine to go down whenever you'd like them to. We usually give Keller a bottle around seven and Jackson likes to sit with him when we do that. Usually, by eight o'clock, they're both asleep, anyway."

Lily nodded and smiled.

"You ready to go?" I asked as I entered. "Hi, Lily."

"Hi, Mr. Taldo." She seemed to be one of those girls that saw growing up as a privilege, and she was going to make it her own. Her parents had to be proud of her.

"Yeah, I think so," Kathryn responded, then looked at Lily. "If you need anything, you have both of our numbers, I think."

"Yes, I do." She waggled her phone in the air, indicating the numbers were saved on her phone. Lily was really very sweet. By the sound of it, she'd been through this before. She knew how parents felt as though it was the end of the world when they left their kids, and it took twenty minutes to get out the door.

She pulled her hair behind her ear and smiled, doing her best to not make eye contact with either of us.

"Alright, let's go." I walked toward the living room and saw Jackson playing with Keller and said "Bye, guys. We'll be home in a little bit." I said "little bit" because I learned to never *ever* give them the actual time. I'd spend the next twelve minutes explaining time and eventually just say "little bit" anyway.

"Okay, Daddy," Jackson replied without looking up. I frowned after Keller glanced my way, giggled, wiped a hand across his snotty face, and looked back at Jackson. His cold seemed to be back.

When I closed the door, Lily was sitting cross-legged as the point of a triangle with Jackson and Keller. She was asking questions about the blocks they were playing with and smiling the way one does when talking to very small children.

Once in the car, Kat and I took a freeing breath. We drove out of the neighborhood and let our red lights illuminate the dark street behind us. There's nothing quite like knowing the kids are safe while simultaneously being able to shuck the mantle of responsibility for a couple of hours.

Kathryn clasped my hand in hers, squeezing it affectionately. "Where do you want to eat?"

Oh boy, here we go, I thought ruefully. "I don't really feel like anything in particular. What do you feel like eating?"

She looked at me with mock disapproval, and I laughed. This was our ritual, whether we wanted it or not, causing many a problem early in our relationship. When my wife would ask what I felt like eating or where I felt like going, it was a very rare occasion when I actually had an opinion on the matter. So when I said that it didn't matter to me, she took that to mean that I didn't care. But not in a neutral way, no of course not. She mistook my indifference for having a bad attitude and petulant frustration of "not caring." Since those early days, however, she's begun to understand that "not caring" is actually my way of saying "my opinion is so minor that it really isn't even worth stating out loud." I have since learned that I can also give an opinion in order to show that I care enough to have a conversation.

Marriage is a dance, and the songs are on shuffle.

We settled on an Italian restaurant called "Noodles." It was one of those hole-in-the-wall places that locals recommended ad nauseum. We'd tried it a few months after moving to the neighborhood and liked it so much that it became the default choice.

We didn't intend for the conversation to center around the kids as we ordered wine and appetizers—fried ravioli covered in melted mozzarella—but they were the most important thing in our collective lives, it wasn't even a choice. And was it ever?

"Do you remember the way that Keller used to babble, and we'd have to ask Jackson what he was saying?" Kathryn smiled over her wine glass, teeth white in the dim light that suffused the restaurant atmosphere.

"Remember?" I laughed. "I asked him yesterday to translate for me." Kathryn laughed, a high and quiet peal that I'd had to get used to, but found incredibly sweet, now.

After she quieted down, she became pensive. "Isn't it interesting how Jackson cares so much for Keller?"

I shrugged. "I guess. But then again, I don't have siblings. I'm not sure what constitutes 'normal' is and 'interesting.'"

"I know that most siblings care for each other, but from the day we found out we were pregnant, it's like he's taken responsibility for him."

"That's actually kind of true now that I think about it. He does look after him quite a bit, doesn't he." I smiled at her and took a sip of my wine.

She nodded, then, "Do you think we did that to him?"

I paused, then asked, "What?"

"I mean, do you think we have made Jackson think that he has to care for Keller? Are we ignoring Keller so much that Jackson feels he has to pick up the slack?"

"Kat, that's a pretty big stretch." I didn't want to make her feel something untrue, but it seemed like a strange place to land. "Do you think we've been such lax parents that Keller has needed another caretaker?"

"Well, no," she huffed, "but what if that's just because we're biased to ourselves?"

The instrumental music playing in the restaurant was barely audible over the quiet din of conversation from other guests. I placed my hands over hers. She was serious about this.

"Kat, listen. Jackson's love for his brother has nothing to do with a lack of love from us. You play with him for hours every day. You take walks with him. I take walks with him and play with him, too. If Jackson feels a need to lavish more love upon him, that's the prerogative of a nine-year-old."

She didn't agree immediately, but she nodded after a few heartbeats. "I guess you're right. I just don't want him to grow up thinking that he had to be a parent."

"I doubt he thinks that. I'm sure he sees it as an honor to help take care of his brother. And he's a natural, obviously. He speaks Keller's language!"

That made her smile, and we were back on track.

We began to talk about his Jackson's love of anything outside, laughing about the time that Jackson had asked to push a dead tree down.

"He grunted and huffed," I was miming the effort of pushing against a tree, "and finally the tree creaked and groaned and went crashing to the ground." Kathryn held my hand across the white tablecloth and laughed.

"I remember. I was standing at the bottom of the little hill with Keller in the backpack. Jack stood on top of it like a gladiator and roared into the forest."

I laughed, remembering the high-pitched "rawr" echoing through the trees. "That was a good day," I said.

Kat nodded at me. "It was. It was a very good day."

She leaned toward me, and I met her in the middle for a kiss. When I pulled back, I nearly tipped my glass of wine over, and it sent us into fits of laughter all over again.

We talked of the nearly boundless patience Jackson displayed. Keller was a great kid, aside from being sick most of the time, but he was also nearly two. In some of his more *passionate* fits, Kat and I were at a loss for what our youngest wanted. After several attempts, sometimes we simply had to hold him—or not, depending on his mood—and go about our day. Jackson, however, would sit with his little brother and try to work out what he wanted. He hated to hear Keller cry and wanted to make him happy.

I grasped Kat's hand and smiled at her. She beamed back at me, and we continued to brag to one another about how perfect our children were.

Dinner came, and it was delicious. We continued talking between bites about work, future plans, and all manner of side topics.

Even when the topic changed frequently, one underlying thought pervaded the rest. Keller *wasn't* perfect. He was a very good baby and toddler, but his constant illnesses were difficult to handle at even the best of times. It wasn't something that most parents would probably admit, at least not in mixed company. But the truth was that I was feeling pressure to fix something that I couldn't fix. Sure, a few days of antibiotics mighty do the trick, but when it came back? What then? We'd already had tubes put into his ears, and that didn't seem to do much.

Kathryn must have been thinking something similar because she squeezed my hand and gave me a somewhat tight smile.

"Do you think he'll grow out of it?" I asked, fearing what speaking it aloud might do.

Kathryn was quiet for a moment and drained the last of her wine. "I don't know, honestly. It's exhausting, but it's not like it makes a difference." She laughed in mild bitterness. "I don't know what I'd do if Keller woke up one day and *wasn't* sick. It's just who he is. Maybe he'll grow out of it. His pediatrician thinks so, but who knows? I guess we'll have to see."

The lights played off her hair, and even in the dimness, I was struck by her beauty. She was right, of course; we'd just have to see. In the meantime, we'd take care of them both. Keller's illnesses would continue, and we'd continue to take him to the doctor when necessary. Until it wasn't.

By the time dessert arrived, the wine had relaxed our parenting muscles and had given Kat and me a pleasant blush on our cheeks. She was beautiful. It's strange sometimes, hearing the way she talked about all the things she despised about herself. I talked about all of those things as some of my favorites, but when she looked in the mirror, all she saw were imperfections. I wasn't sure that would ever change, but I wouldn't ever change, either. I'd love every piece of her, regardless of the opinions of herself. After all, I didn't love her for the way she looked, though that part came easy. I loved her for the way she cared for me and the kids, for the way she worked to help provide for the family. I loved her for the effort she put into making others feel important. She was a best friend to everyone, even if it wasn't always reciprocated.

I'd like to say that was true, that she loved me and I loved her unconditionally through it all, without any deviation. But it would be a lie. There would be a time when I would be hard to love, when I wouldn't give my love freely, and I would begin to give in to the selfishness of my own insecurities. But not for some time, at least.

Our waiter arrived, and we paid the check, leaving a healthy tip more from the serotonin than service. The drive home was peaceful, and I found myself absently stroking the smooth skin of Kathryn's inner thigh. She stroked the inside of my forearm and adopted a coy smile when I glanced at her out of the corner of my eye.

"Mrs. Taldo, you should be careful, or you'll distract me from driving."

She leaned in closer and grasped the inside of my thigh with that sensual pressure that's the bedfellow of desire. "Is that so?" Her whispered words tickled my ear and had the intended effect. I felt the heat rise up my neck and down my legs, and I took a steadying breath.

"When we get home, why don't you go change in the bedroom, and I'll pay the sitter?"

She kissed my cheek and neck and nodded.

Needless to say, I paid the sitter and made sure the night went well, but my mind was focused elsewhere. When Lily left—"They were really wonderful!"—I hastily locked all the doors, turned off the lights, and smiled as the bedroom door shut behind me.

The third, maybe fourth nosebleed that I remember, happened later that night. I remember it specifically because I launched myself up the stairs without any clothes on when I heard Jackson yell for us. I was certain he didn't even notice my nakedness when I helped him to the bathroom to wash his face. Blood was dripping from his face and pooling into his hands, both cupped beneath his chin and filling rapidly.

Kathryn arrived a short time later with some athletic shorts, which I quickly pulled on one-handed while helping clean his face with the other.

I met her eye over Jackson's bowed head, and her pursed lips told me what I was already thinking—we needed to go to the doctor about it.

CHAPTER 9

I struggled with going to the doctor about Jackson's nosebleeds. Kat and I had gone round and round about it over the course of a few days, but we'd both landed on something that resembled agreement.

"We need at least someone else's opinion. It's all well and good that we ask people here and there about their own kids, or dance around it with the pediatrician, but I want you to go get someone else's opinion." We were in the kitchen, and I was drinking a glass of water.

"I know." And I did. I knew she was right. The problem was that I was having to wrestle with the fact that I couldn't do anything for *either* of my sons. I was struggling with that, but I knew that Kathryn might have been as well.

I was still a little in shock. Having researched spontaneous nosebleeds, I found a case in Edmond, Oklahoma—a place just outside Oklahoma City—where a doctor oversaw the case. The article detailed a very similar situation to the one we were experiencing with Jackson: random nosebleeds, no logical cause or precursory event, always at night. Even just finding one or two of those similarities would have been surprising, but as I read the article, I began to have a strange sensation of déjà vu, as if it had been written about Jackson. That also

caused a good deal of fear for Kat and me. The little girl in the article had died after several months of nosebleeds. No matter what they did to stop it, eventually, it was too much strain on the little girl.

I'm not one to make some empty claim, but after reading that, I swore I'd do whatever I could to prevent Jackson from experiencing the same. I called up the hospital where he worked and asked for a consultation. His nurse—or whatever— said he didn't usually do consultations, but I told her it had to do with my child experiencing nosebleeds, and she immediately asked me to hold. When she came back, she had a date and time scheduled.

I had driven through lunch, making my way through Oklahoma, and my stomach was growling petulantly at me. I'd passed plenty of places, but I was too nervous to actually eat anything. The coffee I'd had this morning was enough to tide me over, so I planned to grab something after meeting with this doctor.

I'd received the information for the FAD Field Repair center earlier in the week, as well. I figured that instead of taking a few days to do it all, I'd stay a night in Oklahoma City and kill two birds with one stone. I could drop Gretchen off for repairs, head to the city to talk to the doctor, then pick the FAD up on my way home.

I arrived at the hotel with just enough time to drop off my bags before driving to the FAD repair center.

I put the location into my phone, and it took me a mile or so north. A bright yellow "REPAIRS" sign arched across the front of the building, with Eastwind's logo below it. I gave my information to the tech—Dave—and he told me I could pick it up in the morning. Gianna and Marco had sent in the request, and as far as I could tell, the repair list was based off a diagnostic they ran remotely.

Dave gave me a digital ticket through my Eastwind ID number, and I left, heading toward the hospital I'd called earlier.

A galloping in my midsection reminded me that I was still nervous. I turned down the music as I turned into the hospital parking lot. I didn't want anything distracting me as I once again ran through what my explanation would be. Hopefully, the doctor was someone willing to help.

Hopefully.

I put the car in park and stared out the front window. It wasn't a particularly nice view. Cars zipped by a hundred yards away on the bypass and behind them were buildings that clawed at the gray sky. The sun wasn't shining. Not really. It was daytime, but it was a harsh light, and the cool air cut through my clothes like knives. I turned the car off and saw a couple holding hands and walking briskly, hunching their shoulders against the cold.

I took a calming breath and opened the car door. Its hinges squealed in the sterling light, and the sound echoed across the parking lot. The steady hum of passing cars couldn't even drown it out. I didn't pay it much mind. I stuffed my bare hands in my jacket pockets after pulling my hat lower to cover my ears. A short jog across the asphalt brought me to a sign reading "FRONT ENTRANCE." The pneumatic hiss blew cold air down my spine as I walked through them and into the semi-warmth of the ground floor lobby.

I approached the front desk and told them I had an appointment with Dr. Krist. The woman at the front desk pointed me in the direction of his office up the escalator.

"Thanks," I muttered and made my way up.

I expected it to be more crowded, but then again, I'd never been in a hospital in the middle of a weekday. Some people sat in the stark white waiting room, shifting in their discomfort. Others walked—or limped—around the adjacent hallways. As I entered, the PA echoed around me, and I had the sudden urge to go back down the escalator, brave the cold back to my car and drive home. Lunch *did* sound good.

No, I told myself irritably. I was doing this for Jackson. I could endure the mild discomfort of talking to a stranger if it would save his life. But I was worried. I worried what the doctor would think—worried even more about what he would say. Perhaps, he heard about this, and there wasn't any cure.

A plethora of terrible scenarios whirled around in my head as I picked up a nearby newspaper to pass the time. Most of the headlines reeked of doom and gloom. "I have enough of that in my life right now. Thank you very much," I said under my breath and turned to the comics.

The minutes ticked by. I chuckled quietly to myself to the antics of *Marmaduke* and *The Family Circus*, rolled my eyes at the idiocy of *Dilbert* and *Beetle Bailey*. I'd always loved the comics. When my dad would read the morning paper, he'd hand the comics to me, and we'd gorge ourselves on Cream of Wheat and orange juice.

"Mr. Taldo?" A blonde nurse looked out over the waiting area holding a clipboard. Our eyes met, and I stood up, half waving with the newspaper and feeling like a moron. She smiled and motioned for me to follow her.

"How are you today?" The same question she probably asked every person who walked with her.

"Oh, I'm fine. Thank you. And you?"

"I'm doing well. Thank you for asking."

With the pleasantries out of the way, we could walk to the good doctor's office in silence.

"Here we are," she said and motioned me to a chair in a tiny cubicle of a room. "Dr. Krist will be with you in just a few minutes." And she left before I could even get my thank you out.

I looked around the room. It was tiny, but the doctor probably wasn't in it very often. Or, perhaps he wasn't in it for very long periods of time. There were a number of very official-looking documents hanging in wooden frames on the wall behind the desk. A computer monitor splashed white light over the rest of the cramped desk where a couple of picture frames huddled together. In one, a man and a woman stood smiling on the deck of a large boat, toasting with a flute of golden liquid in each of their hands. Another picture showed the same man holding up a large red salmon, it's dark bulging eye stared back as if to say, "I can't believe I was caught by this schlub."

The door swung open behind me on silent hinges, and Dr. Krist swept into the room.

"Good morning," he said with practiced joviality.

I stood to shake his hand. "Good morning, Doctor." I stood to greet him. "I'm Grant Taldo. We spoke on the phone last week."

He shook my hand, nodding. "Yes, I remember. Nosebleeds, if I'm not mistaken?" His tone was questioning, but his blue eyes were full of confidence. His head was topped with thick silver hair that was moussed to perfection. He was the quintessential rich, white man.

"Yes, that's right."

"Well, take a seat, Mr. Taldo." He gestured for me to resume sitting, and I did. "What can I do for you?" He steepled his fingers and waited, blue eyes sparkling in the anticipation of solving a riddle.

"Well, sir, I had a few questions about a previous case you oversaw. One with the little girl and inexplicable nosebleeds."

He nodded, frowning. "Ah, yes. Tragic, though I wouldn't use the word 'inexplicable.' Sweet little girl died, and there was nothing we could do. Terrible."

I hesitated before continuing. "Yes, it is. Did you ever find anything else out? A root cause for the nosebleeds or anything like that?"

He leaned back in his leather chair until it hit the wall, maybe six inches behind him. "Well, we had a team of doctors and nurses working with that family. We ran several tests and did an x-ray of her nose to see if perhaps there was some structural problem. Everything came back normal, which stumped us. We asked all kinds of questions and, unfortunately, we came to the conclusion that she was probably the victim of abuse."

That was something the article hadn't stated. "But was there any trauma to indicate such a thing? Did you call Family Services?"

"Well, we see all kinds of people here, Mr. Taldo. Some of them are victims of abuse, and I could tell you horror story after horror story of what these people go through at the hands of their abusers. These people get pretty creative in how they hurt, finding ways to inflict pain without leaving a trace. In this particular instance, we had Child Protective Services come in and interview the child and parents separately, which is protocol. Of course, the parents claimed no such thing and the father became very aggressive when we suggested further … services. No surprise considering his background."

I cocked my head. "Background?"

He continued as if I hadn't said a thing. "Without any evidence of abuse and no other accusations that could be made, we had no choice but to send that sweet little girl home. The case stayed open, as is protocol, with regular check-ups scheduled over the course of several months. Unfortunately, none of those came to fruition. The girl died only a couple of days later."

The article had said something along those lines, that the girl had received care at the hospital shortly before dying, but there was no link between any of it. For all intents and purposes, it seemed like she spontaneously bled to death.

"How long was she here, the little girl, before going home?"

He thought for a moment. "Oh, I'd say she was here about a week before we had to send her home. Didn't have a single nosebleed while she was here. Imagine that."

"Did she have a nosebleed when she went home?"

"We had a nurse call the next day and ask about her, the mother was home and said she'd slept soundly the previous night, no issues. Had a nurse call the day after and the mother said the girl had a nosebleed, same night that the dad returned home from work. Seems all too clear to me, but CPS and the courts couldn't do anything about it. The mom protected that son of a bitch, too. She's just as guilty as he is for the death of that little girl."

Krist's eyes sparkled with fierce indignation, daring me to contradict his theory. I decided against it, changing course.

"Well, the other reason I came today was to see what I could do for *my* son. He's experiencing nosebleeds, and we can't for the life of us figure out why. He's not allergic to anything that we know of—we've had a full allergy test—and there's no trauma to his nose that we can remember, not even

when he was younger that may have, I don't know, contributed to nosebleeds now."

The fierceness in his eyes changed to suspicion faster than I could even track. "And your son, does he spend time with anyone else?"

"He goes to school every day, but why does that matter?"

"And does he get nosebleeds at school?"

Now I saw where this was going. I sighed. "No, he doesn't get them at school. He only gets them at night, usually around midnight but sometimes as early as three or four in the morning. There's no pattern to them, at least not that we can pick out."

Dr. Krist just stared at me for what seemed like forever before leaning forward and looking me square in the eye. "I can't do much without seeing him, but my advice would be to get his face—nose, more specifically—tested to look for any abnormalities that could be causing this. There is any number of issues that could be causing it, such as weak capillaries or chronic dryness. If it comes back clean, then I'd start to make a journal of the nosebleeds, try to see how frequently they actually happen, a kind of baseline. A lot of times, we can feel like something is occurring much more than it actually is. A record of the events can help ease us out of the panic we feel when comparing the frequency of events. Keep track of them for a few months, see how many actually occur.

"You may also be able to look at who is spending time him. And Mr. Taldo, if I were you, I'd look very closely at the correlation between who he's with and the nights he gets a nosebleed. I take this kind of thing very seriously and so should you. There are plenty of cases of child abuse that only come to light because a parent picks up on something that just doesn't sit right with them. Do you understand what I'm saying?"

I nodded, unable to muster words. My mouth had dried up, and my throat was nearly clenched shut. I couldn't imagine my son being abused. It was almost too much to even *begin* to play out in my head. I cringed just thinking about it. It wasn't possible, was it? I couldn't be certain until I thought about it a little more, however unpleasant.

"Well, thank you for your time, doctor. You've given some direction, at least." I stood up, and we shook hands. "Um, one more thing if you don't mind."

"If I can, I will."

"The family, can you tell me if they still live at the same address as when..." I trailed off.

"I can't give you their names, though I suspect you already know them what with the access we have to computers and the internet and everything. And unfortunately, I can't tell you that information. Doctor-patient confidentiality, of course." He was silent for a moment. I continued standing, uncertain if the pause would be long enough for me to sit without having to immediately stand back up to leave. Then, he continued before I could make a decision. "What I can tell you is that I keep a very close eye on my patients when I can, you understand. And I'm still able to keep an eye, if you catch my meaning."

I nodded slowly. "Yes, I think so. Thanks again, doc."

He stood, now, his hands in the pockets of his pristine white lab coat. "Anytime. And I hope your boy gets better." He stared at me in that I-hope-you-get-what-I-mean way.

I nodded again and left, probably a little too quickly, and made my way down the escalator and into the cold, gray mid-afternoon light of late winter.

At least I had begun to formulate a plan.

CHAPTER 10

The sun managed to peek out between clouds that resembled lazy gray waves overhead and brightened the piece of paper I held in my shaking hand. An address was hastily scrawled there, and I checked the number on the mailbox outside of my idling car; they matched. I took a deep breath. My heart was galloping inside my chest, no doubt due in part to the conversation I had with Dr. Krist. My stomach—still unfed—was doing somersaults with all the room it had beneath my ribcage. I took a longer look at the house, feeling as if I hadn't already been sitting here for more than ten minutes. It was a modest one-story home. The grass of the front yard was mown short. A paved sidewalk cut the neatly manicured grass in half, from street to front door. The door was aged wood painted a rusty red. An old wooden bench dominated the porch, a pair of muddy work boots stacked neatly at one end. Unlike my own yard, there were no children's toys in the grassy yard and the car that was parked in the driveway was a nice, if aging, two-door sedan. Whoever lived here—and I had a good idea who—wasn't rich, but they weren't destitute, either.

It all seemed very normal. Well, except the signs that pin-cushioned the yard stating "GO AWAY" and "NO INTERVIEWS" in painted red letters. Coupled with the yellow caution tape that circled a tree and trailed its way to the ground, it was obvious that this owner had a problem with visitors.

I took a deep breath and prayed that they would make an exception, then started to make my way up the walkway to the front door. I found the doorbell—a round button set into a yellowing square—and pushed. A distant chime was followed by a cautious scraping sound, what I imagined a chair moved away from the kitchen table. Footsteps approached from inside, and the door shifted slightly as weight was applied to the other side. I pretended to be preoccupied with my shoes, but I could see the peephole briefly darken from the corner of my eye.

A deadbolt thunked after several rattling latches and the door opened a couple of inches. A silver chain inside prevented it from opening anymore.

I couldn't see much through the space, but a single, baleful eye stared out at me from the dimness and a deep, suspicious voice asked, "Can't read the signs or somethin'? What do you want?"

I met the man's eye and could feel my face flush in embarrassment.

"Hi, sir. I'm Grant Taldo." I swallowed hard, my mouth worked to get the words out. "I'm Grant, and I have a couple of questions for you, if you have the time." I swallowed again. God, I was thirsty.

The eye stared me down, briefly looking me over before responding. "I don't wanna buy anything. I'm not interested." A finger pointed out past me toward the "NO INTERVIEWS" sign, and then the door slammed home with a resounding thud that echoed up and down in the silent street.

I couldn't leave this lead untapped, so I starting speaking loudly at the wooden door before the man could walk away. "I came to talk about your daughter. I have a son that has started having nosebleeds like her and..." I stuttered, uncertain of how to continue. "And I don't know really what else to do."

I hadn't heard the man's footsteps retreat, but the thundering heartbeats in my ears could have easily covered it up. I stood on the man's doorstep for what felt like an hour, until I could feel my heart calming down. I took a deep breath and spoke to the door. "Please, Mr. Callum. Just a few minutes."

If he heard me, he didn't respond. I waited by counting to one hundred, then turned around and walked back to my car. I was a stranger. There was no reason he should speak to me. What did I expect? That he'd open up the door and invite me in for a beer?

And this was when my brain caught up and I heard Dr. Krist's voice in my mind. "With his background."

Now it all made sense. Of course, he was suspicious—Mitch Callum, a middle-class black man, had been accused of child abuse by a rich white man and had every reason to be suspicious of me, a white stranger, that came knocking in the middle of the day. What was I thinking?

I had no choice but to head home. I took one last glance at the red door and the muddy work boots before pulling away.

By now, it was coming up on late afternoon, close enough to dinner time for me. I stopped by a fast-food joint for a burger, then headed back to the hotel. I ran through a few emails and called Marco to update him on Gretchen. He hadn't heard anything on the repairs and probably wouldn't until they closed the ticket the following day. I turned the lights off and sent Kathryn a good night message, then went to sleep.

The following morning passed quickly. I still had to pick up Gretchen, which would add at least an hour to my drive home. I headed north to Edmonton, had her loaded into the back, and was on my way after a brief conversation with Dave. I don't remember much of it; it's not my job to worry about the details of how she works, only that she does. Besides, I hoped to make it home before lunch and called Kathryn to let her know that Gretchen and I were on our way.

I did make it before lunch. It was close, and I was greeted at the door with mouth-watering smells and the quiet clatter and murmur of Jackson playing with Keller.

Kathryn was at the stove, wooden spoon in hand and looking very much like a younger, more beautiful Martha Stewart. I put my hands on her hips and kissed her cheek. "Made it just in time, looks like."

She smiled at me and continued stirring what looked like chicken and rice. "You sure did. Mind setting the table for me?"

I set the table and told her about my short overnight trip. I wasn't sure if I should include my brief interaction with Mr. Callum, but I decided in the end that it didn't amount to anything, anyway. So I left out most of the details. She was very curious about the doctor's answers and began making a list of things to buy in between stirring the dinner, in case Jackson's nosebleeds continued.

"A journal is a great idea. I can't believe I didn't think of that," she said with self-deprecation while adding it to the list.

"Yeah for real," I said in mock consternation and called the boys to the table. Hoping Keller could walk into the kitchen like Jackson and *knowing* he would still be playing with his blocks were two completely different things that existed simultaneously. I winked at Jackson as he settled into his place at the table next to Kathryn. Then I walked to the living room where our toddler was stacking blocks on top of each other. He had managed to make a tower as tall as himself, no small feat considering he coughed almost every time he started reaching out to add a block. I watched transfixed. His focus—impressive for a toddler—was remarkable. His steady hands and pudgy little arms stretched, and I could feel the breath I was holding knock at the door to my throat.

Keller settled the block—wooden, with a large capital green "A"—gently on top of the pile and released his hold on it, setting his heels back down as he took a breath and wiped his running nose. I laughed the moment he put his hands on his hips—just like his mother—and he jumped. The tower remained standing, and I walked toward him with a grin. "Keller, this is amazing!"

He grinned and pointed at it. "Big," he said, proudly.

"It *is* big!" I knelt beside him and pulled him close, where he wrapped an arm around my neck and surveyed his accomplishment.

"Are you ready to eat?"

Keller nodded. "Hungee," he said, mispronouncing the word in that adorable way that only toddlers can.

I scooped him up, and he squealed in mock terror, giggling. "Let's get to the table, then!" First, a trip around the living room. I flew him once or twice, making airport callouts and "roger rogers" to which he responded with delighted squeals. We made a landing at his highchair, and Keller smiled as Kathryn squeezed my hand affectionately.

Between mouthfuls of chicken and rice, we talked about the cares and wonders of nine-year-olds, the joys of parenthood, and the delight found in a toddler's eye. The worry and fear that seemed to have been crouching at our door had disappeared for the moment. I could see that Kathryn sensed it, too.

Her smile was genuine, and she was engaging with the boys in a way that I hadn't seen in several weeks. We talked about her job and how well it was going, the relief of only having part-time responsibility, and the freedom it afforded her.

Maybe we were worried about something that was completely normal. Maybe we were on the other side of the difficulty, and it was all downhill from here.

I remember sitting at the table and looking around at my children and wife, thinking it could be over, truly believing that it was a possibility. But I was naïve. Unfortunately for us all, it had barely begun.

Kathryn and I were sitting on the couch later that night when we heard a rustle from down the stairs. We sat still and waited, like deer in a headlight.

"Daddy?"

The soft voice coming from down the stairs was tentative. Kathryn muted the television and we both cocked an ear in that direction.

"Yeah, buddy?" I didn't yell back but raised my voice enough to be heard.

"Can you come here for a second?"

The question was innocent enough, but there was something in Jackson's voice that made my heart begin to race, adrenaline began to flush through my veins in waves.

By the way Kathryn leapt to her feet—not quite running but near enough—I could tell she heard the urgency in our son's voice, as well.

When she looked at me over her shoulder, her eyes were large with growing panic. The lighthearted woman I'd observed at dinner had gone, replaced by a mother who would stop at nothing to protect her son. At the top of the stairs, I put a gentle hand on her arm and made a calming gesture with my other hand. The last thing I wanted Jackson to pick up on was the near-panic we were both feeling.

She nodded, and we both took a stabilizing breath together before walking slowly into Jackson's room.

Jackson was sitting up, the bedcovers draped over his head like a makeshift tent and wrapped tightly around his torso. The dinosaur nightlight cast long shadows in its soft orange glow.

At first glance, I would have thought Jackson was fine, but the gasp from Kathryn clued me in that the situation was more serious than what I initially had seen.

Upon closer inspection, I could see Jackson trembling, the covers dancing and vibrating over his fragile frame. His brown eyes sparkled with unshed tears that would soon spill over his lids and down his cheeks.

I put a gentle arm around my wife as we approached his bedside calmly. I didn't want to plant any more panic in the boy's head than what was already there, and I was glad Kathryn was steady, too. Though I figured she was thinking something similar.

With a deep worry, I disguised as mild curiosity, I asked, "Hey bud, what's wrong?"

Jackson sniffed and blinked, the trembling tears dripped down his face in a sudden gush. One, two, three giant tears.

Neither of us bothered wiping the tears away as they dripped from his chin to his covers. He looked at me, and when he spoke, a chill crept down my spine, and I had to suppress a shudder the need to rush to the balcony door.

"Something's outside my window." His voice trembled with terror to the point that the words were barely audible, mostly pieced together by reading his lips. Jackson glanced out the window and blinked hard, looking away quickly as if he could still see what scared him. I looked, as well, but saw nothing.

I knew there were times when children saw things that weren't there. I remembered times in my own childhood when I had looked outside my bedroom window and would have sworn there was a hand reaching toward the latch. After minutes without something coming into my room, I looked again and saw the same "hand" as nothing more than a branch.

I knew now, listening to my son's shaky voice, that this was not a dream-induced hallucination. Jackson legitimately believed he saw something outside the balcony door.

With only the briefest hesitation, I walked to the window. With the bedroom light off, I could see the streetlamps and the road clearly lit by them. Jackson's bicycle lay in the heap where he left it earlier, and the line of shrubbery that separated their yard from their neighbors, the Shelbergs, was merely a blackish green scar from road to house.

It could have just been a transference of fear, but I felt an eerie unease rise in my throat, too, which settled around my neck like a heavy scarf.

I smiled reassuringly at Jackson and Kathryn, though I didn't feel it.

"I'll go check it out."

Kathryn climbed into Jackson's bed, gently pressing his head to her shoulder and comforting him as he released his hold on the fear in quiet sniffles and sobs.

It broke my heart.

I peeked in on Keller and saw him snuffling silently in his sleep.

The sounds of Kathryn's comforting words faded as I tried not to run down the stairs and out the front door.

I reached for the doorknob and hesitated. On a whim, I went to the fireplace and grabbed the poker, two feet of steel that ended in a hooked spike. Not a weapon, necessarily, but it made me feel better having the cold metal clenched in my fist. I walked toward the door, and before leaving the house, I flipped the porch light on. The bulb must have blown because the front yard remained dark except for a small stretching rectangle from the open front door.

The steps that led to the driveway, and a better look at the balcony window, were cold on my bare feet. The grass was moist and cool, like a thawing fish touching the hem of my pajama pants, the feeling difficult to ignore when they began hitting my ankles with a splatting sound.

Walking briskly with the poker poised above me, I made my way farther onto the front lawn. When I was near the street but directly in front of Jackson's window, I turned back to face the house, looking from one side to the other.

The harsh brightness of the downstairs television—still paused—blended into the front yard with a kind of spectral gaudiness. The light from the open front door faded into the white light from the streetlamp several yards from the house. The balcony was dark, as was Keller's room beyond the railing. The only exception was the occasional flash of color from Keller's mobile light. I noticed some of the front flower beds in disarray and had a flash of frustration at the Ms. Anthony's ridiculously free-range cat, Hazel. Occasionally, I'd caught her having a nice roll in the spring shrubs that Kathryn tried to keep alive beneath the downstairs windows.

Without seeing anything moving or creeping along the balcony, I relaxed and lowered the poker.

Perhaps too soon, though, as a scraping snapped my attention to the roof.

The roof? I thought.

I squinted, trying to get my eyes to focus on what I was seeing in the thin light from the streetlamps and the silver glow from the moon above. The light from the front door failed to help even a little.

I looked carefully along the roof, but I couldn't pick out any movement whatsoever. My heartbeat made my ears throb, and the hem of my pajamas tickled the tops of my feet.

There wasn't anything on the roof, but I thought I saw something near the corner, something crouched there, maybe? It was too dark to know for certain.

A bird suddenly squawked and burst from the cover where I was looking. Its keening cry echoed into the night sky as I followed its flight through the chilly night air and over the roof of a house across the street.

I relaxed. It was just a bird. That didn't make much sense, but there couldn't have been anything on the balcony. I'd have seen it. It certainly couldn't have been a person.

I looked back down at the front flower bed. *Maybe it was Hazel*, I thought with mixed frustration and relief. A cat could climb the tree fairly quickly and stride its way across the balcony. Jackson could have seen it and, in his mind, transformed it into something worse than an ordinary house cat.

I wiped my feet on the front room rug and closed the door behind me, careful to lock it out of both habit and intentionality, then went upstairs.

When I entered Jackson's rooms, I made sure to smile and spread my arms—the fireplace poker back home on its rack in the living room.

Kathryn gave me an exasperated stare, and I laughed, only slightly forced, and I tried to make them both feel better.

"I didn't see a thing out there other than the flowers that Hazel crushed earlier in the evening. No footprints or anything that I could see. Definitely nothing on the balcony. What *I* think it was, buddy, was Hazel. There was a bird that I spooked out of the tree by the balcony, but that was it! Do you think what you saw might have been Ms. Anthony's cat?"

Jack hesitated and looked more intently at me than I thought a nine-year-old could. I wondered if he suspected me of lying, and despite telling the truth, part of me felt like I was. He only nodded, the tears had stopped, but their evidence had polka-dotted Kathryn's yellow blouse. She wrapped her arms around his trembling shoulders and squeezed him gently.

I put a calming hand on my son's shoulder and leaned down to kiss him on the forehead. "I love you buddy. If you need anything else, we'll be here. You're my favorite." I looked at Kathryn. "Do you want to snuggle him for a little bit? Help him get back to sleep?" She nodded at me and smiled a brief but appreciative smile, then laid down next to him.

As I left the room, I could hear the calming notes of a lullaby we'd sung to each of our children. It always helped them go to sleep, and I hoped it would do the same for Jackson tonight.

I plodded downstairs to the couch and sat down, exhausted and feeling every ounce of adrenaline that had packed up and left my body. I thought back to Jackson's tentative but certain statement: *There's someone outside my window.* Those were words you never wanted to hear at any point in your life, but least of all from one of your kids. Too much like a horror movie for my liking.

I replayed the search in my mind's eye, again coming up empty with the source of Jackson's sudden terror.

I let it go and closed my eyes, resting my head on the back of the couch. I intended to merely rest my eyes, but Kathryn's touch brought me back from the verge of sleep. She asked if I was okay and sat next to me, her slim body fitting naturally next to mine.

We sat in silence for several minutes until I understood how I wanted to address my concerns.

"Have you noticed anything different about Keller, lately?"

She looked at me with naked confusion.

"Keller?"

I laughed lightly. "Yeah, you know, our second son?"

She rolled her eyes playfully and said, "I know who you mean, dummy. No, I haven't. Have you?"

"I'm not sure," I said, uncertain exactly how to tell Kathryn what I was feeling. "It feels like he's been feeling better more frequently. It seemed there for a while that every day was a struggle for him, and I've noticed that we've gotten better sleep lately. Well, when Jack isn't spraying blood everywhere."

"I guess that's true," said Kat. "I'm not sure why. Maybe now that winter's over—ending, at least—the cold isn't making him cough or have so much drainage."

"That makes sense, actually."

"Are you worried about something, Grant?"

"No," I reassured her. "No. I just want to make sure I'm paying attention to whatever I can. Paranoia, I think is what they call it."

Kathryn smiled, understanding what I meant. Then she leaned into me and laid her head on my shoulder. "You're a good dad, Grant. Thank you for loving our kids the way you do."

I wrapped her in a hug. "You're a good mom. Thanks for snuggling the boys. They love you, and so do I."

CHAPTER 11

Several evenings later, I was resting my eyes while on the couch, wondering what kind of steps Kat and I needed to take to help our children stay healthy, but in truth, I was having a hard time focusing. I was exhausted. In the darkness of the living room, I believed I could think more clearly with eyes closed and the only sensory input the couch I sat upon and the sullen sounds of the night settling around the house. But even with my eyes closed, the sudden brightness of my phone screen illuminated the backs of my eyelids with a blue-white glow that made me sigh in exasperation.

I raised the phone to eye level and became immediately irritated when it showed an unknown number. While I tend to ignore these kind of calls, I decided on a whim to answer it. It was after normal business hours, so I figured I had a good chance of either getting someone I knew or telling someone halfway across the globe to fuck off.

I touched the green "answer" button. "Hello?"

"This Grant Taldo?" The voice on the other end was gruff and vaguely familiar, but I couldn't place it. There was no pre-amble to conversation, none of the normal social niceties.

"Yes, it is. Can I help you?"

"I doubt it, but I figured I could help you."

I paused for the span of several seconds before responding. I wasn't even sure what to say. When I did speak, it was hesitant. I had heard this person with a southern twang speak before, but where?

"Okay. And what exactly do I need help with?"

The voice on the other end huffed what I assumed was a laugh and said, "When you stopped by the other day, you said your boy had nosebleeds. You wanted to talk to me about it, but I'd already slammed the door in your face."

I sat up, the exhaustion suddenly forgotten. That's where I'd heard it; it was the man I'd visited outside of Oklahoma City—Mitch Callum.

"Oh! Mr. Callum, I'm so glad you called."

"Right. Now listen. I don't know what's going on, and I don't necessarily believe you. I had a lot of people poking around in my family's life with this exact kind of excuse. I'm not sorry I closed the door on you; I'd do it again. But it's been a few years since anyone has even thought of me or mine. If you were a reporter, you're about a decade too late."

"I'm not a reporter, I can assure you," I said with a hint of pleading.

"I hope you aren't. For your sake, you understand?"

I swallowed. "Yes. Absolutely."

I'd like to say that I wasn't intimidated. I was, but I was more excited that out of the blue, an avenue had opened up that could help explain what was going on. If Mitch would open up a little, maybe I could understand and prevent what happened to his daughter from happening to my son.

"Okay, that'll work. Grant." He let it hang in the miles between us for a moment before continuing. "If you actually have something similar going on, I'll meet with you. You can come here, to my home, and we can talk for a minute. Not long, understand, an hour or so, and then you'll be on your way."

It wasn't much, but it was better than the nothing I had right now. "That would be great, Mr. Callum. When?"

"Can you come next Sunday? I have church in the morning and like to lay down until after noon. Can you come by then?"

A little vague, but I'd make it work.

"Yes, I'll be there around two o'clock."

"That'll be fine," and then he hung up.

I gripped the phone tightly in my hands, relief sweeping through me as tears began to cloud my vision. Finally, something that may help. I didn't know what or how much, but maybe, just maybe, it might lead to something great. It would change the course of my life.

I called Kathryn as soon as I'd regained my composure. Hopefully, the work she was doing this late would allow her a break to take a call.

"Hey honey, what's wrong? You usually don't call when I'm at work." Her voice was concerned, but I sensed a deeper fear just beneath.

"Everything is fine. The boys are just fine. They're both sleeping and not a nosebleed in the house. I didn't mean to bother or interrupt but wanted to tell you something."

She hesitated and then her voice became more casual with a hint of irritation in it, "Okay, then. What's up?"

"Well I just got off the phone with Mitch Callum. I'm meeting him Sunday afternoon."

Silence.

"Kat?"

"I'm here. I'm just wondering who that is and why it's important."

"He's the guy whose daughter was having continual nose-bleeds and ended up passing away. I visited him after I talked with Dr. Krist. He wasn't too welcoming, but he called out of the blue to set up a meeting. He could help explain what's going on."

I tried desperately to keep a fairly level tone, but the hope-fulness crept through.

"Grant, that's great. I'm excited about that. Is this the trip you took just a while back? You didn't mention visiting this Mitch guy." Her tone held nothing back.

"No, I just didn't think it would amount to anything. I figured you'd want to know, though I guess I was wrong." Was I being petulant? Of course, I was.

"Sorry, it's not that. It's just that I don't want to get my hopes up. And I don't know what he could tell us that a doctor couldn't, you know? Don't get me wrong, I'm glad that you're going to meet with him, and I do hope that it turns into some-thing good, just—just don't get your hopes up, okay?"

"Right. No, I get it. I understand." I was disappointed and discouraged. But I understood. She was hedging her emo-tional bets, and I could understand why. I decided to change the subject. "You'll be home tomorrow morning around six?"

"Yep, I'll see you in the morning. Fair warning, I'm already bushed."

In the background on her end, I could hear a phone call, someone talk in low tones to her, and Kathryn murmured a response. I knew she'd need to go.

"Okay, babe. I love you."

"I love you, too. See you soon, I hope."

Despite my wife's warning to not get my hopes up, I couldn't help it. I'd finally done something to further our inves-tigation into Jackson's nosebleed issue. It wasn't much and

may amount to nothing more than a trip down the highway, but I felt like I was doing more than twiddling my thumbs, and that was something to feel good about.

As Sunday approached, however, my anxiety rose. Jackson had another nosebleed Friday night. It was a light one, and he was able to go back to sleep fairly easily. I talked to Kathryn the following morning over my birthday breakfast of biscuits and gravy. The conversation was gentle with the boys present, both of them sitting beneath the "Happy Birthday" banner. We discussed different questions that needed to be asked. She wasn't terribly excited, but I always appreciated her perspective on things. I was thinking about asking all questions regarding the cause. She wanted to ask questions about the process: When did they start, what did you do, etcetera.

The morning dawned and washed the incoming storm front with a golden blush. It was going to develop into a day with overcast skies with a chance of rain, but the morning was beautiful and the air seemed to glow with it. It didn't help my anxious mood.

After getting the kids fed and dressed for the day—let's be honest, they stayed in pajamas, most of the day regardless—I went around the room and kissed them all goodbye.

"Where are you going, Daddy?" Jackson was sitting next to Keller at the kitchen table, making Play-Doh snakes and mixing the colors. I learned quickly that there didn't exist a universe where kids didn't mix the colors.

"I'm going to visit a friend that may know how to help your nosebleeds. I'll be back tonight."

Keller lifted his face to mine, and I let his open mouth touch my cheek—a toddler version of a kiss. I stroked his head and thin hair, "Bye buddy," and turned to Kathryn.

"Text me when you get there and when you're headed home. I know it's only a couple of hours away, but I want to make sure you're safe, too."

I kissed her lips and tasted coffee.

"I will, I promise," I said, our lips still touching.

I felt her lips smile and kissed her lightly again. "I'll see you tonight."

She smacked my backside when I turned to leave, and Jackson laughed, followed quickly by Keller. The sound of it followed me out the door and into the car. I loved those kids. They were my favorites.

The drive was uneventful, but it got me thinking about all kinds of things. By the time I pulled up to a familiar yard full of warning signs, I couldn't remember exactly how I'd gotten there, as deep in thought as I had been. I quickly sent a text to Kathryn letting her know I'd arrived, but I was little early. To pass the time, I pulled up the article on Mitch Callum's daughter on my phone. I'd read it before but wanted to make sure I had the details right.

Sandwiched between an ad for glasses and exotic vacation packages was a black and white picture of three smiling faces. The caption read:

> Mitch Callum (left) with his wife Andreya Callum (right) and their daughter Mikayla (6, center) enjoy snow cones on a sunny day several weeks before an accident that would take Mikayla's life.

I stared at the picture. Mitch and his wife looked genuinely happy. He had short curly hair and a mustache that rivaled Tom Selleck's. She had long black hair that even through several mediums shone in that distant sunlight. Both of their teeth stood out stark white against dark skin, but each of their eyes held such joy that, compared to the single eye that I spied through the crack in the door last visit, it was hard to believe this man smiling back at me was the same person.

I scrolled down the phone screen with my thumb. Mitch and his wife Andreya Callum had one child, a daughter named Mikayla. She was six years old when she started experiencing nosebleeds. They began much like Jackson's—slowly and spread apart at first, eventually growing in both frequency and intensity. Doctors couldn't pinpoint the issue, and when staying in the hospital, she wouldn't have any. As a result, they'd send her home, which would result in another nosebleed shortly after. Department of Child Services was called as suspicions grew she was experiencing abuse, but nothing conclusive was found. Of course, that nearly ruined them, and they'd had to move out of their neighborhood into a nearby apartment complex. The nosebleeds stopped for a time, but then they seemed to return with vengeance. She had three nights of very serious nosebleeds. After the way the hospital treated them the first time, they worked desperately to handle the first two on their own. The third was so intense that they had no choice but to go to the hospital where she died later that night.

In the fallout that followed, Mitch and Andreya divorced, with Mitch moving back into their old house and Andreya keeping the apartment. She would later move to another state. *The two have spoken little since that time*, the article stated.

I sighed and locked my phone. It was a sad story, and it scared me that my own story could end up like that, but with *two* children at risk. I could already feel the anxiety and frustrations creep in as a result of restless nights and problems without solutions.

By now the clock was close enough to two that I felt comfortable approaching the front door. I walked up to it and knocked lightly.

The door opened several seconds later and an older, grumpier version of the man in the article stood there, looking me up and down. "Grant?"

"Yes, sir. Hi."

His eyes glanced suspiciously to either side of me, then he looked me in the eye and nodded. "You're even whiter than I remember."

Then turning his back to me, he limped back down the hall, the door open between us. "Follow me. We'll talk in the living room," he called over his shoulder.

A little uncertain, I stepped across the threshold and into the home of a stranger.

The hallway was cramped but tidy. The work boots I'd spied last time sat neatly inside, now, on the dark blue tile floor. The dim walls made it feel as if the farther in I walked, the narrower it became. There were two rooms to the left just inside the front door; I was sure they were a master bedroom and what must have been Mikayla's room.

I ducked my head and followed cautiously. The hallway opened into a bright kitchen lit by a bright bay window and a fixture above the dining table. With the kitchen on the left and a sparse living room on the right, there wasn't much room for anything else. The walls of the living room were bare except for two shelves on either side of a stone fireplace, and both were filled with pictures of the young girl from the article, Mikayla. Some were of her jumping and laughing, others sliding or swinging. In all of them, her smile split her face in the most precious way. Some were of her sleeping, and they tugged at the part of my heart labeled "dad."

Mitch noticed me standing before the frames and said, "Come and sit down, Grant. We'll get to her in a minute. She's not going anywhere." He sat in a blue recliner near a large window that looked out upon his front lawn. His tone was still gruff, but there was such sorrow within that I felt like an unwilling witness.

I walked to the only other seat in the room—a twin to the blue recliner Mitch was currently occupying—and eased myself down. I looked at him from the corner of my eye. His hair was still dark, but there were plenty of silver waves running through the curls. He looked tired, and I guessed that he probably felt it; though, he couldn't be much older than me. His houndstooth shirt was unbuttoned, a white t-shirt beneath tucked into a pair of blue jeans.

"Guess I should have asked if you wanted something to drink before you sat down," he said.

"No, I'm fine, thank you. Really."

"Alright, then. Tell me about yourself, then we'll get to your boy."

I wasn't quite sure where to begin, so I started by telling him a little about my family. First was a bit about Jackson and his birth story, then Keller and his birth story, and finally our recent work-related relocation to the neighborhood. Mitch listened quietly as I tried to describe what I did for Eastwind Energy. I tried not to overshare or get lost in the details, so I contented myself with just labeling my work as "renewable energy."

When I began relating the different nights of nosebleeds and showing him the notebook where Kathryn and I recorded the nosebleeds, intensity, and duration, Mitch perked up a bit. He sat forward on his chair to get a better look at the notebook, and I turned it around so he could read it clearly.

"So they're getting worse, based on what you have written here." An observation, no emotion.

I nodded in response as he pointed to several recent entries.

"Did your daughter's get worse?"

I wasn't sure if it was the right time. He and I both knew it would come up at some point, but I didn't think before speaking, and by the sudden tightening of his lips, feared I'd blown my chance.

He let out a long, drawn-out sigh and sat back into his chair, looking at the ceiling. His dark skin shone in the stripes of light from the window as it shone through the half-closed yellowing blinds. When he looked back at me, there were tears in his eyes.

"Mikayla had always been a sweet girl. She was special to Andreya and I. She was special to everyone that knew her. Didn't matter if you were a stranger at the grocery store or her granny and pop, you fell in love with her the moment you met her." His lower lip quivered briefly, and he pointed at the pictures flanking the mantle with a shaky finger. "That smile there—" his voice cracked and I tried to spare his pride by keeping my eyes trained on the pictures. It continued to shake as he continued, "could bring you out of the deepest, darkest mood. God's honest truth."

The picture didn't do it justice, that I was sure of. But even between the time it was taken and now, I could feel the joy that she must have spread. With her springy, curly hair and her cataclysmically adorable eyes, it was no wonder that Mitch felt the power behind it.

I looked at him and tried to frame my question with care and tenderness. "What happened, Mitch?"

He wiped his nose with his thumb and forefinger and coughed. "Her story sounds an awful lot like your boy's.

Regular life turned into a nightmare. Went from sleeping well all night through to waking up multiple times, her nose bleeding all over the place." He waved his hands in the air as if sweeping the memory to the side. "That's not how it started, I guess. First nosebleed I don't remember since that kind of thing seems to happen all the time with kids. Sometimes it's allergies, sometimes it's dryness, sometimes they go and pick it until it bleeds." He chuckled humorlessly. "What I mean is, I didn't think anything was wrong until the nosebleeds started coming more regular. I vaguely remember early on when she had two nosebleeds in one night. Seemed odd but didn't happen again for a little bit, so the details were forgotten. What I *do* remember, though, is the night she soaked the front of her pajamas with blood. It looked like her throat had been cut, blood pouring out of her nose and down her lips and chin. Had to throw those pajamas out. It stopped after a couple of minutes, we put ice on it and had her tip her head back, you know the drill. That was the night Andreya and I had a long discussion about what to do next.

"You see, Andreya had wanted to take her to the hospital early on. I told her that was an overreaction and that didn't sit too well with her. Now, though." He stared out the window, without speaking. "Seeing the blood covering our precocious little six-year-old, I was more than ready to agree. That's when we took her the first time. Doc said he'd seen a couple of kids with nosebleeds and chalked it up to allergies and dry noses. Simple enough fix—drink lots of water, take some allergy medicine, let him know if it gets worse."

"And did you?" I hated to interrupt, but I could feel my own heart hammering and wanted to know what happened next. "Let him know, I mean."

"We did, but it didn't help. During the day, she was as happy as a clam and most nights, slept like log. But Mikayla had another nosebleed three or four nights later. We told ourselves that if she had another, we'd take her in. Two nights later, we decided it was time to take the trip to the doc again when she woke up bleeding. We told him they weren't going away but getting worse. He checked her nose and was surprised to see how weak the blood vessels were. He spouted some mumbo jumbo about how that's inherited and there's medicine for that. Of course, we were willing to try anything, so we got that medicine and put Mikayla on it. The medicine was supposed to strengthen the blood vessels and reduce the risk of spontaneous nosebleeds—doc's words, mind. And maybe they did, but they weren't spontaneous. They began to happen almost every night after a month or so of starting the medicine. We took her off the medicine, took her into the doc, and that's when they began to suspect me of abusing her."

He shook his head and tears dripped down his face. He took out a handkerchief and wiped them away, blew his nose, and stuffed it back into his pocket.

"Growing up around here, you get used to that kind of shit. People suspecting me of something simply because of the color of my skin. So when he brought it up—by politely asking if he could speak to Mikayla alone—of course, I had to object. I told him I'd stay in the room. Sweet girl didn't know what he was asking at first. She stared at him like he'd grown another head."

Mitch smiled over at me. The smile of a man with regrets staining too many memories. "She asked him what he meant and that white doctor said, 'Does your daddy hurt you?' Mikayla looked at him and started laughing. '*My* daddy?' she said, all sassy-like. 'Only when he sees my hair before mommy fixes it and says it looks like I been struck by lightnin'.'" Mitch started chuckling deep in his chest, and another tear leaked its way from the corner of his eye. "That girl was perfect. Made the doc look like a fool, and I didn't mind one bit. Made me proud, if I'm bein' honest." He shook his head, the wisp of a smile fading. "That girl was a force to be reckoned with. Of course, they thought I had intimidated her. Naturally, DHS was called to investigate and interviewed us all separately, multiple times. Couldn't find a thing wrong with us. I never touched a hair on her head. Didn't need to, you know?" He stared at me with an intensity that underlined his words. "Didn't *need* to. She was *good*. She knew right from wrong, even at six. She was like a little angel child. People always asking how we did it, or telling us that we got lucky." He sagged a little. "Maybe at first we were. Lucky, I mean. That luck turned bad real fast, though."

He stood up, and the chair made a deep *twang* sound as a spring retracted. Mitch walked over to the picture of his daughter laughing in the sunlight, a bright yellow dress flaring out around her. When he spoke, it was mostly to himself, and I had to strain my ears to hear him.

"Few nights later, she had another nosebleed. Next night, another, and then the next night, her last one. Couldn't take her to the hospital until it was too late. She was gone. My sweet, little baby girl was gone."

My heart broke, shattered into pieces. Her story was so much like Jackson's that it terrified me. And yet I couldn't help but feel pity for the man, trapped as he was in so much pain from the past. And then he surprised me.

"But it wasn't that doctor's fault. No sir, not his fault at all. Course, he could be blamed, just as much as her mother and I."

I wasn't sure what he meant. I could understand the senti-ment, but it felt like Mitch and his wife, and especially Mikayla, had been wronged in the worst way imaginable.

"I'm not sure I follow, Mitch."

He paused for a moment, then shook his head as if making a decision. "Not the right time yet. Later."

When I tried to ask again for clarification, he waved it away dismissively. "You have another boy, right? Younger?"

Surprised and trying to hide it, I said, "Um... yes, Keller. He's two."

He nodded as if he already knew, and then sat back down in his blue Lay-Z-Boy. "Tell me about him."

"Well," I began and stopped short. Was it relevant to start when he was born? Discuss all the issues he had when he was born? Or should I just give a general overview? What did it matter, anyway?

"He's two, now. Obviously, I just—I know I just said that." I stuttered a bit. Why was I so hot all of a sudden?

"He and Jackson are inseparable. He—well, *they*—love spending time together. It's always been like that. When Jackson asked to hold his brother, hours after he was born, he cried."

"As in he was overcome with emotion?"

I shook my head. "No. Keller was only a little early. Labor just started and we couldn't do anything about it. He was born through caesarian and went straight into the NICU. Jackson was heartbroken and spent every waking minute staring into the incubator. He asked to touch or hold his hand all the time. The nurses got pretty attached to both of the boys. I don't know how rare it is to find a small boy so inexorably attached to his newborn sibling, but there's something spe-cial between them."

I rubbed my palms together, suddenly finding my throat closing and eyes beginning to sting. "They're very special," I managed to croak out.

The room was silent except for the gentle whirring of the overhead fan and the muted hum of the occasional car on the street outside. When Mitch spoke, his voice was somehow gentler. It still held the gravelly undertone, but now it carried with it a dash of understanding.

"I would imagine their bond is."

It took a few minutes for the feeling to pass, but when it did, I risked a glance over at Mitch. He was staring out the window, and I felt gratitude blossom in my chest for him. He was giving me the time and space to recover and avoiding any further embarrassment by pretending not to notice. I can own my emotions well, but with someone new, I wanted to hold my cards close to the chest, at least until I could figure out where to land.

I coughed lightly and stood up, beginning to pace before the smiling framed faces. "After he was brought home, there was no end to the illnesses. Ear infections, colds, flu, all of it. Some people said he may have colic, and in our naivety, we searched for colic medicines and tinctures. In the end, none of it helped. Well, that's not entirely true, I guess. Some of them helped for a small time, but it seemed like his illness always hung on.

"Jackson held him many times when the fever would rage or his cough would prevent him from sleeping soundly. We went in one night when the coughing had suddenly stopped and found Jackson asleep on the floor next to Keller's crib. His hand was through the slats of the crib, and Keller was grasping it tightly. We knew, then, that there was a special bond between them both."

I laughed and stopped pacing, a memory rising to the surface so clearly that I could almost see it before my eyes. "Another night we heard singing on the baby monitor in Keller's room. The angle was odd, so I walked up to see what it was. Jackson had climbed into Keller's crib and snuggled him onto his lap. He was singing. Singing to Keller. The same tune that Kathryn and I sang to him."

Mitch smiled and nodded. "He seems like a great kid."

"Yeah," I said. "Yeah, he absolutely is. But now there are days when Keller is better. Not just the-medicine-seems-to-have-worked better, but more like sudden healing. I don't know how to explain it, but it couldn't have come at a better time. With Jackson's nosebleeds picking up, I don't think we could handle a chronically sick child and a chronically bleeding one."

Mitch continued to stare out the window, and I stood there wondering what to do with my hands for a very silent span of ten seconds.

His sudden voice broke the silence and made me jump. "You ever notice anything strange around your house? Or anyone suspicious?"

I could hear the words, but my brain couldn't make the transition and my mental gears were sparking and grinding, working to start again.

"I don't—"

"It's a strange question, I know, but I'm just curious what you're doing to keep them safe from outsiders."

Outsiders? I thought for a minute. I was certainly committed to protecting my family, but I suppose a lot of it happens passively. The question Mitch was really asking wasn't "Will you protect your family?" It was "What are you doing to protect them from the unknown and unforeseen?"

"We have a doorbell with a camera, and a fairly rudimentary alarm system that tells us when a door opens or something. But nothing beyond that. I've been considering installing other cameras. I'm just not sure why we'd need them. I'm not sure what that has to do with the boys, though."

He nodded slowly. "Like I said, I was just curious. Living out in the neighborhood, I bet you don't usually get weirdos poking around. Not like living out in the country."

I shrugged noncommittally as I sat back down, realizing I wasn't leaving just yet. "Yeah, I guess we do. There's a guy a block over that gives me the creeps. He's nice enough when we seem him around the neighborhood, and his wife seems very normal. He's just quirky, I guess."

Mitch didn't comment. He just sat in his chair, one leg crossed over the other with both forearms resting on the arms of his chair.

"I mean 'quirky' is one way to put it. He does this thing when he's asked a question. He answers, and to most people, it probably sounds like a standard response, but he pauses just a hairsbreadth too long, like he's—I don't know—*translating* it from 'people' to 'Matt.' That's his name, Matt Brandhauer." I let the name sit in the air for several seconds before continuing on, in more of a rush than I intended. "Like I said, I don't think many would notice, but my wife and I talk about it all the time. He seems so..." I tried to think of the right word. It stood just outside of reach in my periphery, but every time I tried to grasp it, it skittered away.

"Robotic," Mitch finished.

I looked up in surprise. "That's it. That's exactly it." *Robotic*.

He nodded in that way that people do when they get the response they expected. "And this *Matt*," he twisted his face as he said the name, as if tasting something particularly unpleasant, "he knows where you live?"

I shrugged. "Well, I'd be surprised if he didn't. We see him and his wife in the neighborhood all the time. I'm sure they've seen us playing with the kids in the yard or pulling into our driveway."

"You said you have camera on the doorbell. Does it monitor the windows and doors somehow?"

I looked at him, confused.

He sighed in exasperation. "I don't keep up with these things, Grant. I don't know what new gizmo or gadget everybody's lookin' for. I'm asking if your house is safe."

A small part of me tried to smile at the old-fashioned attitude toward electronics, but the seriousness of his gaze stopped it short.

"Yes, Mitch. The house is safe. If a window or door opens, our primary panel says out loud which one did. If the alarm is set, it goes off after thirty seconds. The kids are safe. At least from a break in. If the alarm is disabled and someone answers the door, then there's no way to protect against that."

He nodded that way again. "Right. I doubt you need to worry about that, then."

Silence settled over the living room again. The conversation had clearly come to an end, but it felt as if Mitch had more to say. He was rubbing his knee like some old timers do when the weather changes and their arthritis starts acting up again.

Mitch spoke up again, his tone the type that expects a disagreement.

"That's not exactly what I was talking about, though."

I wasn't exactly sure how to respond to that, so I nodded and waited for him to continue. He continued rubbing his knees and staring out the window.

"When Mikayla passed away, Andreya left shortly after. Our marriage wasn't on the rocks at the beginning, not by any means. But the lengths we went to for Mikayla and the strain those hospital visits took on our finances, we began to resent one another. Our daughter was the only thing tethering us together. When that small leash broke, our desire to be around each other broke with it. I don't blame anyone—I wanted out just as much as she did. But I'd be lying if I said I didn't miss her."

I let him speak. It sounded like he needed to tell this story more than I needed to hear it.

"Once both of my girls were gone, I didn't have much to live for. I could tell that I was starting to fall into a deep depression. I couldn't sleep at night and was tired all day. I hated everyone around me—and trust me when I say there were plenty of people around... what with the media and news people almost wrestling each other to get a picture of me. I knew I was sinking deeper and I didn't want to do anything about it. I figured that it would pass, or I'd at least get used to feeling empty and numb all the time.

"What changed me, though, was when I put a colt .45 under my chin and heard the cold metallic *clack* as I cocked the hammer. I wasn't even drunk that night—plenty of others, but not then. But that sound echoed around inside my head so loud that I thought I'd already shot myself and it was the echo I was hearing.

"When I realized that I was still here and the gun was still pressed to that soft spot under my chin, I started shaking so bad that I nearly pulled the trigger anyway. I put the gun down—cocked and all—and started crying like a baby.

"I was broken, Grant. You understand? I was at rock bottom, and there wasn't anything that would make it better on its own. I'd have to do the work. I'd have to pull myself out of it. I was so busy looking at the darkness that I hadn't realized it was swallowing me."

His eyes had begun to burn with an intensity that wasn't aggressive but instead was passionate. I was drawn in despite feeling a little uncomfortable.

He sat quietly for several seconds, turning to the window and squinting his eyes against the late afternoon sunshine.

"So what did you do?" I asked quietly. I couldn't help it.

Still staring out the window, he continued his tale. "I went on a quest." He turned to me, and the ghost of a smile teased the corners of his mouth.

"I knew there was nothing that would bring my Mikayla back, but maybe I could help some other family going through what I went through. So I began to research, starting with that." He pointed behind me, and I turned to follow it.

Sitting against the wall on a small wooden desk was a laptop computer.

"I used that thing and the internet to find other cases similar to my daughter's. Strange deaths that occurred after a sudden nosebleed or two.

"What I found, Grant, was a whole group of people whose children died suddenly without explanation. Families torn apart by the death of their children. Some of them as young as three years old, some as old as fifteen or sixteen. But not a single child—at least in the extensive research I conducted—fell into this category over the age of seventeen. There was one kid, Dustin Vacaro, an eighteen-year-old boy who died of sudden nosebleeds, but it turned out to be a brain tumor."

He paused, looked around, then stood. I wasn't sure what he was doing and continued to watch him as he went into the kitchen. He came back a moment later, a glass of ice water in

each hand. He handed one to me, and I drank deeply, unaware of my thirst. He sat, leaned back, and took a sip of water before continuing.

"The number of deaths started at a young age—three—and their numbers increased from there, peaking at around eleven or twelve—and then declining again until seventeen. I learned this was called a 'Bell Curve,' and I'm sure you've heard of it."

I nodded, mesmerized in spite of myself.

"Good. I—" He stopped and held up his empty hands, as if praying for something to fill them.

But now when he spoke, the more his voice took on a tone that was both defensive and furtive, somehow. As if sharing a secret that was both terrible and exciting, but for reasons proper people can't voice.

"There's something else out there that wants our kids. The *government* isn't the only thing keeping eyes on us, anymore."

I met his gaze, then.

"Mitch, what do you mean?" The spell that he'd been casting over me while his story was told began to fade. I tried to neutralize the doubt in my eyes but knew the creeping suspicion that I'd suddenly found myself in the presence of a hollow man lingered, I was sure.

He dropped his eyes, starting again the constant motion of rubbing his palms across his knees.

"There's something out there in the world, and it's the reason my Mikayla was taken from me." He stared at me, and the fire in his eyes dared me to argue. "There's something—or someone—that's killing kids, and it starts with the nosebleeds."

My brain came to a grinding halt. I couldn't imagine that he was serious. Of course, my conscious thought argued that he was right. Lions, tigers, and bears came to mind, but there were none of those around here, and there'd be some kind of evidence of an animal attack.

"Mitch, what are you talking about?" I repeated.

He stared at me for a moment, looking for something. Then he nodded as if making a decision and stood up. "Follow me," he said and walked out of the room toward the kitchen without looking to see if I followed.

I hesitated. Was this when I called Kat and tell her "Hey, there's something crazy with this guy," or did I follow and find out what he's talking about?

I made the snap decision to follow him and rushed into the kitchen to see his form near an ancient yellow Frigidaire refrigerator going through a door. I followed him through it and into a dark and formless room.

Mitch's outline was fading from of the light cast by the kitchen and into the darkness of what I assumed was a large garage. I watched his dim form reach up for a string that disappeared into the darkness above. He pulled on it gently, and there was a delicate *click*. Light flooded the room, and I blinked, letting my eyes adjust for several seconds before actually *looking*.

The first thing I noticed was the boxes that lined the gypsum board walls. Some were standard cardboard with black marker detailing their contents as "Mikayla's Things" or "Old Attic misc." I turned toward Mitch and found him standing by a workbench made of four simple legs and several two-by-four planks drilled together. Mitch's back was to me, and he was shuffling through some papers on the bench. The bench itself was stained with what looked like decades of paint. Purple, black, blues, and reds all bled together across its surface. I couldn't tell if it was on purpose or if it had been subject to innumerable projects that it stood simply as a silent witness to its own past.

"What do you think?" Mitch had turned and gestured at the wall behind him. The wall that I hadn't really noticed at first. It was covered with newspaper clippings, their black and white headlines twisting into a linguistic tornado. Strands of yarn connected pictures and articles with a partner on some other part of the wall, some red—which stood out best against the stark white and black—some blue and yellow, colors that blended well with the workbench beneath it. Some of the articles were a block of text beneath a large black headline. Others had pictures interspersed between the text, pictures of children, mostly. My eyes began to blur.

"Mitch, what—" I wasn't sure how to finish. I rubbed at my eyes, which helped with the blurring, but the spinning colors were there behind my eyelids.

I heard him approach and felt his hand on my shoulder. "I know it's overwhelming. But this is what I mean. This is the book where Mikayla and Jackson are just another chapter."

His voice was kindly, understanding, even. But underneath was an edge that once again dared me to disagree, dared me to call him crazy. It was at that moment I recognized the unease that had crept up my spine. *It is understandable*, I tried to justify it to myself. *I'm only uneasy because I'm in the garage of a person I just met, and he's showing me a wall full of newspaper clippings and yarn*. It didn't quite take the edge off, however.

I decided that I needed to be very careful. Mitch may not be violent, but the word *unstable* came to mind; I knew that based on the first interaction I had with him. But this. This was crazy. I could stay for a few minutes, assuage any doubts he may feel about me, and then leave with the excuse that I needed to get on the road; it wasn't a short drive home. I didn't want to dismiss what had obviously been a bit more than a hobby to him, but my discomfort was very real, and I'd be a fool to ignore it.

"Wow, Mitch. This is ... something else." The image in my eyes was a blurry mix of white and black, a few rogue colors here and there, but unfocused as I was, it was workable. My heart was racing. I could feel it beating in the artery next to my ear in rapid thumps.

"This is how I've spent my time since Mikayla died. I've been tracking, Grant. And through it all, I realized that Mikayla wasn't the first. Jackson won't be the last." His movements became larger, his voice more excited. I doubted that he'd had anyone to share this with and since I was the first, I knew the dam had opened.

I cut him off before he could get going. "Mitch, this is really something, but I'm not sure if I have the time to go through it all." I made a show of checking my watch. "Oh man, I'm already running behind. Kat will be expecting me home soon."

He nodded, hands out in front and said, "That's okay, we can pick back up another time. But let me just show you this." He walked over to the middle of the wall that backed up to the kitchen, on the other side of this sanctum of delirium.

I watched him put his palm against the wall, fingers splayed. His eyes burned with an excitement I didn't share. "It started here, about six years ago in Billings, Montana. A healthy nine-year-old little boy. No previous medical issues. He suddenly starts getting nosebleeds. Then dies a month later from it. Doctors rule it 'spontaneous epistaxis hemorrhage.' Sad, of course. But then—" he moved his palm along what I thought was a blue string to another picture, "a few months later in Tempe, Arizona a little girl, eight years old. *She* dies suddenly after a nosebleed that won't stop. Doctors rule it something similar." Mitch moved his palm along the wall and stopped again. "Then over here in Pinehurst, North Carolina, another little boy of twelve—"

I held up my hands. "Mitch, I get it. Nosebleeds aren't uncommon; there are thousands of cases. What makes you think that these are connected? How could they possibly be connected? Even the few you've mentioned are hundreds or thousands of miles apart. If some entity—human or otherwise—is hunting them, it couldn't travel that far in that amount of time, right?"

He waved my questions away, and for a moment, I saw the light in his eyes and the smile of relief on his face. It was the look of a true believer, a *zealot*.

"All of those questions are irrelevant. I can explain it again when we have more time. All I'm saying is that there's more to it than just Mikayla and Jackson." He left the wall and walked toward me, hands outstretched. The limp had disappeared, I noticed. And as he gently grasped my forearms, I was forced to look in his eyes. "Our children are *special*, Grant. There's something about them that makes them targets, or maybe there's more—" His face lit up at this, excitement in finally sharing his theories.

I took a step away from him and nodded, breaking contact. I picked my words very carefully, as if navigating a minefield. "It's definitely a theory—and a good one at that. I can tell that you've put a lot of time into figuring it all out."

He dropped his arms, and I saw the immediate change in his demeanor. The excitement at having a co-conspirator had evaporated.

I was now a doubter.

A naysayer.

An enemy.

Mitch took a step toward me. "You don't believe me." It wasn't a question, and his tone took on a dark and dangerous edge. That dare from before was there and now held the promise of consequence.

I made a placating gesture, praying desperately that I could get out of here before he snapped. Sweat had beaded on my temple and was beginning to trickle down the sides of my face. "It's not that, not that at all." I grasped for something, anything. "It's just a lot to take in." I had to think fast. "You understand that, right? You've been developing this for years and had the time to process it, order it, understand it. I've had all of five minutes since the door to this world was opened. You can't expect me to have the same level of calm understanding that you've achieved, right?"

He didn't respond, and I took that as a good sign. His hands were clenched into fists, but as I continued, they relaxed.

"You're asking me to drink from a firehose, man. I came here expecting to take a sip." I softened my tone. "That's all, Mitch."

He continued to weigh me with a heavy stare. When he nodded and began to glance around, I let out a slow sigh of relief and wiped the sweat off my forehead before it could run into my eyes.

"You're right, Grant. I'm sorry."

I laughed more in relief for myself than for him. "No, Mitch. Don't apologize. This—" I gestured around us both. "This is huge. I'll just have to hear about it another time. That's all."

He nodded once more and gestured back the way we came.

"I'll see you out, then."

I was terrified to turn my back to him, but as I stepped into the kitchen, I turned and saw him pull the light switch and close the garage door behind us. I made to walk down the hall, but Mitch stopped me.

"Grant."

I turned to him and my heart began to pick up speed again.

"I'd appreciate it if you'd keep this between us. I lost myself in the excitement of it all. Having someone else who could understand..." His voice trailed off in a mix of embarrassment and something else I couldn't quite pin down.

I answered without thinking. "Yeah, of course, Mitch." It was sad in a way. This man needed a friend, needed someone to understand, and I'd delivered myself up on a silver platter. I was someone who could understand his fear and hope in a way that very few people in the world could. Perhaps he had come off too strong, but I knew that beneath that excitement was the heart of a father who'd lost his baby, and there was nothing he could have done to stop it. That helplessness changes people. I could feel it changing me.

I put a hand on his shoulder, and he met my eye. "Mitch, it was a lot to take in." I laughed lightly. "But I get it. Really, I appreciate you showing it to me. I want to know more about it. But honestly, I can't believe it right now, but take it as a challenge. Convince me, right?"

He nodded and muttered something like "thanks" and I turned, heading toward the front door that felt like a million miles down the dark hallway. I hoped my body didn't look as robotic as it felt.

I shook his hand at the door, knowing he felt the clammy coldness of it but not caring. I was almost gone. I told him I'd call him when I had another afternoon free, and he said it sounded great.

I took a deep breath when I stepped across the threshold. The change from the dark interior to the almost-bright exterior sent a chill down my spine. It was a pleasant feeling after being inside, and the evening air was beginning to take on the pleasant coolness of spring.

Chapter 12

I made it home without incident. I was hoping to get there before the kids were in bed, but traffic caught up with me when I drove through Tulsa at five o'clock.

When I got home, Kathryn asked me if I'd eaten and told me that the leftover casserole was in the fridge. I told her that I had grabbed a bite on the way home.

"So how did it go?" She was sitting on the couch, Keller asleep in her arms. His little body was long, now. I hadn't noticed it in the last couple of months, but here he was, just growing and growing.

I came over and kissed Keller's head then her lightly on the lips. His breath was coming in rattling gasps that at one time had me worried, but more recently had become normal.

"Rough night?"

She nodded and patted his bottom. "Yeah, he kept coughing and crying so I figured I'd just snuggle him up on the couch."

I smiled and said, "It might do us some good to separate them sometime. Maybe just to give us both a break, you know?"

She nodded.

"I'm going to kiss Jackson. I'll be right back and tell you all about it."

I made my way up the stairs and even still felt an uneasy hesitation turning the corner at the top of them. I knew there wouldn't be something at the end of the hall, but it always felt like there would be. I figured I'd get over it, eventually.

When I went into Jackson's room, I sat on his bed gently, not wanting to wake him. It was always interesting seeing my children sleep. Throughout the day—even the best—I could be irritable, frustrated, and exhausted, but the second they fell asleep, it was like all of that disappeared. I saw the child they are or baby they were, and the irritation evaporates. I'm not sure that ever goes away. I think parents will always see their children as the toddlers they were, the toddlers who needed their mommies and daddies when the darkness overwhelmed them.

I put my hand on his shoulder and squeezed it gently. He was a sweet kid, and even though he was getting close to double digits, he still slept with the bear his grandpa had given him tucked tightly under his arm. I noticed the red and green pattern of Christmas pajamas on his arms and laughed a little. I don't remember when we stopped caring about "seasonal" clothes, but it had to be recent. I bent and kissed his temple and stood up slowly, glancing out the window as the yellow glow of headlights shone briefly on the wall before going back downstairs.

"So," Kathryn prompted the second I plopped down on the couch by her feet.

"So," I began, and then I told her the whole story. I was hesitant to include the bit about his conspiracy theory in the garage, but it was too important to leave out. Her frown grew deeper as I relayed the part about the different cases of kids dying from nosebleed-like symptoms.

"I left as quick as I could, and I don't know when I'll go back. I was nervous, but I really think that he's a good guy, just a little ... socially delayed, having been ostracized for a while." With my story finished, I waited for a response.

She sat and frowned quietly for a minute, idly rubbing Keller's back after he snorted and coughed briefly.

"Well he sounds crazy."

She moved her feet so that I could sit on the couch, then put her legs over mine. I patted Keller's back, and he stirred briefly, then wiped his nose and smeared snot across his cheek.

"But you don't think he could be right. At least about the deaths of the kids being from nosebleeds? I'm not saying I believe him, but—" she swallowed and glanced at Keller, "I'm scared."

I wasn't sure how to respond, so I chose my words carefully. "The deaths of those kids were ruled natural, Kat, and resulted from whatever else was going on. If we look those kids up, I'm sure we'll see that they did die from whatever Mitch said. But I don't think they're connected." I paused. "No, scratch that. There's no way they're connected. It seems too over the top to even be possible."

"It sounds crazy, Grant." Her tone was full of worry.

"I know it does, babe. That's why I'm completely ignoring that part of it." I shifted on the couch to face her more directly. "We are Jackson's parents. We know what's best for him. I'm not going to base the medical decisions of my son on some stranger's conspiracy theories."

That seemed to help her, and she relaxed her shoulders a little, but in a deep place of my chest, the worry remained. Her expression clearly communicated that she wasn't completely convinced.

We sat in silence for several minutes. I was rubbing her feet, and she was rubbing Keller's back.

Finally, I patted her leg affectionately and said, "Let me take that boy up to bed."

She affected a mock frown but smiled as I gently lifted our two-year-old from her chest and laid him on my shoulder. His head lolled comfortably into the hollow at my throat, and I smiled as his limp arms fell to his side.

Even though I'd walked up and down those stairs thousands of times, I was still careful. Several days after we moved in, I walked up the stairs wearing socks, and my toe caught the edge of the next stair. I caught myself but sprained my wrist in the process. It was embarrassing, sure, but now I walked much slower going up and down the stairs.

I laid Keller in his bed and positioned a blanket of alphabetical frogs across his tiny form. He rolled onto his back and snorted once, then snuggled into his bed. His nose was crusty, and I wanted to wipe it, but knowing it could wake him up, stayed my hand. Sleep was precious, and his nose would just get snotty again anyway.

He'll be fine, I thought. Then on a whim, *God please let him sleep tonight and wake up better. I'm so tired of watching him get sick without any way to help him get better. Help Jackson sleep and please don't let him have a nosebleed.*

I tucked the blanket a little tighter around his tiny form. I wasn't the praying type, though I was feeling pretty insignificant in the grand scheme of things. That happens, I've heard, once you have kids. It just brings things into focus that were hard to notice before. Maybe it served as a cautionary tale to some, maybe permission to others. I left the room without deciding which one I believed.

I should have known that praying wouldn't have made a difference. But a fool's prayer is a wise man's fable. A couple of hours later, Kat and I were ripped out of our sleep by a blood-curdling scream tearing its way from Jackson's throat and down the empty stairway.

We both bolted out of bed, throwing the covers wide and all but sprinting up the moonlit stairs. I took extra care not to fall, but I was more concerned with what was happening to Jackson.

We ran to his bed, and I stopped as Kathryn knelt down next to his bed. "Get a towel and turn on the light," she said in a tense voice.

I turned to the bathroom, grabbed a towel from beneath the sink, and flipped on the light switch by the door on my way down to the kitchen. I quickly grabbed a few ice cubes and buried them in the hand towel, taking the stairs two at a time.

When I turned the corner, I had to choke back a cry of surprise. The light had revealed the green and red pattern of his pajamas, but the stripes were clouded by splashes of blood. The whole front of his shirt was covered and the dark, rusty liquid ran freely between his fingers, which were clutching his nose. His eyes were wide with terror and looked feverishly back and forth between his parents.

I handed Kathryn the ice-filled towel, and she gently pushed his hands aside to cover his face with the iced cloth. "Move your hands, baby."

Jackson did and began wiping them on his bedcovers, leaving bloody handprints behind. I could see tears streaming down his face and into the towel that was slowly turning crimson. He was sobbing, and I quickly sat beside him and rubbed his back, reciting calming phrases and telling him all the well-intentioned lies of parenthood.

My eyes met Kathryn's. The fear and uncertainty beneath was obvious. I pursed my lips and shrugged; I was terrified myself. I had no idea what was causing this. I had no clue why Jackson's nosebleeds were so violent and sudden. And unless I was mistaken, increasing in frequency.

On top of it all, I thought they were getting worse, too. Kathryn probably already knew that. She'd been keeping the journal and had written a description of each in the little black journal beside our bed. I was certain this one would have a caption that included the words "gushing" and "copious."

I continued to rub Jackson's back and put my head on the top of his, gazing toward the ruddy glow of the streetlights below. A drop of red on the carpet caught my attention. A single drop had been splattered there when Jackson woke up, probably. I'm sure at the terror of waking up to a ferocious nosebleed like this he'd whipped his hands or head around. I'd clean it later. Or it would turn into just another spot on the carpet that wouldn't come out.

Eventually, the bleeding stopped. Jackson's hitching lessened with each passing minute, and I walked him to the bathroom. He bent over the sink and spit out bloody gobs, turning the clear water into swirls of pink and red. With tears dripping from his cheeks, I couldn't help but feel a desperate pity for him.

"I'm tired of this, Daddy," he said into the basin and began to weep again.

I felt tears sting my throat, and I hugged his shoulders to me as he rinsed his mouth out and washed his hands and face. "I know buddy. Me too. Mommy and I are trying to figure out what we need to do, okay?" I wanted to weep with him. I wanted to plead with him to be strong, that we were trying our best, that we were lost and had no idea what we were doing or what to do next. I wanted to cry out at the unfairness of it all.

But I kissed the top of his head, instead.

He was unsteady trying to get new pajamas, so I helped him change while Kathryn changed his sheets. By now we had a set of twin sheets on constant rotation. This set would go into the washer and dryer tomorrow in the event that tomorrow night he had another. It was unlikely; there hadn't been two nose-bleeds in a row. I had to stop myself from thinking *yet*. I didn't want to think about their frequency increasing even more.

When he was settled back in between his clean sheets, I lay down beside him. He turned over and placed his head on my chest, and I rested my arm across his shoulders.

"I'm going to lie here for a bit with him, if that's okay."

Kathryn smiled sadly and said, "I'll go make some notes. Probably go back to bed, too."

"Okay, hon," I said, and she kissed my cheek, and then Jackson's before leaving and turning out the lights.

As I lay there, I thought about the role of parents. Not anything as mundane as good parents versus bad parents but simply raising children into adults. The process of ensuring their safety for several helpless years and transitioning into a period where they could help themselves with supervision and all the way to the stage where parents set them free—let their kids make their own choices without any say in the matter. What a nightmare. It wasn't that I didn't trust my kids, but that the world actively worked to ruin them. Life was hard enough, but once they were out from under our wings, they had to find their own help. And that was good. What a crazy thought: it was good that they had to find their own way, even if they were lonely and scared. Of course, we don't abandon them, but we certainly don't have eyes on them all the time.

It reminded me of my work with Eastwind. My job was to find some kind of renewable energy stream, to hijack it, really. I wondered if it was the parent's role to hijack the world, or the world's role to hijack the child. The stages of parenthood seemed to mimic that cycle of "find energy, hijack it, move on, find energy, hijack it" ad nauseum.

I shuddered inwardly when I imagined the nosebleeds continuing into adulthood. What then? Would he be able to take care of himself? Would he still feel that bewildered terror at waking up to his nose bleeding freely across his chin and chest? Hopefully by then Kat and I would have taught him how to handle stressful situations.

God, I hoped.

My eyes wandered to that wayward drop of blood on the carpet. I hated that Jackson woke up alone and bleeding, scared and hurting. What could we do about it, though? Watch him constantly?

I thought about that for a moment. I certainly could install cameras. But I shook my head at it. His screams were enough to alert us to the fact that his nose had become a biblical plague. And Keller was a toddler. He'd let us know if he needed something.

So what else was there? Kat or I could take turns sleeping up here. Or he could sleep downstairs. That could work.

My mind buzzed in circles for a few moments. It was only when I woke up at four in the morning that I realized I'd fallen asleep. I groggily moved Jackson's limp body off my own and stepped out of his room. I checked in on Keller and heard him sleeping soundly, so I went downstairs and slipped under the covers, hugging my wife close before falling blissfully into a dreamless sleep.

The next morning showed that half my prayer had been answered. While Jackson had definitely had a nosebleed, Keller woke up bright-eyed and bushy-tailed. His peals of laughter echoed down the stairway as Kathryn changed him and tickled him.

When Jackson came downstairs to eat breakfast, his eyes were ringed with dark circles and his movements were lethargic.

"You okay, buddy?" I asked, knowing he wasn't and handing him a bowl of cereal.

He nodded listlessly and mumbled, "I just didn't sleep good."

I watched him closely. As he ate, his face gained a little bit of color, and by the time he'd finished his orange juice, he seemed to be almost back to normal.

When Keller came downstairs and squealed "Hassin!" at him, he brightened up considerably. Maybe it was some of the sleepiness wearing off, too. He'd be okay.

After taking Jackson to school, I came back to the house to work a little more. Kathryn lay on her stomach in the living room facing Keller. They were stacking blocks and knocking them over—one of Keller's favorite games.

I sat on the couch with my laptop and watched them off and on. "He seems to be feeling much better this morning, doesn't he?"

Kathryn smiled and laughed, keeping her eyes on Keller as he tried to copy her expression. "Yes, he does, and I'm not complaining."

I let them play and continued to work, parsing data from a field researcher's FAD in Iowa for several more minutes before saying, "It is kind of weird, though, right?"

"What do you mean?" she answered in a baby voice to Keller.

I looked at her over my computer, then set it aside and waited for her to look my way.

"I mean that this one," I indicated the laughing toddler before her, "is fit as a fiddle right now, and our eldest," I hooked a thumb over my shoulder, "woke up looking like the walking dead."

She sat up and shrugged. "I don't like that analogy. What's your point, Grant?"

I scoffed at her. "My point, Kat, is that it was the opposite last night. Jackson seemed to be fine, and Keller was coughing and wheezing when I put him to bed. Now, look at him." Keller looked at me, grinned, and blew a raspberry. "Doesn't that seem weird to you?"

She moved her attention back to Keller and adopted that playful baby tone. "No, it doesn't. I'm sure that happens to kids all over the world every single night. Why would it be weird?" She cut her eyes to me and dropped the playful tone. "Coincidence. Don't you dare start entertaining anything crazy from Mitch, Grant Taldo."

I relented by putting my palms up toward her in an "I surrender" motion. She smiled as if she'd won and went back to playing with Keller. I put the laptop back on my lap and continued working.

"Did you log the nosebleed last night?" I asked after some time.

"No, I decided to let it go since it didn't matter."

I sighed and looked at her.

"Of course I did. It's on my nightstand if you wanna read it."

She did that, sometimes. When I asked what she perceived as a stupid question, she defaulted to answering with as much sarcasm as possible. It was infinitely annoying.

I finished up a paragraph where the FAD in Iowa had detected a surge from the south several weeks previous and compared its time stamp to those of Gretchen. They were suspiciously close, maybe the same day. I set my computer aside and retrieved the journal from our room. Sure enough, the little black book on her nightstand had a pen lying on the page she'd filled out the night before.

> *March 21*
> *2:16 am*
> *We woke up to Jackson screaming and crying.*
> *His nose was gushing blood when we got him,*
> *and it covered his pajamas and some of his*
> *covers. Compared to previous nosebleeds,*
> *this one was one of the worst, a 6 or 7 in*
> *severity. After applying ice wrapped in a*
> *towel, it stopped and he was able to go back*
> *to sleep after changing his clothes.*
> *End at 3:21 am*

Well, I was batting five hundred for word bingo, at least.

I thumbed through some of the other entries in the book. Since the doctor had asked us to keep track of the nosebleeds several months ago, he'd had more than seven in that time. Not altogether alarming, but not normal, either. The rating system might be flawed, too, but the descriptions were clear enough.

I looked at the first page of the palm-sized book and read the entry. The month was clear, but the number was smudged beyond recognition.

> *January --*

> *1:43 am*
> *We woke up to Jackson crying tonight. I don't remember his last nosebleed, but it is at least a couple of weeks ago. Tonight's was a drip of blood that ran down his nostril and down his chin. It had dripped a couple of times onto his shirt and a brief cold compress made it stop and he went to sleep almost as soon as we laid him back down.*
> *End at 2:39 am*

Compared to the one last night, it was definitely getting worse. The dates were getting much closer together, and last night's made nearly ten. Were ten nosebleeds in a few months a lot? Well, I hadn't had one in a few decades, so I guessed that it wasn't normal.

I wondered if I should start keeping a track of Keller's sickness. Not just to weigh its frequency against Jackson's nosebleeds, but to compare it to something if he continued to get worse. I decided to talk to Kat about it if we get the chance. Maybe she'd have a better idea.

CHAPTER 13

The nice thing about working from home is that I'm able to, more or less, make my own schedule. After taking Jack to school several days after the worst nosebleed yet, I let Marco know that I'd work the analytics and run a few field tests on Gretchen, but that I'd also knock off a little early. He gave me a thumbs-up response in our virtual chat, and I hammered out a few hours' worth of work, made a few trips around town, then returned home just after Kathryn brought Jackson home.

I made a cup of coffee and sat at the table stirring it idly while Kat told me about her day. It was nice to hear the contentment in her voice, despite the some of the difficulties of raising two boys, not to mention the nosebleed that occurred only a couple of nights ago.

"So *then* I asked Jackson to bring me Keller's sippee cup, which he found underneath the couch, but it was *filled* with old milk. Grant, I'm talking the level of a thick layer on top and liquid underneath. Literally rotten."

I made a sour face. I knew all too well what that smelled like when the lid popped off and the globular mess was poured into the sink with a wet *plop*.

"Well," I said, "then it makes sense why he gagged when he found it." We both laughed and continued chatting until

I drained my coffee cup. I stood, rinsed the cup, and put it in the dishwasher. Then, "Tell me about the rest of your day. Were the boys okay?"

As hard as it was to be away from the boys while I worked, it helped knowing their mother—and the woman of my dreams—was with them most of the days. And since I wasn't around for some of the time they were awake, I cherished the stories of the times I'd missed.

She sipped her own cup of coffee and smiled, grabbing her phone from the counter. "I caught a really sweet moment between them today. Let me find it." She scrolled for a minute, and I was struck by how beautiful she was standing there, phone in hand, biting her lower lip while her eyes moved rapidly up and down searching for a particular picture on her phone. "There it is," she said, and turned the phone so that I could see the picture.

I felt warm affection ease its way slowly through my body. It was a snapshot of the living room, yellow light cascading through the windows to either side of the television. Jackson and Keller faced each other with a dozen superheroes, trucks, and dinosaurs spread around them in haphazard piles and positions. Jackson held onto an airplane, his eyes wide and mouth forming what looked like the sound of an explosion while Keller's eyes were squeezed shut and the soundless laugh that stretched his mouth into a grin was more joy than could be contained within a tiny two-year-old body.

I felt the sting of tears in my eyes and did one of those smile-frown things. It made me incredibly happy and profoundly sad at the same time. It was perfect, and I told her so.

"I thought so, too," she said with the same expression I now wore.

I handed her phone back and walked around the counter to wrap my arms around her waist.

"I can't tell you how happy it makes me to know our boys are watched by their mother. We're so lucky. *I'm* so lucky." I looked her in eyes and smiled. She returned it and kissed my lips. I really believed I was lucky. I still do think I'm lucky, just in a different way.

I stepped back from her, and she continued to tell me about their day, how they played and Keller napped, and how she missed it when Jackson used to snuggle into the space between the cushion and her cocked legs on the couch.

"The Nest, he called it." She laughed, and the sparkle in her eye told me how much it meant to her. "It doesn't matter how often or infrequent I sat like that, he always used to sit there. Keller sits there, now, sometimes. I've noticed Jackson sitting as I do, and Keller crawls into that space. They both call it 'The Nest,' and it makes me so happy." Her smile faded a little, and her eyes grew distant.

"But?" I prompted.

Her eyes refocused. "Well, they're just *so close*. I mean that's wonderful, don't get me wrong. I just feel, I don't know, strange about it. They're *so connected* that I worry that if—well, when—something happens to one of them, what it will do to the other?"

"Jesus, Kat. That's morbid."

"No, not like that. I mean when one of them scrapes a knee or cuts themselves or crashes a car when they're older. Jackson already feels responsible for Keller's well-being regardless of how often I tell him that his little brother's safety is *my concern*. He always responds with a 'I know mom, I just like to help' kind of thing, but I worry that he genuinely feels that it's his job to keep Keller safe.

"My worry is that if something happens, Jackson will feel responsible, and it'll tear him apart." The joy she felt only moments ago was replaced with a kind of irrational anxiety, but I would never call it that out loud.

I took a second to consider before responding, choosing my words carefully. "I can see how you may feel like that," I said. "I guess that's the price of being close, isn't it? The alternative is that Jack doesn't care at all, which is much worse in my opinion."

She sighed and looked out the kitchen window at nothing in particular, tapping her lip with a finger. "You're right, I guess."

I smiled and decided to change the tone a little. "Can you repeat that, ma'am?"

She looked at me with a very unimpressed expression, and I grabbed her waist to pull her toward me.

"I said, 'Can you repeat that, ma'am?'"

She smiled and I could feel the shift. She rolled her eyes and said, "You're right, I guess."

"I know I'm right," I said playfully and looked over her shoulder at the boys. Keller coughed deep in his chest and rubbed his arm across his nose. Jackson frowned a little at him, but he kept playing.

Kathryn followed my gaze and then turned to face them, her back to me. We stayed like that for five or ten minutes, just watching the boys interact. Jackson played gently and easily with Keller, and Keller responded with the deepest, purest delight. Their bond was undeniable.

Something tugged at my thoughts, but I continued to stare at my sons. I thought that my cancer would ruin our plans for a family, and it turns out that everything happened just like it should have.

Well, maybe not *exactly* like it should have. Keller's birth and first few months weren't great. He wasn't an easy baby. He had croup for months and wasn't ever able to keep anything down. My big concern was that my radiation therapy had somehow made him sick. It seems silly, now, but in the middle of a week where Kat and I slept a handful of hours combined, everything seemed to scale exponentially grander than it actually was.

Cancer was scary by itself. Add in a few months of radiation therapy, then a surprise pregnancy, and all the thoughts begin to turn inward. Doctor Keller—obviously, Keller's namesake—told us not to worry, of course. He said the major side effect of radiation therapy was reserved for me. If it affected my sperm, it would just kill it; it wouldn't transfer some kind of sickness to the infant.

Reassuring, sure. But like I said, those first few months were just shy of a nightmare.

Jackson was different, though. He loved every minute of it. Feeding his brother, rocking his brother, all of it. And he was only seven at the time. He wanted to be so big. Honestly, after talking with Kathryn about it, Jackson helped more than we hoped. There were a few times when we'd wake up and Jackson would be rocking him and feeding him a bottle. We didn't know how Jack got Keller out of the crib, but if it let us sleep for another hour, we didn't care. At that point, we were running on less than fumes.

Now, staring across the room at the laughing boys, I couldn't help but smile. What gifts these two were, these favorites of mine. Despite Jackson's random nosebleeds and the frequent nights that Keller had, we led a pretty great life. Easy, some might even say, if they didn't know us.

"Hey, Kat," I said, trying my best at nonchalance.

She turned to me, eyebrow already raised in question.

"Remember when I mentioned maybe separating the boys for a few days? Just to kind of feel out the situation, I guess."

"I mean, 'mention' is about all you did." Then she took a sip of her coffee.

"Well I was thinking that I could take Jackson to Devil's Den for a week or so, kind of have some father-son bonding, and if you were up for it, you could go visit your mom during that time, too. You just mentioned some concern that they're so close, it might do them some good to spend a few days apart."

She nodded her head, thinking silently.

"That," she started and paused, taking another sip. "That is a good idea. Are you thinking this weekend?"

I wasn't, actually. Usually, as most parents know, planning a getaway of any kind can require more than a couple days' notice. I'd planned on working on Gretchen this weekend and running some preparatory field tests, but I bet they could wait, and I was willing to gamble it.

"Well, would your mom be up for it that soon?"

She waved her hand. "Mom wouldn't care if I showed up in the middle of the night as long as I brought one or both of the kids. She'll be fine. Are you able to get enough work done before going?"

I nodded and shrugged. "I'll be fine. I've got a few diagnostics and analytics to comb through, and I need to make sure Gretchen is field-test ready. There's some things I need to work through by the end of the month. I think I can finish it in the next few days."

"And with it being Spring Break, we won't have to worry about Jack missing school at all. You can take your time coming back as long as it's before school starts again."

"That's a great idea, actually. I hadn't remembered it was Spring Break at all."

She smiled at me, though it was a little reserved as if she couldn't quite let herself fully enjoy the small win. "It's settled, then. I'll take Keller with me this weekend and visit mom until, what, Friday or Saturday morning? That would give the boys almost a full week apart."

"Sure, that sounds good. I'll probably bring Jackson back Friday morning from camping, just to get back in the weekly habit, you know." I smiled at her, and she returned it. "It'll be okay."

She nodded, and the tip of her nose turned a bright red. She worked hard to conceal her emotions, but having known her for some time, I could pick this one out easily.

I walked around the counter, and when I wrapped her in a hug, she buried her face in my shoulder and cried softly.

"I'm just so tired of worrying."

I responded once more that it was going to be okay and that we'd be fine and that the boys would be fine. Truth is, I wasn't sure if anything would be fine. As a parent, it's almost impossible to ignore the dangers of what that next minute might hold. With both boys experiencing some kind of sickness, the worst-case-scenarios ran rampant through our minds. I tried to do my best to quiet them, but they were always there, waiting at the edges of consciousness whispering a seditious *What if?*

I accomplished everything I needed to within the next few days. I let Marco and Gianna know my plans—another benefit of working for this company was knowing that off-time usually wasn't a problem.

I was pulling the camping gear off the garage shelves when a man's voice in a thick Southern drawl spoke directly behind me.

"Ya'll goin' somewhere?"

I turned to see Edgar Sandhill standing in my driveway. I plastered a fake smile on my face and groaned internally. Edgar lived a street over and was the neighborhood weirdo. He wasn't a bad, creepy weirdo like Matt Brandhauer. Well, not on purpose. He just had no clue how to be a civilized human. He constantly invaded people's personal space by inviting himself onto their property and into their lives. He was an older man, mid-sixties. He was also a veteran, and he made sure to drop that into every conversation he had. As a result of his service, which I thanked him and others for whenever I could, his right arm ended at the elbow.

Today, Ed wore a bright red button up and a pair of khakis, which fell just above the laces on his old and creased work boots. His white hair, lifted briefly in breeze, reminded me of snow blown off a mountain peak. His eyes were bright and penetrating, and that's probably what made people so uncomfortable. When he looked at you, he resembled a hawk staring down a mouse.

"Hey there, Ed. Yeah, I'm taking Jackson camping for a few days. Figured we'd go out to Devil's Den and poke around for a time."

Edgar nodded and gestured with his stump, "D'ya need some help?"

It was well-intentioned and because of that, I didn't laugh. "No, thank you, Ed. I'm just grabbing a few sleeping bags and the tent. I appreciate it, though."

"Alright, no problem. Figgered I'd ask, even though I cain't do much. Los' my arm when I was in the service, ya know."

There it was. "Yeah. Yep. I remember. Thanks for serving."

"What's yer wife doin' with you gone? She gonna be able to take care of ev'rythang?"

Good intentions, I told myself. "She's able to do more than even I am, believe it or not." He scoffed, and I hoped it was good-natured. "She's going to take our youngest up to her mom's a few hours away. She'll be fine."

"Need someone to look after the house?"

I did my best to keep the annoyance out of my voice. "No, I don't think so. We'll just lock the doors and call it good. We've got an alarm system and the like, so I don't think we'll need anything."

"I'll come 'round and make sure everything is still good, 'nyway." Edgar shifted and looked around at the garage. "Seems like ya need to clean up yer garage."

For fuck's sake. "Yeah, we sure do, Ed. Put it on the list." I smiled at the end and went back to gathering the camping equipment, hoping he'd get the hint that I was ending the conversation.

"Well when ya do need help, jus' lemme know. I may not be able to do much cause of my arm, but I'm a master electrician and master carpenter."

"I'll keep that in mind, Ed. Thanks," I said over my shoulder, still gathering the equipment.

A couple of minutes later when I had finished gathering the camping gear, Ed's voice echoed once again through the garage. Surprised, I cursed and dropped the lantern, expecting the glass housing to shatter on the concrete floor, but it landed on the pile of sleeping bags.

"Have a fun trip."

When I turned around, his retreating back was half a block away. "Jesus," I said to myself and bent to retrieve the camping equipment.

After making sure I'd gathered all the equipment, I packed it into the back of the SUV. It took several trips, and Keller was more than keen on following me and "helping" by holding one end of a trailing rope or walking right in front of me. In addition to watching where I was going around the armload of camping gear, I also had to avoid stepping on him. But that's kids.

Kathryn put her hand on my back as I packed in the final pieces of equipment.

"Well, it looks like you've got everything." She was surveying the back of the SUV in the mid-morning sunlight alongside myself and Jackson.

"Yep, I think so," I replied and motioned to Jackson. "This guy doesn't think we need anything. His idea of camping is driving out to the middle of nowhere with just the clothes on our backs! Not sure we'd last too long, buddy." I ruffled his hair and he giggled.

"I guess we do need a tent and a sleeping bag," he said, the adult teeth in his grin looking too big for his face.

"Looks like you've got a lantern and a few other odds and ends in there, too." Keller cooed on Kathryn's hip. His nose was running, and he'd developed a cough over the past couple of hours but played making faces at Jackson around Kat and me.

"Yeah, we've got enough stuff for a few days of 'roughing it.' It'll be fun, and I think Jackson is really going to enjoy the time."

Keller fussed and reached toward the ground. She put him on the ground and he tottered after Jackson into the yard. "I hope so, Grant. I really do." She crossed her arms and rubbed them. "I'm scared, if I'm being honest."

I put my hands over hers and said, "I know. Me too, since we're being honest. I don't know what the next few months hold, or even the next few days, but I'm going to try to have fun with him, and I know you're going to have fun with Keller. It might offer us a break of sorts, not having to worry about all of these things. What do you think?"

She nodded and took a deep breath. "I'm going to try to have fun. I really am. Mom is already planning a couple of shopping trips, and I'd be surprised if there's not a big present wrapped up by the door for Keller and another to bring home for Jack. It *will* be fun. It's just in the middle of all this crazy, I don't want to miss out on it. I've got two accounts that I need to clear up before I can feel good about where I'm at. That could take a couple of days, maybe some late nights at the office."

She leaned in for a hug, and I wrapped her in it. "Whatever you need. We'll have fun, too. I'll call you if there's reception out there. Or at least keep you posted on when we're close to getting there and also when we are heading back home."

We both looked at the boys playing in the yard. Keller was peeking around one of the small oak trees in the yard, and Jackson was pretending not to see him by peeking the opposite direction. Keller's giggles at his older brother's complete lack of awareness were spectacular.

Jackson's voice echoed across their front yard clearly saying, "Keller? Where did you go?" Jackson would then look the other way, and with the slow reflexes of a toddler, Keller jumped in surprise at being discovered. "Oh, you tricky little sneak," Jackson would say in exaggerated exasperation before they both collapsed in a pile of giggles.

"They're really the most wonderful kids in the world," Kathryn said against my chest.

I grunted agreement and hugged her tight, her fingers pressed into my back in response, and I kissed the top of her head softly.

Devil's Den was a popular local campground and hiking destination. It offered over thirty miles of hiking trails and hundreds of camping spots. When I was a kid, my dad would take me out to Devil's Den where we would hike for two days, spending the night along the river and catching fish for dinner. We had packed hot dogs as backup, just in case we didn't have any luck fishing. But that was one of my favorite memories. It felt so *primal*. So wild to have the chance to find our own food and make our own way through the wilderness. Of course, as an adult, I know now that there was a very specific trail my dad was following and we weren't actually "in the wild." But that feeling of being alone under the stars without a care in the world was exhilarating. I wanted to share that with Jackson, and here I was getting the chance.

The drive was a little less than two hours to get to the park. From there, it was another thirty minutes to find the camping spot I'd reserved the previous day. The trip was full of Jackson's questions. As a nine-year-old, he had plenty of knowledge to gain. I answered them as best and as truthfully as I could.

"Are there bears out there, daddy?"

"A few."

"Really?" His excitement at that was exactly what I expected, and I laughed.

"Yeah, really. But don't get your hopes up. Usually, the bears are attracted by the smell of food, but when they realize there are people around, they scamper off. They're kind of scaredy cats."

"Aw, man. I was hoping to see one."

"Someday, little buddy."

"Are there mountain lions?"

"A few."

And on and on. Spiders, snakes, turtles, and a whole mess of other animals that might even be extinct at this point.

We pulled into our camping spot around lunchtime. We'd have at least five full days here, so I picked a spot that was off the main campground road by a hundred yards or so. The path we drove on led to a dead-end spot that was surrounded by oak, walnut, and evergreen trees that reached toward the sky. The little clearing where we'd park and set up the tent was in the sun only during late morning and early afternoon. The trees weren't thick, so I could see some distance into the forest including another family's orange tent fifty yards away, but it left enough of a screen to make us feel like we were alone.

We spent the next couple of hours setting up the tent and gathering some firewood. Jackson was surprisingly helpful in the process. Not that I didn't expect him to be, but it was nice to have him genuinely try to help—and succeed. He was quick to grab the tent stakes and fabric loop so I could work my way around and hammer them into the soft earth. We laughed a good deal while doing this, however. I occasionally forgot how funny Jackson could be with the usual silly antics of boys his age, but his commentary on the difference between his dad and the other dads, or how many times I would miss a tent stake was spot-on.

It felt good to laugh with him.

When the tent was finally up, we began making a ring of rocks for our campfire. Jackson gathered plenty of kindling and sticks while I worked my way through the nearby underbrush for rocks that were bigger than my head. Once again, his commentary on both his incredible ability to find the perfect sticks and my uncanny knack for finding rocks that resembled his friends' faces provided enough laughs to make our bellies hurt.

Before long, we were sitting in front of a crackling fire on an old rotting log we'd dragged from the forest while evening came slinking through the trees.

"Thanks for bringing me camping, Daddy," he said between bites of hot dog, ketchup smearing the corners of his mouth.

"You're welcome, bud. This has been a fun evening, and we still have a few days of it!"

We talked about the activities we wanted to do before having to leave and settled on hiking, napping, fishing, and digging for dinosaur bones.

"I'm no expert," I told him, "but that last one might be tough."

The next morning was cool and clear. It was the kind of morning where the air was full of that crisp and pleasant bite that wakens the senses instead of dulling them. We grabbed a few packs of Pop Tarts and put them in our packs, along with a bottle of water, a Lunchable for Jackson, and a peanut butter sandwich for me before starting out on one of the area trails. I doubted we'd be gone for any longer than three or four hours but wanted to prepare just in case.

The trail was a fairly easy walk. There were plenty of rocks to climb and branches to swing from along the way, and Jackson reveled in the freedom it provided. His pants and hands were stained brown with dirt, and his face had several smears of it, too. He was more concerned with the next thing he could jump on than he was with his own safety, which was my job, anyway.

We saw several squirrels, and once, Jackson said he saw a lizard scurry into a cleft between rocks. This last encounter

provided him with nearly an hour of conversation that only ended when the trail finally broke through the trees, and we were given a clear view of the hills and valleys that made up the Ozark Mountains.

This early in the year, the leaves were just starting to grow, showing a green-and-gray patchwork across the hills and valleys laid out before us. On a distant hill, we spied a few patches of evergreens that stuck out as great bushy splashes of varying greens.

"Woah!" he said, running out onto a rocky outcropping and away from the shade of the budding maple and oak trees.

"Easy, bud," I said with caution. "There's a hundred-foot drop off this rock. I'd rather you stay away from the edge."

But with most boys of his age, that meant he needed to get closer. I was perfectly fine with it, holding his hand as he stretched his neck out to get a view of the forest floor below. As I gazed down, the trees seemed to stretch toward me, and I could feel a slight sense of vertigo. I stepped back and Jackson, still holding onto my hand, did the same.

"Pretty neat, huh?"

His grin nearly split his face in half. "It's amazing! We're like a million feet up!"

Now that he'd experienced this small measure of danger, he was much more comfortable walking and exploring farther from the dizzying drop. He picked up rocks and threw them over the edge, watching their path arc over the naked limbs that reached like skeletal fingers before disappearing out of sight into the canopy below the edge of the cliff.

I sat on a flat rock in the shade and watched him. He was acting much more like himself—a carefree boy who could let loose and enjoy the wonder of the world around him. I idly wondered when it would stop. I'd like to think that I was able to hold onto mine for a while, even into adulthood. But for most of us, it was a subtle shift from seeing the wonder of the world to seeing the burden of living in it.

I reached into the pack and brought out the sandwich I'd brought for myself and the lunch pack he'd chosen, setting them carefully on top of the bag.

"Jackson, you hungry?"

He looked back over his shoulder, his arm cocked and ready to throw the rock in his hand. He nodded and aimed over the trees, then let it fly. He watched it, and when a satisfying clatter sounded in the distance, he turned and jogged to me, sitting in the shade with a contented sigh and wide smile.

While he tore into his sandwich, I asked if he was having fun.

His cheeks bulged like a chipmunk's as he chewed and nodded his head. Grape jelly dripped down his chin and onto the front of his shirt and all I could do was laugh.

We ate quietly, then, content to sit on a massive rock overlooking hundreds of unspoiled acres of wilderness. I could feel a warmth in my chest that had little to do with the April sun. The worries of Jackson's nosebleeds and the fear he felt the last time—*I'm tired of this, Daddy*—were evaporating. Maybe, just maybe, everything would be fine. Of course, it was only the first day of our five-day adventure. I hoped it would continue to go well.

When we'd eaten everything we packed and nearly emptied our water bottles, I made sure our space was clear of trash.

"You see, Jack, we have to make sure and clean up after ourselves. Otherwise, an animal could come along and find a wrapper or baggie and since it smells like food, gobble it up. The problem is, it's trash, and when they eat it, it can make them really sick."

He nodded and looked around for trash, picking up a translucent plastic bottle cap half-buried in the red dirt. He looked at me with sovereign pride and dropped it into the backpack, a self-satisfied smile spreading slowly across his face.

"Good job, that's right. Now imagine if every person left all of their trash. That would pile up really quick, wouldn't it?"

"Geez, Daddy. That would fill up this whole valley!"

"It definitely would. Everyone has to do their part."

He nodded and stood up, stretching and grinning in the afternoon light.

I walked with him toward the edge of the rock platform. The rusty dirt crunched beneath our boots as we cautiously approached the edge. I had an idea and wanted to try something.

The wind that raced across the valley ruffled his hair and brought vitality to our little trip. I took a long, deep breath and cupped my hands around my mouth. I bellowed into the valley of green-and-gray trees. I felt Jackson stiffen next to me in surprise, then my bellow turned into a laugh near the end.

"What—" he began, but I held up my hand to silence him and cocked an ear toward the valley.

Sure enough, only a second or two later, we heard the echo of my bellow return.

Jackson's expression was priceless; his eyes widened, and a mischievous gleam began to grow there. I smiled down at him and nodded my head toward the valley. He looked at me a little dubiously at first, then squared himself up, took a deep breath, and yelled.

"Helllloooooooooooooooo!"

We waited while he caught his breath.

"*Helllloooooooooooooooo,*" echoed back to us, and if I thought his previous grin was big, this one was enormous. He jumped up and down and pumped the air with his fists.

We repeated this for several more minutes. His excitement never lessened. If anything, it only grew each time an echo returned to us. He roared, screamed, squealed, and shouted all kinds of things. My personal favorite was when he yelled the word "fart" in classic nine-year-old fashion. His giggles were so loud that after hearing the echoing "fart" return, a moment later his giggles could be heard as a joy-filled echo across the valley.

The hike back was filled with a kind of serene acceptance, as if we'd just gone through a ritual. A ritual where a boy enters and a young man leaves. The only curiosity was who the ritual was for. I knew Jackson was growing up, knew he was starting to leave childhood behind—though farts would be funny at any age—and embark on a journey into adulthood. I couldn't help thinking, however, that I was doing something similar. Maybe I was a child on our morning hike, worrying and fretting about all kinds of things. Now, realizing both how small we were and how full of life we could be got me thinking that maybe everything would work out. Maybe Jackson really would be okay. Maybe Keller wouldn't always be sick.

And maybe they were not connected. *God, please don't let them be connected.*

We got back to the campsite well before dark. Jackson wanted to gather firewood in the failing light of the forest, so I told him to be careful and then began preparing a dinner of hot dogs with bags of chips.

A scream from the gloom behind the tent snapped my head up, and I was running before I'd even registered that I'd stood. I jumped over a fallen branch and into the woods, barely acknowledging the few seconds it took for my eyes to adjust to the dimness. I could see a lighter blur through the trees, Jackson's jacket, I was sure of it, and I ran straight for it.

"Jackson!" I screamed, hoping to both reassure him and scare away anything that might be nearby or—God forbid—attacking him.

This thought, this terrible realization, made me lose my focus, and I began to stumble over the edge of an exposed rock. Moss, twigs, and pine needles scattered across the ground and into the air as I windmilled my arms to steady myself.

Jackson was bent double and crying. I skidded to a halt on my knees in front of him and looked into his face, trying to gently move his arms out of the way. I could see tears in his eyes and his shoulders moving with small, reluctant sounds from his mouth, muffled by his jacket sleeves.

When he finally did move his arms, his face had a large, red stripe arcing across the bridge of his nose and onto his left cheek. I realized he wasn't crying. He was laughing. His white teeth shone clear in the fading light and those small sounds I mistook for cries were his chuckles.

"Jack?"

When he spoke, he could barely get the words out between giggles. "A branch slapped me across the face and hurt so bad I screamed." Laughter interrupted him until he could calm down. I could feel the concern leaving my face, replaced with my version of a confused smile. "But the more I thought about it, the more I started laughing. I must have looked like a real idiot and—" He stopped talking and doubled over with laughter, the tears from the sting of the branch replaced with tears of real laughter.

I joined in and hugged him, letting myself finally feel relief.

I held him at arm's length and checked his nose for any sign of a nosebleed. Nothing from what I could tell, but it was hard now that the sun had sunk below the horizon and the forest was nearing full darkness.

I hugged him to my chest again and took a deep breath. "Come on, bud. Let's go eat dinner."

He wiped his arm across his eyes and blinked away the tears, nodding. We made our way out of the trees, stepping gingerly over limbs and rocks so as to avoid a fall in the dark.

The next few days were filled with laughter, hugs, skinned knees, and muddy shoes. We did manage to nap the following day and, afterward, found a particularly excellent tree. Jackson climbed more than twenty feet up its branches before deciding that was far enough. But not until he bragged about being able to see farther than anyone else. It also helped that I refused to climb that high—not only because I'm terrified of heights but also because I doubted the tree's ability to support my weight. I let Jackson have the win.

He dug a trench near the creek and diverted part of it to create his own little world. Over the course of the week, we spent most of our time building rock towers, streets, and lakes for his little village. Each night, he had to nearly bathe in the river to wash the mud and grime from his arms and legs.

When I woke up on the final morning of our camping trip, I resisted the urge to move. I closed my eyes and listened to the wind rattling the tree limbs around me. I listened to the early chirps and trills of the robins and finches. I heard the nearby clattering of other camping families as they packed up, unloaded, or some mix of the two. And I listened to the steady breathing of my son, who lay still beside me. I listened and realized my restful disposition was a result of what people call "relaxing." The worry that consumed my weeks had lessened, mostly due to the absence of the triggers.

And, I noted with a pang of shame, it was over a week of restful nights.

Fast on the heels of that thought, a picture of Keller's smiling, snot-nosed face swam before my closed eyes, and I shook it away. Surely, I wasn't thinking that this confirmed anything. Was I?

I laid in the brisk morning glow that filtered through the tent fabric and tried to decide. Did I really believe that Keller and Jackson were connected? There certainly were some suspicious circumstances that *could* lead one to believe there was a connection.

I listened again to Jackson's breathing. He didn't have a nosebleed all week. The most recent nosebleed happened several days before we left to go camping, that way there would be a period of time between the possibility of another. There hadn't been two nosebleeds within a couple of days together, but one per week wasn't uncommon anymore. Surely, he would have had one by now if they weren't connected to home, right?

I was genuinely asking myself the difficult questions, but the week had been so refreshing that I didn't want to ruin it.

I promised myself that if another nosebleed happened soon after our return home, I'd try to have a serious discussion with Kathryn about it.

I let that simmer for a few minutes. When I felt Jackson stir beside me, I made myself agree to it. A strange kind of internal dialogue, having to make yourself agree to something, but there it was.

Jackson sat up a moment later.

"Daddy?"

I opened my eyes and looked at him. "Yeah?"

He rubbed his eyes in a way that I saw the toddler version of him. "We have to go home today, right?"

I smacked my lips and sucked the air in between my teeth. "Yeah, buddy. We do. We actually should start packing up our stuff. We need to let the dew dry off the tent before rolling it up, or it'll get moldy, but that won't take too long once the sun is up."

He nodded and looked away. "Can we go to Yellow Rock one more time before we go?"

I smiled at him. "Absolutely."

We packed up everything except the tent and a water bottle, satisfying ourselves on powdered donuts before setting out one last time on the Yellow Rock Trail. The tent would be dry by the time we got back in a couple of hours. And *technically*, we didn't have to be home at any particular time.

Once at Yellow Rock where we'd had a shouting contest with the valley, Jackson marched right up to the edge of the rock. Part of me was prepared to grab his jacket to prevent him from walking right off the edge. I felt my muscles tense in preparation, but I relaxed when he stopped a few yards from the drop-off. He took a deep breath and bellowed, "I'm not afraid of you anymore!"

I wasn't quite sure what to think about that, but there was a part of me very near the surface that glowed with pride. I didn't know what he was scared of, and that worried me. Shouldn't I know? As his father, shouldn't I have an idea of what was going on in his head because I had a daily dialogue with him? Was I being as good of a dad as I could be?

All of these questions rang in my head as the echo returned to us, skipping along the white fog that lay in the lowest parts of the valley. Jackson looked back up at me and smiled.

"I'm not afraid anymore, Daddy."

I put a hand on his shoulder and said, "I'm really glad, buddy."

Should I ask?

Should I let him tell me?

Should I just leave it alone?

He answered the question for me by speaking up. "I'm not afraid of going to sleep, Daddy. I have been. And maybe I shouldn't be, but—"

"Hey," I said, sinking to one knee and turning him to face me. "You're allowed to feel whatever it is you feel. Whether that's being afraid, being sad, angry—whatever it is. And you don't always have to tell me. I'll always be by your side and do my best to help, but you tell me only if you want to. Okay?"

My son nodded. "It's just that I've been afraid of the nosebleeds. And I've been having bad dreams. Before this weekend, I mean."

I hugged him close to me.

"In my dreams," he continued, speaking to the side, "it's like I'm running but not going anywhere. There's something chasing me, and I don't know what, but I know that if it catches me, it will suck all the blood out of me."

Jesus, I thought.

"Daddy?"

I looked down at him and cupped his cheek. "Yeah?"

"I'm sorry, but—" He looked away, his chin quivering.

"It's okay, buddy."

Nodding, he said, "But sometimes I feel like it's Keller chasing me."

With that, he broke into uncontrolled sobs. His shoulders shook and I felt his body melt into mine.

What was I supposed to do with this? How was I supposed to help him manage his fears when they were untouchable? I couldn't fight this. I couldn't do anything about this, but my heart ached, and I felt my throat begin to constrict.

I cleared it and picked him up, setting him on my hip just like I used to when he was three.

"That's a lot to carry, Jack. I'll always listen, and I'll do whatever I can to help you."

We walked back, and I carried him most of the way. I could feel him calm the closer to camp we got, and when he asked to walk, he seemed his normal, chipper self.

But I knew. Underneath it all was a little boy facing some unseen terror, and there was nothing I could do.

CHAPTER 14

I called Kathryn when my phone changed from showing "No Service" to three little bars of service. I first had to ignore the multiple messages that came through; it chimed an alert with each one. Most were unimportant, but a few were from Marco and another California number, probably Gianna. We were a couple miles from Devil's Den, but nestled in the mountains as it was, there were only a few spots where we had service. I tried to send a text here and there, but I doubted any of them went through until we were out of the valleys.

She answered on the third ring. "Hey babe!"

"Hey hon, how you doing?"

The phone crackled as it sounded like she rearranged it on her shoulder. "All good here. We're planning on heading home tomorrow morning, but I'm not sure yet. Are you boys done camping?"

I looked over at Jackson, who was staring out the window watching the trees as they blurred by. I was struck at that moment how the sun dappled his face very much like the morning I went to the doctor for test results.

"Grant?"

"Yep," I continued, blinking away the moisture that appeared in my eyes. "We're headed home. Figured it was better to head home now and prepare for school tomorrow, rather than miss a regular day right after Spring Break, and this late in the school year." He looked over at me then, and he mimed gagging with his tongue out.

"Well, how was..." she hesitated. "Were there any nosebleeds?"

I took a breath and let it out, hoping my tone of nonchalance carried through the airwaves. "Nope. No nosebleeds. He did get in a fight with a branch, but he showed it who's boss." I punched his shoulder playfully.

"Good. Good." I could tell she was probably biting her lip or her fingernail.

"What about on your end? How's Keller doing?"

I could hear her take a deep breath before answering, too. "Well," she began slowly, "he's alright."

"Good alright or bad alright?" I prompted.

"He's gotten worse over the past few days."

I glanced over at Jackson, who was staring back out the window and ignoring my conversation. To him, this was all "adult talk" and didn't concern him in the slightest. *If only that were true, buddy.*

"That's not completely *abnormal*, though. Right? There have been times when he's gotten sicker over the course of several days. Weeks, even."

"Yeah, that's true." She didn't sound convinced. "But Grant," I could hear her tuck the phone closer to her mouth and when she spoke, it sounded like she was cupping her mouth over the phone, "he keeps *asking* for Jackson."

"What do you mean?"

"I mean," she said with a little more emphasis that was necessary, "that Keller keeps waking up in the morning asking for Jackson. He doesn't sleep well, anyway, regardless of what medicine we give him. His nose is a runny mess, and the cough he started before you left seems to have moved deep into his chest. His eyes are watery, his voice is scratchy, and through all of that, he says 'where's Jackson' in his little, raspy voice. 'Need Jackson' he keeps saying. I don't think it means what we think it means. I guess... I hope it doesn't. But it gives me goosebumps."

The line was silent for a full thirty seconds while I processed this.

"Grant? Did I lose you?"

"No, Kat. I'm here. Just ... thinking."

"Yeah," she responded glumly.

"Yeah," I repeated, "I don't know what it means. Honestly, how often are they separated though? There's been, what, a whole three days outside of this week where they weren't in the same space for more than a school day? It makes sense that Keller doesn't understand. To him, Jackson's presence is as permanent as yours, especially with summer break starting just a few weeks from now."

"Yeah, I guess that's true." She sounded *slightly* more convinced this time.

"Besides, we'll see you tomorrow, right? And nothing bad has happened. Our little theory might have just been shot to dust."

"Honestly, Grant, I hope so." She sounded exhausted. I figured she was. No, I *knew* she was. Between Keller's lack of sleep and her worry about the theory I'd come up with, she'd been "on alert" for several days.

"Listen, get some rest today. If you want to head home tomorrow morning, great. If you feel like you need to come home tonight, do that. Whatever you need is great with me."

She sighed on the other end. "Okay, babe. I'll let you know what I decide."

"Sounds good. I love you, Kat."

"I love you, too, Grant."

Jackson looked over at me when I put the phone down on the seat between us.

"How's Keller?"

I hesitated, trying to find the right words. "He's doing okay. Not feeling great. You know how he can get sometimes."

Jackson nodded and looked back out the window. I looked at him and felt my heart begin to ache. Patches of alternating sun and shade flashed across his thoughtful features as the SUV roared down the road.

I knew that Jackson carried some kind of burden that involved Keller's well-being. I knew he tried to be the kind of big brother that was able to carry that burden. But I also hated it because it wasn't his burden to carry; it was mine. It was a burden that should have been reserved for parents. A young child should never have to shoulder the wellness of another. To this day, I ask myself if I should have done something differently, if I should have acted or told him differently. I don't think I could have, but nevertheless, the regret remains.

We drove home in silence. Jackson closed his eyes at the halfway mark, and I turned the radio on for some background noise. I tried to empty my mind, but my thoughts continued to return to the relationship between Jackson and Keller. I didn't see any way around having the conversation when Kathryn and Keller returned home, and I was trying to prepare my opening statement when we pulled into the driveway.

"Hey buddy, we're home." I gently patted Jackson's shoulder and then rubbed his chest. "Jackson, wake up."

He blinked blearily and looked around, then stretched and yawned.

"Let's unpack real quick, and we can put on a movie or something until mom gets home. Sound good?"

Jackson nodded mid-stretch. The door squealed in protest as I opened it and stepped out into the afternoon sunlight.

By the time we put everything away and unpacked our bags, it was nearly five. The washer's rhythmic thumping was the soundtrack to which we made dinner. We laughed and joked with one another, pretending to have a food fight. It only turned into a real food fight for a moment when Jackson "pretended" to throw a handful of flour at me and "accidentally" released it all. It hit me square in the chest, and the subsequent cloud of cloying powder got us both coughing and laughing. It was good to see him unafraid. Too often over the past few weeks, I saw in my mind the boy bent over the sink, bloody pink water dripping from his chin as he said, "I'm tired of this, Daddy."

We cleaned up the flour mess, ate some chicken nuggets and mac and cheese, then settled down in front of the TV for a movie. I knew he'd pick a superhero movie before we even sat down, which was fine with me. I loved the story, and he liked explosions. It was a win for us both. Though, I did see him pay special attention to the scenes with the female lead.

Off and on throughout the movie, I messaged Marco in our virtual office, who was two hours behind me and still technically on the clock.

[6:41p: GTaldo – Saw a few of your messages pop up. I was out of town without reception with Jackson. What's up?]

[6:42p: MRiviera – nm, dude. Gianna was curious where you were at with the FAD. She wants it up and running this week since some of the FAD-B test results are swinging.]

[6:42p: GTaldo – Does she want me to run some tests at the same Intersect where it blew?]

[6:43p: MRiviera – idk, man. I think she probably just wants SOMETHING from you. I know you've been busy with your kid being sick and shit, so I've kept her off your back. I'd advise you to at least get some kind of reading from Grendal or w/e you call her.]

[6:44p: GTaldo – Gretchen, Marco. Her name is Gretchen. And I appreciate you covering for me. I didn't think it was a big deal, though. She find something in the data?]

[6:44p: MRiviera – not sure, maybe? I heard her talking to the big man about getting a team out here if you can recreate the results. Idk if that means another FAD blowing up or the reading itself. My guess would be that she'll tell you that when you talk to her.]

[6:45p: GTaldo – Alright. Thanks for the heads-up. If you see her before I talk to her tomorrow, just let her know I've got the FAD set up to run the same test as before. But between you and me, the signal on the FAD-B shows that it's barely even an Intersect anymore. Either the original signal frequency was off—which I know it wasn't—or whatever happened did something to the Ley Line.]

[6:47p: MTaldo – Will do. Talk to you tomorrow.]

[6:48p: MRiviera – Peace, bro.]

When the credits began to scroll up the screen, I told him to go get ready for bed and brush his teeth. I cleaned up the dinner dishes and made my way upstairs to tuck him in.

He was sitting up in his bed, a reading lamp perched on the headboard behind him with a book held in front of his nose.

"Whatcha reading?" I could read the title, of course, but why not let him tell me about it?

"One of your old books, *The Hardy Boys and the House on the Cliff*."

"Oh, that's a good one. I read that when I was about your age. What part are you at?"

His eyes moved back and forth as he read. I waited for him to answer, and just when I was about to stand up and leave, he responded. "The boat just blew up in Barmet Bay."

"Ah, getting to the good part. I'll leave you to it. Lights out after this chapter, okay?"

He nodded in response, and I patted his leg before standing up. I couldn't tell if the bed creaked or if it was my muscles. I looked out the doors toward the neighborhood and then back at Jackson. My eyes hesitated on the small brown circle of dried blood a few feet from the bed. I'd forgotten to clean it up, and it was probably stained, now. I made a mental note to clean it while he was at school tomorrow, and then I walked out of the room, forgetting completely.

My phone rang while I was flipping through the channels in search of something to fall asleep to. The display said "Kathryn," and I picked it up, but not before thinking about a worst-case-scenario.

"Hey babe, everything okay?"

"Hey," she said a little breathlessly, and I held mine. "Yeah, everything is okay. I just wanted to tell you that I've decided to head back tonight, that's all."

I let my breath out away from the receiver so that she wouldn't get an earful of windy static. "You hate driving at night. Are you sure you want to come home tonight?"

"I know I do, but I made an appointment with the doctor tomorrow morning, and I sure as heck ain't waking up early to make it back to town on time. No, this is easier, I promise."

"Alright, if you think so. He's gotten worse?" I could hear Keller cough in the background, and it sounded like a wet bark.

"Yeah. His sinuses are almost completely plugged, and if you can't hear it, his cough is really deep in his chest. His nose bounces between either crusty and plugged or running like a faucet and somehow still plugged. I hate to see him like this. He's miserable; I'm miserable, Mom tried to give me a break and stay up with him, but then she started feeling sick from not getting enough sleep. Honestly, it's just better for us to be home; I felt like I was intruding last night and today."

"Yeah, of course. Come on home. I'll wait up for you."

"Thank you. Yes, please wait up for me just in case I need to get ahold of you."

"No problem, babe. I'll put on a movie and just keep washing and folding laundry."

I felt her smile across the distance. "That's only one reason I love you. I'm not looking forward to laundry."

"Then consider it done."

"Okay. I'll see you in a couple hours."

"See you then, hon."

Well my night wasn't going to be as relaxing as I'd planned, but the laundry did need to be done, and I didn't want Kat to have to wash our smoky camping clothes.

Remembering that a load was done in the washer, I moved the wet clothes to the dryer, turned it on, and put a new load in the washer. Then I sat down on the couch and turned on my computer until the timers went off for both. I traded out the dry for wet, put a new load in, and started folding.

Between transferring dry clothes to the couch, transferring wet clothes to the dryer, putting a new load in the washer, and then folding and putting away the dry load on the couch, I looked at the data from Gretchen. Nearly six months since the spike in energy blew her up and threw Keller in the air. The data was still intact; that wasn't a surprise. It was connected wirelessly to my phone, which I had in my pocket, and both cached locally and uploaded to Eastwind's servers immediately. I could follow the timeline down to the second.

A green line began at the base of a graph indicating when I'd turned Gretchen on and begun the frequency sequence. The line crept up each second that passed. It dipped once, but I could see the accompanying frequencies that it scanned, looking for the right frequency at which the Ley Line reverberated; there would be drops in efficiency as the sequence recognized a longer distance between the one it emitted and the one it was trying to match. The line had an upward trend, though, as Gretchen's frequency emitter calculated the frequency adjustments based on the results of the previous iteration.

There was one point where the graph suddenly spiked significantly and then turned into a straight horizontal line. Gretchen had matched the frequency of the Ley Line perfectly.

I stared at the line, looking for any kind of hitch. I zoomed in, down to the millisecond, but there was nothing. A straight green line stretched across my screen. I pulled up a secondary graph that was the Polarization Sequence. Gretchen had initiated the sequence that would detect what charge the Ley Line carried. The issue that I previously struggled with—how Eastwind knew the Polarization Sequence would work—I'd resolved.

The Sequence began, and instead of a steady green line, there was a cone that stretched from the bottom to the top of the graph. It shrank into a very fine point when the exact polarization frequency was determined.

Gretchen had done it. The FAD had found not only the frequency of the Ley Line—which I'd seen before—but it had also matched the energy charge, polarized itself to begin siphoning the energy from the Ley Line. It was like the Ley Line was a garden hose, and we'd tapped into it with a hammer and nail.

A third graph appeared when I selected it. The energy cells of Gretchen's Charge Retention went from a literal zero to some number off the charts, there wasn't even a number on the y-axis that reached that high. The line was almost an instantaneous increase to infinity, which looked like a single vertical line.

There wasn't some kind of failsafe or restrictions on the amount of energy that could be absorbed at a time. It made sense to me that if I were tapping the actual planet for its energy, I'd make some kind of limit on the amount of energy that could be accepted at a time. It seemed like Eastwind hadn't, maybe because they hadn't expected success. Gretchen's mechanisms were overwhelmed with the sheer amount of energy that was being stored and replaced in an infinite loop that Gretchen became unstable. The constant discharge and gathering of energy was too much. The housing cracked, the gyroscopic wheels were turning on an uneven axis and scraping one another, sending metal filings into the gears and spindle array. They weren't able to twist, turn, and rotate with all the metal gumming up the works and eventually stopped, making the gyros bend and snap with the bulb housings following. I didn't even want to think about the tiny cogs and parts that were housed beneath the glassteel globe. The kicker was that the Energy Retention Cells had been overcharged. They'd had such a massive amount of energy sent to them that they'd literally exploded.

It was all there. The energy transfer was instantaneous, but without anywhere for it to go, or a shut off valve of sorts, it just kept absorbing it and sloughing it in an endless loop. Gretchen couldn't keep up, and she blew. The graphs told the story of a machine that successfully tapped an infinite energy source. It could change the world. *If, just if, I can recreate it without blowing up again.* That was the key. Duplicate with different results.

I guessed all I could do was try. Maybe I could get with Marco and let him monitor the sequence while I ran it. Surely there was something he could do within the machine to stop the endless loops.

I decided to write Marco before I forgot. I included the images of the graphs and described what I assumed happened because of it. I'd see what he had to say in the morning as I wasn't too worried about it now.

Kathryn arrived a few laundry loads later. I helped tuck Keller into bed, cleaning his nose and frowning at how pale he was. He coughed feebly, then gagged in a wet retching sound. I didn't want to worry, but he wasn't doing well. I decided to take him to the doctor tomorrow with Kathryn, then added another blanket to the few he already lay beneath.

I jogged out to the car and brought her bags inside while she hopped in the shower to wash off the day. Well, that's what we called it. Sometimes it was just a regular shower, sometimes it was crying in the shower, sometimes it was sex in the shower. It just depended on what we both needed at the time. This time, it seemed like she needed to take a shower knowing everyone was safe and where they needed to be.

When she walked into the living room in her pajamas and her hair wrapped in a towel that stood another foot off her head, she was visibly better. She took a deep breath and sighed as she sat on the couch and leaned her head on my shoulder. She really was my favorite.

It was nice, sitting there and letting the energy from the day kind of settle around us. My breathing began to even out, and I could tell that Kathryn had closed her eyes. It wasn't a terribly long drive from her mom's, but it was still energy spent, energy she didn't have. I didn't want to bring up any topic of conversation that would burst our calm little bubble.

Unfortunately for us both, bursting the bubble wasn't up to me, and it happened regardless of what we wanted.

The scream that tore down the stairs went beyond terror. It went beyond fear and fright. It was despair on a level that young children should never experience.

Kathryn jerked awake, panic and determination clear on her face.

I took the stairs two at a time with Kathryn not far behind me. Jackson continued screaming uncontrollably.

When I grabbed the doorframe and rocketed into the room, blood covered his face and mouth, dripping and oozing endlessly into his lap. His eyes were wide, and even though he was looking at me, I didn't think he could see me. Even in the dark, I could see the contrast of the crimson streaming down his chin against his pale white cheeks.

"Fuck!" I screamed. I took it in as I closed the distance to his bed in only a couple of rapid steps.

"Kathryn, get a towel, please."

I tilted his head back and pinched the bridge of his nose. His eyes stared, unseeing, at the ceiling and his breath came in ragged gasps. When Kathryn handed me the towel, I tried to ignore the blood I accidentally spread around his face trying to clean him up, all while keeping his head back and nose pinched.

In a matter of seconds, the towel had turned red, and in a terrifying development, blood began leaking out of the corners of his mouth.

"Jackson?" I did my best to keep the fear from my voice, but even I could hear it plain as day.

I could feel Kathryn lean over my shoulder, and from the corner of my eye, I saw her cover her mouth. "Oh my God, Grant. We have to get him to a hospital."

I didn't want to agree with her, but I was terrified. "Just-just a second. Get some toilet paper, and I'll plug his nose with it. And some ice, please."

While she did that, I tried to calm Jackson. He seemed to be more present but no less afraid. I took the towel away from his nose, relieved to see the flow of blood had slowed. "It's okay, buddy. Mommy went to get some ice. You're going to be just fine, I promise. Okay?"

I could feel him nod his head a little, and even that small movement was enough to start fresh rivulets of blood running from his nose.

Goddammit.

"Kathryn!" I yelled, understanding but not caring that it was out of fear and not anger.

"I'm coming!" Her tone matched my own as she rushed up the stairs.

She'd put the ice in a new towel, and I traded those out and told Jack to hold it on his nose while I made plugs out of toilet paper and positioned them to stop the nosebleed.

Almost immediately the white plugs turned crimson from nose to tip.

"Hold these here," I said in a near-panic. "I'll go get Keller, and we'll go to the hospital."

We switched places, and I could see that same panic in my voice reflected on her face.

What was I doing to my family if I couldn't keep even my voice from betraying me? Wasn't I supposed to be the strong one? Wasn't I supposed to be the foundation for everyone to build upon? How in god's name was I helping right now except in feeding their fear and terror?

I didn't know the answer to any of those questions that ran through my mind in the few steps to Keller's room.

When I stepped into his room, I was expecting to see him curled up beneath the blankets. What I saw instead was a bright-eyed toddler standing in his crib with his blankie clutched in one hand. His breathing was even, not even a hint of drainage. His pink cheeks were clearly visible in the light mobile's glow.

"Dada," he whispered in what normally would be innocent excitement. But now, it set my teeth on edge.

There was no denying that Keller was feeling much better while Jackson's life leaked out of him in the next room.

I couldn't think about it right now. I scooped Keller into my arms and walked down the hallway to Jackson's room. Kathryn held her hands out for Keller, and when I handed him to her and she saw the change in him, our eyes met. The fear that had been for Jackson changed somehow in her face. I nodded and picked up Jackson, making sure that he was keeping the cold compress on his nose. He asked to spit when we walked through the kitchen, and a bright red glob of blood was washed down the sink a second later.

CHAPTER 15

The drive to the hospital was much faster this time. Turns out that when the speedometer is pushing ninety, the miles seem to click by at an alarming rate. It wasn't really even necessary, at least not to stop the bleeding. By the time we'd made the drive all the way to the hospital and I parked, his nose had long since stopped. Kathryn still wanted to get him checked out, and I was inclined to agree. She sat in the backseat of the SUV between Keller and Jackson, the latter laying his head on her shoulder and a look of worry creasing her features. Keller kept looking around the edge of his car seat at Jackson and saying his name. When Jackson didn't respond, he looked at Kathryn's face. To her credit, she smiled weakly at him and held his little hand the rest of the way when it was offered.

Checking in was a slow process since there was no immediate danger. By a stroke of luck, Dr. Krist was on call that night. Thankfully, there weren't many others in the waiting room, so we only had to wait an hour or so. Jackson fell asleep in my lap, and Keller did the same in Kathryn's. Even sitting there, the remnants of panic and fear roiling around in my midsection, I stared at both of my kids. I was reminded of the innocence in the world, of what peace is. It wasn't always the quiet of the empty house, or at least not quiet on its own; it was the calm in the middle of chaos. Peace by itself is nothing more than silence or stillness, but it transforms into peace when chaos and upheaval whirl around it. So many times we chase peace but mistake it for calm and quiet, forgetting that the unknown wild winds are what give us the circumstances in which to recognize it.

If I'm being honest, I felt a little ashamed with myself. Any parent would have probably acted in a similar fashion, but I could have done better. I wondered if I was searching and requiring the quiet in order to feel at peace when I should be searching for peace amidst the noise.

My thoughts were interrupted when a nurse called our names. We stood carefully and walked to a door she held open for us. I smiled a tired smile at her, and she returned it.

"Right this way."

We followed and sat in a room for a while. I sat on the gurney with Jackson while Kathryn sat in an adjacent chair with Keller. She sighed and hugged him to her chest. I saw a tear make its way slowly down her cheek, and I reached for her hand. She looked at me a moment later and grasped my hand.

"What are we going to do?" she asked, lip quivering.

I could feel my throat tighten. I wanted to ask what she meant. I wanted to let her know that everything was going to be fine. I wanted to tell her there was nothing to worry about.

But then I looked down at Jackson. I saw the dried blood around his nose, mouth, and chin. I saw the dark circles beneath his closed lids and the weak breaths that he drew in. I patted his hip as I held him and looked back at Kathryn.

"I don't know." I doubted the doctor would give us any information we didn't already have, but I hoped. I hoped desperately.

I was dozing off when the door creaked open and Dr. Krist walked in, tablet in hand.

"Sorry for the wait, Mr. and Mrs. Taldo." He looked at us, and I saw his eyes widen. "Woah, there. What's going on with this little guy?"

He stood in front of Jackson and me, lifting the useless, bloody towel and peeking around at different angles, like a bird deciding how to catch a fish beneath the water's surface.

"I don't know if you remember me, Doc. I came to your office a few months ago to discuss my son's nosebleeds. You had some recommendations, and we've tried following those. But tonight..." I trailed off.

"Yeah, it looks like he had a pretty bad one, here. How long did it bleed for?"

I looked at Kathryn. I hadn't paid any attention to the clock, so I shrugged at her.

"About seven minutes," she said confidently. "It stopped but we still decided to come all this way."

Krist puffed his cheeks out, still looking at Jackson's nose and prodding it gently before settling his stethoscope around his ears. He checked Jackson's breathing by placing the circular metal his chest and back, then got out the tool used to check ears and noses. He knelt down a little and poked it gently into Jackson's nostrils. Jackson stirred a little but remained asleep.

After checking both nostrils, he stood up and tossed the cap of his tool in the trashcan.

"Has he been hit in the nose recently? Like with a baseball or maybe his little brother tossing something at his face?"

"Not recently, no. I don't think so. Kat?" I deferred to her again, knowing she spent more time with them than I during the day.

"No, I don't think so. And if so, Jack never mentioned it. Why?"

"Well, Mr. and Mrs. Taldo, I won't bore you with any of the technicalities of it. But what it looks like is that Jackson's capillaries are very raw, like they've been injured recently."

We both sat and looked at him, waiting for him to continue.

"Nosebleeds can happen by themselves: it happens all the time. Now forgive me, Mr. Taldo, but I don't remember our conversation exactly from several months ago. I know we talked a bit about frequency, and I assume that I recommended you keep a journal of some kind regarding their frequency and intensity. Then we could establish a bit of a timeline and see what we needed to do."

"Yes, that's right," Kathryn said, as she dug around in her purse. "It's right here." She offered Dr. Krist the little black book that she kept beside her bed.

He took it and flipped through the first few pages. "And you've written down every nosebleed?"

Kathryn nodded. "As you'll see, I noted the date, time, and description. I tried to be as accurate as possible."

"Yes, you did a very good job. This is very detailed." He flipped through a few more pages. "And the most recent one appears to have happened more than a week ago? And before that was just a few days?"

We nodded.

"They seem to always happen at home. Seems like they happen overnight." He met our eyes. "Exclusively."

"That's right," was all I could think to say.

"Don't you find that a little suspicious?"

I looked at Kathryn, confused. "Suspicious?"

"Yes, that they only happen overnight?"

I could feel my stomach tighten in prickled irritation. "Why should we be suspicious? This is the first time we've been parents of a child with spontaneous nosebleeds. We'll have a little more experience the next kid whose nose spontaneously explodes."

I saw Kathryn's lips purse in disapproval out of the corner of my eye, but the doctor's condescending smile made my cheeks flush in anger.

"Mr. Taldo, I don't mean to challenge you in any way. I only mean to offer my *expertise* as a physician." *Oh, so it was going to be like that,* I thought while he continued. "I see kids with nosebleeds hundreds of times a year. Oddities tend to stand out, and I've seen this only once before, several years ago."

The heat that had suffused my cheeks moments before drained and a chill curled its way down my spine.

Kathryn looked from my face to the doctor's and then asked, "That's great. Can you tell us how you helped them?"

The doctor held my gaze for only a moment longer before answering. "I remember you now, Mr. Taldo. Our conversation revolved around the only other case of nosebleeds that mirrored yours."

Again, Kathryn looked from my face to Dr. Krist's before saying in an exasperated tone, "Okay. Great! How did you help them?"

"He didn't." I spoke to Kathryn but held the doctor's eyes, a knowing smile tugging the corners of his self-important mouth.

"He didn't what?" Kathryn was growing frustrated, and I couldn't blame her.

"I mean he didn't help them."

"What..." she trailed off, confusion and irritation intermingling.

"He didn't help them because he believed the father was abusing the daughter and the mother was letting him. Instead of looking for ways to help, Dr. Krist here decided to call CPS on the family." I looked at Kathryn. "The daughter died shortly after from excessive blood loss."

The look of revulsion she gave Dr. Krist gave me no small amount of pleasure. He put his hands up in mock defense, no doubt believing himself to be well above reproach.

"It is my job to help those who need it, to protect those who cannot protect themselves. I saw a dangerous situation, and unfortunately, those, whose job it is to *remove* the helpless from dangerous situations, didn't follow through. It was an unfortunate situation, but that little girl wasn't suffering from nosebleeds, and I don't believe that Jackson, here, is either."

I saw Kathryn stand and clutch Keller close to her chest. I stood, thankful that I was holding Jackson or I'm certain I would have attacked the man.

My voice trembled as I spoke with ill-concealed rage, feeling the heat of it rise again through my cheeks and neck. "You have no idea who we are or what we're doing with our children. You're blind and stupid if you think that we would ever hurt our children." I stepped closer to him and he stared me down, raising his chin. "We came to you for *help*, and you have the nerve to call us child abusers, instead." I gestured to the small black book he held. "Do you think we'd keep track of the times he had a nosebleed if we were the ones causing it?"

He shrugged, uncaring. "I've seen worse."

I was stunned. I was hurt, too, but I'd never admit it to that man.

"Feel free to get a second opinion, but I'll be writing up my recommendations all the same."

"How dare you," Kathryn spat as she walked briskly past him to the door, snatching the black book viciously from his hand. "You make me sick."

I followed her out the door and tried to catch up. She stalked down the hallway and past the reception desk, and by the time I caught up, I could tell that she was holding back more tears of anger and helplessness.

We walked through the dark parking lot to our car and buckled the kids in their seats. Kathryn sat between Jackson and Keller again, and as soon as I sat and buckled my own seat belt, she reached around Jackson, pulled him as close as she could in the confines of the car, and wept into his hair.

CHAPTER 16

I slept for three and a half more hours after arriving home from the hospital and tucking the kids into bed. Kathryn wanted the boys to sleep in our bed, and of course, I couldn't say no. Keller woke up feeling fine as far as I could tell. Jackson wasn't feeling well at all. We let him sleep, and I called the school to say he would be out for the next couple of days.

I had to work and so did Kathryn. She went into the office for a couple of hours and would be back around lunchtime. Her meetings at eight and ten couldn't be moved. I could tweak Gretchen and prep her for a sequencing run, then when Kat came home, she could watch the kids while I ran Gretchen over to Corner House.

I'd tried explaining to Kathryn what had happened and why I needed to go back, but she said she was too over-whelmed to process it.

"I'm sorry, Grant. My brain just can't handle it. I've got to get these meetings off the ground, and just like you, I'm run-ning on pretty shitty sleep. I love you, but I just don't have the capacity for it right now."

I smiled and told her it was fine then gave her a kiss before she walked out the door.

Keller munched happily on a breakfast bar while I pulled up my email.

One new message from Marco, a response to my explanation last night.

> 2:48 am CST
> Re: FAD/Intersect Data
>
> Yo,
> This shit is crazy. If you hadn't attached the images, I wouldn't believe it. Smart of you to show all the grids at the same time. Guess that's why you get paid the big bucks. Holler at me in the morning. I know you're central, but I'll probs be up, girlfriend is out of town, so I'll be up early cleaning up before she gets back.
>
> Warm Regards,
> Marco Riviera
> Team Lead

Despite my fear and exhaustion, I smiled at his email signature. I'd eat my shoe if Marco ever used "warm regards" as a way to say goodbye.

I looked at my watch. It was eight-fifteen, which meant Marco was sitting at just after six. And based on his email, he'd at least been up at nearly one.

It was a guess, but he did say to call him. Well, "holler" at him.

I dialed up his cell and waited.

Voicemail picked up.

"What's up! It's ya boy Marco. Leave a message, and I'll holla back."

I waited for the beep.

"Hey, Marco. It's Grant. Just giving you a call. Got your email, I know you may still be in bed—"

My phone began to beep, and I pulled it from my ear to look at the screen. Apparently, Marco was up. I ended the voicemail and switched to the incoming call.

"Marco, good morning."

"Hey bro! Sorry for missing the call. I was vacuuming the living room, and my phone was charging in the kitchen. Got the notification on my tellie."

I didn't want to ask what a "tellie" was, so I just let it go.

"Yeah, that's good. I'm glad you got back to me. What did you think?"

"Oh, dude. It's wild. You nailed it though. The descriptions you gave fit perfectly with what I see on my side as well. I bet you didn't know this, but we have internal cameras mounted within each FAD's glassteel casing. Funny thing is, you told it like you saw it, but I know you field fellas don't got access to the feed. But I do. Watched the whole thing. All kinds of metal and shit flying around inside. Crazy thing, too. The charge displacement—that's what you called the energy housing or whatever—was cracked and was leaking energy all over the inside. Bits of metal were actually floating and hovering around inside. The FAD—Gretchen, right?—was rocking because of the inconsistencies of both the mechanisms grinding and the fact that it was blowing off energy in waves. I think you said the actual explosion was a wave that popped your kid into the air, right?"

"Yeah, that's right."

"Nice. At that point in the data, there was what we call a Causal Nexus."

"What's a Causal Nexus?"

"Glad you asked." It sounded like he sat down on the couch because this explanation was going to take some time. "A Causal Nexus is a never-ending loop of action and reaction. In our FAD data, you can see it as the exponential increase in energy despite the system registering a massive amount of energy being discharged and dumped. So we have this cause and effect happening forever. The energy is dumped, more energy fills the space, it dumps it, it fills it, blah blah blah. You get it?"

"Yeah, actually, I do get that."

"What you described about needing the loop—the Causal Nexus—to short-circuit somehow isn't something in the FAD's code."

That was disappointing.

"Well, what do we do, then?"

I heard the smile as he spoke. "Just because it's not in the code doesn't mean it can't be put there. And if you're looking to mess with code, you came to the right place."

"You know how to do that?"

"Bro." The disbelieving condescension made me laugh. "You don't know this about me, but over here in Cali, I'm a fuckin' celebrity when it comes to coding shit."

"Marco, you are a fucking liar is what you are." He barked a laugh and then went on.

"Aight, check it out, Grant. I've already got access to the FAD's code sequence, so I can debug it and shit. All I need to do is find where the code tells it to keep dumping without recognizing any other option. I'll put in a tri-catch and run the deploy. Gretchen should be down for a minute or two while she updates, then she'll be good to go."

"How long will it take to write the code?"

"It shouldn't be too long. It'll take me a couple of hours, probably. Guess it's a good thing my girl is out of town. I pulled an all-nighter to clean the house so the rest of my morning is clear."

"Yeah, good news for both of us, I guess."

"Aight, let me get a good look at this. I'll let you know when it's done and when I'll start deploying it to the FAD."

"Sounds good." I stopped short. "Hey thanks, by the way. I really appreciate your help, Marco."

"Yeah dude, anytime."

I hung up and looked through my notes. There wasn't a lot for me to do, but I decided to call and leave a message for Gianna.

I kept it short and sweet, simply telling her that Marco and I were booting up the FAD for a test run and then an actual frequency sequence, that if she needed me for something else, she could get with me.

By that time, Keller had finished his breakfast and was playing contentedly with some of his dinosaurs. When Jackson finally rolled out of bed, he asked for something to eat. A good sign. Keller ran and wrapped his big brother's legs in a hug. Jackson bent at the waist to hug him back, and then clutched his head and stood up.

"You okay?" I put my hand on his shoulder and felt his head. He was warm, but not feverish.

"Yeah, Daddy. I'm okay. My head is just throbbing."

I filled a glass of water from the sink. "Drink this, buddy. You're probably dehydrated."

He took a few sips at a time, but eventually, the glass was empty.

"Want to work with me today?" There wasn't *really* a choice, but he nodded without enthusiasm.

"Sure. But didn't Keller work with you one time?"

"Um, yeah." I secretly hoped the result would be different this go around.

He shrugged and then I loaded Gretchen into the SUV. While I struggled to lift it—because of its awkward shape, of course—I wished that the hovercars of my childhood imagination would have been invented by now. We were planning on going to Mars. Why couldn't we fly on Earth yet?

The boys sat unbuckled in the car for the short two-block drive at ten miles per hour. They thought it was quite the treat. Even Jackson cracked a smile when Keller jumped onto his lap and flailed about as if we'd just experienced the crash of the century.

I put the SUV in park by the curb of the Corner House. I looked up into the empty stare of its eyeless windows. A cat—one of Muriel Anthony's I was sure—watched us from one of the top windows.

At least it wasn't raining this time. The sun was shining, and while it was a little chilly, the sun was warm enough to avoid jackets. I was glad for the slight chill when sweat beaded my brow unloading the FAD.

I set it up in the same position on the porch, careful to avoid the steps which looked even less stable than they did the first time I was there.

Jackson and Keller played in the front yard, but with the house looming over us, they were contained and quiet, as if they were afraid of disturbing something.

Keller would stop every few minutes to stare up at the house, no doubt feeling that uncomfortable sense of being watched. He reached upward at one point, and Jackson and I shrugged at each other. Maybe he saw the cat.

My phone trilled and I answered.

"Hey Grant, it's Marco. Turns out I'm even better than I thought. Only took about an hour to find the recursive action in the FAD's code. Another fifteen minutes to write a stop-sequence, slot it in with a conditioning phrase, and bam, we're set."

"I only understood about fifty percent of that, but it sounds like we should run the frequency sequencer again."

"Boom, you got it. Give me a few to deploy. Gretchen will boot up with a yellow folder on the touch screen. Don't mess with it. Once the folder disappears and the version shows zero-point-eight-point-two-zero, you'll know the deployment was successful, and we should *hopefully* have a sequence ready to run with the changes that will prevent the result you got last time."

"Okay, that's great, Marco. Stay on the live feeds and let me know what you see. I'll run on test sequence, you tell me things are good, and I'll move her to the same location and run the frequency sequence for real."

"Sounds like a plan, boss. Marco out."

The folder had appeared on the interface and my heart was starting to beat a little faster.

"Hey Jack, will you take Keller to the car and wait for me there? Shouldn't be long."

He nodded to me, took Keller's hand, and led him to the SUV where they sat looking longingly out the window. I could tell they were looking for the cat based on how often they gestured toward the top of the house behind the tinted glass windows. They really were my favorites.

The folder disappeared, I checked the version number, and it read zero-eight-two-zero. So far so good.

I booted up the test sequence, ran it, and waited for a message from Marco. My results seemed normal, but he might have access to additional information.

My phone buzzed and the virtual office message from Marco said, "Green Light Go." I took that to mean everything worked as it should, and I moved Gretchen into the Corner House.

I sat Gretchen in more or less the same place. The house was quiet except for the occasional sound of the cat moving upstairs. I hoped that the test wouldn't affect it. Poor thing didn't need to go back to Muriel with a third eye or something.

The dimness of the house, even at this time of day, seemed to press in upon me. The lights from the FAD illuminated some of the darkness inside, but the touch panel beamed a ghostly light across the wall and my face. The "Initiate Sequence" button lit up on the touch screen. I selected the correct sequence and tapped the "start" button.

I didn't *run* out of the house, but my walk was meant to put as much distance between Gretchen and me. I made it to the SUV and leaned on it. I could see Gretchen from this vantage point and for the next several minutes, there was nothing but a distant whir coming from Corner House. The boys asked about the cat—they called it a dog, but it didn't look like a dog to me—and I told them it probably ran off.

My phone chimed and the message read "Sequence is over. Looks like everything came through, but the data is still rendering so give me a few."

I waited and felt the tension creep into my shoulders and back as I leaned against the car, making faces and playing peek-a-boo to pass the time. I wasn't nervous, not really. But I was worried, I suppose. I was working to make the world better, wasn't I? That meant that whatever I was doing needed to make the world better for the boys. I had to ask myself that whatever I was doing right now was going to set them up for success, not just for short-term gain.

I jumped when the chime came from my pocket.

"Dude..." was all it said.

I called Marco immediately, and next, the boys bore witness to their dad jumping up and down, pumping the air with my fists.

CHAPTER 17

There was something in the air when Kathryn came through the door that evening after a day at the office. She greeted me with a peck on the cheek and asked if we could talk after the kids went to bed. I nodded, but the anxiety that blossomed in my belly settled there until the kids were sound asleep, nightly rituals complete.

Kathryn and I sat across from each other on the couch where so many times we'd snuggled up to watch a movie, or the few times we'd made love on it after a glass or three of wine, certain the kids were asleep. Her legs were crossed behind her, making The Nest where Jackson or Keller would snuggle if he were here. Her nose was red, and her eyes were swollen from crying. A cup of tea cooled in front of her, untouched.

"Kathryn, I'm not sure what you're trying to say."

She looked at her hands, folding and re-folding a used tissue. "I'm not even sure, Grant. But you aren't making me feel any better. You're making me sound like I belong in the loony bin." She wiped her nose. "I'm saying the boys are close, but it seems like there's some other bond between them, something... Jesus, Grant, some connection, I don't know, okay?" She sniffed and wiped her nose with a tissue.

Her silence seemed to be less reluctance and more a cue for me to continue.

"What I'm saying is that I'm just having a hard time understanding what exactly you're pointing out. You've said that the boys are close, and I've never argued that point; they don't really have a choice. But to say that they're—" I made a hand motion that I hoped conveyed the same meaning as the word she had said.

She looked at me with a look of muted betrayal. "Grant, I said that I've always suspected there's something more to their relationship than just a regular brotherly bond. I said they're *connected* somehow. Don't make it sound like I said something crazy."

I bit back my response and took a breath, instead. "That's not at all what I'm saying. I'm just saying that I don't understand how it's possible, that's all. I'm glad that I'm not the only one that thought of it, but I'm not sure what to do with the information."

"Well I don't know if you just refuse to see it or you really are that blind, but it seems pretty obvious to me." She held her fingers out as she ticked off points. "Keller has always been sick. Maybe not deathly ill, but not carefree and well, either."

Thumb.

"Jackson has always been well. That is, until recently."

Forefinger.

"Keller had a cold or some kind of sinus issue one night. Jackson had a nosebleed that same night, a bad one. Next morning, Keller is happy as a clam, no sickness in sight."

Middle finger.

"Almost the same scenario happens again a couple of weeks later."

Ring finger.

"I take Keller to my mom's house. He's sick almost all week. Jackson doesn't have a single nosebleed while you take him camping that week. I come home on Friday, and he has a nose-bleed that night. Guess who wakes up without a single cough or sneeze?"

Pinky finger.

"Do I need to continue or does that lay it out clear enough for you?"

When she put it like that, it was suspicious, to say the least. But what was she saying?

"So you're saying that our kids have some kind of *connection* that, what, makes one sick?"

She leaned forward so intensely that I felt my face flush.

"I'm saying that our younger boy is *feeding* off our older one. When he's sick, I don't know how, but gets better by sucking the life out of Jackson, and that causes some kind of nosebleed."

I was dumbfounded. With all the evidence she presented, I knew it was something like that. But to hear it spoken out loud was—

Crazy.

"I know how it sounds," she said, calming a little. "But I don't know what else it could be. If it was just a nosebleed here and there, or Keller was still sick the next day ... or if taking one of the boys made a lick of difference, I'd call the whole thing off." She licked her lips. "But it's not just a nosebleed here and there. And Keller *isn't* sick the next day. And it doesn't make a difference if the boys are away." In an uncharacteristically gentle move, she grasped my hand. "Our baby is hurting our firstborn, and I'm scared."

Now the tears refused to be stopped. Kathryn sobbed into her hands as I pulled her close to me, moving so that she could lean on me comfortably. She cried into my shoulder, and I could feel her cold tears leaking through my shirt.

She was right. Even then. It was hard for me to believe, and I wanted to scream at her that she was crazy, that there was no way our kids were connected on some supernatural-voodoo-magic level. But the numbers didn't lie. Jackson's nosebleeds *did* coincide with those mornings when Keller woke up well. That's what was most telling. Keller, in his toddler mind, could do the only thing he knew how to do: survive. How could he survive when he was feeling ill? Take the wellness of the one person he knew would give it: Jackson. It didn't feel like Jackson knew or was okay with taking part, so maybe there was more to be figured out there. But the bottom line was that Kathryn was onto something, and it scared me too.

When Kathryn's sobs turned into the hiccups that followed a hard cry, she sat up. "I don't know what to do, Grant."

"What makes you think that there's something that we *can* do?"

"Because I'm their mother," she said fiercely. "I'm the one that's supposed to kiss their skinned knees, hug them when the world hurts them. How am I supposed to fix this when one of them is the reason the other is hurting?" She almost made it through without crying, but the last word caught in her throat, and tears began their stolid march down her cheeks.

I tried to comfort her by wrapping my arms around her and holding her close. What was I going to say, that everything would be fine? Frankly, I was getting sick of that word. *Fine.*

"Well what, then? What do we do? Separate them?"

I could feel her shake her head on my shoulder. "No, I don't think that's going to work."

"Why not?"

"Grant," she said in a voice dripping with impatient disbelief, "if what we suspect is true, then separating them will take away the one source that Keller has for health."

I wasn't sure there was an alternative to what she was saying. "Well, right. But if we leave them together, we're risking Jackson's health every single night. Eventually, and if it wasn't obvious before it should be now, Keller will suck the life right out of Jackson until there's nothing left."

Kathryn's back straightened and her eyebrows rose. "I should have known that's what your thought would be."

"What do you mean?"

"Your first concern is Jackson, always. Oh, don't give me that look. I love Jackson just as much as you do, but have you thought at all about what will happen to Keller if they're separated?"

"Kathryn, that's exactly what I'm saying." Was I really going to have to explain this? "Jackson is our first child. Of course, I'm thinking of his well-being, just as much as I'm thinking about Keller's. But this is a no-win situation!" I couldn't believe what I was saying. "You're so concerned with Keller's health that you're willing to risk Jackson's."

"And you're so worried about Jackson's health that you're willing to risk the life of our toddler!"

I threw my hands up. "Exactly. Like I said, a lose-lose situation. If we separate the boys, Jackson will continue to get better, and Keller will get worse. If we keep them together, Keller will get better, and Jackson will get worse. What are we supposed to do, here? Pick our favorite kid and spend the rest of whatever short lives they have left together?"

Her mouth dropped open in stunned horror. "Don't you even say that! We're their parents. We don't have favorites!"

"Oh really? Is that why your first thought is Keller and mine is Jackson?"

Her mouth was making sounds, but none of them were words.

"No, of course not." I forged ahead, though I wanted nothing more than to go to sleep and wake up from this nightmare. "Of course, we love our children the same. Of course, we don't have favorites. But what are we supposed to do? If what we're saying is true..." I let the consequence hang in the air, unspoken.

"Grant, don't you dare put that out there."

"Kat. Listen to me. I don't think we have a choice. We—" Was I really going to say it? "We may have to—to choose."

She shook her head firmly. "No, I am not going to do that."

"We can't go to the hospital. They'll throw us in jail. Or at least take the kids away, which is a death sentence for one of them, no matter what the result."

She covered her eyes with her hands and began to weep. "I don't want to do this."

"Neither do I," I said as gently as I could.

She sniffed loudly and wiped her eyes. "There has to be something we can do. There has to be something we can try before we jump to that awful conclusion, right? What if we watch the kids somehow? Can we install cameras or something? So that even if we fall asleep, we'll have a record of what happened that night? We can watch and see? Maybe..."

"Maybe what?" I prompted when she didn't continue.

"We're already talking about crazy supernatural stuff, so just go with it, okay?" I nodded, and she continued. "What if there's something else going on? What if there is... god, this is insane, and I can't believe I'm even saying it. But what if there

is like a vampire or magic something-or-other going on that's making this happen?"

I tried not to laugh. The anger bubbling beneath the surface helped temper my tone into a stunned kind of deadpan. "You cannot be serious."

"Well, I don't know, Grant. If Keller is sucking the life out of Jackson just by being near him, certainly that opens up other possibilities, right? I know how that all sounds, but maybe our kids are being hurt by something else."

I didn't feel the need to reiterate that one of our kids was definitely being hurt by the other. But, in my need to accept any other scenario than the obvious one, I agreed.

"You're right. I'm sorry. That was mean of me to say. What does that look like, then? Us watching the kids, I mean." I held my hands to forestall her next question. "Yes, I think it's a good idea to get some cameras up. I'll go get them this week and install them. But should we stay in their rooms?"

She crossed her arms and looked away. "We can try it. Maybe it will help."

We moved the rooms around that afternoon. The extra twin bed we'd stored in the attic for Keller was coming out a little sooner than anticipated. It was strange, we'd both mention later, that we both hoped for and feared the resolution.

That night, after bathing both boys and toweling up the splashed mess, I tucked Jackson into his covers.

"I'll be right back. I'm going to check on mom and Keller, okay?"

He nodded and watched me walk out of the room.

In Keller's room, Kathryn was lying down, knees drawn up nearly to her chest, our toddler curled up beneath her chin. Her left hand was stroking our second son's hair, and she was humming an old church hymn. His eyes and mouth were open, his breath coming in hollow wheezes.

I bent and kissed his forehead and whispered how much I loved him, then kissed Kat on her forehead and told her that she was amazing.

She closed her eyes and smiled. "I love you, too." When she looked at me, there was a determination in them that made me nervous, and I didn't know why. "Stay awake, Grant. Watch out for Jackson."

I nodded, a little taken aback. "I will, Kat. Let me know if you need anything." I had more to say and wasn't quite sure how to say it.

"Kathryn," I began.

"What is it?" She blew a wayward strand of hair out of her face.

"Our goal, however long we decide to do this, is to watch the kids, right?"

"Of course."

"Right. So I am curious what your thoughts are on whether or not we should stay separated tonight."

"I don't know what you mean," she said, her face screwed up in confusion.

"I mean," I honestly wasn't sure what I meant. "I mean that it would be an opportunity to get hard evidence of the extent of their ... bond."

Her expression was frozen for only a moment before falling into stone-cold control. "You're saying that you want me to stay in here while Jackson bleeds so I can watch Keller. To see if he gets better in that moment. To confirm that he's actually stealing Jackson's ... health."

I straightened and ran my hands through my hair, unsure of what to do with them. "Well ... yeah."

She set her jaw and shrugged. "Fine by me. If you think it'll be worth it. It might even be." Her expression softened, and she reached for my hand. "Grant, I really do hope we're wrong."

I knelt; my knees cracked too loud in the silence. "Babe, so do I. I want nothing more than to be wrong about this."

We squeezed our hands, and I kissed her once more on the forehead, whispered "You're my favorite" and returned to Jackson's room.

He was breathing evenly, and I thought him asleep, but when I sat on his bed and swung my legs onto it, he opened them and said in a groggy voice, "Are you staying in here with me?"

I wrapped an arm around his shoulders and hugged him closer. He lifted his head and laid it on my chest in a way that he hadn't done for some time. "Yeah, bud. We're gonna figure this whole nosebleed thing out."

He was silent for a long time, long enough that I thought he'd fallen asleep. "Why is momma with Keller?"

My mind whirled for an answer that wouldn't give him a reason to believe he was at fault. So of course, like any good parent would do, I lied.

"Oh, she was going to be so lonely falling asleep in our bed that she wanted company. She didn't think it was fair that I got to have a sleepover, so she and Keller are having one, too."

I could see his cheek smile, and I grinned as he wrapped his arm across my chest.

"I love you, daddy."

"Love you, too, Jack." I rubbed and patted his back, much like I used to on his diapered bottom when he wasn't much younger than Keller. Perhaps it was fear of the unknown, or perhaps it was the closeness, but my throat began to constrict, and I could feel tears welling in my eyes.

I took some deep calming breaths. Eventually, the emotion sank back down into my chest, but I was stricken by the power of nostalgia, of how quickly the years pass.

I thought back to the day when Jackson was born.

It was early morning when I heard movement in the master bathroom. I'd asked Kathryn if she was okay, knowing full well that she may not be okay.

"I think I'm in labor." Her tone was matter of fact.

"Probably not," was out of my mouth before I could stop it. In my defense, it was two in the morning and sleep was an unforgiving master.

Turns out that she was, in fact, in labor.

I chuckled to myself, returning to the present, and I continued rubbing Jackson's back. If I'd known that in twenty-three hours I'd meet my son, I would have been much more excited. But the labor and contractions lasted so long, that by the time Kathryn was ready to push, I was falling asleep between contractions. Again, an unforgiving necessity.

I rested my hand on his sandy-brown hair, smiling as I remembered watching him transition from a resident of Kathryn's womb to a full-blown, bawling adult-in-training.

It was love at first sight, no doubt about it. After he was cleaned up and nursed—with Kathryn crying in relief—I held him on my lap and cried. I stroked his smooth cheeks and couldn't stop telling myself that he was mine.

You know, they say that a baby can't really see anything beyond a few inches those first few days, and their eyesight progressively gets better the more time that passes. But as I sat there and stared into his dark eyes, I could tell he knew me. He was a beautiful baby. Oh, I know everyone always says that their baby is "the most beautiful," but mine *actually* was.

Perfect eyes, perfect little nose, perfectly round head. He was perfect.

I sighed deeply, relishing the feeling of having Jackson close and enjoying the silence of the night. It was a good thing that I'd had a couple of cups of coffee in preparation for this. Well, it would help keep me awake, but I had a feeling I'd be taking a few trips to the bathroom before the sun hounded the night away.

After about an hour of blinking my eyes awake, I felt pressure in my abdomen and decided it was probably time for one of those bathroom trips.

I crept next door to Keller's room and waved and flashed a thumbs-up when Kathryn looked my way. She nodded and put her head back down. I was amazed that she could look so comfortable and be wide awake. I was in danger of falling asleep while sitting up.

After relieving myself and splashing a bit of water on my face, I went downstairs to grab my phone off the kitchen counter and made my way back to Jackson's room. When I laid down, I moved slowly as not to wake him.

I pulled up the photos app on my phone and scrolled back through until I started seeing pictures of Keller as a newborn. Truth be told, I didn't remember a whole lot of details from the day he was born. Thinking about Jackson's birth made me miss those first few days when I was getting used to caring for a new human.

Just about the first thing I remember about that day is labor starting in a similar manner, then telling Kathryn that "it's probably nothing." Well, it was something. I was oh for two on that front.

I remember spending some time laboring at home, then going to hospital when Kathryn began feeling unwell. If it's something I've always trusted about her, it's her instincts. Until recently, maybe.

When we arrived at the hospital and they checked her, there were only a few minutes of checking her vitals before she was rushed an emergency C-Section, with very little in the way of explanation.

I was allowed to accompany her after washing and donning the very flattering blue medical gown. I held her hand, stroked her cheek, and told her what a wonderful mother she was. Stupidly, I checked behind the curtain they'd erected below her chest. I was rewarded with a perfect view of my wife's insides, but on the outside. I can confirm that curiosity did indeed kill the cat, though I believe there's another half to that saying.

After choking down the bile that rose suddenly in my throat, I went back behind the curtain and stayed there until Keller was brought around it to us. Kathryn stroked his cheek and kissed him and then he was whisked away to be cleaned and checked.

Turns out, Kathryn's instincts were spot-on. The umbilical cord had been wrapped around his neck and was restricting the flow of oxygen to his brain. There was no way to tell what the effects would be, but the doctor was kind enough to give us a host of things to watch out for. Delayed speech, delayed milestones, and the like.

We didn't have much of those. Delays, I mean. What we did discover is that Keller was susceptible to every kind of seasonal allergy. Once spring rolled around, his nose mutated into a faucet that didn't stop running even after taking medicine specifically made for it. His eyes were an angry red and some days nearly swollen shut. In the summer, it was ragweed;

in the fall, it was flu; in the winter, it was a cold, and then, it started all over again.

The one thing we didn't anticipate was how quickly Jackson would jump into help his little brother. Incidentally, the coughs and runny nose would lessen—not stop—but lessen. I suppose hindsight is twenty-twenty, and it should have been a sign to us both. As his parents, we did all that we could. Or at least all we thought we could. We've never been averse to medicine, but that wasn't our default option, either. There's always an attraction from the option you don't take, and I don't think it ever goes away. The grass is always greener, you know. It could drive a man insane, if that tugging was paid more attention. All those decisions, all those strings stretched across time and tied to those instances when we opted for one instead of the other. You don't feel them at first. But now, two years later, there are hundreds of them. I can't imagine the weight of ten years, or twenty years' worth of *other* decisions.

I shook my head and checked my phone. Two twenty in the morning, and Jackson slept soundly beside me. I was thankful for that and decided that I'd use the restroom again and check on Kat and Keller.

Kat had changed positions but was fast asleep. Keller was still wheezing, but I thought he might sound a little better. I hoped it wasn't wishful thinking.

When I crawled back onto Jackson's bed, I wrapped myself in a blanket and closed my eyes. I thought sleep would come quickly, but perhaps the coffee lingered, or I was more jazzed up about keeping watch than I'd thought. Either way, I ended up staring out the balcony glass door, watching the stars circle the earth. The red brake lights of a car would flash every so often, and it wasn't until I could pick out the gables of the house across the street that I realized it was morning and the sky was shifting from the deep velvet of night to the uneasy gray of pre-dawn light. Keller's cries brought me to full wakefulness shortly after. He seemed particularly fussy this morning as I could hear Kathryn trying to calm him with gently shushing. By the way the sound changed every few seconds, I could tell that she was either rocking him side to side or pacing with him on her hip. Probably both, actually. His cries were interrupted by deep, dry coughs that sounded painful.

"I know, baby. I know that's no fun." Kathryn's voice echoed through the open bathroom door, and the tender eternal patience I heard in it made me fall in love with her all the more.

When Jackson began to stir, I got up to make a pot of coffee, then sat down at the table to go through the data Marco sent.

I wasn't sure how many more nights I'd be able to do it, but I'd chalk up this first one as a success. I wasn't sure how long it would last, and while part of me hoped that it would last and Jackson wouldn't have nosebleeds, another part of me hoped that it wouldn't, and we could see if something was happening to Keller when Jackson's nose began to bleed.

It wouldn't. Three long nights of very little sleep later—thank god for paid time off—it happened again.

The time between that first night and the next nosebleed were uneventful but tedious. Much of my time spent poring over the data that Marco sent and trying to align the charted results, compare them to the previous test, and all manner of detail work that I loathed.

I began to measure the days not in twenty-four-hour periods, but in "how many days since the last nosebleed" and an accompanying dread of "when is the next?"

I'd like to say that I enjoyed lying in my child's twin-size bed and doing everything in my power to avoid closing my

eyes. But the truth was it was terrible. Oh, sure, I tried to enjoy the quiet solitude of listening to his breathing. I enjoyed the ridiculous amount of time I had to think about my work, or home projects, or any number of things on the growing "To-Do" list. I was able to finish one of those projects, though. After our conversation about installing cameras in the boys' room, I took an extra hour on a Tuesday morning and went to the hardware store and found the two most expensive brands. I opted for the second most expensive, for no other reason than I didn't want to spend the extra sixty dollars for the name. Installation was simple. That isn't to say there was a fair bit of cursing and loud, irritated sighs. But the cameras were up and tested by the second night. Seven cameras total, which cost a pretty penny. One on the front door outside, one in the living room facing the front door and hallway, one in our room facing the front hallway, another in each of the rooms, one above the garage and one above the balcony facing the street so we could keep an eye on them when they got a wild hair and ventured out to play there. Kathryn was pleased, which meant I was pleased. "Happy wife, happy life," right?

We'd both agreed that, should a nosebleed occur, our best bet would be to remain with our respective charges for a few minutes, and then if needed, Kathryn could come help me clean up Jackson. Easy in theory, but in practice it was much, much more terrifying.

I had gotten up to go to the restroom a little after one in the morning several nights later. By now, we were both tired and expectant. If a nosebleed was going to happen, it would be soon. I'd been uneasy, sitting in the room with him. The silence that settled over the house that night seemed to also include a bit of my anxiety. The waiting was the worst. Waiting for the bad to happen, knowing it was going to descend on him any minute. And the previous two nights were weighing heavily on my soul and on my eyelids. Despite the pale glow from the moon and streetlights casting a shadow here and there, it was too dark to really see anything that might hold my attention. The tops of the trees outside, barely reaching the balcony, swayed in the midnight wind and early breeze. It was hypnotizing, and I found myself jolting awake several times.

After going to the restroom, I went downstairs to check on things. Kathryn caught me at the top of the stairs before going down.

"Everything okay?" Her whispered voice carried easily through the empty gloom.

I nodded and gave a thumbs up, then mimed getting a drink. She nodded and went out of view, presumably back to Keller's room as I descended the stairs.

I filled up a glass of water from the sink despite not feeling particularly thirsty. I figured the cool water might help shock my mind and wake me up a little. After two sips from the glass, I put it on the counter.

Downstairs was silent. I walked through the rooms, checking doors and windows to ensure they'd been locked, and then splashed some water on my face. The towel that should have been hung on the small silver ring by the sink was lying in a heap on the floor. Keller, it seemed, had either conned Jackson into reaching it for him, or the stool beneath the sink provided just enough height for him to pull it down. I picked it up, dried my hands, and hung it neatly over the porcelain basin.

Keller was reaching the age where the desire to do things on his own overwhelmed his desire to do the thing quickly. That, in turn, translated into many more instances of having to check my patience while he fumbled with whatever he was working on. Any attempt to help by someone other than Jackson resulted in ear-splitting screams of protest.

I walked up the staircase with leaden heels, feeling barely more awake than when I'd descended them.

Shadows danced on the floor outside of Jackson's doorway, but I barely noticed them as I turned the corner. The movement of the trees outside the balcony caught my eye briefly, and another long, thin line of shadow seemed to flash across his floor and was gone. I sat down on the edge of his bed and noticed a redness on his upper lip.

I took a closer look and positioned my body so that the weak light from outside washed across his face. Sure enough, there was a tiny trickle of blood coming from his nose. It wasn't a lot, not nearly as much as his previous nosebleeds. I was alarmed, but Jackson was still sound asleep. Except for a brief stirring and a wince, which I assumed was from a dream, he was still.

I carefully got up and went to the bathroom for a wet cloth. The dread I'd been feeling earlier seemed to have abated a little. Perhaps his nosebleed wouldn't be as bad. Maybe this was the first step on the road to never having to worry about them again. Was this little nosebleed what we'd been so worked up about?

When I came back to the room, Jackson was sitting up in his bed with his eyes rolled up in the back of his head and his back arched, spasming in brutal bursts. I lunged for his bed, catching the glowing eyes of the neighborhood cat from my peripheral vision and subsequent scurrying sounds out on the balcony before completely discarding it from my immediate memory.

I could hear movement from Keller's room but was focused solely on Jackson's shaking body.

"Jack? Jackson? Can you hear me, buddy?"

His eyes rolled in their sockets and a grunting gurgle escaped from between his clenched teeth, which were turning red from the blood dripping from his nose.

His arms lay at his side, but with his body shaking, they were doing a morose caricature of a dance. I put my arm on his back and tried to help him lie down, but his muscles were tight across his whole body, like a coiled spring, and he wouldn't budge.

The blood that was previously leaking down his lip had become a steady flow. It wasn't gushing, as in previous instances, but was oozing off his lips and chin, mixing with spit that ran from his bottom lip. I resisted the urge to cry out for Kathryn.

"No, buddy. I know. I'm here. I'm here for you, buddy. Daddy's here." I didn't know what to say, but I knew if I didn't say anything to him, I'd begin cursing and crying.

I hastily wiped off his nose, chin, and mouth. His convulsions were lessening in intensity, which relaxed his body inch by inch. His shoulders began to slump and his back straightened. When his eyes stopped rolling and focused on the ceiling, I took a deep breath.

He blinked a few times, still staring up, then moved his arms purposefully into his lap and met my eyes. The paleness of the left side of his face was awash in the dull glow from the streetlamps and sickle moon outside. The right side was hidden in shadow.

I held the cloth beneath his nose and smiled at him, trying to reassure him.

"Hey, buddy. I'm here. Are you okay?"

He nodded weakly and tried to swallow, gagging on what I could only imagine was a sickening mixture of blood and spit.

I told him to spit it into the rag and schooled my expression as he did it.

I told him I was going to get him a glass of water and check on Keller. He reached for my hand and shook his head. "Please don't leave me alone, Daddy."

Tears began to fall down his cheeks.

"Okay, bud. Come on, then."

I picked him up, enfolding him in my arms. He wrapped his legs around my midsection and laid his head on my shoulder. I'm sure he was exhausted, but I also took a little comfort in knowing I was needed, too.

I glanced out the balcony door, thankful that there was no sign of that damn cat. The last thing I wanted to do when I was exhausted and scared was to confront the neighbors about their stupid pet.

Kathryn was holding Keller in the bed when I carried Jackson in. He was laying on her chest, but when he sensed another in the room, he sat up and blinked blearily, then smiled. "Dassin!" he croaked happily.

I ruffled his hair as he laid back down—fell, more like it— on Kathryn's chest. She looked at me with a weary smile, her lips pressed tight. "Jackson, how are you?"

Jackson lifted his head and answered, "I'm okay. A little nosebleed, but not as bad as the others, I think."

I shrugged in half agreement and smiled at Kathryn, "Yeah. It wasn't like the one from a few nights ago, but it made him shake a little, and scared me just a little, too." I hesitated, somehow knowing the answer before even asking the question. "What happened with this one?" I indicated the snuggling little toddler that had crawled into her lap and was now laying prone from her breast to her thighs.

Kathryn patted his bottom affectionately. "He'd been coughing, and I'd had to wipe his nose with toilet paper because I can't find that stupid bulb syringe to actually clear it. But when I checked on him, he wasn't asleep. He was awake and looking over at Jackson's room. Or through the wall, I guess. I heard you go into the bathroom and knew you were probably dealing with something. I heard you talking to him but couldn't make out the words."

I nodded and waited for her to continue.

"But before you went into the bathroom, he sat up and focused on the wall. It was strange, his body was tight. I'm not sure how to describe it. Kind of like..." She trailed off, searching for the word.

"A coiled spring," I finished for her, the thought from only moments before crossing my mind.

She looked at me with something approaching surprise. "Yeah, that's exactly it. For the record, any other time, it would take every ounce of self-control to not rush over and help. This time, though..." She looked at Keller's still form and as gentle as a breeze, brushed hair from his forehead with her fingertips.

"As you can see, he's feeling much better. His cough is almost non-existent, and his airway is completely clear. His nose isn't plugged or running, no thanks to the bulb syringe, and the color is back in his cheeks." She snapped quietly and raised her hands in a sign of resignation. "Just like that, he's perfectly fine." Her eyes were drawn to the lanky child in my arms. I patted his back, understanding what she was saying without any words passing between us.

Keller's illness disappeared the second that Jackson began having a nosebleed. I can't understand how there seemed to be two separate nosebleeds, and I was kicking myself for

leaving his side at the exact time when the nosebleed started. It was as if his body sensed my absence and reacted.

Regardless, I couldn't deny the connection, now. We had actual evidence of a correlation between our kids. How could we explain this to anyone? We certainly couldn't go to the doctors, anymore. Not since our last visit ended with the doctor accusing us of abuse.

It was ridiculous. It was a travesty. But we were alone now. No one in the neighborhood was a close enough friend to divulge this kind of information. Mitch came to mind, but only briefly.

I squeezed Kathryn's hand affectionately before taking Jackson back to his room. The sheets, thankfully, weren't soiled but his pajama shirt was. I helped him change it and laid him down, searching in my mind for some resource we could use, someone we could talk to about it.

His name popped into my head, again. I discarded it and continued searching. After walking around the room several times, I settled on standing before the balcony door and staring out into the murky purple night. I came up empty every time I thought about going to someone. Well, almost empty; Mitch may be the only person to not consider us crazy. Though, Kathryn may not be on board. Then again, she did bring up the whole "connection" thing.

But what if it was the only option?

I sighed heavily. The mental weight of carrying Jackson's well-being and the suspicion it cast on Keller was almost overwhelming. But I was the dad. What else was I supposed to do? And if there was someone who might be able to help, shouldn't I at least try it out?

I thought hard for a moment, searching internally and trying to separate the knot of emotions that seemed to be dragging my stomach across bones and through the carpet beneath my bare feet.

Could I consider myself a good father if I didn't attempt *every* available option? I wasn't sure if I'm honest with myself. But I did know that if there was a chance, I had to take it.

I made the decision there, staring out the balcony windows at the pale sliver of moon hanging in the deep starlit night.

Tomorrow, I'd call Mitch Callum.

CHAPTER 18

I did end up calling Mitch the next day, but he didn't answer, so I left a voicemail. I expected a call back later in the day, but by the time that Kathryn and I were ready for a night out, I still hadn't heard from him.

Lily had come over again to watch the boys. Every now and then when we needed a night to ourselves, we'd invited her over and she'd been more than willing. She'd watched the boys several times since her first night at the house and as far as we were concerned, it was working well. Kat and I really liked her and so did the boys, which is what really mattered.

We gave her the nightly run down despite knowing she'd done it enough that we didn't have to, and then kissed the boys and left. We needed a break. After last night's events and our realization that maybe we were on to something far beyond our understanding, we needed to go out.

Matt Brandhauer was out sweeping his sidewalk of grass clippings as we left the house. I waved, and he only stared back. *Weirdo*, I thought.

Our Saturday evening out wasn't as enjoyable as it could have been. The previously pleasant coolness of spring was being replaced with the waxy, unrelenting heat of summer. The kind of heat that made me irritable and unpleasant to the people around me. That in turn made things like date night even *more* uncomfortable. It felt like we just couldn't get past it. The worry and anxiety that came with being parents was compounded when impending medical events seemed to always be on the horizon.

We ate dinner mechanically, with little conversation. Each of us had a glass of wine before asking for the check without dessert. We left the restaurant in relative silence.

It wasn't that we were mad at each other. Not really. The good times that come in marriage are always accompanied by difficult times. Then there are times when you're not even sure why things are strange or why you feel disconnected, but you find yourself in an awkward silence and no understanding of how you got there. That's where Kathryn and I found ourselves now. In one of those strange twilit seasons of our marriage. I loved her, I knew she loved me, but it *felt* low.

When we turned into the neighborhood, we were met with a barrage of blue and red lights that lit up the entire block. Despite the chilly dinner, Kathryn reached over and grasped my hand tightly.

We drove slowly and stopped when a policeman blocked the road, his hand upraised. I rolled the window down and could feel Kathryn's hand tighten on mine as he approached the driver's side.

"Evening, folks," he began, friendly enough.

"What's going on here, officer?" I could feel the lump in my throat and hoped my voice didn't shake.

"Road's closed for now. As you can see," he gestured behind him, toward *our* home, "we've got a situation we're dealing with at the moment."

I gestured to our home that was just around the corner where it appeared most of the police vehicles were parked,

their lights winding relentlessly against the neighborhood homes. "That's our house, there. We're the Taldos."

The officer looked behind him and walked a short distance away from us. He bent to speak to the walkie-talkie on his shoulder. I couldn't hear what he was saying, but his sideways glances at us made my heart sink.

He walked back over to us, his midsection pushing the uniform to capacity. "Mr. and Mrs. Taldo, I'm afraid there's been a situation at your home."

"What kind of situation? Our kids are there with a sitter!" Kathryn was leaning across the vehicle and almost into my lap, her voice teetering on panic.

The officer waved us on and said, "They'll explain it there. I don't know the details. Just pull through and find the investigator at your home. He'll explain everything."

Kathryn's grip had tightened as he spoke, and even more so as we rounded the corner and our eyes finally saw a half-dozen police vehicles parked crookedly around our home. Kathryn started crying and asking what was going on. I drove as fast as I safely could the remaining hundred yards or so and put the SUV in park. A man in a long brown coat approached us as we were getting out and stopped us.

"Mr. and Mrs. Taldo?"

We tried to walk around him, to get to the front door, but he held up his hands to stop us. "The house is empty right now. There's been a situation."

"Empty?" Kathryn shouted and clutched the sides of her face. I felt my own urge to push the man aside and rush ahead. Kathryn pushed the man's hands down, and he frowned. "Where are my children?!" she shouted, nearly hysterical. If she hadn't asked it, it was going to the next thing out of my mouth, and I'm fairly sure it would have been a shriek as well.

"Your children are fine. They're being seen by the paramedics over—"

"Paramedics?" Kathryn walked past the investigator despite his attempts to corral her, and his huff that followed nearly made Grant slug him in the face. A stern look as we passed would suffice.

Kathryn found the boys sitting on the back of an ambulance with a blanket around each. Keller was holding Jackson's hand, and both boys looked terrified. Keller's face was stained with tears, and Jackson's nose was bright red. Not with blood, thankfully.

When they saw their mother, they lit up, and Jackson yelled, "Mom!" He jumped off the back of the ambulance despite the paramedic's attempt to dissuade him. What the hell was up with these people trying to stop us from getting to our kids?

Keller started crying as soon as I picked him up. His nose was a sticky mess, and he'd developed a light, phlegmy cough.

Jackson hugged Kathryn so tightly that she had to pry his arm from around her neck. He was whimpering when she picked him up, and we held each other for several moments.

The investigator had caught up to us, and after several seconds of ignoring him, he finally said, "Mr. and Mrs. Taldo, I need to speak with you about the sitter, Lily Carlisle."

We both looked at each other, having completely forgotten about her.

"Is she okay?"

The investigator shrugged and said, "Can we please speak privately? I'm not sure the kids need to hear this."

If his goal was to scare us, it was working incredibly well.

We told the boys to wait for us, which they weren't too keen to do, but the paramedic told Jackson that he could play

with some of the tools in the ambulance, and Keller was willing to follow Jackson, anyway.

"What's going on here?" I didn't mean to be rude, but the fear that was twisting my guts into knots wouldn't allow me to be calm at the moment.

"Mr. and Mrs. Taldo, I want you to know that Lily is stable, but she was transported to the hospital."

Kathryn seemed a little relieved, but said, "Oh my god, why? What happened? And why would that require all of these officers?"

The investigator nodded. "Lily fainted and hit her head. The paramedics who arrived at the scene said she suffered a concussion and would need to be monitored overnight. Her parents were notified and are going to the hospital with her."

"You didn't answer the question. Again, why all the police?" Kathryn was getting impatient at this point.

"I'm getting there, Mrs. Taldo. She fainted because there was an intruder in your home that threatened to kill her."

We answered with shocked silence. Kathryn gasped but nothing more.

"We don't really know what the circumstances of this intrusion were," he continued, "but the identity of the intruder is Matthew Brandhauer. He lives a few houses down at 4122 Steeple Tree Lane."

It felt like someone punched me in the gut. Matt had always rubbed me the wrong way. There was always just something off about him.

"Jesus," I whispered. "Wait, I saw him on our way out of the neighborhood, maybe a couple of hours ago."

"Did he harm Lily? Or the kids?" Kathryn looked over her shoulder at the boys, whose attentions were fixed on all of the equipment they were being allowed to play with.

"From what we can tell, no, Lily was the only one injured. The boys were asleep until our team of officers came into the house to arrest Mr. Brandhauer. Lily was able to tell us that he threatened her with a weapon—a knife—but beyond that, we don't know much more at this time."

I held Kathryn close to me, and she began to sob into my chest. If she felt anything like me, it was more in relief. I could feel the lump in my own throat threatening to crack my façade of strength into gut-wrenching tears.

"I'll leave you both for a moment. If you have any questions, you can contact me." He handed over a card that I glanced at just long enough to read the name—Raul Martinez—then put into my pocket.

We gave ourselves a couple of minutes to feel all of the emotions washing through us, then walked back over to the boys. There were a thousand questions careening through my mind, but my focus was on the kids and that they were okay.

I couldn't tell if I held her, or she held me as we approached the ambulance. Their backs were to us, and the paramedic was showing them all of the ways the bed could sit up and lay down. They laughed and giggled, completely ignorant of the danger they'd been in.

"Hate to interrupt, but are there two really rotten boys around here that need some parents?" Kathryn sniffed and smiled at them, holding out her arms.

"Daddy!"

"Mama!"

They jumped up, and from that moment on, they completely forgot about the fun of the moving bed. The paramedic smiled, and I forced one, mouthing the words "thank you" as we carried the kids toward the house.

It was nearly 1 a.m. when we tucked them into bed, more than two hours after our eyes were assaulted with the flashing lights of the police force. It's interesting when the job as a parent becomes downplaying what may be a very strange or even scary occurrence. Jackson was at the age where he knew more than he let on. We weren't able to simply gloss over the fact that police had barged into the house and arrested a stranger.

"So he was a bad guy? Like the monsters we talked about before?" I was tucking him in when he decided to rock my world with a very adult question dressed in child-like understanding.

I sighed and met his eyes, deciding in that moment to treat him not as a child, but as someone who would become an adult. "Yes. That's exactly it."

He nodded, and I was stunned at how he seemed to suddenly age another year before my very eyes. He wasn't scared or worried, but very pensive, as if he had expected this answer and now had a great deal to think on. His brown hair stood at all kinds of messy angles, and his cheeks were hollow, all of what made him a baby, gone.

"Are you going to be okay, buddy?"

"I think so." He yawned and settled into his covers.

I kissed him on the forehead and whispered that he was my favorite, then walked soundlessly from the room. I glanced at the camera above as I did. I'd almost forgotten.

Kathryn was rocking Keller, who was out like a light. I bent to kiss him on the top of the head, and in a surprising turn, she bent her head to give me a kiss.

"I love you, Grant." She smiled half-heartedly.

"I love you, too, Kathryn."

"I'll be down in a while. I think... I think I just want to hold him." Her eyes couldn't hide the truth of a mother.

"I understand. Take your time. I'll be downstairs."

I gave each of them another kiss. I decided to make myself a cup of coffee, too. Not out of necessity to stay awake, but in hope that the warmth would soothe me into a state of rest.

After it was brewed and steaming, I sat on the couch and booted up my laptop.

Before doing anything, I decided to send a message to Marco and Gianna. I gave them a brief overview of what happened and told them I'd be out of pocket for a couple of days. Seeing as it was Saturday, I didn't expect much of a response.

I was wrong. I received a response from Gianna almost immediately.

> *1:24 am CST*
> *Re: Family Emergency*
>
> *Grant,*
> *I'm so sorry to hear that. Please take as much time as you need. I'll just assume that we'll talk sometime next week. Maybe Thursday we can chat about some ideas I have for sending out another team of field agents? If you need more time, I understand completely.*
>
> *Sincerely,*
> *Gianna Rossi*
> *North America Project Lead*

That was nice. Thursday would give me plenty of time with the kids and I wouldn't have to worry about the test results until then. That new team had me mildly worried, but I didn't need to think of it right then.

Marco would respond with a similar message by Monday.

With that out of the way, I was able to actually address what was on my mind. A thought hit me as we were talking with Officer Martinez. I had set up cameras before Matt's intrusion and confrontation with Lily in the house. I should be able, at the very least, to see what happened in the rooms where the cameras were. As it turns out, that was pretty much everywhere in the house.

I pulled up the application where the recordings were stored and found the second on the list. The program saved the files in the easiest way possible, with the date range of a week followed by the start time—always 00:00:00—and a dash followed by the end time, which was always 11:59:59.

I began to scrub through the video until I saw Kat and I leave. Then, I continued on at double speed. I didn't know the exact time that the bastard Matt Brandhauer had come into the house, but it was after seven o'clock. I slowed down, dragging the viewing windows from Cameras D and C, the two upstairs bedroom cameras, Camera A in the living room, and the Camera B in our bedroom. They made a tiled quartet view of each room on my screen. The two with lights on—both downstairs—showed in color, while the upstairs two showed in black and white as the night-vision mode kicked in without sufficient light.

In double speed, I saw Lily get off the couch and hesitate, looking briefly between the blinds by the door. I stopped the video, bracing myself and toggling the speed to "normal," then clicked "resume."

Lily stepped back from the window and walked to the couch. She bent to pick up her phone, glanced quickly at the screen, and then put it back on the couch. Her body jerked in surprise, and her head whipped around to the door. He must have knocked again.

The door opened a crack as Lily peeked through the space. I couldn't make out the face of the man at the doorway, but I could see enough of his outline to see he was swaying drunkenly on his feet and had to catch himself several times on the doorframe.

I paused it there, looking intently at every detail I could. I could see that Lily's foot was wedged against the door. It was good that someone in her life had taught her which precautions to take. I hated that everything I was seeing was taking place in my living room. I hated more that it took place in the first place.

I started the playback again.

The conversation couldn't have lasted more than a minute. I saw Lily's head bob in response, then shake in a negative response. I was terrified for her. The part of me that was a father yearned to see this recorded video play out some other way. But I had to watch it, had to see. This was my penance.

There was what seemed to be a lull in their conversation. Lily looked over her shoulder and then back, her lips saying something, perhaps an excuse trying to get Matt away from the house, away from *my* house.

There was a sudden jerking motion on the video as the door surged forward, then Lily was pushing against it with all her might, trying in vain to stop it from inching open. Her body, unencumbered by an aging metabolism, showed the outlines of flexing muscles along her arms and legs. Like a scene from a horror movie, though, a hand pushed its way through the opening Matt created. He grasped the inside of the frame, and

I saw hungry eyes through that tiny opening. All rage and grim determination despite the perspective of the video.

He was enjoying this.

I watched, transfixed, as Lily heaved the door nearly closed on Matt's claw-like hand. I tried to will it, but there was no way to make it so. I could feel myself sweating with dread when Lily's socks—yellow with Tweety Bird outlines—began sliding backward on the floor. Matt shouldered the door open an inch, then another, and another. He looked like something vile hatching and ripping its way into the world. In a way, he was. He was tearing his way through Lily's sense of self-preservation, the fucker.

Our babysitter's head came up and not even the medium of video could hide the tears running down her face. My heart shattered, and I wanted to reach out and take her into my arms, to save her from the predator that was carving his way into her psyche.

The door continued to slowly open, and despite her weight against it, Matt finally squeezed through, his shirt catching on the large wooden door that pinned him briefly against the frame.

Then the door slammed home, and she fell forward, barely catching herself on the doorknob.

Matt was standing over her, his back to the camera, all pretense of the swaying drunkard evaporated. I couldn't make out what was being said, but by the look of desperate terror on Lily's face, I knew it wasn't good. His hand came down on her shoulder in a mockery of familiarity. Lily tried to recoil, but the fingers clasped her firmly and I saw her wince in pain.

His confidence in the power he held over her made him a villain, but it was his clear disregard for her humanity that made him evil. He walked over to the kitchen counter and out of the camera's view.

I looked toward the camera video that showed the hallway and our bedroom, hoping to get a glimpse of what he was doing, but it was a bad angle, and I couldn't see the kitchen, either.

Matt Brandhauer came back into view of Camera A holding something in his hand. It glinted in the video, and I could identify it immediately. Matt motioned for her to stand up, a lazy flick of the knife blade that said, "You'll do what I say because I'm powerful and you're not." Lily, thank goodness, did what he said and stood.

He sauntered closer to her, the knife poised to strike at her throat. To her credit, she didn't flinch. I could see both faces clearly, now. Despite a slight tremble in her lip, Lily's was a mask of stoicism despite the monster before her. Matt's was a sly grin that didn't touch his eyes.

I felt my face suddenly flush as Lily's form began to tremble, and a colorless pool began expanding around the smiling birds on her socks. I was sick to my stomach, enraged, and miserably helpless all at the same time.

I watched as Matt looked down at his feet, smiled back at her face, and took a step *closer*. He wasn't put off by the urine that was puddling around his own leather shoes. While I couldn't understand what he was saying, his posture spoke volumes. I could nearly hear him croon, "I don't care that you pissed yourself. In fact, I like it. It makes me feel good. It makes me feel powerful. And it shows me that you're nothing but a scared little rabbit afraid of the big bad wolf."

I paused the video and took a shuddering breath. I had to finish it. I had to see what happened to Lily, to this girl that had been entrusted to *my* care. After all, wasn't this *my* fault?

To try and wash away the bad taste in my mouth, I took a sip of my coffee, cooled now to an unappetizing temperature. I grimaced and set it down, then resumed the video.

Matt gestured with the knife, his lips moving in the dim light of the video and Lily sat with mechanical effort. She didn't seem to notice the wetness of her pants or the sardonic grin that spread across the predatory features of my neighbor. I could see his face and mouth a little more clearly as he circled Lily. When I read his lips, I chill washed down my arms and back.

Good girl, he said to the trembling teen before him.

His eyes moved up the staircase on his right, and for a moment, it seemed that he looked straight into the camera. What I saw there was not the gaze of a man but the gaze of a monster.

Lily's lips moved, but they were difficult to read. I saw her say "me" but the rest was impossible to make out.

Matt turned to her and tapped the knife on the top of her head several times in a cadence that matched the movements of his lips. He was playing with her, the way a cat plays with a mouse that doesn't know it's already dead.

Lily nodded, her back straight despite the fear she must have been churning her insides. I felt a disconnected sort of pride in that display of bravery in the face of such cruelty.

My eyes, however, were drawn to Matt as he began making his way up the stairs. Dark footprints of urine remained on the kitchen tile and carpeted stairs as he stalked his way toward my children.

I quickly switched the feed to Cameras C and D in the boys' rooms.

It was several more seconds before I saw a shadow creep its way into the frame of Jackson's room. My blood went cold and beads of sweat popped out on my forehead and upper lip. I wasn't aware of this development; there would have been no way that the officers could have known.

My palms were a clammy distraction. I wiped them on my pants without thinking as the shadow elongated, its source the imposing form of Matt Brandhauer. He stood in the light of the doorway, every inch an intruder.

He stood motionless for several minutes. Then, without an indication, the form retreated, the elongated shadow following on his heels. I expected to see it crop up in Keller's room, but instead, the movement of the front hallway camera caught my eye. It wasn't Matt's self-satisfied smirk that walked down the stairway; it was Lily. She was up and racing toward the couch. She slipped once, almost sprawling across the tile floor in her sodden socks windmilling for balance and righting herself.

I watched in disbelief as she rallied, picked up her phone and tapped it rapidly, then put it to her ear. Her hand cupped the speaker, and I could only assume this was when she called the police.

Pride blossomed in my chest, and I knew she'd just saved my children's lives. There was no doubt about it—her quick thinking saved all of their lives.

After several seconds of her head bobbing in the affirmative, she put the phone back down and ran back to the kitchen, sitting squarely in the puddle on the floor as if she'd never left it. The only clues were her footprints, now quickly fading dark slashes of moisture that led to the living room and back. I prayed Matt wouldn't notice.

I looked back at the children's rooms, and I watched with confusion as the shadow appeared again, this time in Keller's room. There couldn't be any more than a dozen yards between

their two doorways, and I hoped that he hadn't stopped to listen for movement downstairs. Regardless, he now stood once more in a doorway, watching the sleeping form of my toddler. The knife, perhaps forgotten in his hand, glinted in the shifting colors of the mobile's light.

I held my breath, waiting for something to happen. I expected him to walk slowly toward Keller and reach into the crib, intending to hurt or—god forbid—kill him. Even knowing the outcome, my heart raced faster than it ever had. I knew that neither of my children were aware of the stranger in the house, knew that they would come out unscathed, but still, my mind issued tricks of restless horror upon me.

I finally relaxed the grip on my own hands when the shadow retreated once more, bleeding its way out of the frame as Matt walked away. I didn't know where to look for movement, but the dark leather shoes of the intruder appeared next on the stairway, stepping slowly down the stairs, ensuring that each step was noticed.

Once in the kitchen, Matt stopped and stared down at the floor, then looked over at Lily's trembling form, and then back at the floor. My heart sank as the movement of his head followed the nearly evaporated footprints on the floor. Another minute upstairs and they'd have been nothing more than texture. Though, I couldn't stomach this man spending even that much time in the same room as the kids.

Matt turned to Lily, and he spoke through pursed lips, no doubt angry that she had the audacity to defy him. Her head shook in denial, and the knife came up in Matt's hand. He pointed it at her, accentuating each word with a jab of the knife. Lily winced each time the knife moved toward her, but she didn't cower or cry out a single time.

Have you ever seen a deer cross the road in broad daylight? They are remarkably fast. One minute they may be grazing contentedly in the grass, and in the blink of an eye, they're bounding through it, over the road, and into the distance.

Lily was that deer. One moment she was sitting cross-legged on the floor, and the next she was up and running toward our bedroom. Matt, who must have suspected something like this, reached out for her, his fingers raking the air behind her. He would have missed if he'd been a millisecond slower, but he wasn't. His hand closed on a fistful of hair, and he yanked back so viciously that had I been watching this unaware of the outcome, I would have believed he broke her neck.

I gasped as her head snapped back, and I could almost hear her scream of pain and despair. Her feet came out from under her, and the only thing that kept her from landing on her back was Matt's fistful of her russet hair. Instead, her rump hit the ground hard with enough force that I could see her face contort in pain.

With another violent tug, he turned her around, no thought to how her small arms whipped through the air or how her feet left the floor briefly.

His face was inches from hers, and from the way he was holding her, I could only see her wide, terrified eyes. The knife came up slowly from where he was holding it at his side. Lily's eyes caught sight of it, and they widened farther still. Her mouth opened in a scream, and Matt jerked her head several times, no doubt in an effort to scare her into silence.

Matt Brandhauer got more than he wanted. The third or fourth jerk of her head, with a knife poised inches from her face, Lily's features changed. With what she might have believed was her final act, she reared back as best she could and spit in his face. I clapped my hands and smiled. The fucker deserved more than that, but Lily deserved different than this too.

Matt's face contorted in rage, and he raised the knife with fatal purpose.

The body in Matt's grasp suddenly slumped in response as Lily passed out. Now faced with either letting her fall to the floor or holding on to her hair, he looked derisively at Lily's lax features. He released the fistful of hair, and she dropped heavily to the floor. I'm sure he thought himself successful, probably strong and efficient. With his back to the camera, I could only watch his shoulders rise and fall as he took several deep breaths.

I glanced at the other camera that would be facing that direction, but once again they were too far in the kitchen, and I could only make out his shoulder and Lily's limp form at his feet.

It did, however, provide the perfect angle to watch the police slam through my front door.

I watched both camera angles as splinters from the door-frame rocketed through the air in a movie-like rescue. Flashlight beams cut through dust particles, flashing briefly across the camera lens and creating a light show that rivaled a rock concert. Pistol barrels glinted in the chaos, the hollow deadly eye of the barrels trained on the man standing in my kitchen.

He had turned enough in one of the camera's angles that I could see his very surprised and very frightened face. It wasn't much, and would certainly never be enough, but it was satisfying to see the callous, self-assured mask melt away. Where Lily had been the escaping deer, Matt Brandhauer was now the one that was caught.

The lights from the police flashed across his face, and he winced away from them. His arms lifted in slow resignation as his dumbfounded eyes glanced at Lily's limp form.

Matt's fingers slowly uncurled from around the knife as the officers surrounded him, no doubt shouting variations of "Drop the weapon" and "Drop it now," as it clattered on the tiles of my kitchen floor.

Movement in the other two windows caught my attention, and I saw Jackson sit up suddenly. Keller was jumping in his crib, both hands grasping the rail tightly, and he was crying.

I followed a woman in uniform go up the stairs and again as she entered Jackson's room. He recoiled and screamed. She put her hands up and pointed to her badge, then approached him calmly. I could tell that she was trying to do everything in her power to ensure that my boy knew she was a safe person.

When he'd calmed enough, there were some words exchanged between them. Jackson pushed the covers aside, and together, they walked to Keller's room.

Keller reached for the officer the moment she entered the room, and she scooped him up. She walked downstairs with them, one hand under Keller's bottom and the other holding tightly to Jackson's hand.

They entered the kitchen where Matt Brandhauer was cuffed and lying face-down on the kitchen tiles. The officer did her best to shield the scene from the two boys. They were dazed enough with being woken in the middle of the night and dazzled by the commotion all around them that I wasn't sure if they would have seen him anyway.

I stopped watching the recording after I saw Lily stir beneath the attention of several paramedics. She appeared dazed, but she gradually became aware that her nightmare was over. Well, part of it, though I feared that the nightmares might just be starting.

I resolved to bring the video over to the detective in the morning. It wouldn't take long and would certainly show enough information to convict the bastard, I hoped. And I was fairly positive that Mr. and Mrs. Carlisle would be pressing charges, as they should. I'd encourage them to do so.

Kathryn came to bed sometime after I was already asleep. I felt her wrap her arm around my midsection as she made me the little spoon. I didn't mind. Her warm body pressing against mine felt good, calming me and coaxing me back asleep.

CHAPTER 19

After letting the boys sleep off some of the previous night's excitement, we ate lunch and brought flowers to Lily in the hospital that afternoon.

A few of the neighbors came by and asked if everything was okay. The police were still parked at the Brandhauer house and most—if not all—of the neighborhood bore witness to the commotion. How could they not?

The Uptons stopped by first. Their concerned questions danced politely around their interest in the actual story. The Shelbergs stopped by as well, along with their yippy little dog. And just as we were walking out the door, Greg McKahee stopped by, a cup of coffee steaming in one hand and Daisy in the other. Jackson was ecstatic, and the dog's stub of a tail was a blur as Jackson cupped her face and she licked his.

"Oh yeah, everything is fine, Greg. Just a bit of a scare. Matt Brandhauer—apparently—had too much to drink and forced his way in last night when the boys were here with a sitter. She's okay, but she fell and had a concussion. We're going to visit her, now."

"That's terrible. And the boys? They seem to be okay." He smiled down at Jackson and poked Keller playfully in the stomach.

"Yep, boys slept through most of it. Biggest fear they had was waking up to the police in the house. Other than that, just a little shaken up from it all."

Mr. McKahee sighed and sipped his coffee. "Well I just wanted to drop by, see if Alice and I could do anything for you."

"I think we're okay," Kathryn said sweetly, "but that is very kind of you to offer. If we do need something, I'll be sure to let you know."

Greg and I shook hands, Jackson kissed Daisy on the snout, and then Keller made the attempt to do the same but got a mouthful of puppy tongue instead, which he thought was the funniest thing on the planet.

My main concern, which Kat and I discussed on the way to visit, was that Lily might lay some of the blame on us. I hoped desperately that she didn't, but I understood that she may.

"I'm not sure she would do that," Kathryn huffed, just as anxious as myself. "It's not like it was planned or anything."

I nodded in agreement. "No, I think you're right. Lily doesn't strike me as the type to hold grudges, especially since she's been our regular sitter for a while now. Her dad, on the other hand..." I let that hang in the air for a moment.

"I hadn't thought of that. You don't suppose he would try to convince her to lump us in with it?"

"I don't know. I'd like to think the best of them, but honestly, who knows." I shrugged. "I guess we'll find out when we get there." The rest of the drive we were relatively quiet while the boys fired off questions to no one in particular.

Lily stayed overnight for observation at the Northwest Medical Center. Either the violent yank of her hair or the subsequent fall to the floor resulted in a mild concussion. I was more than a little anxious entering the hospital, even more so as we stood patiently as the elevator climbed its way to her floor.

When we arrived, Lily greeted us with a smile, and the boys walked cautiously to the bed. Jackson handed the flowers to her, and she thanked him profusely. He returned to our side glowing a bright red and stood just behind me. Keller handed her a single flower, and she beamed up at him. He smiled crookedly in return and put his fingers in his mouth, of course.

I greeted Mr. Carlisle with a firm handshake. "Hello, sir. I'm Grant Taldo. This is my wife Kathryn and our two kids, Jackson and Keller."

He returned the shake with a tight-lipped smile and introduced himself. "I'm Dan Carlisle. This is my wife Rosa." The woman at Lily's bedside nodded a similarly tight-lipped smile and said, "Pleasure to meet you."

"Lily," I began with a bit of hesitation, but she held up a hand to forestall me.

"Mr. Taldo." She stared at me with a very adult expression despite her youth. "Please do not apologize. That man made his own choices. I could never blame you or your family for his actions. You have always been kind and fair to me, and if I'm being completely honest, I like your children quite a bit."

I smiled at her and laughed, relief washed over me, and by the look on Kathryn's face, she felt the same way.

"I'll admit that I'm relieved to hear that, Lily. But I'm still sorry for what happened to you." I wasn't sure if should tell her that I saw almost the whole thing on the cameras; a small part of me saw that as an invasion of her privacy. I wanted her to keep some of it to herself. Should it come up, I'd share, but otherwise, I'd act none the wiser.

"I accept your apology, Mr. Taldo. I expect to watch the boys next time you have a sitter, if you still need one."

I laughed with relief at her resilience. "As long as I get the go-ahead from the Head Honcho, then I'm sure we can work something out."

Dan Carlisle's tight-lipped smile from before was gone, and he was grinning in good humor alongside Rosa. I was glad to see that. I can't imagine the fear that shackled their minds as they spoke with the police and heard the story from Lily herself.

I made small talk with Dan and Rosa while Kathryn filled Lily in on the "fun" the boys had after we returned home to a squad of police cars blocking our road.

Dan had grown up on the west coast and met Rosa on a trip to El Salvador. They fell in love and eventually Rosa moved to America to be his wife. Dan was in banking, and Rosa worked as an office manager for a local hospital. They were a sweet couple, and I apologized once more to them before we left. I'd expect the same had our situations been reversed. I know it wasn't *my* fault that Matt Brandhauer decided to traumatize their daughter, but I also knew that she was in our care when it happened, or at least at our home, which was supposed to be safe. Because of that, some of the responsibility had to lie with me.

"Let us know if there's anything else we can do. Please." I'd heard Kathryn tell Lily the same.

Rosa waved it away. "We can take it from here, Grant. Please know that we hold you responsible for nothing. Our Lily is strong; she'll be okay. Even if she isn't, we'll be here for her."

I shook her hand and thanked her for her kind words, then shook Dan's hand and said again, "Let us know." He laughed and winked at me when he said, "Okay, Grant," and we left with smiles and waves.

We dropped by the police station on the way home from the hospital. Jackson's temperament changed from one of excitement to nervousness after he read the giant silver letters adorning the red brick wall of the low building.

"Police Station? What are we doing here?"

"Just dropping something off to one of the detectives. Making sure that Lily is safe." I opened the door and gave him a wink. "I'll be right back."

I asked for Detective Martinez at the front of the building, and few minutes later, a squat familiar man waddled down the hall toward me, his bulk swaying side to side with each step. Maybe it had been the trench coat, but he seemed to have gained twenty pounds overnight.

He reached out a hand, and I took it.

"Mr. Taldo, nice to see you again. What can I do for you?"

"I wanted to bring you this," I said, handing him a USB drive.

"What's this?" He turned it over in his hand and popped the cap off the top.

"That's a recording from all the cameras inside our home. It shows almost every second of what Matt was doing in my house. I think you'll find it very telling."

He looked at me for several seconds before responding slowly. "Thanks, Mr. Taldo."

I nodded and turned to leave.

"Uh, Mr. Taldo?"

"Yes?"

"Why do you have cameras mounted *inside* your home? Usually people have cameras mounted on the outside of their home to catch burglars or porch pirates."

"Well, we don't order too many things, so we don't worry about porch pirates. As for burglars, I think you'll agree that it's a good thing we had them on the inside. If they were outside, you'd miss out on an awful lot of information, regardless of whether or not it's usable in court, or whatever."

The detective nodded in an I-guess-so manner, then held up the USB device. "Thanks again. I'll reach out if I have any questions."

He never did, and I never saw Matt Brandhauer again. I was able to draw my own conclusions from that.

Both boys fell asleep on the way home, most likely still hungover from their late night of excitement. We made the decision to let them sleep and lay down for a nap ourselves, with both of us experiencing just as late of a night.

Instead, they woke up when we got home, and we had a quick snack before the boys were bouncing off the walls.

The afternoon was spent riding bikes around the neighborhood, chasing bugs—and making sure Keller wasn't eating them—through the nearby park. We were enjoying one of the rare days where the previous night's rain cooled the earth instead of turning it into a greenhouse. By the time we went inside for dinner, the boys were covered in grassy sweat and red-faced.

After a dinner of leftovers, Kathryn sent Jackson up to put on his pajamas.

"Can I get Keller ready for bed?" he asked, adopting puppy eyes and a pout.

"Sure, bud, that's fine. But don't let him play with the toothpaste this time, deal?"

Jackson smiled sheepishly and agreed, then held his brother's little hand and guided him upstairs.

"Would you mind putting them to bed tonight?" Kathryn began cleaning up the table as I began cleaning up the dishes. "I would really like a break from the bedtime routine tonight."

I nodded and smiled a winning smile. "Of course, babe. I'll put them to bed."

I found Jackson chasing a fully naked Keller around the room, pull-up in hand and both giggling raucously. Jackson, grateful for the help, allowed me to finish the task while he brushed his own teeth and put his own pajamas on. I snatched Keller as he tried to run out of the room and slipped his jammies over his head. These were printed in such a way that his own head sat atop a bear's body on the shirt, and of course bear legs on the pants.

Keller complained briefly when I sat in the chair to rock him. "Mommy, no Daddy." The pacifier bobbed with each syllable of his baby-faced complaint.

"Yeah, yeah, yeah, I know buddy. But Mommy needs a break, so you get Daddy tonight."

He shook his head, and I laughed at the stoic expression that was only offset by the rhythmic sucking of his pacifier.

He leaned against my chest, and I began reading him *Where The Wild Things Are*, which was always a favorite of Jackson's. I was pleased to hear him chuckle a few times at the gnashing of terrible teeth and roaring of terrible roars, even though they were a little close to a cough. But by the end, his eyelids were drooping dangerously close to sleep. I kissed his cheek and laid him gently in his crib. He fussed a little, but I patted his rump until he quieted and covered him with his knitted blanket, told him he was my favorite, and that was that.

I walked to the large window in his room and gazed down at the street below. I realized that I tended to do this frequently, thinking and working out what I did well and what I should have done better on that day. There was something serene about the view from the second-story windows, the way the sky was just angled lines and treetops as far as the eye could see.

"Daddy?"

Turning contentedly, I saw Jackson standing in the doorway of the jack-and-jill bathroom. He wasn't bleeding.

"Yeah, buddy?"

"Can you tuck me in?"

I smiled. "Of course. Let's go."

Jackson hopped into bed more energetically than I thought possible based on how exhausted he looked at the dinner table.

I sat on the edge of his bed and tucked the covers in around his not-so-little body.

"How's that?"

He smiled and nodded. Then, I saw him bite his lip.

"What is it, bud?"

"Can you tell me more about what happened to Lily?"

I took a deep breath, trying to figure out what the right answer was in the three seconds that it took to exhale it out.

"Yeah, I think I can tell you a little more of it."

"Leave out the scary parts, though. Please."

Nodding, I told him about how someone had come into the house and tried to hurt Lily, but she had been very brave and called the police before he could. I had not wanted to tell him any of the part where Matt Brandhauer had stood not ten feet from we were sitting now and feet from where his brother slept. But it would be a disservice to believe him too young to discuss what he needed to discuss.

"Was that Mr. Matt who did it?"

"It was," I said, nodding once.

"I never liked him." Jackson shivered. "He gave me the creeps."

I smiled knowingly, but it was more of a sad realization that the world was full of creeps, and this was just exposure to the first.

"Yeah, me too." He smiled, and we laughed a little. I didn't want to end on the subject of the "creep," so I tried to turn it around a little. This time, the police were the good guys. And Lily, too. They were here to save the day and protect you boys."

Jackson began to think hard about it, then, "And Mr. Matt was the monster?"

I felt my throat tighten as I said, "That's right, Jackson." It wasn't fair. I don't think it ever would be fair, but it was the way of things. "I'm sorry you had to go through that. I'm sure it was kind of scary."

"That's okay," he said quietly. "It wasn't too bad after the cop lady told me that she was there to make sure we were safe."

I nodded again. "Yeah, that's their job. And mine. And Mommy's, too."

"I'm tired," he said without preamble and closed his eyes.

I kissed his forehead and told him he was my favorite, then left his room.

Kathryn was on the couch with her phone in hand when I descended the stairs.

"Everyone good?" she asked looking up briefly.

"Yep, both are asleep. Or close enough."

"Thanks for doing that tonight. I think my heart and brain just needed a break."

I reached for her hand, taking a risk that she might not put hers in mine. "Happy to give you a break, Kat."

But her hand closed around mine, and I felt myself relax. We were going to be okay.

"Hey, I was thinking."

"Uh-oh," she said with a wry smile.

"Ha-ha." I said tonelessly. "Seriously, I was thinking about maybe talking with Mitch Callum again."

Kathryn dropped her phone into her lap and looked at me with an are-you-kidding-me expression. "I thought you said he was a little off his rocker?"

I shrugged. "He is. But he's also got a better handle on this. And having experienced it, I think that he may be able to provide some insight into the situation for us. And don't you want to make sure we're doing everything we can for the boys?"

This second look she gave me was more of the are-you-sure-that's-the-direction-you-want-to-take-variety.

"Okay, point taken on that. But I don't think it could hurt."

"Fine. But I don't actually think he knows what he's talking about."

That was fine with me because she didn't actually know the half of it.

The next day Jackson was back at school. Kathryn and Keller went to the park to play with some of the other moms and kids, so I had the house to myself. Deciding to be very adult, I opted to work a bit. But not before giving Mitch a call.

It rang twice and then, "Hello, Grant."

"Oh," I said, momentarily taken by surprise. "Hi, Mitch. How'd you know it was me?"

He chuckled. "I got your message before. I just... I just been busy's all. I saved your number in my phone last time you called. Now I got two numbers."

It was my turn to chuckle. "Well, I'm honored."

"You calling about something specific or just shoot the breeze?"

"Well..." He seemed busy, but I knew better. At least I hoped I did. "Kat and I are still figuring this thing out. We haven't made much progress, but I wanted to ask you what you would do differently. I know you're aware of everything going on with Jackson and Keller, but..." I trailed off. This guy was unreliable at best. Did I want to divulge the biggest secret in my family to him?

"Well? Out with it." His voice held a small bit of gruff amusement.

"Jackson's nosebleeds have gotten worse, and you remember my younger son's ... illnesses." Was I really going to say it? "Well, we... we think they're connected somehow."

Silence was the only answer for several heartbeats. I heard him breathing on the other end and then a thoughtful, "Hmm."

I breathed a sigh of relief. At least my admission wasn't answered by a zealot hearing a disciple's encouragement. "Yeah, that's about where we're at, too."

"What gives you the idea that they're connected?"

I rubbed the back of my neck with my free hand. "Well, the nosebleeds seem to happen around the same time that Keller—that's the younger—begins to feel better. We don't have confirmation. It's really more like a hunch."

"Yeah, that's sometimes all we get." Again with several beats of silence. "What's your wife think?" Straight to it, just like last time. I could appreciate that about him.

"She is ... hesitant. She doesn't want to believe it, but we didn't get any answers with the doctors."

He scoffed, and I remembered a little too late what a sore subject that was to him. I decided to take a few minutes and explain where I was at. As a fellow father, he'd at least understand the mental load I was under in trying to balance the health of both kids with worrying what the increased frequency of nosebleeds to illnesses could mean.

"That's some heavy stuff, man," he said when I'd finished.

I sighed, feeling a little lighter. "Yes. Yes, it is."

I heard a scratching sound, and I could almost see him rubbing the stubble on his cheek. "You asked earlier what I'd do differently. You still wanna know?"

"I—" I wasn't sure if I did or not. Would I be met with zealotry or lucidity?

"Sure. Yeah, I want to know."

Without any hesitation, he said, "I'd have loved them more."

I felt like my brain had taken a hard left. "What do you mean?"

"I wouldn't have worried so much about the things I couldn't change. Andreya was upset about how much I was trying to 'solve the problem,' but you know, now that I'm on the other side of it all, I can see how much time I spent away from them both. Maybe—" His voice cracked, a deep tremble of emotion followed when he began talking again. "Maybe things would have turned out differently for us if I would have just spent my time loving on them before they left me. In their own ways, of course."

I can say without any irony at all, that I had not expected that.

"So you think that's what I should do?"

Hesitation this time. "Well, that wouldn't be fair to either of us, would it? I can say all day what would be good for me. But that doesn't mean it's the same for you. I've been thinking about our last interaction, and I'm a little embarrassed by it. I've since taken down most of that stuff in the garage, and I actually called Andreya to apologize. She was ... suspicious, at first." He laughed, then. It was mostly good-natured, but I could hear a tone of bitterness within it. "She asked if I was plannin' on dyin' any time soon. I assumed she was really asking if I was calling to apologize before offing myself." He laughed again in the same tone, and I suspected that perhaps the thought had crossed his mind despite his assurances to the contrary when we last spoke. "Took a while to convince her."

A sudden thought struck me, and I figured it would be the best option for everyone.

"What are you doing for dinner next Tuesday?"

I heard the smile through the phone, and it warmed my heart. "You know, I don't think I've got any plans. I'll have to check my schedule." He chuckled at the joke.

"Why don't you come over and eat with us? I'll send you my address. Maybe we can talk about this in person finally. Maybe understand it a little more."

"That sounds real nice, Grant. I'd love that. It's been a while since someone invited me over, especially after ... you know."

"Yeah, I bet. We'd love to have you."

"That so?"

It was my turn to smile. "Well, *I* would. And Kathryn will come around."

"That sounds alright to me. Just let me know what works for you and your family. I don't want to intrude or throw a wrench into things."

"No, of course not. I'll talk with Kathryn, and then I'll let you know. And thanks, Mitch. Thanks for hearing me out and talking to me. Doesn't feel so lonely, now."

"Hm. Yeah, that's what we all need. You let me know. I ain't busy 'cept when I get a wild hair to do some gardening."

Laughing, I said, "Alright, that's fine. Talk to you soon."

After hanging up, the reality of having to convince Kathryn that Mitch would be joining us for dinner soon hit me. I hoped it would easy, but I knew better. I knew *her* better.

CHAPTER 20

"**A**bsolutely not, Grant." Kathryn slammed a plastic cup into the sink with much more force than was necessary, causing excess water from something to splash onto the counter.

"Kathryn, think about it—" But she didn't let me get started.

"I don't need to think about it! The last time you were there earlier this year, you told me he was a grieving father that had lost his grip on reality. I understood; I said it was fine but that I didn't want anything else to do with him. What did you two talk about last night? You're telling me that you want to ask his *opinion* on something? Like actually take it seriously?"

Well when you put it like that, I wanted to say, but instead opted for, "In not so many words, yes."

Exasperated, she threw her hands in the air and grabbed an empty bowl from the table. Keller tottered in the living room, coughing and drawing in wheezing breaths between.

"If there's even a slim chance that someone else can help, doesn't it seem worth it?"

She glared at me, then. "Don't you dare hijack the moral high road by implying that I'm not willing to do everything I can to keep our children safe."

I put my hands up as if I'd touched a hot stove. "That's not at all what I'm saying. All I'm saying is that I'd like to simply talk to him face to face, all three of us. That's it. I just want to hear him out after we get the chance to explain what's going on. Explain everything. Okay?"

During my speech, she'd begun cleaning the counters with a hand towel. Now, she tossed it on her shoulder, tossed the hair out of her eyes, and stared me down. "When, Grant? We don't have time for anything else. You've already taken time off from work, I've taken time off from work—which has consequences, you know. But sure. Fine. Mitch can come over for dinner. But I swear to god, Grant, if you start talking crazy, I'll take you out behind the barn and put you down."

I smiled, which was infinitely better than an outright laugh, but Kathryn didn't crack a smile before returning her ire to the counters.

The day continued on without much in the way of conversation. She technically had said yes, but I knew what she really did was tell me that she didn't want to say anything definitive. Not yet.

Over a cup of coffee later that afternoon, however, she grabbed my hand and said, "Grant, I think Mitch should come."

In one of the biggest underdog stories of the century, Kathryn agreed. Of course, I was suspicious at first, but when she explained that she'd done some thinking, and even though she didn't want to admit it, I had been right. I asked her to repeat that part just for good measure and she did, rolling her eyes.

"I guess I just didn't understand what you were feeling. I suppose there's a part of me that's hoping it will be an absolute disaster, and I'll be here to witness it. Just a small part

of me, though." She said the last bit in a tone that was only half-joking.

I called Mitch to confirm the date and time. He agreed and asked what he could bring. I told him to bring a bottle of wine, if he felt so inclined.

Tuesday rolled around without any preamble. Jackson, thankfully, didn't have any nosebleeds leading up to the date. Keller was under the weather, as usual, but was in high spirits. He tottered around the playroom with the sitter—Lily, again, who had fully recovered—and Jackson.

When Mitch arrived, I introduced him to Kathryn, who to her credit, embraced him in a warm hug after taking a bottle of wine from him and placing it on the counter. Mitch was taken aback by her warmth and thanked her profusely for the welcome. He apologized for his "charismatic" first impression, and she waved it away, saying, "It's all water under the bridge as far as I'm concerned." She gave me a wink over her shoulder.

Thankfully, dinner wasn't a disaster, as Kathryn had partially hoped. We avoided conversation about kids almost entirely, except when our own needed something.

Mitch was very forthcoming about his life with Andreya and their daughter. He skirted the end of her life with as much grace as was possible. Kathryn was enthusiastic when the conversation turned to parenthood and pleasant memories. Mitch was a wonderful guest. And when we ran out of dissimilar topics, the conversation naturally turned toward the common ground that brought us together in the first place.

"It does seem suspicious," Mitch said after we gave a bit more detail about the way Keller's sickness and Jackson's nosebleeds coincided. While we didn't want to *hide* things from Jackson, we also didn't want to scare him. The conversation had become more serious, and while Keller wouldn't understand it, Jackson certainly would.

"That was our thought," Kathryn said after calling Jackson into the kitchen. She handed a sippee cup of water to Keller and asked Jackson if he and Keller could watch cartoons in the living room "while the adults talked." He skipped away, gleefully corralling his little brother toward the couch.

"In your readings of similar cases, did anything like this crop up?" I wasn't sure how to ask what I felt in my heart. "Anything about a sick brother or sister? Or even a sick mom or dad? I mean, I don't even know the boundaries of this."

Mitch rubbed his chin. "I can't say I've run across something like this. At least not in the few cases I've read." He sat up a little straighter and met our gazes. "That's not to say something like this hasn't happened, you understand. I could always do a little more research."

"How many cases of children and nosebleeds did you find or read through?" Kathryn looked at him curiously.

Mitch took a deep breath in and held it, thinking. The sounds of cartoon crashes and horns drifted in from the living room accompanied by the giggles and whispers of our boys. When Mitch finally spoke, it seemed as if he was trying to downplay the effort he put into it all.

"I had a lot of time on my hands, and it wasn't hard to find things online about kids getting hurt. The media eats that stuff up, trust me. In the end," he sighed and puffed out his cheeks, "I looked through probably two hundred articles. The ones that I kept totaled close to fifty or so." He looked at me. "Those were the ones on my garage wall."

"What did you find in your research, Mitch?"

We talked then for another hour or so. Kathryn, who was only slightly less suspicious of Mitch's intentions, talked animatedly with him about his findings. Many children in the articles were the only child of the family, there weren't any others who had a sibling with reports of chronic illness. Mitch and Kathryn were discussing the similarities of one particular case in Georgia when I stopped them.

"Kathryn, I'm going to put the boys to bed. You and Mitch keep chatting; I'll be back in fifteen minutes or so."

Mitch nodded, and I kissed Kathryn on the top of the head.

I found both boys snuggled up and nearly asleep on the couch. Keller lay across Jackson's lap, snoring contentedly despite his congestion. Jackson's eyes were drifting closed when I said, "Hey Jack, let's get to bed."

He nodded groggily, and I lifted Keller to my chest, cradling him in my left arm. His head lolled into my neck, and I could feel sticky snot smear coldly beneath my jaw and ear. I grimaced. He was sweet, but also a little gross. I think that's an apt description for kids in general, though, you know?

Jackson lifted his arms, and I cradled his bottom in my elbow, lifting him to my shoulder with more effort than I expected. His head lolled the same way, this time without a snot streak.

"Can you carry me to bed?" Jackson mumbled into my shoulder.

I knew all too well that he was getting to the age where carrying him to bed was not only difficult for me, but something he'd desire less and less. Soon I'd be waking him up and simply helping him to the stairs; he'd do the rest on his own. One day, I'd carry him to bed for the last time and neither of us would know it. Maybe it would be tonight.

"Yeah, buddy."

Jackson's room was the first stop, and he was already asleep by the time I laid him onto his bed. With Keller holding one arm hostage, it was tricky to pull the covers over him, but I managed, like every father does.

I bent and kissed Jackson's forehead, "You're my favorite," and then walked to Keller's room. But before settling him into the crib, I pressed my face against his slightly feverish head. A wave of mild sorrow washed across me as I realized that I hadn't had much opportunity to hold him lately. Life and work took up all the hours, and suddenly, he was two. He wasn't as little as I remembered, and I could feel myself getting a little choked up. Was that regret that was creeping up my throat? I had never participated much in the rat race, but I had to make a living for my family. Was my time being spent well? I wasn't sure. Now, I'm even less-so.

I remembered walking around Keller's room in-between feedings during those first few months, the roughest of them. Kathryn was exhausted from feeding him and worrying about him all day and night. The few hours of sleep she was able to get in the middle of the night were the only thing that kept her sane. I took the night shift since he didn't seem to want to eat as often, and I could adjust my work schedule much easier.

I would walk in a circle, slowly swaying my body from side to side as one hand cradled his head and the other patted his bottom. Some nights I would hum, other nights I would shush in rhythm with my steps, and sometimes we'd both be quiet. Keller's nearly white hair was wispy then. Now, he looked very much like a little boy. I wondered when that happened. So many people would tell us to "enjoy it while you can" or remind us that "it's gone in the blink of an eye." I *knew* it on an intellectual level; I *knew* that time was fleeting. But to have it seem to pass before my very eyes in this moment was almost unbearable. The recent fears for Jackson had compounded our fears for Keller, as well. What were we going to do? Were

we going to have to *choose* which of our children would live? Surely not. No, there would be another way. Jackson's nose-bleeds could be sickness-related for all we knew. Keller's increases in health could be circumstantial.

Even as I said it in the middle of the room, slowly rocking Keller's sleeping form in the mingling lights from the mobile beside his crib, I knew it was a lie. I wanted to believe it so badly, wanted to allow myself to believe it, to jump in and make it true. But it wasn't. I knew it wasn't, and perhaps that's what scared me the most.

I hugged Keller tightly to myself and took a deep breath. They say that babies have a certain smell, and it's a good one. I wasn't even sure of that. Toddlers have a smell, too, and it's usually a mix of dirt and wet diapers. But not tonight. Keller smelled like home when I kissed his little head. I was reluctant to put him in his crib. Reluctant to let today's little boy become tomorrow's slightly older little boy. Like the biblical story of Abraham and Isaac, we sacrifice them. Each night when we put them on the altar of sleep, they're sacrificed for the version that replaces them in the morning—hopefully a better version, a version that learned from the lessons of the previous day. An endless cycle, incremental forward progress. The inevitable evolution called "growing up," cataloged in the pictures taken over the years, or the hashes on the doorframe inching further from the ground. Today's kids are gone forever, replaced by tomorrow's new and improved version.

I laid him reluctantly in the bed. Bless him, he was amazing. I kissed his wispy hair and whispered, "You're my favorite." Then said goodbye to the Keller that lived today.

With that unhappy thought rattling around in my brain, I made my way back downstairs where Mitch and Kathryn continued talking about a case in Michigan. Mitch was explaining a few similarities to Jackson's case, namely the progression of nosebleeds over time.

"It seemed to have started in a similar way, maybe a little slower. Just a few nosebleeds here and there, almost nothing noteworthy that the parents remembered only after the fact. Then they started increasing in frequency to something like two times a week. The kid was a little younger than Jackson, maybe seven, I think.

"The parents, thinking it was something to do with the house or air, decided to move. This was only a few years ago, mind, so I was able to call 'em and talk to 'em. They said that after they moved, it stopped. They moved out to the country, a hundred miles outside of Flint, and hadn't had a problem since. 'Course I said I was a reporter following up on it to get to talk to 'em, but they didn't mind. Their case didn't have a bad ending like some," he gestured to himself, "but they said it musta been mold or somethin'."

Kathryn nodded. "Yeah, that was my first thought as well, to be honest. But the house is only a couple years past the inspection we had before moving in. There's no way the problem grew that bad in two years, surely?"

I shook my head. "I doubt it. Cases where the black mold has taken over the basement and stretched into the rest of the house through the walls take five or ten years of persistent problems."

There was silence for a minute, and then I asked Mitch, "What do you think we should do?"

He shrugged. "Honestly, y'all, I don't know. Keep an eye on your kids. Make sure they're safe at all times. Have the house checked out again. Who knows? Maybe the original inspector missed something. I hope that's the case for y'all."

He stared down at his coffee for a minute, the calm within the house felt out of place after being filled with the noise of children of the day.

"I heard about your neighbor, Grant. Kathryn told me about it. How are the boys holding up?"

I shrugged. "Honestly, better than me. I find myself checking the doors, worrying about them almost constantly. They don't seem to have been affected much at all." I turned to Kathryn. "What do you think?"

"Yeah, Grant's right. I think he and I are having a harder time believing it happened in comparison to how the boys are dealing with it."

"That's good," said Mitch softly. "I'm glad they're doin' okay."

He drained his coffee in a final slurp and said, "I better head home. Isn't a short drive, you know."

"Of course," said Kathryn, and we stood up.

"Thanks for coming, Mitch. Appreciate your time."

"Yep, happy to help. And you let me know if there's anything I can do."

"We will." Kathryn surprised us both by reaching up to hug Mitch. "I'm glad you came."

We waved goodbye to Mitch as he walked toward his maroon Oldsmobile.

Kathryn gave me a glance when the door closed. "It wasn't as bad as I thought, honestly. And as much as it galls me to say it," she hesitated and rolled her eyes, "I'm glad you invited him over. I feel better about it, now. Maybe we aren't so alone out here."

That made me feel particularly good about myself, but it didn't last very long.

Kathryn began to walk away from me, but over her shoulder she said, "I still don't like the idea that there isn't a solution, though. I want to take Jackson to the hospital and see if they can cauterize his blood vessels."

CHAPTER 21

Getting an appointment with an Ear, Nose, and Throat doctor wasn't as difficult as we'd anticipated. We put our names on the cancellation list at the Children's Hospital and, a day later, received a call with an opening that evening.

Kathryn and I waited after checking in at the children's hospital front desk. The woman there was nice enough but forgettable. I was so anxious that I barely remembered giving her the information so that we could check in. Keller wriggled in my arms as I hugged him close to me. Jackson clung to Kathryn's leg and looked all of his nine years, that cusp of becoming a "big kid" replaced by the fear and anxiety of the unknown.

After sitting for a few minutes, Jackson asked if he could play with Keller, who had found some tinker toy and was moving different shapes along its twisted colored metal bar.

"Sure, honey." Kathryn smiled and nodded at him, and we watched the two boys play eagerly together as the evening sun suffused the waiting room with a dull orange glow.

There are occasions that I know occur between husband and wife where she may ask what he's thinking and his response of "nothing" is met with doubt. It's true, though. There are times when my mind is completely blank, devoid of thought. Not because there's nothing to think about but because I turned it off. In my case, Kathryn is quick to point out all of the things that she has to think about. In our current state, however, my mind was flitting between multiple subjects: fear for Jackson, worry about Keller, anxiety about what the future would hold. All of it. Based on her own facial expression, her mind was bumping against something similar.

Hopefully, the cauterizing would make the nosebleeds stop. Kathryn and I had spoken with our family doctor, and he'd sent in the recommended paperwork and signed off on it before we'd finished the call. Kathryn was quick to mention the nosebleed log in her little black book, including some new entries. He was surprised by the number of nosebleeds, so it wasn't hard to convince him.

That still didn't explain the relationship between Keller and Jackson, though. If the nosebleeds stopped, would Keller continue to improve incrementally? Or were the nosebleeds a requirement? It was impossible to know, but we had to try. We had to try *something*.

I'd mentioned it to Mitch, and he said it was a good thought and to keep him updated. I promised I would. Mitch's zealotry that I'd witnessed at first had been replaced with a kind of sage-like temperament. Admittedly, I did see him in that light, now. He'd been through what we were going through now and could offer advice. He'd asked about Kathryn and our relationship, but I changed the subject. He knew it was taking a toll on us, and I assumed it was because he knew separation or divorce wasn't off the table, despite what may happen to Jackson.

A chunky-sounding sneeze brought my gaze to Keller. Jackson ran to the counter to get him a Kleenex before Kathryn or I could even move. It was so strange to see their relationship

grow and bloom in the best kind of way and know that, deep down, they might be better off apart. Or separate. I don't know, but a different way than they were at the moment.

I chuckled as Jackson held the dirty Kleenex at arm's length and searched for a trash can. Kathryn rolled her eyes and asked for it, which Jackson relinquished easily. She stuffed it neatly into her purse, and Jackson and I exchanged looks, then he mimed gagging. Kathryn smiled tightly and said, "It's just snot. I've wiped worse from both of your faces and one of your butts."

Jackson straightened up and pointed at me, and I pointed at him, laughing. Kathryn's smile was a little more genuine this time. I laughed for Jackson's benefit, but a part of me was irritated. I wasn't sure why, but maybe the stress was starting to alter the way I viewed her. She was a good wife; she was a loving mother. My own stress was probably getting in the way, and I didn't know how to stop it.

She caught my eye and the smile slipped a little. I looked back at the boys, hoping that all this would be over soon.

"Jackson Taldo?" A voice rang out through the waiting room.

Our heads turned in unison, and Kathryn stood to begin ushering the kids toward the nurse who'd called us.

We were led through several doors and hallways, the nurse making small talk that we answered with half attention. Keller tottered beside Jackson, who walked slowly enough to hold his hand.

Kathryn reached out and grabbed my hand, surprising me so much that I jumped.

"Sorry," I muttered.

"It's fine. I just need you to calm me down a little."

I squeezed her hand and whispered in her ear, "Everything is going to be okay, Kat."

She flashed a smile at me that was probably meant to convey gratefulness, but it was too obvious a mask to be heartfelt.

I squeezed her hand again and rubbed the back of her hand with my thumb. "Let's hope this works."

Nodding, she followed the doctor and kids into a room that felt larger than a standard room. There was a curtain on a track that was pulled around to cover the bed. The nurse began taking Jackson's vitals and writing the results on her tablet while making small talk the whole time.

"How are you today?"

"Fine."

"That's a cool shirt. You like dinosaurs?"

"Yes."

"What's your favorite?"

"Quetzalcoatlus."

"Wow, I've never heard of that one."

"It's a flying one."

He was nervous. I'm sure Kathryn could see it, too. He answered the questions but didn't offer much else.

When the nurse was done, she told us the doctor would be in soon to perform the procedure. Since it was an outpatient procedure, we'd be nearby while they cauterized his poor little nose, and then we'd go home together.

While applying a small topical anesthetic to his nose, she explained that the procedure wouldn't hurt at all. She tried to give details of the procedure in a kid-friendly manner by picking up a few tools and explaining their purpose. Admittedly, she did a great job. She'd probably done this a thousand times, and I could tell. After explaining the doctor's tools, she put her own down and made some notes on the table. I pictured Jackson coming home with a giant gauze bandage on his nose and said, "Jack, you remember that book we used to read about the daddy bear getting chased by bees so he had to jump in the pond?"

He nodded distractedly.

"The only problem was that the bear had to breath and so he left his nose above the water. He came home with that big bandage on his nose, remember?"

A nod.

"Maybe you'll look like him?"

The attempt was only mildly successful. He smiled a little, but both the nurse and Kathryn gave me disapproving stares. The nurse even said, "Dad, that's silly."

Jackson's smile widened, and he pointed at me as if I'd gotten in trouble. Kathryn surprised me again by rubbing my back affectionately. I could appreciate the gesture... I hoped she realized I was just as nervous as she was, but I didn't want our kids to be freaked out by both of us clamming up. One could hope, as she always said.

The doctor came in and after a brief introduction, showed Jackson the tool he would use. It resembled a miniature soldering iron to me. Then, he explained the procedure to Kathryn and me; it would take no more than half an hour. Jackson's nose was already being numbed thanks to the nurse applying the anesthetic.

"I'll just stick it up there, and with the help of this tiny camera," he tapped a small divot in the metal pipe, "heat the ends of your blood vessels. This will hopefully stop the nosebleeds, and you'll finally have some peace." At least, that was the goal.

The doctor asked one of us to sit outside the curtain, which made Jackson immediately stiffen. Kathryn and I both put a reassuring hand on each of his shoulders. "I'll be right outside this, just a few steps away," she said, indicating the tall green curtain.

He nodded and gulped. "I'll sit with you while it happens, Mr. Bear." I hoped to get a smile out of him with that, but he just nodded again.

The doctor smiled pleasantly at us as he closed the curtain behind Kathryn and Keller. I heard the machines beeping and whirring to life and held tightly to Jackson's sweating palm. To be fair, I wasn't sure who was sweating more.

The doctor wheeled his round stool to the other side of the bed, the black cord of the tool trailing behind him like a thin black snake. He told Jackson to close his eyes and that it shouldn't hurt at all. If he did feel something, he just had to raise his hand and they'd put more anesthetic on it. Jackson nodded and closed his eyes tightly.

I squeezed his hand, and he clasped my hand back, not relaxing his hold at all.

The procedure was relatively fast, with only a few breaks between when the doc would give Jackson's nose a moment or two of rest. It bled a little, which seemed odd to me considering the procedure, but I had been reassured it was completely normal. The long silver tool went into his nose much farther than I thought it should, followed by a few wisps of smoke, and then it would come out again. The doctor would watch the screen that displayed the insides of Jackson's nose in hi-definition. I wondered if Jackson could smell his own skin burning but didn't want to distract him. I hoped he didn't, but I knew that he probably could. I could, and it was not pleasant.

After both nostrils had been given a once-over, the doctor sat back and turned his machine off. "They both look good. I've cauterized a lot of noses in my life, but this one was probably the one that needed it most. If I didn't know better, I'd say that he'd gotten into something and had an allergic reaction to it. His nerves were incredibly swollen and seemed ready to burst at the slightest touch. It's no wonder they bled so much."

The curtain had been pulled back by this point and Kathryn stood holding Keller on her hip. "Is that bad? That his nose was like that?"

The doctor shook his head vehemently. "Oh no, not at all. Every kid is different. Some don't have a nosebleed their entire life. Others," he indicated Jackson sitting up in the bed, "have nosebleeds frequently. It's just the way it is." He shrugged helplessly.

After waiting a few more minutes to make sure nothing else would come loose and that Jackson's sense of smell was returning, we thanked the doctor and left. There was no giant bandage, much to the disappointment of my earlier joke. Instead, he had both nostrils stuffed with gauze and strict instructions to leave them in tonight.

By the time we pulled into the driveway, Jackson and Keller were joking in the backseat, with Keller reaching for the gauze plugs and Jackson pretending to sneeze them into his hands. Despite his sniffling, sneezing, and gagging cough, Keller's laughter was contagious, and all four of us were chuckling along with him.

Dinner was a quick round of macaroni, green beans, and chicken nuggets. Both boys brushed their teeth and Kathryn read a book to Jackson while I rocked Keller. It was a nice change of pace, but I could feel the anxiety of the night begin to creep upon me. What if Jackson had another nosebleed? Would it undo everything the doctor did today?

And the worst thought of all, that wouldn't go away—what if Keller was the reason Jackson was bleeding every night?

I couldn't let myself go down that path, there were too many "what ifs" for my liking, and it would do no good.

Keller fell asleep despite several coughing fits and one gag that sounded very close to vomiting. He rested his head on my chest, and his rattling breath was unnerving in the quiet. I turned the sound machine on to "white noise" after laying him in his bed, hoping that the constant noise would help him relax.

Jackson had snuggled up to Kathryn and was fast asleep, the gauze plugs still stuffed into his nose. She had her arm around him and smiled pleasantly when I looked at her.

I hesitated before leaving the room, unsure of what I wanted to say.

"We're okay, aren't we?" I didn't know what else to say but figured that was a good place to start.

She hesitated before answering and said, "I think we're in a bad spot right now. But it won't last forever. Let's just get through these next few nights and see if the nosebleeds stop, okay?"

I nodded, unsatisfied with the answer and feeling the sulky part of me wanting to take control.

"You don't think that Keller's sickness is related, do you?"

She took a breath and looked away from me. "I don't know. I want to believe they aren't related, but..." She shrugged. "Who knows?"

"If they are," I began, but didn't finish, uncertain of what the consequences would be.

"I don't want to think about that, Grant. Please don't make me."

I nodded and left the room, but I knew she'd already been thinking about it; her foul mood all but screamed it.

CHAPTER 22

O n Jackson's birthday, July 26th, the sky opened and
released the rain that had been threatening for several days. We hung the same multi-colored "Happy Birthday"
banner we did every year. He opened a few presents after
devouring a dozen miniature donuts, and we snuggled up on
the couch to watch a movie. It wasn't much. Having a birthday
in the summer had always been a bummer for me as well, since
all your friends are gone on vacation or just plain busy. But he
said he enjoyed it, and so did I.

Now, later in the evening, both boys were sleeping contentedly in their beds while a storm brooded outside. Lightning
flashed in the distance, illuminating the dark angry clouds that
stretched across the horizon. A low rumble followed a few seconds later and the windows rattled lightly. Summer storms in
the dark were always a little spooky, but this one seemed to
bring with it an extra dose of unease that increased each time
the thunder grumbled in the atmosphere. I had a clear view
through the tall windows of the living room and enjoyed the
sight. As much as I could in my current state, at least.

Kathryn sat at the other end of the couch. She'd been
broody all day, with off-hand comments and snide remarks.
I knew better than to ask if she was on her period, but I had

caught myself multiple times wanting to say it out of spite. I was becoming quick to judge her, but I recognized that I was also kind of an asshole.

Our sleeplessness was making itself known in frustration and anger over little things. But they were all piling up, and soon, the pile would topple over and scatter its contents.

Since his nose had been cauterized, Jackson had four nosebleeds over the course of three weeks. We were at our wits' end. We weren't going to re-cauterize them, and we certainly weren't going to take him to a hospital that suspected us of abusing him. The boys would be taken from us—and worse, each other—and we suspected that would be the worse of the two.

Add on to the fact that each time Jackson's nose bled, Keller was wide awake and immediately better. There was no way they weren't connected, and I was terrified that one night a nosebleed would result in Jackson's death.

The fake fire within the glass fireplace cast flickering shadows across the living room floor and on our faces. Several times I tried to open a conversation, only to have Kathryn give a one-word response or no response at all. The latter were hard to handle, and I bristled at each response. We had to talk about it, I just knew we didn't want to. Neither of us wanted to. We suspected the outcome, and it was a loss all around.

Thunder rattled the windows, a little louder and deeper this time.

"Kat," I began once more, hesitantly.

It seemed like she made special effort to avoid looking at me, finding the fire much more interesting.

"Kat, we have to figure something out." I tried not to plead.

This time she did look at me, and I wished she hadn't. The cold desperation and anxious fear I saw in her eyes broke my heart, and I hated myself for it.

She pursed her lips and looked back at the fire, which highlighted the tears in her eyes with an umber glow.

"We can—"

"No," she said, still looking at the fire, her voice thick and controlled.

"Kathryn, we—" I tried again.

"I said no."

I wanted to tell her that I didn't want to, either. I knew what she was feeling, inasmuch as a husband can. But I also knew that if we did nothing, our boy would die. I wasn't willing to risk that to avoid a hard conversation.

"I know you don't want to, Kathryn. But Jackson—"

"Don't you think I know what you're going to say?" The tears were streaming down her face now, but her voice was hard as steel. "Don't you think I know that we're in a lose-lose situation? Don't you think I wish I knew what to do here? I'm so completely lost and afraid and scared that no matter what choice I make, it's the wrong one?"

"Babe, it's not just up to you. I'm—"

"Of course, you're here, too. But your choice is automatically to make sure Jackson is okay while Keller wastes away. Your only thought is that Jackson gets better. It feels like you barely even care that Keller is getting better."

I stopped, momentarily stunned. The anger that had been churning in my stomach flared at the same time as a flash of lightning lit up the living room in harsh, white lines. "At the cost of Jackson's life!" I could barely believe she was taking this stance.

"We don't know that!" She was nearly yelling, now.

"We absolutely know that, Kathryn! Or are you blind? Just a few nights ago, and even times before that, you saw it with your own eyes, though maybe you didn't want to admit it. Jackson had a nosebleed, and Keller *magically* gets better in the exact instant. Not only that," I continued, unable to stop, "but you said that he was awake even before the nosebleed. He was looking at Jackson through the wall while I was dealing with Jackson, who was trembling and bleeding all over the place."

She wiped her eyes and sniffed. "We don't know that. He could have just been listening to you." She didn't sound like she even believed that.

"Kathryn," I said, dripping with doubt.

She turned to me then, cheeks flushed and tears pouring down her face. "Grant," she said, trying to mimic me with sarcasm and succeeding only in sounding defiantly heartbroken. "You've always loved Jackson more. You love Keller, I know. But your love for him is different. It's like he's your favorite, and Keller just gets seconds."

I blinked and did my best to not show the hurt on my face. "My..." *favorite*? Surely she didn't just say that. But she had. I heard it again in my head. I wish I could say I approached the situation with calm and cool logic, but when your heart's involved, logic takes a hike.

Thunder rumbled, and I felt it in my chest.

"I can't believe you just said that. I suppose that would make Keller your favorite, wouldn't it?"

She scoffed. "That's absurd."

"Not any more absurd than saying that Jackson is my favorite." She didn't respond as she stared into the fire. "But you know what?" Apparently even *I* didn't know I had more to say. "It doesn't matter at all. I can't imagine my life with *either* of them gone from it."

She rolled her eyes and shook her head, her hair shaking lightly across her shoulders. Rain began to patter the windows with large, angry drops.

"Fine. You know what? I would save Keller. I'd save Jackson if I could, too. But if I had to choose, and it looks like we have to, I choose Keller."

This time I did gasp. "You'd choose to let Keller slowly leach the life from our oldest?" I couldn't believe it. I couldn't allow myself to believe that she was that coarse, that cruel.

"Oh, and you're so high and mighty yourself?" She turned to me, and I braced myself against her rage. "You say that like what you'd allow isn't just as bad. You'd take Jackson so that Keller would simply waste away, getting worse and worse until his body broke down and refused to keep working. *You'd* be the one leaching his life away, then." She stabbed a trembling finger at my chest.

I didn't want to hear it but was guilty of the harsh rebuke. She was right. That was what hurt the most. We both knew we were in an unwinnable position. If we have to choose—when we had to choose, one of the kids would die. I would choose Jackson, and knowing that decision condemned Keller to death twisted my insides in an excruciating way.

The room went white as lightning flashed outside. Almost immediately a clap of thunder soared across the sky and through the house. We both jumped, choosing to ignore one another instead of laughing together, which is what we would have done under normal circumstances.

Why would it come to this? How could it possibly have come to this? All those trips to the hospital for both boys, and they amounted to nothing. Keller's scans came back clear; he was just prone to illness. Jackson's scans came back clear, as well; he was just prone to nosebleeds. The doctors seemed so unconcerned, and now it had come to this. Their two parents, unequipped and ignorant of so much, were required to choose who lived and died.

The rain was lit outside by another flash of lightning. It was a downpour, raining cats and dogs, my dad would say. The street was covered, and in that half-second image of everything lit in a silvery wash, I could see the neighbor's cat standing on the sidewalk across the street.

In a strange way, didn't we choose our children's lives for them? We conceived a child and chose to let it live? Isn't this just the second part of that choice?

"This is just so fucked up," she whimpered and buried her head in her hands. A deep vibration and clatter of the windows ended the discussion, thunder rolling through the sky unhindered.

CHAPTER 23

Kathryn decided to take Keller away for a couple of days while I stayed home to work. She worked remotely on a few cases, and I needed to go through some training for a new employee, Sanjay Priyap. He was a nice enough guy, but training was usually boring.

Jackson played on a tablet while I worked through the magic of video calls. His previous nosebleed was only a few days past, and the anxiety of an impending follow-up nosebleed was clouding every happy moment that I felt.

But after only two days away, Kathryn called and said that Keller was really sick—fever, vomit, diarrhea—the whole nine yards.

She came home, and we gave him a cool bath and some Tylenol. After an hour of worsening symptoms, we decided that choice had already been made for us.

I buckled the car seat straps over Keller's chest and clicked the two metallic points at his waist. I tried to control my breathing, but worry was crashing in waves across my cranium. Keller's breathing was coming in rattling gasps. He was pale, and his eyelids were an angry red, which gave him an alien, diseased look. His nose was a mess of dried snot, and the red tip matched his eyelids

"Grant?" Kathryn sat in the front seat and was looking back at me, concern clear on her face.

"Yeah, coming," I said.

Jackson sat in the minivan seat beside Keller, worry plain on his face. He carried Keller's blanket for him, and as I backed out of the driveway, I could see him tuck the blanket between Keller's face and the car seat.

The doctors were fairly unconcerned, at first. We waited a nominal time in the waiting room, which seemed busier than expected at half past midnight. Jackson was content to lie on my shoulder as Keller slept on Kathryn's chest. He looked pitiful, and Kathryn rubbed his back and kissed the top of his head several times a minute. She was scared, more scared than I was, though I did my best to hide it. I'm not sure when I decided that I had to keep a level head no matter what, but I only knew I had to. Kathryn was doing a bang-up job of keeping it together, but her anxious mutters of "it'll be okay, baby" gave her away.

When we finally walked into an exam room, the nurse asked for symptoms and issues. I did my best to explain it all without letting in on the suspicion that there may be a link between our two kids.

The nurse checked his vitals, frowned, and wrote something down on the clipboard she carried.

"The doctor will be in shortly." We nodded as she left and then looked at each other. I shrugged and patted Keller's back. Kathryn wrapped her arms around our toddler, and a single tear dripped from her trembling lip into his sandy hair.

Jackson, having fallen asleep in the waiting room, was resting his head on my shoulder and breathing evenly. It had been a few days since he'd had a nosebleed, a blessed relief considering Keller's rapid decline.

We rocked our children gently while we waited on the doctor. I smiled at Kathryn, and she returned one, weak as it was. I was at a loss. I didn't know what to do or where to turn. Keller was struggling to breathe, but not so much that it was an emergency. Jackson's nosebleeds were increasing in frequency, but not so much that they were an emergency. It was like there needed to be a place for "almost emergencies." The emergency room was too much of an emergency, and the general practice family doctor didn't seem terribly concerned. "Take some Tylenol and put a band-aid on it" is what I felt like their default prognosis was.

A gentle knock at the door was followed by a tall, red-haired woman with a hawk-like nose and bright green eyes staring down at our sickly group.

"Hi there," she said quietly after noticing the sleeping children on our laps. "Tell me what's going on with this little guy." She sat on one of those same circle chairs that exist in every doctor's office and hospital, the ones that the boys always loved rolling around the room and rolled closer to Kathryn and Keller.

Kathryn told her a bit about his health history and more recently about his continued illnesses and how medicine wasn't really helping.

"Hm," the doctor replied when Kathryn finished. "Yeah, that doesn't sound fun at all." I could tell that she was used to addressing the kids instead of the parents, which in my book is the sign of a great pediatrician.

The smiling face on her ID badge named her Monica Haber. Dr. Haber took the stethoscope from around her neck and listened to several of Keller's breaths. He coughed once, ending with a wet choking sound. Dr. Haber looked in his ears, up his nose, and tried to look down his throat. She checked his pulse again and frowned, much like the nurse before.

"What do you think, doc?" I asked.

"Well, I can tell he's not feeling well. His throat is really red, his nose is really messy as I'm sure you've noticed, and it looks like he's getting an ear infection. A lot of times it could start out as an ear infection, but because the drainage builds up, it can often become more of an infection of the upper respiratory system, a lot of pressure around the nose, cheeks, sometimes even the jaw and back teeth can hurt. My gut says it should clear up in a couple of days with some strong antibiotics. I was mildly concerned that his pulse has slowed just by a very small amount, but that's not at all abnormal for a kiddo that's trying to sleep *and* under the weather." She clapped her hands on her thighs and looked from me to Kathryn. When we looked at each other without answering, she said, "Is there something else?"

Kathryn cleared her throat before speaking. "It's just that he's had ear infections before. The medicine doesn't help. We've had tubes put in his ears, and that didn't help. I would say that we could just take him home and let him heal like ... before, but his breathing is off. Something is wrong, and I can't tell what... it just feels like something is worse this time."

Dr. Haber nodded and, thankfully, didn't ask about what made him better last time, because we didn't know. What we did know is that if we told them being home made him better, they wouldn't try to find the source of Kathryn's suspicions.

"Dr. Haber," Kathryn began again, "can you run some tests on Keller? I don't want to subject him to being poked and prodded, but there's something inside of me that just doesn't sit right." Her voice began to shake, and I reached for her hand.

She grasped it tightly, as if I were a lifeline. But maybe she was mine.

After thinking for a few seconds, Dr. Haber nodded. "If that's something that you think will help, we can absolutely get those done. We can do a full workup, or a partial, what do you think will do the most good?"

It was then that I recognized the feeling that had been itching the back of my neck. I had my suspicions, but it seemed like Kathryn was so much more in-tune with Keller. I realized I'd been dreading this. The doctors will find something. Something terrible like they did with me. Just something as innocuous as light-headedness became a cancer diagnosis. Is that what they'd find with Keller? Perhaps it would be blood disease. Or even worse, they'd find nothing. There would be no sign of any negative disease or curable issue, and we'd be back at square one.

Kathryn shrugged in response to the doctor's question. "I don't know what any of that means. I just want the ones that cover the biggest issues and can give us the best chance of finding out what's wrong with my baby."

She blushed, and I squeezed her hand, hoping she took it for a burst of affection instead of something else.

"Yeah, we can certainly do that. We'll start with some bloodwork and then do a couple of scans. It may take a couple of hours to get them all done, and we won't know much tonight, but at the very least, you'll have some answers tomorrow or in a few days at most."

I nodded and squeezed Kat's hand again as the doctor told us where to go and what would happen.

It wasn't going to be fun, not for any of us. But, perhaps, we'd finally get some answers.

In the end, we returned home several hours later, none of us very happy. The initial tests had shown nothing more than some inflamed organs, most likely due to the sinus infection that were either caused by the ear infection or causing the ear infection. No elevated white blood cells, which I was thankful for. They asked us to return tomorrow to discuss the findings and get Keller checked out once more. They wanted us to come back several days in a row to monitor several things. They wanted to check whether or not the medicine was having an effect, they wanted to monitor any changes in his behavior and illness, and they wanted to review the tests that took longer to get results back.

We slept most of that day back from the hospital. Other than the occasional medicine dose and snacks or meals, even Jackson was too exhausted to do much other than lie on the couch and fall asleep watching cartoons.

That evening, Kathryn took Keller back to the hospital, and they noted that he wasn't any better and that his symptoms had gotten incrementally worse. Nothing to be afraid of yet, but something to keep checking. Kathryn had told me this after putting both kids to bed. She'd taken Keller by herself to the doctor while I stayed with Jackson and fed him dinner. She said she wanted some time to herself—or themselves—and I was apt to give it to her.

But when Jackson had another nosebleed that same night, our suspicions were all but confirmed.

Kathryn had fallen asleep rocking Keller, and after everything was cleaned up and set back in place, Keller's whole affect had changed. He was clear-eyed and smiling. His giggle didn't have a hint of sickness to it, and his flushed cheeks bounced when he blew raspberries at me.

When Kathryn took him in the next afternoon, the doctors celebrated that the medicine had worked despite taking a couple of days, and that we didn't need to keep coming back. The test results and scans hadn't shown anything of concern, anyway. They said we could come back anytime we thought we needed something, but they felt confident that he'd continue to show gains in his health.

Truth was, we hadn't given him any medicine. Sure, that sounds like a pretty shitty deal, I'll give you that. But Kathryn was adamant about it. She didn't want to put medicine in his body that he didn't need. I tried to argue that the doctors may know more about it, but when she asked if I was challenging her motherhood, I conceded. Besides, if he needed it, we could always start giving the medicine.

No, what was concerning was that he was not only better without taking any medicine, he was better at *the exact time* that Jackson had been stricken with another nosebleed. As much as I hated it, my brain drew the line in bright red permanent marker; it wouldn't go away... not now.

Chapter 24

The sky was dark and sinister as I stood on the front steps, staring at it with my hands in my pockets. There was always something endlessly intriguing about late summer storms. They did seem to chase some of the heat away, the wind that preceded the rain often cooler and bringing with it the electric scent of churned earth and subtle vitality.

I'd spent the day running tests all around the town, actually, trying to determine where the Ley Line sat both on latitude and longitude. It could be assumed it stayed more or less along the same gravitational degree of the planet.

I heard the front door open behind me and turned to see Kathryn looking at me, perplexed. "What are you doing?"

I shrugged, a little chagrined and irritated at her for making me feel it. "Looking at the sky, I guess." Did I mean to add that little bit of challenge in my voice?

She sighed and said, "Well, dinner is ready if you're done looking at clouds."

I nodded, but she'd already closed the door. When did we stop liking each other? Seemed like so much of the last few weeks or months were a steady decline. I hoped that the destination was our current emotional predicament; I wasn't sure we'd survive too many more steps down toward indifference with one another.

Dinner was mostly uneventful. There was some laughter from the boys as they did what brothers do. They made all manner of noises and faces while being chastised gently by Kathryn. Any words from the two of us were playful and fun—as long as they were directed at the boys. If we were forced to talk to one another, a coldness crept into our tone, and I could see Jackson look at us cautiously and then back at Keller. I hated that he noticed. I hated that Kathryn wasn't doing more to make things more normal. I hated that I wasn't able to keep the irritation from my own voice when I had to respond to her.

When they boys finished eating, I cleared the table, and Kathryn asked them to go upstairs.

I kissed Jackson's forehead. "Love you, buddy. I'll see you in the morning."

"Love you, too, daddy."

I couldn't believe how sunken his eyes looked. They looked as if they'd been pummeled, the resulting black eyes showing clearly in the paleness of his sallow cheeks. All because Kathryn wasn't willing to work out whatever Keller was doing to him. Did I hate her for it? No, I don't think I could ever hate her. But I could certainly hold her responsible. Maybe that, in its own way, was worse. Hate might be able to change, but I don't know if I'd ever be able to forgive her if something worse happened to Jackson. I loved both of my kids, but it seemed so obvious that Keller was the problem.

When I walked into Keller's room, Kathryn was rocking him gently.

"Anything I can do to help?"

She didn't even look at me when she responded. "No, I've got it." Her tone gave no indication of needing anything from me ever again.

Keller was fast asleep in her arms. His breathing had improved over the past day, which was strange considering Jackson had come home from staying with my parents in a nearby condo they'd rented for the weekend. My parents made the round trips like it was nothing. Retirement had its advantages, I guess... well, *rich* retirement. Maybe Keller's improvement was because of the couple of walks we'd made around the neighborhood. Maybe it was the change in weather. Regardless, I didn't have the mental capacity to work it out, so I just nodded and kissed him on the temple, then went downstairs.

I sat on the couch for several minutes, thinking. If I'm being honest, I was pouting. I didn't want to do anything for Kathryn. I didn't want to do anything that would make her think I was trying to fix something. She'd probably fall asleep with Keller and then come down when she wanted to go to bed. She wouldn't care if I joined, and frankly, I didn't care to.

So instead, I grabbed my computer and logged in. I opened the camera recording folder and scrolled through the cached files until I found one of the nights where Jackson had his nosebleed. One of the worst ones. Incidentally, it was the first entry because it was one, maybe two nights, after I'd installed the cameras.

I watched the video version of myself at double speed moving in ways that would have been comical if I wasn't in such a foul mood. And it was only funny because of the robotic motions of a video at double speed. Having mounted the cameras in the position I had, Jackson's bed was clearly visible, as was the balcony door and most of the bathroom. It reminded me of the night I watched Matt Brandhauer stand in the doorway of each room, his shadow stretching across the floor toward the balcony door.

I slowed it down to normal speed when I saw myself get up, the clock in the upper right corner of the image showed 1:42 a.m. I didn't want to remember this night, but I watched it with intensity as the other viewing pane showed Kathryn lying down with Keller, her movements now normal speed. I watched as Keller sat up suddenly, just as she'd said. It was about that same time when I emerged from the jack-and-jill bathroom with a cloth in hand. I backtracked in the video to the point where I noticed the light nosebleed and watched from there. I paid special attention to Keller's room during this time. Kathryn was right, their toddler was awake. In the grainy black and white, it wasn't easy to tell. But after watching it back several times, the camera angle showed his little eyes were open and staring at the wall that separated their rooms. Much like the camera angle in Jackson's room, it was mounted in the corner where the wall to the bathroom and the wall where the door to the room met. And like Jackson's, it gave a full view of Keller's bed, the balcony door, and most of the bathroom entrance.

When Keller sat up in the viewing panel, I rewound it a few seconds and looked to Jackson's room. My back was to the room, but what I saw was hard to watch. A shadow stole across his face, and his back arched suddenly, making his torso rise from the bed with nerve-wracking speed.

I paused the video and rubbed my eyes. What was I trying to find here? What was I looking for? More evidence that Keller was killing Jackson? I didn't want to find that, but I had to. I had to prove that Kathryn's favorite child was killing mine.

So I hit the rewind button again until I went into the bathroom for a washcloth, looking rapidly between the two views. A flash of movement caught my eye in one of the panes, and I paused the video. I wasn't sure what I'd seen, so I rewound it again, and when I hit play, I made sure it was set at one-quarter speed. The video version of me now moved to the bathroom in the incremental progress of jerky slow motion.

There it was. A flash of something on the glass to the balcony. A reflection, I thought, probably headlights from below.

I rewound it again and hit play. This time, I could see it a little better and thought back to that night, remembering something I'd barely even registered at the time.

I'd come out of the bathroom, and before I had seen Jackson painfully dealing with a convulsion, I had seen something in the glass door to the balcony. Only, it hadn't been a reflection, it had been something on *the other side* of the door. I remembered seeing the neighbor's cat on the balcony.

I let the video play forward for several more seconds. Keller was reaching toward Jackson, his pudgy little fingers splayed, palms reaching toward his older brother. It was obvious what he was doing. Even as I watched, it seemed that his demeanor changed. As he lay on Kathryn's chest, he was pale and lethargic, even in the black and white of the playback. But now, with his palms outstretched, his posture had improved, and he was noticeably more *aware*.

I knew that a single occurrence wouldn't be enough to convince her, so I closed that night's video and began watching every couple of days' entries, choosing dates randomly but unable to ignore the list of dates, the gaps between them shrinking with each entry. They showed night after night, some with nosebleeds and some without. Those same nights with the nosebleed I watched Keller's interaction. Just as in the others, he was awake when it happened and was reaching toward his brother when the worst of it happened. And if I was right, I'd see that Keller was better the morning after. It was simple. Terrible, but simple. Keller had to stop. Or be stopped. I didn't know which.

And to my shame, I found myself entertaining the idea of what life would be like without him, and I hated myself for it.

The last entry on the list of recorded videos showed yesterday's date. I opened it and sped up the playback. While I certainly didn't feel the need to do much else right now, I also didn't feel like sitting through twelve hours of recordings.

I reverted the playback to normal speed when I saw myself sitting on Jackson's empty bed. Jackson had been feeling better that day, having spent several nights sans-nosebleed, and that particular night he'd stayed at Grandma and Poppy's. I couldn't speak to whether he was well that night or not, but we hadn't received a call from them. No news is good news, right?

Keller, on the other hand, had gone to bed with watery eyes and a rash all over his chest and back. Kathryn had given him some medicine for itchiness, and it didn't do a thing for it. Not that we expected it to, medicine never seemed to touch his mystery illnesses. Whether we liked it or not, we knew he'd get better. He always did, and by doing nothing, we accepted the cost.

I was bothered by the fact that Keller had improved without Jackson being present. I was hesitant to let him go with my parents in the event that his nose decided to become the sprinkler from hell. It turned out fine, and he came home several days later with all kinds of memories made.

Our theory—the one that had driven a wedge between my wife and me—was built upon the fact that Keller was getting better only when Jackson was around. It was built on the fact that he was in fact *stealing* his older brother's health in order to maintain his own. He wasn't doing it on purpose; he was a toddler for god's sake. But everything pointed to it, supported it, and verified it. So what did this mean? Was it possible that Keller had gotten better on his own? Maybe. That would be a welcome change, but I doubted it, and I wasn't going to expend any of my already-depleted energy figuring it out.

I mostly ignored the image of myself in Jackson's room. Instead, I focused in on Keller. I don't know at what time he started feeling better, or if in some insane normalcy, he just needed a good night's sleep, and I wouldn't see a thing. That's what I hoped for.

I sped the video up past Kathryn rocking him and tucking him into his bed. I followed along as, in true toddler form, he woke up several times, and Kathryn gently laid him back down. Until finally he tossed once, twice, and then was still. I watched nearly an hour in triple speed and was beginning to doze when I saw Keller sit up in his bed. I felt a clashing flash of fear and affection for him as he turned his tiny body in the clumsy way only toddlers can do and still be called "cute." I watched in mild confusion as he looked toward the wall and a tiny palm reached out through the wooden slats of the crib, stark white in the night-vision grayscale of the video.

I looked over at The Jackson panel somehow expecting to see Jackson there, his ghostly form arching and bleeding wisps of ectoplasm. But there was nothing there, it was empty.

I looked back at Keller's room and saw him drop his hand to his side and then lie back down, his small pajama-covered bottom tucked into the air.

I paused it, confused and irritated with myself. It didn't seem like anything, and I wouldn't have thought anything of

it if Keller's actions didn't mirror the exact behaviors he exhibited when Jackson was violently bleeding in the next room.

I hit rewind and watched Keller's room twice more, coming to the same conclusion.

On the third pass, I noticed something else and paused it.

There, staring intently through the glass panes of the balcony door of Jackson's room, was the blurry form of what I believed was Muriel Anthony's stupid cat.

CHAPTER 25

The next morning was Wednesday, and before dropping Jackson off at school, we celebrated Keller's third birthday. In classic Taldo tradition, we decorated the table with age-appropriate cartoon items, hung our gaudy "Happy Birthday" banner, and opened presents over breakfast. Now that Keller was three, he'd be talking even more and his sleepy toddler face was just too cute. We spent much of the time snapping pictures with our phone.

"Iss my birfday!" he said multiple times between mouthfuls of donuts and ripping open his gifts. Jackson had picked out a new stuffed animal for him—a raccoon that by the end of the morning would be covered in donut crumbs.

"Dasson, I lub it so much!" He hugged Jackson and before parting, wiped his mouth on his brother's shirt.

"Kel Kel!" he protested, but without any edge; he laughed it off.

We cleaned up, and I got everyone dressed, then ferried Jackson off to school. As I was backing out of the driveway, I heard an ungodly rattle, followed by a clunking *scree* beneath the car. I slammed on the brakes and put the car in park.

My suspicions were confirmed when I saw Jackson's blue bike twisted and bent beneath the back tires of the car, its handlebars angled both toward and away from the bike itself.

"Goddammit," I muttered under my breath. I sighed and pursed my lips, wondering how much of my anger needed to show to get the point across while trying to avoid making him distressed. I clawed the bike from under the back of the car, wincing as it scraped and creaked against the chassis and concrete.

When I got back in the car, Jackson—with his uncanny ability to sense emotion—immediately paled.

"What was it, daddy?"

I looked in the rearview mirror with disapproval. "Your bike, bud. You left it out last night, and I ran over it."

He paled further and swallowed hard. "I'm sorry, daddy. Is it broken?"

I nodded and exhaled. "Yeah, bud. It's pretty torn up."

Luckily, I didn't have to lay it on thick at all. He got it. Maybe at his age, he understood the implications, despite having said very little about it.

"Don't worry about it, Jack. We'll figure it out." He nodded and looked out the window, obviously emotional about the loss. It was a silent drive to school... outwardly, at least. Internally, I was trying to figure out if I'd said the wrong thing or acted the right way. The whole goal was to get him to understand that all manner of things—bikes, in this case—were transitory and would eventually break on their own. We didn't need to help them along. But would it take more lessons like this for him to learn it? If so, would he remember how angry I had become or that I was forgiving?

All of these questions rattled around inside my head until I told him to have a good day and left him at school.

Kathryn stayed home with Keller to clean up the morning's mess. I helped finish it off when I returned, but before getting to work on a new set of analytics to test, I walked down the street to Muriel Anthony's home. Kathryn had left for work at the same time I took Jackson. We said goodbye to one another, but that was it.

My stomach turned somersaults as I pushed Keller down the sidewalk, the straps of the stroller making his jacket gather up around his chin. I didn't want to confront Muriel about her stupid cat roaming the neighborhood like it owned the place. I especially didn't want to confront her about her stupid cat playing around on my balcony like it owned *my* place, either.

Keller sniffled, his eyes peeking out from beneath a blue fur-lined toboggan. Maybe overkill for a chilly day, but it was the first one I found. I hastily wiped his runny nose, then rang the doorbell—a practice I found immensely more invasive than knocking. As I waited patiently, I looked at the window, fully expecting to see the same cat that stared in the video last night, staring at me with deep reproach. But its perch on the chair in front of the window was empty. The only signs of the overfed hissfest were strands of dark, coarse cat hair that clung to the carpeted tower and stuck out at odd angles.

I heard the locks clicking on the other side of the door and forced a smile before the door swung inward.

Muriel looked at me sternly from sunken sockets surrounded by wrinkles, and I realized in that instant where her cat had learned it. Her sharp, hooked nose looked very witch-like, and her hair was thinning, brown strands listlessly framed her face without her shoulders. She stood in a black dress with bees flitting around the hem. Her ankles sprouted from fluffy white slippers and resembled tree trunks in a snowbank.

"What do you want?" she croaked, scratching her neck with a long-fingered hand. I noticed a gaudy pink handkerchief on her wrist and was reminded of the generations between us.

"Hi, Muriel. I hate to be this kind of person, and please understand that I didn't even want to. But I just wanted to come by and ask if you wouldn't mind keeping your cat inside at night."

She blinked and frowned, deepening the lines around her mouth and eyes. "What?"

"Your cat, Ms. Anthony. Harriet, or Harley or whatever her name is?"

"Hazel?"

I nodded. "Yes, that's her name. Sorry. Hazel. Would you mind keeping her in at night?"

I don't know what it was, but at that moment I actually *looked* at her face. The wrinkles on her face began to change and her appearance shifted from stern to solemn. Her eyes softened and tears began to well within them. She sniffed and took the handkerchief from under the bangle at her wrist to dab at her nose and eyes.

I swallowed. "I'm sorry, did I... did I say something?"

"Hazel isn't here, Grant."

I didn't even know she knew my name. "I don't understand. Did she run away? I'm sure we could get a few people together and—"

She honked into the handkerchief and tucked it back under her wrist. "Hazel passed away several weeks ago. We buried her underneath that maple tree." She gestured to a tree several yards behind me. Sure enough, there was a scuffed patch of dirt about three feet by two.

That didn't make sense.

"Are you sure, ma'am? I would swear that I saw her this week."

She sniffed, and a tear fell down her ancient cheek. "I'm sure, young man. Edgar helped me bury her. He was kind enough to carry her and lay her to rest."

I nodded and gave my condolences, then thanked her and began to turn toward home.

I turned back to see her watching me. "Do you know of any other families with cats in the neighborhood, ma'am? Or if there are any strays that hang around?"

Edgar. The neighborhood weirdo. Maybe I should ask him. *But*, I thought, *there'd be little reason to do that.* Muriel had no reason to lie about her cat, and Edgar was even less believable than that.

She thought for a moment and blew her nose again. "I can't say that I've seen other cats around here. So many of the families in this neighborhood have dogs. I would guess that any stray cats would be afraid of coming around."

I nodded and thanked her, apologizing once more before she shut the door silently.

No. Muriel was telling the truth. At least, she believed she was. But if Hazel had died weeks ago, what had I seen in the video last night? A different cat? That was certainly a possibility, but I'd seen the cat on the balcony at least twice. What are the odds the same cat came to the same house around the same time at night? Especially when we haven't invited it back by feeding it or caring for it any way. *Maybe I should watch the videos again and see how often it pops up,* I wondered. That might give me an idea of how often it comes around. After all, it could be just those two instances.

But even as I thought it, I had the creeping suspicion that I was already wrong. I had to find out tonight if Hazel the Cat was actually dead. I didn't want to, but I had to know.

The rest of the day was spent writing up a report of what I could share with a new team of field agents that would be arriving soon to study the Corner House Intersect, as it had been named, as well as the report of my recent readings around the city. It was getting tricky balancing work and home, especially with not one, but two ill children. The randomness of it all was what cost the most energy, waiting and waiting, wondering when the next bloody sleepless night would occur. But the report wasn't hard, only time-consuming.

I waited until that night to become the gravedigger. Kathryn had some friends over, and I was instructed to stay out of the way. Not in so many words, but the message came through loud in clear. I took this as a perfect opportunity to see if Hazel was really lying cold and stiff beneath that tree. Everything pointed to "yes," but I had to be sure. I knew what I saw in the video. Thought I did. Believed it enough to base the decision off it. If I dug up the cold corpse of Ms. Anthony's cat, then I'd take a closer look at the footage.

After putting the kids to bed, I told Kathryn I was going for a walk.

"Right now?" she asked, incredulous.

I stopped with my hand on the doorknob. "Well, yeah. The boys are in bed, and it's a nice evening." It wasn't really a nice evening, and she knew it.

She shrugged after giving me a suspicious look, then went back to talking to her girlfriends about some reality show they watched.

The garage was cluttered and rapidly approaching messy. It took me several minutes wincing between clatters and clunks as I searched to find the only shovel I owned. It had been a gift from Kathryn's father when we got married, with some witty remark about how much I'd need a shovel to dig myself out of the hole my mouth put me in. Hardy-har-har.

I figured at first that I'd need a light, and I dug around in the tubs and baskets that held a random assortment of accumulated junk. After a few minutes, I remembered that there was a streetlight near her home, and I abandoned that hunt.

I made my way down the sidewalk, careful to avoid yards where dogs might alert their owners to my presence. I must have looked pretty ridiculous carrying a shovel over my shoulder, but I hoped that by this time, everyone was settling into their pre-sleep routine, and some passerby was of little concern to them.

When I reached Muriel's house, I was pleased to see that the light from the streetlamp pooled on the ground near the patch of freshly turned dirt. Not perfect, but it would do. I took a few steps forward, glancing around at the dark windows of the nearby homes. My breath was coming faster, now; fear and excitement burned in my chest. Little traffic down this corner of the neighborhood, especially this late at night. I bent over the patch of dirt and hoped she didn't have one of those lights that turned on when it sensed movement. She didn't.

The shovel made a deep scratching sound as it sank into the soft dirt beneath the tree. I wasn't sure how much I'd have to dig, but I wanted to make sure I dug deep enough to either uncover the corpse or clearly show the lack of one.

It didn't take long. After removing three shovels of the red stuff, the tip struck something a little softer. The dirt moved an object longer than the dirt I was trying to lift, and my heart thundered in my chest. I knelt down, ignoring the wetness of the soft earth beneath my knees, and inspected the hole. Half a foot down, I recognized mud-clotted fur extending down a nearly exposed bone that ended in tiny little toes with pink pads beneath.

Hazel was dead. Muriel was right.

I swallowed hard and felt my ears thumping with every heartbeat. My hands shook as I wrapped them around the wooden shaft of the shovel's handle, then made to begin covering the dead cat once again. A voice spoke in the darkness behind me and my blood run cold.

Caught.

"What'n Sam Hell are you doin'?" It was an unmistakable voice. A tenor tone and a southern twang that betrayed his upbringing as much farther south than Arkansas. The hunk of a dip in his lip usually changed his words slightly, as well, and this time was no different.

I plastered a smile on my face, hoping that in the pale light of the streetlamp, along with the surrounding darkness, was enough to hide how scared I was.

"Oh, hey, Ed. You scared me."

The issue was that Ed would talk to anyone around, especially something as juicy as seeing me with a shovel in a neighbor's yard late at night. I had to give him a good enough reason to repeat my made-up story and not his opinions on the situation itself. If it was believable enough to him, he'd exaggerate enough to make it seem like he confirmed it *with* me, making himself a character in the story too.

He spit a brown gob of dip onto the ground. "Well imagine me walkin' over here' n' findin' some guy standing with a shovel over the grave of an ol' lady's cat!"

I tried to laugh in a light, disarming way. "Oh this. Yeah, weird, huh? I saw some dogs digging over here earlier and heard from Ms. Anthony what happened. I put two and two together and realized they were trying to get to the body—corpse—or whatever."

He eyed me suspiciously, glasses reflecting the same eerie way a cat's might, similar to the animal I saw on the video.

When he didn't answer, I continued, making it up as I went along. "Not wanting her to deal with something like that—or you both, actually—I figured I'd do my part to help. Thanks, by the way, for being so kind to her about this. You're really a big help around here."

That should do the trick. He was just insecure enough, I thought, that a little shot of praise would make him forget that I was suspicious at all. And while I made up the scenario on the spot, Ed always wanted to be seen as the hero. Maybe it's what made him so keen to be involved in every little thing going on.

"Oh yeah. I think I seen 'em around here t'other day." *Bingo.* "And I didn't want her to deal with a dead cat. You know, I dealt with dead things all the time when I was in the service."

I let him drone on while I finished burying the cat again, smacking the once-again freshly dug grave with the back of the shovel like I'd seen my dad do hundreds of times, though it felt a little less natural when I did it. While he continued, I used the time to think of an excuse to get back home, and fast.

"You know, Ed," I interrupted after his second mention of being a master carpenter, "I wanted to take care of this and head back home. Now that it's done, I'm gonna do that. You have a nice evening walk."

"Alright, you too." And he continued up the street away from Muriel's as if I hadn't just ended the conversation mid-sentence. More importantly, he walked the opposite direction I was headed. The last thing I wanted to do was tell him goodbye and end up walking the block and a half side-by-side back to my house.

After putting the shovel back, I realized that it might actually be a good time for a walk. The girls were a bottle of wine into their conversation, and I had no desire to sit in the master bedroom to try and work while they put a dent in their second and third bottles. Kathryn glanced my way when I came in, but I lifted my jacket off the coat rack and smiled at her, then went back outside.

The pale glow of the streetlamps illuminated the bare branches of the trees that lined the road. In the wan light, shadowed on one side as they were, they resembled skeletal fingers reaching out of the darkness, like the hand of the undead stretching toward daylight. It was unsettling in a sort of foolish and childish way, and I shook my head to clear it as I plodded along the sidewalk.

The late summer night air was cool, a hint of what the new season would shortly bring. Not cold, certainly not enough to merit a hat or gloves, but the chill that crept into my skin through the jacket was unexpected, and I hunched my shoulders against it. Brown leaves, those early casualties of the war of the seasons, skittered across the ground in light, papery applause as the wind ushered them along into the darkness. The sound reminded me of mandibles clicking in the air around me and the cold sank deeper into my skin.

As I walked along the deserted street, I began to feel my shoulders relax a little. Not just from my body warming with the exercise, but from the clarity that began to spread through me. The lack of sleep and fear that I'd felt building over the last months was beginning to take its toll on me. I knew parenting would be difficult, knew it would be "the best worst-night's sleep" as my friend JD would say, but no one ever told me the constant worry that would accompany it. Well, I knew it wasn't always constant, but for the past few months, it had been.

Where once our nightly ritual had been bed for the boys and then a couple of hours of uninterrupted adult time, followed by a good night's sleep of seven or eight hours, it had now turned into bed for the boys and what felt like nightly yells for help from the bedroom. We'd changed our own schedules to account for this, opting to go to bed early to get as much sleep as we could, but it didn't make much of a difference. If anything, I'd grown *more* tired and *more* irritable by the lack of sleep. The fear was just the logical next step. What if this never changed? What if Jackson had nosebleeds for the rest of his life? Or the worst question that held a significant portion of the Fear Pie: What if the nosebleeds continued to get worse and the unthinkable happened?

I took a step over a crooked branch lying across the sidewalk, its bark a soggy green that twisted along the length of it in the pale light from the streetlamps like an old, arthritic snake. I had a sudden impulse to move it. To take my hands out of the relative warmth of the fleece-lined pockets of my jacket, grasp hold of the cool wetness of the lichen-coated stick, and toss it heedlessly into the grass a few feet away. The neighborhood was that kind where kids and parents alike dressed in tight pants and either sports bras or tank-tops and ran a few miles before meeting friends at the country club. I was of more common stock, but even I didn't relish the idea of seeing someone tumble ass over teakettle. But I left it lying on the damp concrete, the impulse ignored.

I stopped and stared at the sky for a moment, trying to steady my breathing. Puffs of wispy vapors rose from his mouth and writhed momentarily before blending into the night. It was dark tonight, the new moon was getting dressed and wouldn't show up for a few more nights. The stars were out but hidden behind a thin blanket of gray clouds. More like trailing wisps than clouds, I noted.

I turned my gaze to my surroundings and realized with some surprise that I had been walking at brisk enough a pace that I slightly out of breath. I now stood several blocks from home at the edge of the neighborhood.

I was standing at the corner of Wisteria Lane and Poplar Street, the main thoroughfare of our little neighborhood. The house across the street from me was dark and dilapidated. A forgotten FOR SALE sign stood askew in the yellowing grass of the front yard with a smaller REDUCED sign hanging listlessly from only one corner hook. The realtor's name and company had been completely bleached by the sun and weather, and the only thing readable were a couple of fading letters that I didn't have the interest to decipher.

I hadn't really looked at the house the few times I'd come here to measure the Ley Lines. Well, that's to say that I'd looked at it, but hadn't really *seen* it.

A wooden railing ran the length of the house's second-floor balcony. Between two of the posts, however, it sagged dangerously where the supports below had rotted away. The gables above each shuttered window in the third floor were speckled with chipped and peeling paint. Many of the shingles were broken; some were sliding their way down the roof in jagged black fragments. Across one stretch of the roof, I could see that some of the shingles had come off completely, the tar paper beneath shredded to little more than fibers and flapping in the chilly night air with an eerie *whap whap whap* sound. The windows of the second floor were all but empty, their glass long since shattered by bored children or the occasional storm.

I was reminded briefly of the scene in *It's a Wonderful Life* where George Bailey and Mary make wishes after throwing rocks through the windows of their future home. I had the sudden urge, so I picked up my own rock to make my own wish.

After a moment of introspection, rock clattered to the pavement near my black sneakers. This home didn't have any wishes left. No, this house was all that remained of a forgotten life, a monument marking the futility of effort. The specters that no doubt once drifted through those dark and musty corridors had long since departed, leaving rusty hinges and the hollow rattle of lonely cabinets behind.

Perhaps I was being too harsh. Maybe I was being cynical because of how I felt about Kathryn during this difficult time of our life. If I was a house, I might look very much like the one before me now. No more windows left. No more wishes. The proverbial home we'd built had been reduced to the simulacrum I saw before me. Laughter and joy forgotten, replaced by an empty, chilly wind. I was worried about us. Would our marriage survive? I wasn't sure. Mitch and Andreya's didn't. By all intents and purposes, it seemed like that's where ours was headed, despite our best efforts.

That thought itself scared me the most. The fact that I was seriously considering what life would be like *after* one of the kids was gone showed that I was already in the process of resigning myself to it. If not completely, then enough to consider it a serious possibility. Perhaps if I could prepare myself for it, however ignorantly, it would soften the blow. Truth was, I was scared to my bones.

I stared, unmoving and unseeing into the darkness for several minutes, my breath coming out as a briefly visible puff of air.

Movement caught my eye on the front porch, and I peered into the dimness. The porch swing moved dolefully in the chilly night air. There was a small breeze, at least one that I

could feel brush across my cheeks. Enough movement for the swing to move the few inches back and forth, giving it the illusion that a tiny form was rocking it back and forth, the broken chain whining in haunting squeals.

Life seemed to have caught up with me, then, and a sadness settled around me. No doubt there had been laughter at that house, once. Perhaps even children bounding down the porch stairs and giggling as they sat on the oversized wooden planks of that swing. Kicking back and forth as it soared into the air above the front yard. I could almost hear the gales of laughter as the mother or father chuckled with them. Children had the innate gift to disregard all reason, to be swept up in the joy of each moment. How I envied them. And still do.

A wind kicked up briefly, and I shivered despite myself. I glanced once more at the house, sitting forlorn and forgotten across the street from me, still bathed in that same ghostly glow from the streetlamps. Someone must have fixed the one outside the house, as it now glowed moodily nearby. Feeling my walk had accomplished nothing, I began walking back toward the warmth and light of my own home.

Before I'd taken a dozen steps, however, I felt one foot connect with something. Before I could react, the other had connected with it as well, preventing either of my feet from moving. I had time to think *my hands are stuck in my pockets* before the ground rushed up to meet me. I turned my face hastily to avoid crushing my nose and tried to scream before the absolutely rigid concrete connected with my head; I was, in fact, screaming inside of my head.

Then everything went black.

I opened my eyes groggily, blinking against the pallid light washing across me and pouring across the sidewalk at eye-level. The gritty feeling beneath my temple was irritating and with monumental effort, I untangled my hands from my jacket pockets, cursing myself in a kind of muddied feverish grunt as I tried to sit up. The sidewalk and sprigs of grass I could see began to spin wildly and my stomach lurched and tried to empty itself. Allowing the feeling to pass, I clamped my eyes shut before slowly opening them again. The world spun, but for now, it was bearable. I was able to lift my head a few inches off the ground without feeling the vomit creeping up my throat, so I took several steadying breaths and continued to inch up very slowly.

Now that my hands were free, I was able to push my torso off the ground. My legs, however, were still twisted around whatever had tripped me up, and I couldn't quite blink away the giant gray parentheses that bordered my vision. I put a hand to my head and felt a sticky coolness there. It came away covered in bloody dust. The gaudy brightness of it startled me in the pale light, shocking the haze away. I looked closer at my hand. There wasn't just some blood, there was a lot of it. Enough that I could feel it running down my cheek and into my beard, a disconcerting mix of warmth and cold.

Completely forgetting why I was on the ground in the first place, I looked down at my legs and saw what had tripped me up. That stupid branch that had caught my attention on my walk was now resting at an angle, half beneath my right foot and half on top of my left. The left part was broken, exposing a rotten, gray center of splintered hash marks.

With no small amount of frustration at myself, I kicked the stick away and threw the broken pieces into the grass near a tall privacy fence that ran to the corner and curved out of sight. I stood shakily and hesitated before doing more, just in case the Tilt-a-Whirl came back. It didn't. The blood continued pulsing down my face, and I tried to wipe it away from my eyes before

taking a small step forward. My head responded to each plod-
ding step with an angry echoing *thump*, and I winced in time
with them.

It was a longer walk home than I hoped, and by the time I
spied my front porch washing a bright yellow across the empty
street, my head was throbbing without the steps. The bleeding
had stopped; that was a relief. Even still, I knew my face looked
far worse than when I left. I was preparing my speech when I
saw Kathryn come out on the porch and glance around. She
didn't see me at first as she wrapped her arms around herself
and peered up the dark and empty street.

She froze when her gaze landed on me, though.

"Grant?" Curious panic eased its way through her voice in
that single syllable. And before I knew it, she ran to me.

I lifted my hands toward her in a warding off gesture when
she reached me and began peppering me with questions, a
look of desperate concern marring her features. Her voice
was frantic, and with the rush of wine from the evening, she
seemed to be quickly descending toward hysteria.

"I'm fine, Kat, really," I finally managed to get in between
her concern. "I took a tumble when my stupid feet got tangled
in a branch on the sidewalk. I had my hands in my pockets and
couldn't get them out fast enough before I kissed the pavement, that's all. It looks much worse than it is; I promise."

She touched my forehead delicately with her fingertips,
gauging the exact location of the wound. She managed to stick
a fingernail right into the center of the throbbing static in my
skin and with a sharp intake of breath, I winced and pulled
back. "Yep, that's it." I was uncertain she'd care at all, what
with us being at odds so much lately.

"Sorry," she muttered quietly. "I'm just trying to see how
bad it is. There's already a goose egg rising on your head." She

clicked her tongue in disapproval. "And you're still bleeding, but it looks like it's easing up." She placed her hands on my cheeks and planted a tender kiss on my surprised lips.

"Do you feel alright?"

I smiled reassuringly. "I feel right as rain. Almost. Nothing to worry about." I hugged her close and turned her toward the house. We were still standing in the street, and I hadn't forgotten that she didn't have a coat on. Kathryn let me take her under my arm, and she hunched herself into my warmth as we hustled through the cold night air. It was as if the veil of apprehension that had settled over our life had suddenly thinned. However briefly, I'd take it.

In the house, she told me she was going to get me an ice pack, and she didn't want any arguing. I told her that was fine and eased myself down to the couch.

"Where are the girls?" I asked, trying to make conversation in the hope that Kathryn had somehow, miraculously forgotten that we'd been fighting all week.

Between clattering utensils in the kitchen she said, "They left a while after you went out. I started getting worried when you didn't come back. I'm glad I went and checked."

I yawned and nodded, despite knowing she couldn't see me.

"Babe, do you want a cup of coffee?" Her voice came from around the corner in the kitchen, but it held a suspicious amount of nonchalance.

"Coffee? Now? It's almost time for us to get some sleep." When she rounded the corner with a washcloth and Ziploc bag of crushed ice clamped in her fist, her forced smile confirmed my suspicion.

She sat next to me and refused to look me in the eyes. She was blushing, only a little, but the rosy glow in her cheeks stood out in stark contrast to her light hair and pastel shirt.

"You worried I may never wake up?" I'd meant it as a joke, knowing full well that's exactly what she was worried about, now.

Instead of answering she pursed her lips and smacked me playfully on the arm so quickly I didn't have time to even flinch away.

"Ow!" I said with a light-hearted laugh.

She glared with both embarrassment and consternation. "Of course, you know I am. Just because we've been ... off doesn't mean I've stopped caring for you." She spoke with a low voice. Not anger, but maybe a small shadow of hurt within it. "I don't want you to have a concussion." I chuckled again, all in good nature, but it only made Kathryn more obstinate. "It's not a joke, Grant! I'm serious." And she was. "You're not going to sleep, not for a little while. At least until we're sure you're not just tired from falling and getting a concussion."

My mouth dropped open in mock surprise. "Honey, I'm tired from working all day and trying to be a good father and husband. I was this tired yesterday, and I'm still tired today! The hit on the head is just one more example why I should go to sleep sooner; I'm practically asleep already. My body just doesn't know it yet."

She pretended to ignore this and put the cloth-wrapped bag of ice directly on my throbbing wound. My head felt sticky. Before I put any bandage on it, it would need to be cleaned. But the ice felt good.

I waited for her to speak up, and she didn't disappoint. "Well, will you please at least just have a cup of coffee and watch TV or something? I'm exhausted, too, and I know we're both always tired." She was hedging against the ever-present and never-winnable argument of "who worked harder today."

"But it would make me feel much better if you just stayed awake for another hour. Or two. Three would be best."

"Three hours? Seriously?"

"If you love me, you will."

I smiled and rolled my eyes. It was a phrase that I knew could be used as a weapon, the kind of weapon that forces a person's hand, a person who cares deeply for another. In this instance, though, despite everything else, I could sense that it was being used out of playfulness. My wife of eleven years was acting serious, but the slight upward tilt of her ruby lips, along with the playfulness in her eyes told me she was using it as a last-ditch effort. I couldn't help but concede.

"Fine. Yes, I'll take a cup of coffee." She bounced on the couch and stood up to go get it. "No sugar, though! Only cream, please." I raised my voice so that she could hear me from the kitchen and wished I hadn't. My head punched my brain as if to say "Cut it out!" I closed my eyes and laid my head back until it stopped.

Kat returned with a steaming mug of coffee. I smiled gratefully as she set it on the coffee table before me and leaned over to kiss her on the cheek. She let me, too.

When she turned back to me, where there was once light apprehension, there was now barely an echo of it. "How do you feel?" she asked.

I reached for the coffee, feeling the warmth of the mug seep through my hands. "I feel pretty good, honestly. I mean, my head is pounding like the drum," I shrugged, "but overall I feel pretty good." She raised an eyebrow at me, and I continued. "Good enough to even stay up for a couple of hours." She nodded. "I could use the time to go through some of the recorded video of the boys' rooms again. I've been wanting to do that for a while, and this is a good opportunity."

She patted the hand I wasn't using to hold the mug of coffee. "I think that's a good idea." She stood up with a deep breath and exhalation of finality. "I have to get to bed. I have an early meeting tomorrow and—this is a long shot, but—hopefully I won't have to travel next month. The board is deciding exactly how much travel is within reason for an employee in my position." She shrugged. "We'll see."

Kathryn was an integral part of their company, whether they knew it or not. She not only was one of the most well-known marketing researchers in the area, but she'd also been published in several online journals because of her expertise in the field. She worked hard when she needed to, and when she didn't need to, she still worked hard. I was damn proud of her. I know that much of the time she spent at work also had her own worries in the background. Many of our conversations touched on her ability to multitask not only physically but also emotionally. She was an incredible woman and much better than I was at handling the stress of the kids. I wanted to be more like her, and I wanted the boys to be more like her, too.

"Yes, we definitely will see," I answered and raised my mug in a half-hearted toast before taking a tentative sip. The swirling heat seemed to banish some of the fuzziness in my head, and its warmth spread pleasantly down my throat and into my midsection. "Goodnight, babe. I'll see you in the morning."

She leaned over and kissed my swollen and blood-matted hair tenderly before squeezing my shoulder affectionately. "Goodnight, honey."

Before turning away she said, "You know, Grant, I *do* love you. It's just that this whole *thing* has been hard." She looked at me, silently assessing me in the way women can sometimes do. Then, "I hope you know that I still love you."

I sat on the couch contemplating how much energy it would take to reach for my laptop without having to get up. I should have asked Kat to snag it for me before she went to bed. While I made the calculations, I finished the cup of coffee. Now that it sat pleasantly in my stomach and spread its caffeinated tendrils into my brain, I decided I could if I moved slowly enough. So I stood and snatched it from the side table two feet away.

I opened the small computer and found the monitoring program that stored the recorded video files already open from the last time I reviewed them. I navigated to the dates with the most recent nosebleeds.

As it was, I opened the first file that was recorded in June. From what I remembered, the nosebleed happened sometime in the early morning. I remembered getting back to bed and glancing at the clock where it read 2:38 in digital cherry, so I cued up the video a few hours prior to then.

I saw the usual pantomimes happen while Jackson had a nosebleed, but I paid them little mind, not only because I was there but also because that's not why I was watching them.

The balcony door windows were my focus. I made sure to cue up each video several minutes prior to the actual nosebleed. The current video, from later in June showed the same scene as all the others, but through the balcony doors, black and white from the night-vision mode, I saw movement and paused it. Was I ready for this? Was this something I was prepared to see? I already knew it wasn't the cat that I'd assumed it was, it couldn't be a dog unless one had learned to climb vertically. I feared what I'd see, feared what conclusion I'd come to, but maybe it would offer an explanation.

I un-paused the video with no small amount of apprehension and watched as the movement stopped on the balcony.

There was a form on the balcony, I could see it there, but not anything concrete about its shape, size, or purpose. An almost imperceptible flicker of movement inside of Jackson's room caught my eye just before he sat up with blood dripping down his face. I rewound the video, but I was unable to see what was causing the movement, only that *something* was there a shadow only, so I moved on.

I continued watching the video until a final flicker of movement occurred outside the balcony doors, the same time that Kat and I ran into the bedroom. The motion was so fast that it was impossible to tell what it had been. I was betting, perhaps stupidly, that the other videos would have something more useful.

I queued up several in a row, comparing their dates to the little black notebook I'd had to go get from the bedside table. Kathryn was already asleep, but with the caffeine and something to chase on the videos, sleep was the furthest thing from my mind. Some of the notebooks entries were easy to remember. I just didn't trust myself to remember all of them in detail. So many I knew as just another entry on the list of long nights of bloody sheets and interrupted sleep.

The first two showed almost the exact same mysterious flickers of movements on the balcony just before a nosebleed occurred. The third, however, finally gave me something useful. It happened to be the nosebleed from late September, one that was particularly difficult. It reminded me of the one where I noticed a drop of blood on the carpet and chalked it up to just a far-flung drip from Jackson's nose or chin.

While the movements on the balcony were the same shadowed impressions, there was something new *inside* that provided something. A wire or string of some kind caught the light in such a way that I could see it stretched across the room, from the balcony door to Jackson's bed. Well, not exactly from the door, it was from the door frame itself, or rather, a crack between door and frame. It took a dozen times to finally understand what I was seeing. A thin strand moved from outside of Jackson's room, across the distance and over to Jackson.

I couldn't believe my eyes. It was awful. It was exciting. It was frightening.

I had to see more.

I went back to the first video, now armed with this new information. Sure enough, it seemed not to be a shadow, but the movement of the strand retracting back through the crack in the door.

I watched the next video with a fresh perspective. This time, it was easy to pick out the string as it extended into the room from the doorframe. This video also gave me the first glimpse of whatever was on the balcony. Before, it had been a formless shadow, something that I knew was there, but couldn't identify.

It was also the first time I truly felt afraid.

Whatever it was, was the size of a cat. A large cat, sure. But its eyes, which glowed like a cat's in the moonlight, were a foot or more off the ground, giving me a general idea of its height. The light from the moon reflected off some part of it, and I could see the length of the animal, which is why my brain translated the input into a cat. It had a long slender body, four feet, and a tail that flicked back and forth, very cat-like. But hairless, I realized. It wasn't bushy or furry; it was sleek and smooth.

I feared that I was dealing with something completely alien.

An impossible new thought cropped up quickly on the heels of the first. A thought that I grabbed and held onto as if it were a lifeline, something that provided us all an alternative to the reality we'd reluctantly accepted. Maybe Keller *wasn't* causing Jackson's nosebleeds. Perhaps this thing, this *visitor*, was the culprit.

CHAPTER 26

The next morning before Kathryn had to go to her meeting, I tried to talk with her about what I'd found. She wasn't exactly in the best of moods, and it felt as if the walls were back.

Instead of bringing it up and showing her the brief snippets of video I'd recorded and compiled as evidence, I decided to buy another camera. This one, I'd install on the balcony in such a way that it would hopefully capture the approach of the creature, if it remained true to form and stood in mostly the same place.

This way I'd get a perfect view of it, and there'd be no doubt of what it was. She'd have to believe it, then.

What worried me was that the nosebleeds had gotten significantly worse, and much more frequent. The first nosebleed happened sometime at the beginning of the year and the next didn't follow for nearly a month. Now, we couldn't go a week without a nosebleed, and sometimes, they were separated by only a few days. They were getting more violent, too. What would happen with the next one? I knew what would happen *eventually* but when did eventually become immediately? I prayed it wasn't now.

It had been several days since the last nosebleed, so I set everything up with the expectation that it would happen soon.

If it was indeed this creature that was causing it, I may not know why, but I knew that it was on some kind of schedule.

If it was an animal of some kind, it had an instinct to feed, to survive. Was it hunting multiple children and Jackson was just one of several in a rotation? No, that didn't feel accurate. Could it be that the creature was *requiring* more? That would certainly account for the increase in frequency, but not for the severity.

Unless...

Unless it was becoming desperate. I knew a thing or two about desperation. When the cancer threatened to overtake my body, I drank deeply from desperation's cup. Would I need to again? Wasn't that same cup poised against my lips even now? I felt it was.

Regardless, I had to wait for another nosebleed. It felt odd, using Jackson as bait for this, especially in his condition. But I had to know. I had an idea of what I was looking for, but I had to *see* it. I had to get a good shot of the animal before I brought it to Kathryn's attention. Otherwise, I'd be dealing with a Doubting Thomas and not my wife, though perhaps these days they were one and the same.

I checked the cameras almost constantly for three days, then spent most of the fourth waffling between the worry that a nosebleed would occur and hoping one would.

Sure enough, that night Jackson had another nosebleed. I was watching Jackson intently, hoping against hope that he wouldn't be hurt too bad, but knowing that the longer the creature was present, the better chance of catching a good shot of it in the video. Unfortunately, the longer the creature was around, the worse the nosebleed.

This one could have been as bad as any. Kathryn was in with Keller when it started, but I'd been ready, and I ran into his room as soon as it started. As I wiped a few wayward drops of blood from Jackson's chin, I could imagine Keller reaching through the wall. I was excited and distracted but made sure to avoid checking the cameras until after we were back in bed and Kathryn was asleep, though I doubted she'd care.

I opened my laptop, ensuring it was on mute and dimmed the brightness. It still washed over the bedroom and her still form beside me with an unearthly glow, but I had to know.

Just as in the others, Keller had been awake by the time the nosebleed occurred. The creature was there, though. And the camera showed it all, and the creature's face became clearly visible in the recording.

I watched the video from the freshly mounted balcony camera, and just before the nosebleed, the creature turned its head straight to the camera. Perhaps it was reacting to the sound of the passing car, or maybe it noticed the new addition. Either way, it was just enough to catch my first real look at it.

At first, I assumed what I was seeing was simply a result of the grainy video. Each time I rewound and re-watched it, I became more and more certain that what I was seeing was the truth and not a trick of the camera to be simply discounted. My mouth dried up immediately, and I began shaking.

The creature stood on all four feet, between one and two feet tall from paw to cranial ridge, with an earless, hairless body and head. At least, that was the impression I got. Its eyes were set on the side of its head as two dense, black orbs. But that isn't what made me question my sanity. Its mouth, or where its mouth should have been, looked as if it had swallowed the head of an octopus and left the tentacles dangling out of its mouth. Dozens of the things in varying thickness hung loose from its face. But even as I watched, they began

to writhe and dance, with one or two actually becoming rigid and then relaxing.

The worry and fretting I'd done over the past year seemed suddenly insignificant and misplaced. This thing was the reason. It had to be. Of course, it wasn't a sure bet, but it would explain a good deal of it. I just had to make sure. I wasn't sure how to do that, yet. And it didn't solve all the problems. It solved the problem of Jackson's nosebleeds but not of Keller's sudden wellness. But if his wellness coincided with these visits from the creature, could he and the *creature* be linked, somehow? Had my assumption that the link between brothers been wrong, and instead, it was a link between Keller and this thing?

The next question, then, was discovering Keller's role in all of this.

I had to determine a timeline, and fortunately for me, one had already been established.

I threw back the covers and crept to Kathryn's side. Taking extra care to avoid unnecessary noise, I eased the nightstand drawer open just enough to remove the little black book from within.

I opened it to the first entry once I was back on my side of the bed. The header matched the date that Gretchen blew up at Corner House. Knowing there were few things more consistent than email, I opened the account for work.

I scrolled hastily through the emails I'd received. I wasn't sure what I was looking for until I saw it.

From: GScotelli@eastwindenergy.com
To: GTaldo@eastwindenergy.com
3:48 pm CST
(No Subject)

Call me when you can.

Sincerely,
Gianna Scotelli
VP of Field Research

There it was. The date of the first nosebleed matched the date of an email Gianna sent to me. But this particular email was in response to when Gretchen blew her top. When the FAD finally hijacked a dissonant energy stream. But how could they be related? No matter how much I wracked my brain, I couldn't come up with an explanation of why or how those two dates were related. There wasn't any reason to believe they *could* be, but I felt a deep resonance that there was something there.

I checked the clock, 12:42. Nearly 1:00 a.m. But in California...

I sent a message to Marco.

[GTaldo 12:48am: Hey. You awake?]

I waited, feeling my heart thumping up and down my limbs. It skipped a beat when three little dots blinked in response, and I let out the breath I'd been holding.

[MRiviera 12:48am: Hey bro. Yeah, just gaming. What's up?]

I typed rapidly, trying to convey what I knew I wanted to say without actually saying what I had to say.

[GTaldo 12:48am: Can I call you? It's a lot to type.]

My phone rang five seconds later. It was Marco.

"Hey, dude. What's got you worked up?"

"You could tell, huh?"

"You're pretty straight-laced, my dude."

"Can you tell me if there's ever been a successful Dissonance Extraction like the one Gretchen had before blowing? I know that Gianna said she was the only one, but I'm just curious, I guess."

"From what the records show, yeah, Gretchen is the only one that's been successful."

That was what I expected, but I was still disappointed.

"Damn. Nevermind, then."

"I said that was what the records *show*. Do you want to know what the *logs* say?" His tone told me there was more.

"Logs? I don't follow."

"Every FAD is equipped with an uplink node that sends its data straight to HQ here in Cali. It can't be moved or deleted. It can be appended, but only to provide additional notes. And … it's all encrypted."

"Yeah that would be great. Can you do something with it? Are you able to, I mean?"

"Dude. You know I'm a celebrity over here, right?"

"Right. I forgot, Mr. Celebrity. Do your stuff."

"Already done."

"Jesus, that was fast. And?"

"And it looks like there was a successful Dissonance Extraction back in '24, somewhere over in Europe, a place called Sardinia. More specifically, in a town called Castelsardo *in* Sardinia."

"Sardinia?" I'd never even heard of the place, and I told him so.

"Yeah, not much interaction with the teams in Europe, but they're out there. Looks like the logs show a spike similar to yours, but I don't know why this wouldn't be in the records. Gianna would go apeshit if she knew you weren't the first."

While he was talking, I was opening my web browser and looking up Castelsardo. There wasn't much. It was a beautiful ocean-side city that clustered up and around a massive rock formation. It couldn't be very large, at least by the looks of it.

"What else do the logs say, Marco?"

He was quiet for a second and then, "Not much, man. There's another two tests on the two days following the first with similar results and then nothing. The logs are empty until a message that just says the machine was purged and reconditioned."

Castelsardo was a quiet city, nothing noteworthy ever happening there.

Except one thing.

While Marco continued on, I read the article before me. In 2024, an unnamed energy corporation began conducting tests across the region. It went on to describe the tests to have "zero environmental impact" and were "completely localized."

> *The tests continued until the midyear, when the company suddenly closed the local office citing that the tests were complete and their results were inconclusive. However, during their withdraw and subsequent liquidation of assets (the office and hardware included) Castelsardo noted a significant increase in pre-adolescent*

nosebleeds, though after the initial spike, no
subsequent cases were reported.

My blood ran cold.

"Marco, can you search for any kind of internal report or, what was it, a log about Castelsardo?"

"Um... Yeah I can, but if I go digging around, there's a chance I'll get in some serious trouble."

"I wouldn't ask if it wasn't important. Please. There's something that I have to know. Can you?"

"Alright," he said reluctantly, "it'll take me a few minutes. Ten, tops. But I'm sending this shit from a spoof account and masking all the DNS records."

"Alright." I didn't know what that meant, but he was a celebrity, right?

"Thanks, Marco. I... I really appreciate it. I'll talk to you later."

"Peace out."

I read on about the "unnamed energy company" and its presence in Castelsardo. There wasn't much else in the way mysterious energy companies and the goings-on of a town. I was hoping that Marco would come through for me.

Not even ten minutes later, the mail notification blinked on my computer.

The sender was a masked email address, but the subject was clearly from Marco.

Subject: TO MY DUDE AND NO ONE ELSE

Marco was a good guy—or dude.

My hands were shaking by this time, and it took a few clicks to open the new message. It was a list of incident reports that were mostly unintelligible to me, but I was relieved to see that Marco had taken the time to draw a large red box around an incident report in the middle of several pages. Why he didn't isolate the single one, I didn't know. At this point, I didn't care. I was close to a solution. I could feel it.

The report said a little of what Marco had told me, but in a kind of internal syntax, which I ignored. I was looking for something causal, something that would bring an investigative field team to a full stop and subsequent withdraw.

I found the date of the initial test, with its spike, along with the two subsequent tests, both with spikes of similar intensity. The logs around those bore nothing noteworthy except a single asterisk.

The asterisk was noted at the bottom of the page. This must have been the note that Marco was talking about earlier because while the logs were mostly robotic gibberish, the note itself was obviously written by a human.

> *Testing period ending prior to scheduled termination due to external and unknown biological interference. Testing may continue elsewhere, but Dissonance Extraction cause of differential tear in conjunction with Ley Line Polarization Process. Unknown entity affecting local population. Dispatched and disposed of by EE Periphery team. RF

The letters at the end were probably the initials of the person entering the note, but that didn't matter. There was something similar that happened elsewhere, and it was shut down, and the—what was it—"unknown entity" was disposed of. Was that what the field team Gianna assigned was coming to do?

I didn't know, but I wasn't going to wait for them. I was going to take care of this myself, and I was going to do it the next time it showed up.

I wouldn't have to wait long.

CHAPTER 27

As luck or fate would have it, the team came by the following day. I'd emailed Marco and Gianna, letting them know that I was getting to work that day. I think Marco knew something was up, but Gianna simply responded with "Sounds great, can't wait to see the results, Grant!"

I didn't trust her, not anymore. I suspected the team she was dispatching soon would be to take care of the "unknown entity" and wasn't a research team. My guess was that this was a Periphery Team, and I could only suspect what they did. She hadn't let on that she knew anything when she knew exactly why I was having to take time off to go to the hospital and the reasons for my child's sudden illnesses.

The remote team had shown up and stopped by the house on a sunny September day. The air was cool but comfortable. They were staying in a hotel not far from us and wanted to introduce themselves before they started their own work.

The team lead, a stocky man with glasses and a large mustache, stepped out of the truck. His large belly bulged over his pants, and I could see the buttons on his shirt squinting with the effort of holding itself together.

"You mus' be Grant." His voice was deep and carried with it strong "country boy" vibes.

"Yep, that's me." I held my hand out, and he took it, pumped it a little too forcibly, and then introduced himself and the other two on his team.

"My name's John Huxley. This here's Mendoza." He gestured vaguely to a man with dark hair and eyes. He smiled warmly and rubbed his stubbled jaw before shaking my hand. "And this here's Elliot Bardaferra." Again, he gestured vaguely to a short young man with wide blue eyes and long blonde hair.

"Barda-*fierra*, actually," the young man said in a European accent to clarify, then shook my hand genially.

John continued, then. "My understandin' is that we're gonna be workin' together over the next little while, tha' right?"

I nodded. "Based on what Gianna sent me, yeah. I'm guessing you've read my outline and process notes?"

The bulky man took a lighter from the front pocket of his Eastwind Energy monogrammed shirt, but he shook his head after lighting a cigarette he produced from behind an ear.

"Nope. That's their job." He cocked his head behind him.

"I read it, Mister Taldo," Mendoza responded, his Latin accent very light. "Very thorough and intriguing. I'm very much looking forward to working with you on it, sir."

"Yes," Elliot piped in. "Yes, sir, very interesting stuff."

I didn't want to, but southern hospitality and all that. "Well, do you gents want to stay for lunch?" I prayed they didn't.

John shook his head, smoke puffing from his nostrils as he exhaled. "Naw, we cain't stay. We gotta unload at the hotel and make sure ev'rything's set up for the work."

Whew. "Well, no problem. Thanks for stopping by. I should be at the site tomorrow morning around eight-thirty or so, after dropping my son off to school."

"Sounds good, we'll be there 'round nine." John dropped his cigarette and smashed it between his boot and the sidewalk, then put the lighter in his pocket, though it stuck out an inch or so.

I shook their hands again, spending more time telling Elliot and Mendoza how much I appreciated them, seeing as the team lead hadn't even bothered to do his homework on why he was here. I hated people like him.

I waved once when they pulled away from the curb and then walked toward the house. I kicked something that went skittering across the sidewalk. I bent and picked it up. It was a lighter. John's lighter, actually.

Unsurprising, it was covered in pictures of naked women in seductive, unrealistic poses. I put it in my pocket intending to return it to him in the morning and continued inside, forgetting it completely for the moment.

I told Kathryn everything. I was happy to be wrong about the boys. She wasn't a Doubting Thomas; she was ecstatic that there could finally be a solution. Her initial fear and disbelief about *what* it was could be worked out later. She didn't balk at the fact that something was feeding on our child, and I was jealous of that. I told her that I was sorry that I didn't believe her, that I had ridiculed her ideas. That, in the end, I had been an asshole about it all.

"I know it's probably too late now, but you were right, and I should have listened."

Kathryn graciously picked up my hands and kissed the backs of them.

"Grant, we didn't know what to do. And I wasn't *right*. It's not a vampire."

I chuckled, and so did she. We both felt a little better despite the fear and anxiety that crept beneath the calm surface.

I showed her the videos, then. She was appalled, scared, and intrigued in a way that I didn't expect. She cried when she

saw how frequently it had shown up and how close we were to blaming Keller for it. It was good to hash it out, but when we were done, we knew there was work to be done.

"I think we should tell Mitch."

I'm sure the surprise was plain on my face. "Are you serious?" I asked, thinking that she was certainly joking.

"Yeah, I think so. I mean, he was right, wasn't he?" She looked at me with a sincerity I'd missed in the recent months.

"Yeah. Yeah, I think you're right. Should you call him or should I?"

She looked pensive for a minute, then said, "I'll call him. It'll mean more coming from me, I think."

I don't know when she called him, but I heard her working on the phone throughout the afternoon.

Kathryn ended the day with a call to her boss. She told him she'd be out until Monday. Not altogether strange since she was part-time anyway. The rub was the lead time, I think. He wasn't happy about it, but all she had to point out were her current numbers compared to the rest of the team.

"Milton—" she started, and I mouthed her boss's name and made a face. She turned away from me to avoid the distraction. "If the team can't afford for me to be away for a few days a year, that's not a *me* problem, that's a *you* problem." Yeah, she's a badass, I know.

Milton reluctantly agreed, but not without some grumbling. Then we set to work. I made sure the cameras worked and put the kids to bed, just like normal.

With the excitement of it all, we didn't really have time to let the truth settle in. There was a monster hurting our kid, killing him, and now it was time to face it. But how? Kill it? Hurt it? Make it run away so it could do this to some other family? I wish it were that easy. Even now, I wish it had been that easy of a choice.

True to form, the visitor showed up on the camera just after one in the morning.

It was time. I paced confidently through the kitchen, seeing the events unfold on the live feed of the cameras. Before it knew what was happening, I watched Keller wake up and reach out toward Jackson's room. In that instant, I looked at Kathryn, who began to run up the stairs and I ran out of the house, searching the balcony for any sign of movement. My eye caught some movement and could see the now familiar form of the animal slinking along the balcony railing.

"Hey!" I wasn't sure what to do, but I'd grabbed the fireplace poker and now realized how useless it was. I knew I had to get it away from the boys.

It turned and met my eyes, then hissed at me. The tentacles on its face extended outward and danced, small specks of saliva danced in the lamplit air before it, revealing rows of razor-sharp teeth beneath. I took a step back in surprise, but I could feel the tension building to a point. It was almost over; I was close to the end. *We* were close.

I searched for something, anything, to throw at it. I could launch the fireplace poker at it like a spear but knew that I was no Olympian and that I'd probably end up hurting the house more than the visitor. Instead, I found several rocks on the ground near my bare feet. I reared back and launched them at the creature as it tried to keep its balance along the balcony railing, no doubt looking for its path back up onto the roof to escape.

The first two rocks missed. The third hit it in the hind quarters with a loud *clack*. I'm sure it wasn't hurt, but it must have messed with its balance enough because it fell from the

second-story balcony and landed with a *thud* on the ground mere feet from me. Now that it was close, I was hesitant to approach it, though part of me wanted to rush toward it and pummel it to death with the poker. Maybe that would have been the better option.

Before I could make a decision, it scrambled to its feet with unbelievable speed and disappeared around the corner of the house toward the front yard. I ran after it, hoping to chase it down and realizing how out of shape I was.

As I rounded the corner, however, I heard a cry of surprise and saw the creature skid to a halt, its feet slipping on the sidewalk as it tried to course-correct around a figure blocking its path. The figure—a man—cocked his leg back and swung it forward with more force than I thought possible from the weird, old, crippled war veteran that wandered aimlessly through the neighborhood.

The kick sent the animal into the air several inches and landed awkwardly on its front shoulder. It let out a barking hiss of pain at the man before continuing in the direction it was headed, now with a significant limp.

I approached the man while keeping one eye on the retreating creature. Adrenaline made my breath come in short gasps.

"Thanks for the assist, Ed. You alright?"

The grizzled face lifted in a smile, flecks of tobacco crisscrossing his lips and teeth.

"Oh, I'm fine as frog hair, Grant. Jus' glad I could get a lick in. What was that thang?"

I hesitated, but what the hell? "I don't know, Ed. Something that's been hurting my kids, I think."

He nodded as if this was the most reasonable explanation in the world. "Yeah, I seen things like that before. Well, not exactly like that, but there were bigger boys over in China when I was there." He met my eyes, all lack of social grace replaced with a serious kind of camaraderie. "Ya need help? I can go get my gun from the house?"

I was touched, but didn't think that was needed, or what I wanted. I appreciated the hand—or foot—that Ed had lent, but thinking of him patrolling through the neighborhood with a rifle might just bring the wrong kind of attention.

I put my hand on his shoulder and shook my head. "No, but thank you, Ed. Really. I need to chase this thing down. I'll take it from here."

I started off at a jog, searching the ground for tracks and finding those bloody scuffs across the concrete. Then turning, I said, "Hey, Ed?"

"Yeah?" His southern drawl echoed across the empty street.

"Make sure Kathryn got Mitch. Tell her I'm headed toward Corner House, but she and the boys need to *stay away!*"

He raised his crippled right hand in acknowledgement, but I was focused back on finding the visitor. I had a sneaking suspicion where it was headed. I wasn't sure how I knew, but something told me that was where I'd find it.

Where I'd find and finish it.

CHAPTER 28

I approached the house with more than a large measure of caution. After Ed had kicked the *thing*, I'd run after it, barely catching a glimpse of it retreating in a shambling gallop. Its form could be seen ahead, lurching beneath the streetlights and leaving oddly shaped bloody footprints on the stark white of the sidewalk's concrete.

I stopped in front of the snaggletooth fence of the old house on the corner at the back of the subdivision. The forest behind it was a dark velvet backdrop. The house itself was silent, but the trail led right to the rickety gate at my feet. The house before me seemed to reserve some of that darkness for itself. Its eyeless windows were sockets full of ill intent, and the front yard pickets stood as silent sentries for the children who would never play through the poorly manicured grass. Most of the pickets leaned at odd angles; others were broken off in cracked and splintered designs. Together, they created the jagged image of vicious unwashed teeth, a warning I would have heeded if I'd had the choice.

It seemed that in the couple of weeks since I'd last visited Corner House, time had been unkind to it. The air was still, and at this hour of the night, I doubted there was going to be anything that broke the silence.

It was difficult to admit to myself that I was unsettled and scared, that I was facing something completely foreign to me. But we don't have a choice, many times, do we? As parents, our job is to face the danger regardless of foreknowledge. And right now, I was in the dark.

I could feel my heart beating, and if I was a betting man, I would have said that anyone nearby could have heard it. I took a breath and prayed for bravery before grasping the gate and trying to gently push it open. It skittered across the stone walkway and fell with a squealing clatter into the grass. The rest of the fence, jostled by the disruption, shook and rattled. It brought to mind the image of bleached and chuckling bones, hanging limply from the fence instead of wood.

I made my way carefully to the front door, stepping over the occasional stone that no doubt was the precursor to the wayward shards of glass scattered across the walkway or half buried in the decomposing grass.

I hadn't noticed it before, but I thought of it now despite the fear that was coursing through my veins. Every person that threw a rock at the house or busted a window probably thought themselves brave. But now that I looked, not a single spray of graffiti marred the exterior of the house. The sidewalk was as far as anyone went, as far as I could tell. It was enough to toss a rock at the window from thirty yards away, but there wasn't a chance in Hell anyone was getting within arms-reach of this corpse of memory.

The bloody footprints from the creature—shaped like overlapping hearts—led toward a busted window to the right of the front door. Knowing I would prefer to avoid the vulnerable position of crawling through the window on my stomach, I stepped to the door. It was still unlocked, even after the months since I'd first called on it. I guess property being stuck in litigation for years isn't always a bad thing.

The door seemed to be stuck, though. Perhaps the rain and cold had warped the already-warped doorframe since my last visit inside. I pushed, but apart from a reticent creak, nothing happened.

At this point, I knew there weren't a lot of options. I put my shoulder against the door and pushed. It still didn't budge.

My heart continued to pound, and I could feel my breath catching in my throat as the fear tried to steal my courage. Every second that I waited, the creature was steeling itself, or healing or escaping or something else that I couldn't stop.

I shook my head and took a small step back, keeping my hand wrapped tightly around the brass doorknob. I readied myself and stepped quickly to the door, closing the distance in a millisecond and positioning myself so that my shoulder would hit as close to the doorjamb as possible.

The door gave with a deep and mournful snap. The doorjamb had broken in two, falling inward with my momentum as the door swung inward on hinges that had only moved once in probably a decade or more.

I stepped into the house as dust motes floated around me. Despite the darkness outside, the streetlights lit enough of the house that I could get a vague impression of the interior of the house.

It was exactly the same as before—when I'd brought Gretchen into this foyer, and she'd thanked me by exploding. This time, however, it *felt* different. It still stank of stale air, rotten wood, and sodden walls, the kind of smell that seemed sweet and pleasant at first, but beneath it sat something deeper and more sinister. The air was heavy with it, and I felt the spirit of the house settle across my shoulders.

I tried to find a trace of the blood trail, but it was either too dark in the house or there weren't tracks to follow. I peered around the front room walls, walking gingerly and preparing myself for something to leap out at me, but nothing did.

A rustling scuffle above me snapped my head up, and I got a face full of dust and grime. I coughed and tried to wave it away, running a hand through my hair as I imagined bugs falling and tangling in my hair.

The thing was here, and now I knew it.

As quickly as I'd begun to pursue the creature, I hadn't thought about what I'd do when I caught up to it. I looked around for something to use as a weapon.

My eye found the doorframe that had cracked and splintered in two when I hulked my way into the house once again. It wouldn't have been my first choice, but the splintered point of the wooden frame would do if it came to that. I found a small measure of comfort in the smooth wood, though.

I scooped it up and felt it in my palm. It wasn't comfortable, with the coarse side that had been forcibly separated from its seat, but that was fine. I'd do what I could with it. I intended to end this thing, whatever it was, and send it back to wherever it came from.

As my eyes adjusted to the darkness, I pulled my phone out and turned the flashlight on. I'd have to figure out what to do if I needed a free hand because I wasn't going to drop my sad excuse for a weapon, but I needed to be able to see. Either way, I'd figure it out later.

I was able to spot some scuff marks in the dust that carpeted the floor past the entryway. They led to the rickety staircase where the banister, no doubt once an ornate piece of craftmanship, lay in a jumbled heap across the stairs. I didn't remember it being like that before. The creature must have

been small enough to wriggle its way through, but I wasn't able to. I shined my light onto it, working out how to climb over or through it, and finally, I decided that the best option was to simply remove it. I put my phone against the wall, adjusting it so the light shined on the staircase and then dropped the spear. Gripping the banister with both hands, I heaved it upward. Either I was stronger than I remembered, or the wood was completely and utterly rotten because it rose easily—too easily—and slid off the staircase with a terrific crash that reverberated through the house. Dust erupted into the air, and I closed my eyes and covered my nose and mouth with my shirt to avoid a coughing fit.

And, if I wasn't mistaken, I felt the stairs shake ever so slightly. The sound of scuttling above made the hair on my arms stand on end. It was as if the creature that waited for me suddenly understood on a primal level that it was, without a doubt, in trouble.

I bent down and retrieved my phone and the splintered doorframe, once again feeling a measure of security in its weight.

The stairs moaned like lost souls as I ascended them to the forgotten second floor. I sidestepped a particularly rotten-looking step halfway up the staircase. The wood was dark and looked as if it would collapse with merely a touch.

When I reached the landing, I would have had to choose a hallway to the left, which led to several closed doors, or to the right, which led to a single large room. The choice was made for me when I looked down. The creature's tracks made a sideways jag through the dust. I could see it clearly though, as if a recording was playing in my mind. It took the corner too quickly, its legs slipping out from beneath it before slamming viciously into the wall, where a streak of blood was drying. The tracks after the spill were more irregular, and I imagined—hoped—it was badly injured. I followed the trail, bracing myself for what lay ahead.

The corridor ahead ended in dark opening and a darker room beyond. A window at the end of the hall was partially covered with a rotting curtain or cloth. What little light did bleed through the moth-eaten drape created a surreal kind of glow that gave small hints at what remained within the room. A corner of something tall here, a rounded edge of another object there.

The room was full of things that were very old.

And something that was even older.

I took a hesitant step forward and halted. In trying to identify the stuff in the room, I'd nearly forgotten my purpose. In the center of the room, a pair of silver eyes gleamed in the light from my phone. I tried to calm my racing heart, but it did nothing. The eyes were staring at me for the moment, but I realized soon enough that the eyes were staring *into* me. I gripped the spear and took a step, intending to simply walk up to the wounded creature and sink the wood into its beating heart, but the eyes disappeared in a wisp of smoke.

In a sudden, dizzying display that made my stomach lurch sideways, I saw something else begin to form around me. I was still in the upstairs hallway of the decrepit old mansion, but as I stared, the peeling wallpaper and peeling paint disappeared, replaced by something else, somewhere *outside* of what I knew.

I was standing in an empty field, but when I looked hard around me, the vague outlines of the upstairs corridor shimmered distantly. The sun—or *a* sun—shone down on me in a warmth that was both familiar and alien. I tried to reach out and touch the wall that was nearby, but my shaky hand moved through it without any resistance. Like a sunspot on a camera,

it was there but insubstantial. I began to register something else that was missing from before: sounds of nearby animals and a buzzing in the air that penetrated my skull. It made me want to shake my head, displace the sound and its source.

In the upstairs corridor, I *did* jerk my head, and the phantom grassland disappeared as quickly as it had come, replaced by the wreck of a hallway.

This time, when I reached out to put a steadying hand on the wall, my fingers pressed against rotting plaster. I ignored it, mostly. I couldn't reconcile what I'd just seen, and for a moment, I satisfied myself with an imagined truth that would let me address it later.

I tried to shake the feeling of vertigo that came over me as I tried to catch my breath, and I was mostly successful. I was left with only a subtle discomfort.

The light from my phone illuminated the hallway again, and I could see the two small silvery globes floating against a backdrop of thick shadows. Again, the streetlight marked the ghostly outlines forgotten treasures. But those eyes, they bore into me. I took a single step forward, trailing my hand across the papery walls until this time, I felt *something* touch my mind.

I was once again in the field—

—*in the before*—

—and could see creatures that were familiar, lazing around a pool of what appeared to be water, or some close approximation my human mind could grasp. My gaze roved around what I understood to be a watering hole, and I began to see small glowing orbs through the grass. Some were large, and I reacted with tense avoidance—an evolutionary flight-or-fight response which transcended time and space—while others were small but no less bright, making my body shudder in pleasant expectation.

My vision changed rapidly, blurring as if in high-speed transition, and I was suddenly running through the grasses, chasing something that glowed faintly as a yellow sunburst through the reedy vegetation ahead. I could actually feel the stalks of it brush my legs and face as I slowed from a run to a stalking crawl.

I stopped at the edge of a small clearing and could see my prey. It was a small furry mouse-like creature that glowed with an effervescent light. Except, it wasn't actually glowing. There was something *within* it that glowed, something I could sense and see, something I could taste on the air. It was the same way I feel when I smell freshly baked bread.

My mouth began to water as I burst from the safety of the grass and into the clearing. The creature scuttled as quickly as it could, but it was trapped, backed into a corner where two giant rock outcroppings met. I could feel my heart—hearts?—speed up as I approached the thing. It cowered and trembled, its tiny whiskers vibrating.

It knew it was trapped. Its black snout sniffed the air with bouncing rhythmic surety, and its eyes darted back and forth in terror.

I opened my mouth toward it and as I did, two thin strings—

—*chaffara*—

—that hung loosely inside my mouth reached, flexed and stiffened, then began feeding. The animal's eyes rolled in their sockets, but it was momentarily paralyzed. The glow that had covered the animal in bouncing, shifting light began to fade alongside the satisfaction I felt of feeding.

A dark red liquid began to ooze down the creature's snout.

I resisted the satisfaction and wasn't surprised to find revulsion beneath. I gasped, trying to shake away the pleasure of it, then with some effort, I pushed the presence from my mind and found myself in the dank hallway of Corner House once again.

The walls of the Corner House felt closer together, now, and whatever I'd just experienced seemed to have knocked the wind out of me. I couldn't catch my breath.

The eyes at the end of the hallway were larger still. They hadn't come closer; I was sure of that. But whatever lids had previously hidden parts of them were now stretched wide.

I could faintly make out the outline of a head, the top of one, at least, just above their silvery glow. The light from outside lent the outline a primal, reptilian evolution.

I stood panting in the hallway, one hand steadying me against the wall. I wondered what I could do next while also knowing what had to be done.

Initially, I suspected the creature had something to do with the visions I began experiencing only moments ago. Now, I was sure of it, and I knew that if I let it happen anymore, I wouldn't live to finish what I started.

When I had enough breath to feel confident in my ability, I pushed away from the wall and gripped the spear in my hand. I wasn't sure what to do, if I'm being honest, but I knew if I wanted a chance at ending all of it, I'd have to run. I played it out before moving, planning to sprint to the cloister ahead and spear the creature through the heart or whatever its equivalent.

"Get out of my head, you son of a bitch," I whispered.

Then I sprang forward, ignoring the initial touch on my mind, and took two bounding steps. I was in the room now, nearly there. My eyes had adjusted to the dark just as my muscles locked up. My legs came to a skidding halt, and my mind was hijacked once again. I was transported to the other place. I could feel my momentum carry my body forward and the ground came rushing up to meet me.

In the same vein of terrible unreality that happened moments before, I was suddenly transported to a wasteland. The previously pleasant sights, sounds, and smells were gone, replaced by a landscape of ragged black rocks and a wind that was sharp and cold. I could feel it, brushing against my skin in raking waves. But at the same time, it was also distant, as if I were *remembering* the feel of a wind in a dream, instead of experiencing it firsthand. Clouds billowed through the space above me and across the horizon, angry purple shifting between shades of blue and dark red to black. It was the same place as before but another time. I think. At least, that's the best I can come up with.

After. The world bubbled up unbidden from my subconscious. No, from outside of my subconscious.

I could feel the hold on my surroundings slipping, as if I were leaning back in a chair and very close to tipping.

I blinked once, trying to clear my eyes, and suddenly, they were; I was standing in the grit of a forgotten dim corridor in the house on the corner, staring at the smoking orbs in the room beyond the hall.

The eyes shifted slightly, moving left and then right in a hypnotically feline motion.

I was tired of this. And to be honest, I was scared. Terrified, really. I let my hand fall away from the crackling wall, and still shining the light ahead, I took a tentative step forward, looking intently at the silvery specks lingering in the darkness.

When nothing changed around me, I took another.

I had just enough time to hear the dust crunch beneath my shoe before the eyes shifted once again into smoke and I was surrounded with that landscape that felt like dried blood and splintered bone. It was more real than it had been a second ago. The wind, which whistled in my ears, brought with it a new sensation, a sound that I couldn't put a name to. Was it a scream? No, not quite, but close. It was *wailing*. Yes, that was closer. I turned my head in the direction I thought the sound originated, and in the distance, I thought I could make out hazy figures. Movement, at the very least.

In some unreal reality, I took a step toward the figures milling about in the distance. I felt the change in my body as steps propelled me forward, but my shoes within the Corner House hadn't moved. And in the wasteland, I wasn't taking steps or moving at the speed of a walk; I was gliding forward on unseen tracks, rapidly approaching the bulky figures who were no longer vague outlines but had shifted into humanoid shapes. It quickly became apparent to me that something was wrong—terribly wrong—within the group of beings.

—*Shagatir*—

The vista faded, with that word—*Shagatir*—echoing faintly. The bleak scenery was replaced with the concrete clarity of being in my own body and seeing with my own eyes, but they were watering.

Later, I felt myself think. Or perhaps, was thought for me.

I looked again toward the alien shape. Closer, now. The eyes which had appeared silver from the top of the stairs were actually black orbs reflecting the light from my phone in this wasted ruin. There was something off about that thing, something powerful and eerie and strange about it, and I couldn't let it continue.

I straightened my back, lifted my foot and stepped forward. I hefted the spear in my hand, readying it for the final fatal blow.

This time, when the eyes disappeared in a swirl of glowing eddies, I was able to prepare myself for what would come next.

I closed my eyes tightly and leaned against the wall before it was replaced.

The wasteland was back, but it was dark, now. Not just in the sense that it was night, thought. There was a sense that something had changed in the makeup of this world. I could feel it in the air and in the grit beneath my feet.

A few small primitive huts stood in the darkness ahead, lit by the shifting shadows of a fire as it played around their corners. The vision—my vision—swung toward one house that showed a familiar glow in one low corner. I slunk through the shadows, avoiding the firelight as much as possible, staying hidden and still when any sounds were made.

When I approached the corner of the house where a gold light shone through wall, I knew something I needed was on the other side. My stomach rumbled and hurt in its emptiness. My mind back in The Corner House connected the earlier vision, and I thought that small animal must be inside, some kind of rat or something.

I moved around the house searching for an entrance and was rewarded with desperate relief when I looked up and saw an opening in the side, a window of sorts. Using razor sharp claws, I scaled the wall of the hut—little more than grass and sun-baked clay bricks—and made my way to the window. Peeking through, my eyes settled on the source of the glow. A small bundle lay in the corner, covered in a hairy hide blanket, one pudgy nose and the top of a scaly head were all that were visible, but I knew it wasn't an animal—well, my human understanding of one. It was a young Shagatir. I also knew what accompanied that glow—food.

I felt myself extend the *chaffara* toward the sleeping body. They wormed their way up the child's face, whipping more frantically the closer to the holes in its snout. There was almost immediate relief as I felt warmth begin to seep into my weary body, washing away the exhaustion and fear that comes with starvation.

When I was full, the child's glow had dissipated to an almost imperceptible light. It was actually more of a hum. I realized, then, that I could return if I didn't suck it dry. I could let it rejuvenate and feed again, later.

I retracted the *chaffara* and made to jump off the window. I was caught short, however, as a shout of anger and surprise came from inside the home. A larger Shagatir was staring at me, a look of disgust and fear marring its already reptilian features into something much more primal. Teeth as sharp as daggers caged a wiggling tongue as it barked at me in some kind of guttural language. The young Shagatir raised its head lethargically, and a steady stream of blue liquid coursing down its face. Seeing this, the larger Shagatir bent to retrieve something. I watched in frozen terror, curious as to what would happen next. At this point, I couldn't tell if I was feeling the fear in my human mind or this creature's memory.

A stone hurtled through the air at blinding speed, crashing into the wall next to my head and cracking the sun-baked brick. Clay chips glanced off my shoulder but as surprised as I was by the blow, my grip slipped, and I fell to the ground outside the hut. My shoulder was wet and warm as the blood ran freely down my leg. When I tried run, pain like nothing I'd ever experienced lanced across my shoulder and down the ridge on my back. I stumbled into the grass and continued as best I could, limping away as the sounds of searching Shagatir urged me on.

The scene changed again, and my stomach threatened to empty itself fully as my vision settled once more upon the vast wasteland. The sun was back, as were the Shagatir, which scurried about the landscape. I was beginning to understand that I was seeing through this creature's eyes in a different time or living a memory of one like it.

I was still as stone and watching movement through tall blades of pale and wilting grass. The Shagatir were searching for something, using blunt-ended tool with a sharpened blade to part the blades of grass before moving to another spot to do the same. I watched, and while I knew it wasn't my human emotion, I could feel a heart thundering in my chest with fear and uncertainty of this strange new development. The image of that shining furry creature that I'd devoured in a distant sunlit field rose in my mind. Now I was the creature—caught and trapped, no way to escape.

As I watched, one of the Shagatir parted a swath of grass, and its arm pistoned down, lightning quick. It lifted its weapon out of the grass, and its muscles flexed beneath scales as it hauled out its catch. Wriggling and writhing and skewered on the end of it was one of my brethren—or its brethren, rather. It was held aloft for the others to see, and they cheered and clapped. I felt a sudden pang of longing and defensive aggression rise up in my chest, but I stayed hidden, knowing that would be a death sentence.

Several other Shagatir came over to the one holding the creature, which was now rasping a high-pitched squeal. I knew—or whatever was showing me knew—that it was crying and in pain. It was terrified; it knew its death. I couldn't take much more of it and could feel tears stinging my human eyes a million miles away. It didn't last long, thank goodness. A larger Shagatir came over to the one holding weapon and ripped it viciously from the others' hand. My kin was forced to the uneven ground, and its whipping tail was stopped with a vicious stomp. This new Shagatir raised its own weapon and brought it down with a nauseating and meaty *thunk*. The squeal cut off abruptly, and the eyes through which I looked were turning through the grass and fleeing, leaving both its kin and the Shagatir alike.

The image faded, and I found myself sprawled on the floor, the spear lying an inch from my outstretched hand just over the threshold to the creature's sanctum. My mouth was dry and my head was throbbing. I tasted blood on my tongue and wiped my mouth. Then I turned to the side and spit a mouthful of bloody bile onto the bone-gray wood beneath me.

I struggled to my knees and reached for the spear, clutching it tightly in my fist. Whatever this thing was, it was powerful. *Or desperate*, a small part of me thought quietly. I tried my best to ignore it. My phone lay nearby, its light shining up toward the ceiling and illuminating much of the room.

I risked a glance to where the eyes had been before. My face felt heavy, like the skin was being pulled toward the earth and was ready to separate from my skull at any moment. My eyes, watery and buzzing simultaneously, didn't even have the energy stay focused. I was afraid *I* didn't have the energy to stop the attacks. I just stared open-mouthed at the eyes that hovered feet from my own.

They were black as midnight and held no emotion that I could find. They were set in a face covered in black and purple scales that rippled in the weak light. The lower part of the face was a mass of tentacles, with only a small bump that could pass for a nose. Beneath those tentacles he knew there were rows of razor-sharp teeth set within a mouth that could open as wide as his head. I also knew that's where the *chaffara* lay. The very tool used to suck the lifeforce from the creatures in the Before. *And my son.*

I tried to make an assessment of my body. From the way my knees were trembling on the ground, I couldn't stand.

There was no use in trying to get to my feet. Instead, I leaned forward and pulled myself onward, using my left elbow as leverage while grasping the spear in my right hand.

The eyes that held an infinity of space and time seemed to re-assess me and then my heart had a moment to sink to the floor as they vanished again. I felt myself being pushed and pulled and sent and summoned all at once. I closed my eyes against the incoming shock that would happen when I knew I'd open them on an alien landscape.

When I felt the cold pain of that ghostly wind, I opened my eyes. The light was familiar but changed. It was lower, now, more a tragic kind of perpetual dusk.

I was rushing through the grass, approaching something. I smelled death nearby, and my heart beat dramatically in my chest. It was near; *they* were near. The Hunters.

I used my tentacles to part the tall blades of grass before me and was greeted by a grisly reception. Groups of my kin lay scattered across the ground. Their blue-green blood dried, now a dark slick that reflected the grim and brooding sky in its shimmering splatters, coated the grass and rocks in the clearing. The bodies of my kin lay at unnatural angles, heads and limbs broken or missing altogether. In a recessed corner of my own mind, I tried to count them but couldn't. There were hundreds.

I made my way through the carnage, stopping here and there to sniff at a corpse. Whatever passed for fear or terror began rising inside me. My joints, as alien as they were, began to tremble in terror.

The skies overhead, once filled with light that washed the fields below now flashed ominously with electric blue light and a rattle shook the ground beneath me. The crack that followed echoed across the vast emptiness.

Fear and terror gave way to resolute defiance, and I began to lope across the gray plains, sidestepping bodies of my fallen kin and looking for shelter from the approaching storm. I moved my head back and forth, searching, using my ability to see prey but finding none. My tentacles tasted the air, but desperation sank in as the skies opened and a torrent began to beat the ground.

A guttural shout rose up to my right, and I shied away from it. A spear clattered across the ground where I had just been, followed by another. The trembling in my legs was forced away, and my survival instincts took over. The Hunters were here—they were here for me, and I had to escape.

The rain made the uneven ground even more untrustworthy, and I slipped twice. The first was merely a stumble, and I could maintain my stride. The second was an all-out spill that caused me to slide painfully across the jagged rocks. I felt gashes open up on my side, and with those new wounds, the fear seeped back in. The tentacles around my face spasmed with each breath I huffed out. The starvation was doing no favors as my already weakened body was pushed beyond its limits.

The Hunters were gaining on me. Their long reptilian stride allowed them to bypass many of the things that could trip my body up, low to the ground as it was.

When I was up and running again, the thunderous cascade blurred my vision, and I searched frantically for a safe space. Distantly, I saw a glow. This one was different than food and one that I'd never seen before, but it was something. I ran that way, dodging spears and Shagatir that came close.

When I could feel that I was out of time, the glow had grown into a cave. It hummed invitingly within my mind, and I sped toward it.

The cave was close, and I knew I might make it if I could push myself a little harder.

It loomed ahead of me, darkness glowing as if lit within by an ethereal fire. I didn't stop when I heard the splashes behind me slow and then stop although I did have a flash of concern that an even larger predator had taken their place. I didn't have the time to latch onto that thought, though, and I galloped ahead.

The sound of the storm stopped abruptly when I entered the cave, and the glow disappeared, becoming more of an emanation rather than a projection. I was *within* the glow, now. Something that hadn't happened before.

I turned to look at the entrance and could see the Hunters standing several yards from the dim mouth of the cave, shifting warily on their large, clawed feet and pointing at me. One reared back and launched a spear. I didn't wait to see where it landed, choosing to turn and run toward the back of the cave. I was fully expecting to hit a wall at any moment, to once more be trapped and cornered like the prey I had become. Instead, I found that with the flashes of light from the storm, I could run at almost full speed through a large tunnel. It curved slightly this way and that, angling downward part of the way before angling back up. The glow guided me, in a way, and I made the decision to run until the cave walls stopped me.

Twice, I thought my flight was at an end when an outcropping of stone obscured the tunnel's path. But after passing the massive formation, I continued my retreat as quickly as I could.

Finally, the tunnel opened up into an enormous cavern. The glow, it seemed, was coming from this place. It wasn't brighter here, but it was *more present*. These emotions came to me in flashes of intent, not as thoughts themselves. Perhaps,

I was misunderstanding what was being shown to me, but my human mind was translating it as best it could.

My footfalls, soft paddings that barely disturbed the blanket of dust and scree that littered the cavern floor, stopped. Three new tunnel entrances faced me. My animal eyes blinked in confusion, and something akin to panic began to creep through my scales, which rippled in discomfort and uncertainty as I shifted my gaze from each of the new cave mouths.

Knowing I couldn't go back, for both fear of the Hunters and knowing there wasn't any food left, I had to move forward. In the final days before the purge, my kind had decimated the remaining vermin in desperation, leaving a completely depleted food source and hundreds of hungry mouths.

My tentacles felt the air, feeling for any kind of movement and coming up empty.

I launched myself toward the middle tunnel and, just before I entered it, made a sharp turn, entering the tunnel on the right. I don't know what it was, some ancestral instinct, perhaps. I was immediately plunged into darkness. There was no going back. The familiar and comforting glow that my vision had used to light the way was now gone. When I looked back, there wasn't even the entrance I'd just used. The eerie blackness of the cavern was all that was left. No light penetrated the inky depths, and I only knew my feet were below me because I could hear the shuffle they made as I plodded somberly forward.

I traveled for an interminable amount of time. The black void that now embodied this reality was my only companion as I marched forward. Hunger and thirst clenched my body and muscles, but I marched on, pushed by some hope of salvation, either in death or discovery. Sleep would not come. Anytime I closed my eyes to rest, there was a jarring insecurity that I hadn't yet closed them, and I sat in the dark just staring ahead. Blinking several times forced the feeling away, but it returned as soon as I stopped. For this reason, I didn't stop to sleep again. I was beyond the bounds of tiredness and near death, but sleep wouldn't come as long as there was uncertainty in my own decisions.

So I continued on, one step at a time.

A dazzling brightness suddenly grew before me after what felt like weeks of traveling in the dark. Even though I was walking excruciatingly slow, the glow raced toward me and enfolded me, nearly blinding me. I felt myself being pulled, compressed, then released time and again in a cycle of mystifying agony.

When I was able to blink away the sting to make my inky eyes refocus, I was met with the now-familiar view of the same hallway where both of me now lay. The same emptiness and dimness surrounded me, but as I turned, spinning on the spot and searching, my eyes caught the faintest distant glow through the wall. For the first time in a very long time, my tongues tasted saliva, and I knew I was saved.

CHAPTER 29

I tasted blood and dust, my breath came in ragged gasps against the dusty floorboards beneath my face. I tried to groan, but my throat was dry as parchment, and it crackled painfully as I tried to swallow spit that wasn't there. A second and third attempt gave me the freedom to lick my lips, and a croaky groan finally escaped my lips.

The tendons in my neck resisted, and I could feel myself grimacing when my face seemed to stick to the floor. Drying strings of blood, drool, and snot had all but glued my cheek down, and while it hurt to raise my head, I forced myself to get up; I had to see.

I blinked the dust away from my eyes and glared as best I could at the creature that lay not five feet away. I hoped desperately that this other-worldly abomination was dead. I thought I was spent after the first flashbacks, but this last one had knocked me out cold, and from the look of the beast before me, it had cost it dearly, as well. There was a dark slick dripping from beneath the mass of tentacles on its face, which now lay still, not even twitching the slightest bit. They looked like large, discolored worms hanging across the floor. They were lifeless.

My face throbbed in time with my heartbeat, which pounded out a steady, quick rhythm. The drums in my head made blurred my vision with each pounding beat. I spit a red gob of mess onto the floor in front of me and then stared at the creature's dark eyes.

"What do you want?"

The creature, surprisingly, chuffed something from beneath the tentacles, making them flutter as if in a breeze. It seemed to me that it took every bit of energy for even that small motion.

"I don't understand," I managed, just before my heart sank in despair. I tried to scream as I saw the eyes ghost away once more and felt my own mind tether itself to the alien perspective, but I only heard a weary groan issue forth from my mouth.

I was once more under attack by the creature, viewing something through its eyes. This time, though, the view was familiar. It should be... it was my own house. The only difference was a gentle glow emanated from a second-story window—from Jackson's window.

At first, I saw it as a distant lamp. It could have been, I suppose, if the glow was seen through a window. But it wasn't. I was seeing it through the walls of the house where no window was cut.

I—in the creature's body—moved cautiously across the ground, making sure to stay in the shadows. I was wary of the glowing lights suspended in the sky.

The moon and stars.

They shouldn't be there, I thought. It was the creature's thought. But it was more of a hesitant fear of this new, unknown world. I was in a strange place without any knowledge of what to do or where to go, but I knew one thing: there was food in the dwelling ahead, and that would suffice for now.

I crept to the side of the house, and using my razor-sharp claws, I climbed the tree nearby to leap nimbly onto the roof. Here was easy access to the opening where the glow originated, but there was no shelter from the floating glow of the ghostly disc above. I had to risk it. My lithe body scampered across the roof until I was just above the window to where the glow originated. The body I now inhabited might be from an alien landscape, but it was designed for sneaking, and its reptilian paws made barely a whisper on the shingles beneath me.

Once at the edge of the roof, I carefully leaned over. What I thought was merely an opening in the wall much like the ones in the dwellings from the Before—*windows*—had a transparent barrier covering the opening—*glass*. While surprising, it was only a minor setback. I was equipped with a remarkable tool that could fit through the tiniest cracks and still function, my *chaffara*.

I looked through the pane of glass and saw, to my immediate relief, a small sleeping creature, glowing with that undeniable source of sustenance. The creature resembled the Hunters from the Before, but looked ... softer. There were no scales or teeth that I could see, and its snout was short and stubby, almost non-existent.

Even still, I was cautious as I extended my *chaffara* toward the glass. They felt tentatively along the edges until they found purchase in the tiny lip where the windowpane joined the wall. They slipped through easily, changing shape and thinning until they were nearly transparent themselves, a fraction of a their original thickness. Still, they extended far enough to reach the creature—*Jackson*—and found the nostrils, in the same general area of the Shagatir. I engaged my ability to siphon and immediately felt the relief of feeding racing up the barbed extension. The pain in my midsection eased, and even though it was glorious, I stopped and retracted the *chaffara* with no small amount of longing. But just as in the Before when my kin would feed endlessly by allowing their prey to regain strength, I would do the same with this one, The Jackson.

As I looked, a darkness began leaking out of The Jackson's nose—*blood*—and onto its chest. This Jackson would do well. I would make sure to leave it well enough to regain its strength easily; perhaps I could make this feeding last for many days before needing to return to feed again.

As I sat on the edge of the roof overlooking the minia-ture stalks—*grass*—and the black stream—*road*—that ran down between the large dwellings, I felt a sense of ease come over me. I was safe. I'd survived, and while I didn't know exactly where I was, I could continue to survive here. There was a food source, and as far as I could tell, there were no Hunters. The prey was easy, and perhaps, I would find more as time went on. For now, I was *alive*.

As I turned to go, I felt a tug on my consciousness. The beast's, not my human mind, which a distant part of me real-ized in a confusing sense of schizophrenic mental vomit. The tug was gentle at first but grew in intensity until I felt the fresh comfort and fullness from my recent meal leave in a burst of hollow emptiness. And just like that, I was hungry and weak again. My back legs collapsed in fatigue, and I nearly rolled off the high roof, my front claws ripped into the material, stopping me from plummeting to my death.

After catching my breath and regaining enough of my strength, I looked over the edge where The Jackson had slept while I fed. There were two more larger creatures there, sitting close to the glowing one and interacting with him while another, the female I was sure—well, the creature was sure—helped clean the young one's face and hands, which were covered in its own blood.

There was no sign of anything that could have stolen my own essence but stolen it had been. In a confusing mix of irritation, fear, and resignation, I left the house and retreated back to my den. The glow was faint, now, the one from The Jackson, but it was still there. I—it hoped this strange occurrence wouldn't last.

In quick succession, I witnessed, night after night, the visitor siphoning Jackson's essence and in turn losing the fullness of its meal. It was a confusing, stuttering light show that spanned months and seasons. There was a growing sense of desperation, and the visitor's interactions increased despite the fear of knowing it would only be fulfilled for the briefest of moments. It even tried running as soon as it was fed, but to no avail, it was siphoned just as easily regardless of distance.

However, being the only food source that he had found, there was no other option. In its animalistic brain, it knew that at some point, it could be successful, and so it continued. Only sporadically at first but more frequently the more desperate it became, culminating in tonight, where I watched myself discover the visitor and chase it down the street and into the Corner House.

I came back to my own body, this time propped against the doorframe to the room where the creature lay. Blood ran freely from my nose, soaking the front of my shirt. My breathing was labored, and I felt like I was on the verge of passing out, blackness coalescing at the edge of my vision. I had to calm down and take a break. The psychic barrage I'd just received was too much, and my mind was reeling with everything that came with it. This creature had been feeding on my child for months. Some of those visions, quick as they were, had something else with them. What was it: affection? That couldn't be right. This thing couldn't feel affection for Jackson; he considered Jackson food. Was it gratefulness? No, that wasn't right, either. *Preference*. That was it. This creature *preferred* my son over the food that had come in the Before.

I made the great effort to sit up and grabbed the spear that now lay across my knees, uncertain of how it got there. This thing didn't get to have a preference. It was a parasite, something that required another to survive. It was no different than a giant flea or tick that you picked off your dog and smashed.

I stumbled the last few feet toward the creature, leaning on the spear for support. It hunkered beneath what looked like a decomposing table in the center of the room, one leg cracked, causing the boxes stacked on top tilt and lean precariously. The creature's scales were a sickly yellow, and from the visions, I knew they should have been a vibrant, pearlescent lilac. I stepped around a fallen stack of papers and books that spilled across the floor like a deck of cards and felt something brush against my neck. I spasmed and whipped my head around only to find a moth-eaten and musty material hanging from a rotting coat rack. In my shambling stride, my make-shift spear caught on the edges of boxes and trunks that crowded the room, making it almost impassable except for the clear trail from doorway to table, where the source of all our misery now listlessly lay, obscured by shadows.

The creature's black eyes, now a milky charcoal, rolled toward me, and I knew that the last vision—or visions—were delivered in desperation and had sapped all the remaining strength from it. There was a small part of me that cared, but I silenced it with brutal swiftness.

If I had faced this creature in any other circumstance, I was certain that I would have been disgusted and unsettled by its

likeness. But here, in the darkness of the room and knowing that this... this visitor from another plane of existence, was now harmless, I was numb to anything about it. It was a creature, an animal, and it had little bearing on my own life apart from needing to be expunged from it.

I bent close to the creature; it smelled of death and slow decay. I positioned myself astride the visitor and held the spear tip to its chest, pricking the scaleless flesh there. A buzzing skittered through my mind, then, a low hum that sent goosebumps down my arms and raised the hairs on them. But something akin to pleading bounced within the periphery of my consciousness. I felt sudden disgust at the thought of the thing before me. It was trying to bargain. It was asking for mercy.

Or was it?

That could be bargaining, yes, but it felt—I clenched my teeth as the buzzing moved behind my eyes and into my sinus cavity. It felt like a *pleading*. Just as the thing before me had communicated its journey through pictures, it seemed to be communicating emotions in the same way.

I closed my eyes against the rising hum in my mind, and at the same time, I saw the creature limping away. A form that I knew to be the creature's interpretation of Jackson sat on the ground and watched it go, a black spear grasped in its hand.

The thing was asking for mercy. It was asking for freedom.

I shook my head and could feel my vocal chords engage but couldn't hear them. The hum overpowered every other sound until I opened my eyes and rolled them until the creature came into view. Its heaving sides shone pale in the dim light. The metallic spheres, which had seemed to be two dark portals were now two dull pewter orbs hidden behind translucent lids.

"No," I managed to growl. I pulled himself up onto my elbows, getting a better grip on the spear and better leverage against the beast before me. I felt like a knight come to slay the dragon, but the scaly monstrosity before me was no larger than a small golden retriever.

I felt the buzzing begin again in my head, and I shook my head and screamed at it to stop.

"No!" I was panting now. Spittle flew from my mouth as my chest heaved. Blood continued to leak from my nose and down my lips. I tasted the metallic warmth coating my teeth and knew I looked like something from a nightmare. Maybe that's what it took, a nightmare to kill a nightmare. There was a mental toll, one that was quickly burning a hole in my pocket. This had to end, and fast.

I was now faced with a choice. Where before the lives of my children were at stake, now there were the lives of other children at stake. And this thing, too, I supposed. Not that I cared. Not really. But either way, I had to decide. Let the beast go to potentially harm some other family, maybe even killing a kid like Mikayla. Or I could kill the visitor and end it once and for all.

Could I?

Sure, I thought, *I can do that.*

But will you?

That was the question, now. Not if I could or not. I could do anything if it meant the safety of my children was assured. Well, if not assured, then more likely. Hadn't I proven that already?

Had I?

My vision suddenly went swimmy, and I felt myself falling. I put out a hand to steady myself against the wall and closed my eyes as the world went on a tilt-a-whirl. When I felt the swaying subside, I looked down at the creature. Its lids were

now open, and the pewter orbs had faded to a kind of matte steel, gleaming dully in what little light shone from my phone.

I felt the buzzing begin, but it was weak, a final attempt of the creature begging for mercy.

I heaved another great sigh and nodded, finally making my decision. I pushed off the ground and stood, slowly making my way to my feet. The ground lurched only once as I looked down at the pitiful creature before me. The warm air in the musty old house swam through the beam of light as small glowing motes.

I took a deep breath.

The visitor turned its head to look at me with its dull gray eyes. The decision had been made, and it must have known. Its emaciated sides rose and fell in what seemed like resignation to me. The same way a sigh of relief is huffed when the finality of a task is settled.

I plunged the spear tip down unceremoniously, aiming for where the line of purple scales met the soft underbelly skin, just behind the visitor's foreleg and between what appeared to be ribs. The wooden spear sank easily into the skin with a meaty *snick*. The creature jerked, and its head whipped around. The tentacles on its face spasmed briefly, revealing a mouth agape, full of needle-like teeth as it tried to bite at the spear.

Dark, black blood oozed around the spear and began to spread across the floor in a viscous, reflective puddle.

The buzz that previously had felt like a kind of begging was back, but it held something akin to what I would later describe as disbelief. And anger. And pain. It hurt my head, and it was the start of a migraine, but I'd made my choice.

A nightmare to kill nightmares.

I held the spear firmly, even though I felt unsteady on my own feet, effectively pinning the writhing mass of scales and tentacles to the floorboards. The creature's claws raked feebly across the floor, expanding like a cat's and retracting, but gouging small tracks across the aging wood. Its tail whipped back and forth, forming lazy arcs through the air and thumping against the floor as death began to finally take hold.

Its head turned once more toward me, and I thought, as crazy as it sounds to me now, that I saw a look of betrayal there. But that would be impossible. We would have had to have been on the same side in order for me to betray it.

And we weren't.

A nightmare to kill nightmares.

I leaned heavily on the spear and bent over, getting within a foot of the tentacles that flicked back and forth, spasming feebly. "You don't get a second chance," I spit viciously. "You almost killed my son. You don't get to do that to anyone ever again." I stood up straight, once again closing my eyes against the nausea that crashed against my temples.

I didn't know how long I stood there, but when I opened my eyes—slowly, at first—the world had stopped spinning and the house was quiet. I looked down at the thing before me. It was still. The eyes, which once upon a time born witness to the rise and fall of worlds, were now a flat gray, glazed and glassy. The tentacles lay limply across the animal's mouth and floor. The feet and tail were still, and the black blood that had pooled near the animal's mortal wound had stopped flowing, too.

I wasn't sure what to do about the visitor. After pulling the spear free and prodding the beast—just to make sure, I told myself—I was certain it was dead. I couldn't bury it, not in the ground. But this place had been abandoned for years. Maybe—

I lifted the lighter from my pocket, the one John dropped in my yard earlier in the day, what felt like a lifetime ago.

I looked around. The still air seemed inviting, but the stench of death and infinite distance filled my nostrils, and I didn't like it. There was a strange smell in the air that I hadn't noticed before, but it brought to my mind the image of Gretchen exploding. I wasn't sure why, but it gave me no love for this place.

No, this house had to go.

The room was filled with all manner of flammable objects. Old books and papers, tattered, moth-eaten clothes. There would be little suspicion if this house suddenly caught fire. All it would take would be one small spark; it could be explained away in a magnifying glass concentrating the sunlight into a single, devastating circle of white fire.

But in the middle of the night? That seemed suspicious at best and downright obvious at worse. But this place was a relic, forgotten by its owners and stuck in legal purgatory for years. Maybe I was doing them a favor. I told myself that because when we're desperate, the worst ideas sound good.

I opened the lighter. It popped with a light metallic *click*, and when I spun the wheel, the *Schick* that preceded the tiny flame was satisfying and welcome. Here was the end of the journey. It started in blood, now it would end in fire. Wasn't that the way of things? Wasn't that the price the world asked of me, of everyone? You come into this world bloody and leave it as ashes.

I picked up my phone and turned the flashlight off. The sudden darkness was disorienting, but after letting my eyes adjust, I was able to relax a little.

My battery was low, but I had enough to make a call.

"Grant?"

"Marco, hey. I've got a problem."

"What the fuck, man? It's like … super fuckin early for you and super fuckin' late for me." I heard rustling and a yawn. Then, "What's up?"

"You know that report that showed the weird shit in Castelsardo? They called it 'biological interference.'"

"Um… yeah… I remember."

"Something like that happened here, when Gretchen blew up from hijacking the ley line."

"Wait, what? You pulling my leg, bro?"

"No."

"Holy shit. Dude, you gotta tell Gianna."

"I can't."

"Why not?"

"Because I just killed it."

Silence.

"What was it?"

"It was a… a nightmare, man. But it's over, now. I think. I hope."

"What do you need from me?" He was serious, now, his tone changing quickly from groggy curiosity to grim acceptance.

"I need you to send the team that Gianna was going to send. But I need you to send them as a cleanup crew. I'm going to burn the house down with the creature inside it."

"Grant, that's some heavy shit, dude. You sure that's the best option?"

"No. But this house is abandoned; it has no ties to anyone around here, and the only people who care about it have been dead for twenty years. It's been stuck in mortgage or deed of trust or something like that for over a decade. And once this place burns down, any evidence of the visitor goes with it."

"I can't say that I agree with you on this, but you know better than me. I'll send out the request right now. They'll get it in a few hours when they wake up and will probably arrive there tomorrow. But like, tomorrow-tomorrow, not today-tomorrow."

"Yeah, I get it. Thanks. You're a good friend."

"Anytime, bro."

And that was that. The only thing left was to start the fire and run.

Something bothered me still. Something about the visions the visitor had shared with me. It always ran away, unsatisfied, but why?

I tried to ignore it; it didn't matter, now.

I bent to the nearest stack of books and papers. The wan light gave everything around me a ghostly glow. I smelled the small flame, fueled by a tiny amount of propane and oxygen.

The paper curled away from the heat, darkening. But before it could catch, I released the switch.

It always ran away *empty*.

What was it that it told me, or showed me? It fed, and then was drained. It was as if it were being fed upon.

Weren't there animals in its world that it feared? Those large glowing lights it could see but instinctually avoided because *it* was prey to *them*?

But those weren't here. It would have seen them. *I* would have seen them through its visions.

I thought I actually heard the audible *click* of the final piece falling into place.

It was Keller.

It was Keller all along.

Keller wasn't feeding off Jackson—we knew that once we discovered the visitor. But what we *didn't* know was that Keller was still a piece of the puzzle. The creature would flee, but not because of anything we were doing or because of something it had done. It was fleeing because it was being fed upon.

My mind flashed with the instances of seeing Keller reaching toward his brother. Now however, with this new understanding, it made total sense. Keller was reaching for *the visitor*, was feeding up on the visitor's life force in order to heal himself. The visitor was healing Keller, not Jackson!

And now the visitor was dead.

Oh, god, it was dead. If what I suspected was true—it had to be, I felt it—then I'd just sentenced Keller to die.

What could I do about it? Could Keller still drain the energy from the creature even though it was dead?

No, that was a stupid thought. How could I have been so thoughtless? If only I'd have seen it sooner, I could have come up with a better plan, something to save both of my kids.

But it looked like I wasn't able to do that.

There was nothing for it, then. I'd taken out the nightmare—ended one and secured the other. The nightmare might be over for Jackson, but it would continue for Keller.

I flicked the lighter on again.

I'd have to figure it out later.

The flame touched the paper and began to climb up the edge. It climbed faster than I thought possible, and suddenly, the box of books beside it wasn't filled with books anymore; it was filled with leaping flames. I watched it, transfixed by the power of its rapidly spreading maw. Fear began to rise within my chest.

I have to get out or I'll burn alive, I thought. But my legs were sluggish in responding. The loss of blood, perhaps.

A nightmare to kill a nightmare.

I turned on my heel, and using the spear as a crutch, I limped from the room. There was plenty of light, now. I could hear crackling and popping from behind me, and decades-old wood burst into flame. Heat from the tiny fire was washing across my back, and I knew that it was no small flame.

I made my way to the stairs and chanced a look back. The entire room where I'd been standing was ablaze. The heat was immense. The creature, little more than a sizzling mass in the middle of the floor, was surrounded by orange and blue flames. They danced across the ceiling and began to make their way out of the room even as I watched. My final image of the creature was of its scaly skin bubbling and steaming as flames licked hungrily in the space around it.

The crackling heat that began to buffet my backside as I made my way down the stairs was a ticking clock. My time was running out, and I knew it.

Once at the bottom of the stairs, the true price of my actions were laid bare. Angry orange sparks rained from the ceiling all around me. Wallpaper around me bubbled and warped, burning and melting as the heat peeled it from the wooden slats beneath. Boards and molding sizzled and steamed as the fire tore its way through the weak or rotted spaces between the floors. The fire was spreading with unnatural speed, and if I didn't get out of the house in a matter of seconds, it was going to take me with it.

It was getting hard to breathe, and I covered my mouth and nose with my shirt, but it didn't do much. A glowing timber dropped to my left, and I sidestepped it, knowing that if I took one of those to the head, I was done for. The sidestep, which I planned based on my knowledge of the house, would have taken me away from the stairs and farther into the foyer. What I'd forgotten to account for was the banister that lay in that space, rotten and splintered and very much a hazard. My foot tripped over the mass of wood scattered across the floor, and instead of taking a step, I took a fall.

At that same moment, the ceiling in the adjacent room disintegrated. Burning wood, sparks, and smoke poured across the floor toward me.

I tried to catch myself but flailed helplessly and landed amidst the splintered wood. Pain stabbed through my hip and midsection, forcing me to suck in a deep breath. Instead, I inhaled a lungful of hot air and ashes that were billowing across the floor. I coughed, unable to hold it in and began gasping for breath. I was caught between the pain in my side and the pain in my lungs, and each was causing the other. I tried to roll onto my back and disentangle myself from the bars that pinned me, but a single movement sent jolts of pain lancing across my side.

Flames began to lick down the stairs and across the ceiling. Their orange danced across the walls, giving me a front-row seat to my own agony. The air was heating rapidly, and the moisture in my skin evaporated, leaving my body feeling dry and stretched like canvas.

I could taste the smoke with every breath. Even with the knowledge that it was poisoning my lungs, I couldn't help but gulp in great lungfuls of air. The pain in my side made me pant, and the lack of oxygen was making me dizzy. My vision began to blur at the edges, and I couldn't tell if it was the smoke obscuring my vision or if I was passing out. I couldn't stop coughing or heaving for breaths, even with the pain, and I suppose at this point, it didn't matter.

Cancer tried to burn me from the inside out and failed. This fire though.

This fire should do the trick.

The last thing I thought before everything went black was that today was the anniversary of my final chemo treatment. Instead of my veins filling with medicinal poison, my lungs filled with noxious, boiling clouds.

CHAPTER 30

I woke up an interminable time later in a place that was all too familiar. The sterile smell that accosted my senses overcrowded my senses alongside the cloying smell of flowers. The white linen sheets were too commonplace for me to wonder long where I was.

I made to look around the hospital room, but my eyes resisted opening at first. I worked at opening them slowly, building up their tolerance for the light and the colors until I could focus them on a form sitting in a chair near the bed. I tried to speak, but my mouth was void of moisture, and it took several minutes of working up spit to be able to lick my lips properly. The sandpaper-y feel of them made me cringe, but I spied a cup of water on a tray lying a few feet away.

I heard one of the machines beep an angry warning when the small IV tubes in my hands reached their limits, and they tugged uncomfortably under my skin. It was still several inches away from the cup, and I let my hand fall listlessly to the bed.

The angry beeping continued until an orderly came into the room and pressed a few buttons on a monitor.

The form curled up on the chair next to the bed stirred and then sat up abruptly.

"Grant?"

Kathryn's near-frantic voice helped anchor me, and I found it easy to focus on her form as it changed from a haze of colors into my beautiful wife.

"Oh my, God. How do you feel?" She was up now, standing next to the bed and holding my hand.

I blinked and looked at the cup of water. She followed my gaze and snatched it quickly and thrust it at me, too much familiarity in this situation, I think.

"Of course, here, honey."

She touched the trembling cup to my chapped lips, and I gulped greedily. The relief was immediate, and it was followed quickly by immense pain in my throat, as if I'd swallowed razorblades. I coughed and choked on the water and a moan escaped my lips.

The orderly, who had been standing to the side, approached the bed and wiped my face.

I met her eyes. She had big, beautiful brown eyes that exuded kindness. Her black curls framed a beautiful face that smiled easily at me.

"Mr. Taldo, you've suffered some injuries from smoke inhalation and a gash on your side. We've got you on some pain meds, but if you need more, you can just let us know, alright?"

I nodded my understanding and tried to reach up to tap my throat.

She nodded, her hair bouncing along with it. "That's part of the injury. Your throat is burned from the hot air and smoke that you breathed in that house fire. Do you remember that?"

I nodded and squeezed Kathryn's hand.

My cracked lips had absorbed the water, even if I hadn't been able to swallow much. I was able to form the word "How?"

Kathryn squeezed my hand back.

"How did you get out? Is that what you're asking?"

I nodded again, not wanting to risk the pain of speaking because even that small movement of my head felt like I'd thrust it into a jet engine.

"Ed gave us the general direction of where you went. But it was Mitch who pulled you out of the house, Grant. Mitch ran in despite the fire crawling out of the cracks and windows of that old house. It collapsed only a few minutes after. It's just a pile of smoldering rubble, now."

"If I'd been even a few minutes later, I wouldn't have made it."

The voice came from my left, the opposite side of the room. I turned slowly and saw Mitch leaning against the windowsill. I smiled at him and felt that all too familiar buzz move from my eyes into my nasal cavity. The appreciation I felt for him was unexpected. I hoped he knew how thankful I was. He had to know, even though I don't think I ever voiced it.

I closed my eyes and lay back on the pillow. It was over. Finally, the nightmare was done.

Kathryn bent and kissed my forehead. "Get some rest, babe. I'll have Mom bring the kids up later today or tomorrow."

I nodded. Rest sounded good, even though I knew I'd already slept today. I closed my eyes, and I don't remember thinking much else except a brief prayer that the remains of the creature wouldn't be found and that we'd find some way to help Keller.

True to her word, Kathryn brought the boys by the next day. She said she'd come back later that first day, but I must have been asleep because I don't remember seeing her until the next time she came the following day. I watched both boys step into the room cautiously, autumn sun slanting across the room, illuminating dust motes and worried eyes alike.

"Hi, Jack," I said with excitement when his head peeked around the corner. My throat was still scratchy, but I had been able to eat breakfast and had very little trouble drinking the water they gave me.

A grin spread across his face, and he walked over to my bed and hopped up on it. This was old hat for him, seeing his dad in the hospital. He leaned into my chest. I was able to hug him awkwardly, confined by the tubes as I was.

"Hi, Daddy." He wasn't as scared as the first time he saw me in the hospital, even though it wasn't that long ago. I suppose I still saw him as a kid, but that wasn't true. He was growing up, despite my best efforts. "How do you feel?"

I looked down at my arms, the hair singed off. "How do I look?" I was genuinely curious. If it had been as hot as it felt, I wouldn't be surprised if I was now bald and waiting for eyebrows to grow back.

He looked me up and down in mock seriousness. "Well, you look mostly like you. Your face is red, and you have a bald spot on your head."

"Oh yeah?" I asked. "Where at?"

He reached up and poked above my right temple. "Right there."

I reached up and felt the spot. Sure enough, there was a definite smooth patch of skin surrounded by hair.

"Mitch said that side of your face was exposed to the flames; that's why it's singed on one side and not the other." Kathryn was still in the doorway, Keller on her hip.

"Makes sense," I said, speaking to Jackson and answering Kathryn. "Bring that baby over here."

Kathryn smiled and walked to the bed. Keller's eyes widened a little when she handed him to me, but he smiled a second later, said "Dada!" and laid his head on my chest. He was a sweet kid and kept growing sweeter.

"Hi, my big three-year-old. How are you today?" My throat was already starting to hurt, but I ignored it.

"Dood," he said in his toddler tone and smiled.

"Good? Good, I'm glad." I hugged him to my chest and felt my throat constrict with emotion. I'd almost been killed in a fire. A fire that I set to kill something hurting Jackson. But what was I going to do with Keller's sicknesses?

Kathryn had brought books and toys for the boys to play with to avoid boredom. They were content to sit and listen while I read to them. When my throat couldn't tolerate any more work, we played little games for the remaining hours they were there.

"Doc says you'll be discharged in the morning. They're running some final tests but don't foresee any issues. You'll have some discomfort for a couple of weeks, but they're pleased with the progress you've made today in both talking and swallowing food and drink. So I'll pick you up in the morning. How's that sound?"

I smiled at them all and hugged the boys tightly before kissing Kathryn. "That sounds great. I miss you guys."

I watched the lights of the city battle the light of the stars as night fell, thinking somberly about my brush with death. Well, second brush with death, if I'm being honest. The cancer didn't take me those few years ago, and this fire tried and failed. But what was I leaving for my children?

I thought about all the lives bustling a few stories below me. How much longer would I be around to teach the things that fathers teach their boys? Two near-death experiences in less than five years didn't bode well for the next five, or ten, or fifty.

I took a deep breath. I felt like I was on the edge of a cliff looking down at the ground hundreds of feet below. It was the way of the world. If I did my job, I'd raise my children to not only think for themselves but also to improve upon those lessons so that their children could allow them to pass into obscurity, and on and on.

But if I was going to pass into obscurity, I'd at least give them a record of it. I decided then and there, in that fifth-story hospital room, to write down the story of my boys, their health, and the visitor. I wanted—and still do—to hand something down to my children, and their children, and so on. While lying on the hospital bed, I knew that I wanted to remember every detail, and I think I did a pretty good job of it. Grandpa Grant, they'll say, was a crazy old kook. But it was not because of the stories he made up. No, it was the stories he lived that made him crazy.

Kathryn arrived the next morning and took me home. I was sore, too sore to do much. Marco and Gianna sent flowers and well-wishes and told me to get back to work when I was up for it. When we left the hospital, we hadn't received the results of the tests I took before leaving. At that point, there was still a point to healing.

After a few days of being able to totter around the house without needing to take a break every other step, we decided to take a walk. I wanted to feel the late autumn air on my scorched skin and let the kids run around.

Now that the constant threat of a nosebleed had gone, the chains that had hung around my neck seemed to have gone. They'd been replaced, however, with an old rusty chest that held all my worry for Keller. With the creature gone, I wasn't sure what would happen to him. Would he continue to worsen just like when he and Jackson were away from the house?

I was still in a kind of shock. Keller's sickness was very real, but so was his ability to somehow siphon health from the visitor. It explained everything but still made no sense. Where we once thought that Keller's illness and Jackson's nosebleeds were linked, now we understand that there was another player all along. Jackson's nosebleeds were a result of the animal that visited every few nights. Keller's wellness occurred because he siphoned health from the animal when it would visit to siphon from Jackson. It was all a twisted, convoluted and impossibly delicate balance. I couldn't hardly believe it.

But now, what would Keller use to get better? Was there another animal? Another creature out there that would let him feed?

I put a hand to my head. The possibilities and fears swirling through my cranium were too much. I was also kicking myself for killing the beast. If I'd taken more than a second to think about it... I guess it didn't matter, now. My goal was protect the kids from it, and I had. Only now that Jackson was well, we were faced with a larger problem, and one that didn't have a solution.

Kathryn laced her gloved fingers through my bare one as I limped down the sidewalk, my free hand grasping that old familiar cane I used after cancer treatments. The air was crisp but not uncomfortable, and I could feel it seeping into my weary bones. She walked with her other hand on the stroller where Keller sat beneath his froggy blanket. When Jackson would pass in front of him with his bike, a little red nose would lift above a grin that split his face in two. He sniffed, sneezed, coughed, then smiled up at Jackson and giggled, then babbled something that Jackson could understand, and we could only partially decipher.

The leaves had turned, and we walked beneath them. The sun attempted to shine through them, but it gave the illusion that the ground or air around us was on fire. It would have been unsettling to me if I hadn't come to terms with my mortality in the charred ruins a short distance ahead.

We slowed when we approached Corner House. Well, what remained of it. It was nothing more than a smoldering ruin. The blackened skeleton of Corner House was a testament to the havoc its inhabitant had wreaked on our family. From the nosebleeds, to the sicknesses, to the burn and hospital visits, I was glad to see it go.

Cleanup crews from both the fire station and Eastwind Energy were on site, though the Eastwind team were there only as "volunteers." There would be legal issues if they found out that the fire was set on purpose.

"Hassen!" said Keller's little voice to his brother.

"Yeah, Kel?" Our eldest propped his bike on the rickety old fence and bent over, hands on knees to get eye-to-eye with our youngest.

"Up-it," Keller piped.

Jackson obliged, unbuckling his little brother and lifting him to his hip.

Keller pointed with a mittened hand toward the blackened wooden struts jutting up from the singed front yard. "There," he said, but it came out more like "dare" with his toddler-talk and stuffy nose.

Jackson walked awkwardly with Keller on his hip up to the fence, and they stood there for a moment, looking quietly at the remains.

I squeezed Kathryn's hand, and she put her head on my shoulder.

"I'm still so sorry for all of this." I didn't know what to say, and even knowing it was all completely out of my hands, I still felt so sorry.

She hugged me tighter with her other hand. "Grant, we couldn't have known. It will all work out. You did all you could to keep our kids safe; you know that."

I did, in fact. It seemed so little and unimportant, but maybe I was being too harsh on myself.

We watched the boys converse in their little language—I didn't know how Jackson could understand half of what Keller said, but he responded as he did. Then Keller did something I hadn't seen recently but was very familiar. He reached out toward the ruins, fingers splayed with both palms out.

"No, we can't go over there buddy. It's not safe." Jackson was patting his brother's bottom in a very parental manner, and I smiled, but my eyes were focused on Keller.

Our toddler shook his head, restrained as it was by the hat and coat he wore. "No, go derr," he said and tried to lunge in that direction.

Kathryn and I approached them, and I took Keller from Jackson. "I'll take him, buddy," I told him.

"Grant, I—" Kathryn began.

"No, it's okay. I think he wants something from it."

Kathryn's eyes betrayed her doubt, but she nodded.

The firefighters were there and warned us of getting too close, but I told them I was dragged out of there and just wanted a closer look. I promised we'd stay well away from the house itself.

I could feel a strange ribbon of hope begin to wind its way through my core, and the butterflies began to join it.

The gate creaked on its hinge as I opened it. Keller was still reaching toward the rubble several yards away. I wasn't sure what I'd do when I got there, but maybe Keller would?

I walked carefully along the stone path, avoiding large shards of shattered glass as best I could but hearing it crunch beneath my shoes nonetheless. Shattered wooden timbers blocked much of the path and littered the front yard, but I wove my way around them to the steps. When we stood facing the remains of the front door—

—and the doorframe I used to kill the visitor—

—Keller reached out, his little eyes squinting toward the middle of the blackened ash pile and as if giving the ghost of Corner House two high-fives.

I watched him closely as his nose turned from red and runny to pleasantly pink. Then he turned to me and smiled. I could feel tears welling in my eyes at the thought that perhaps, somehow, impossibly, there was residual energy here that he could use. Would it be just this once?

He placed a mittened hand on each cheek and touched his nose, no longer a runny snotty mess, to mine and spoke softly. His gentle voice, to me at least, sounded full of relief, as if he was finally sated. "I good, Dada."

I was stunned. Did he know what he'd done? Did he know that this place could be a kind of well for him? Surely not. But...

Kathryn called from the other side of the fence, worry thick in her voice. "Grant?"

I cleared my through and turned, hoping that she would see Keller's color change even from the dozen yards between us. "We're okay, babe."

Her face paled a little after she nodded. Yeah, she could see.

How? she mouthed.

I shrugged, possibilities trying to find purchase in my brain and coming up with none. One thought did come through clear as day, though. If Keller was able to use whatever energy remained here, then we'd have to do more than just pass by this place every now and then.

We finished our walk, Kathryn and I talking in hushed tones about it while Keller tottered as Jackson walked his bike ahead of us.

I explained a little of what transpired between the creature and myself in that dusty upstairs room. I told her how the creature had shown me some other place, and then how its home had changed and how it had to run away. I explained that it showed up in Corner House by accident, but that maybe—and it was a big maybe—the rift or portal or whatever that led the beast here was still present somehow, and Keller was able to use link from that other place to heal himself. It didn't make sense to me, or her for that matter, but we understood that if there was a chance it was true, there was only one thing we could do.

We'd have to stay near Corner House.

EPILOGUE

Kathryn Taldo closed the book and looked at her husband, now nervously biting his fingernails as he stood in the middle of the kitchen.

"It's really good, Grant. Almost every page reflects your love for them."

Grant rubbed his palms together. "Yeah, that was the point. I wanted to let them have something if... you know." His voice was scratchy.

Kathryn nodded, but she wouldn't meet his eyes. "Yeah."

"Do you think they'll like it, hon?" He shifted his weight from one foot to the other, waiting.

She stood and walked to him, wrapping her arms around his frail frame. "Grant," she began but couldn't continue. She held her husband as his bony shoulders shook with the effort of crying. He was able to stand on his own for now, but only just. She supported some of his weight, and she felt tears seep out of her eyes to drop forgotten on his shirt.

She held Grant's hand, barely more than skin stretched over bone now, and walked to the living room where Jackson and Keller were curled up asleep on the couch. They sat next to one another, each cradling a boy on their lap. "They'll love it, Grant. It'll be one of the greatest treasures they could ever have. The greatest thing their dad could have done for them, all wrapped up in a tidy little book. Well, not little, I guess." She laughed and rapped her knuckles on the stack of typed papers.

She tried—unsuccessfully—to avoid looking at the *other* stack of papers nearby. The ones that detailed the test results after the house fire. The ones that Dr. Keller had to present before Grant left the hospital. The ones that showed elevated white blood cell count and several suspicious spots on his lymph nodes.

She blinked away the tears and stared around the room. The lights of the neighborhood bled into the kitchen, every surface reflecting the glow of streetlamps and stars alike with a dull, silvery light. Grant preferred the lights in the house to stay off since he'd come home from hospice the previous week. The light only amplified the mountains and valleys on his weakening body and gave him a headache almost immediately, which led to vomiting, and he couldn't handle that, not anymore after he nearly broke a rib from retching so violently.

"I do have one question, though," said Kathryn, who gently stroked Keller's straw-colored hair.

"What is it?"

"The part where you fight the ... visitor. And then after when we saw Keller reach out. I thought..." she trailed off, not really wanting to say it out loud.

He nodded weakly. "Yeah. That's the only part that isn't completely accurate. What I didn't say in the story is that includes lying to them."

She nodded, trying to understand. "So you didn't really experience those hallucinations?"

He turned to her in surprise. "Oh, I absolutely did." He swallowed and coughed. "That's what I think caused the cancer to come back so quickly. Something about the energy the visitor forced upon me. Or maybe it's that I was exposed in some weird way when I was in the Before. But that's not what I'm talking about changing a little."

"Well I know for a fact that the house burned down, and Mitch pulled you out. So what was different?"

He sat for a minute, his breath coming in short, rattling gasps. "You really want to know?"

Kathryn nodded, but her stomach churned in anticipation and uncertainty.

"I think Keller can heal me," he said plainly.

"You..."

"Think he can, at least. I'm not sure how or why, and I'm not certain how to ask him or show him what to do, but I think he can make me better. For a little while, maybe."

Kathryn sat up, hope blossoming in her chest.

"Grant if that's true, why didn't you include it in the story? Why finish the story at all? It's not done!"

He hesitated, trying to work out the gentlest way to explain it. "It's not in the story because the story *might* be complete. He *might not* be able to heal me, and I don't even want to take the chance that he would carry the weight of what *might be* considered failure through his life." He coughed, a deep hack from his chest. "I don't want to write that he could have and didn't. Now, if I ... don't make it, he's none the wiser. If I do make it because of him, then we can add another chapter."

She nodded in understanding. "That makes sense, honey. I'm not sure what I think about that, but I do know that no matter what decision you made or what you wrote, your kids and I love you no matter what. We know that you would do anything to keep us safe, and that's exactly what you did."

She was quiet for a minute, both of them enjoying the silence and the peace. "Thank you for doing what you did for the kids. I won't lie," she paused to wipe a tear away, "I'm angry. Angry that all of this is because of your job. I wish it had never happened. I wish we'd never moved here." Grant tried to reach across and comfort her, but she was just out of reach. After a moment, she quieted. "But I'm glad we went through it together."

Grant nodded and tried not to let the tickle in his throat grow into another coughing fit. Kathryn could see the effort it took, and it broke her heart into a million pieces.

Eastwind Energy, mostly Marco and to a lesser extent, Gianna, had been sad to see Grant give his notice and even sadder to hear of his new diagnosis. Despite their efforts to duplicate the initial test, the field team they sent had been unsuccessful. Grant also confronted Gianna about the "biological interference," and having nothing to lose, he was pleased to give the ultimatum that Eastwind buy Corner House out of the legal quicksand it had been mired in or he'd reveal every single detail of both his incident and the one in Castelsardo. She reluctantly agreed, and he was given a hefty severance package in addition to the deed of the house, all to keep him quiet. It was enough that Kathryn and the kids would be taken care of for a very long time should he be unable to. Marco recommended that Grant stay on as a consultant, and he let Marco know that he'd consider it.

She smiled, and they leaned in for a kiss. His lips were chapped, but she didn't care; her tears stained his shirt when they parted.

Grant stared down at the ten-year-old on his lap and stroked his cheek. It seemed like yesterday when they were moving into the neighborhood, wondering about all the

different things they'd do together, the adventures they'd have. When he met Kathryn's eyes again, there was an unfathomable sadness deep within his sunken sockets.

"When I'm gone, you'll make sure they know how much I love them, right?"

She nodded and tried not to cry, distrusting her voice. She tried to be strong for him, but she loved him too much, and he, her.

Keller stirred on Kathryn's lap, his clear nose and pink cheeks still coming as a surprise after so many months of living with the soundtrack of coughs and sneezes. The relief in the house each night was palpable. There hadn't been a nosebleed since Grant killed the visitor. They began going on daily walks, even in the rain, to the husk of Corner House. Once he'd turned three, it was as if Keller's mind had opened up like a book. He was able to communicate quickly and understood that the walks were more for him than anyone else; he knew what to do. His words were still more than a little confusing, but day by day, they were hearing the boy behind the toddler.

So they sat in the dimness of the night, stroking their sleeping children's heads and holding hands. Each of them silently prayed for one more moment as a family. They would get every one they asked for.

Even the last one.

BOOK CLUB
DISCUSSION QUESTIONS

1. What emotions were brought up around the story's "favorite child" plot?

2. If you found yourself in a situation where you would have to choose between two loved ones, what would you do?

3. How does our society treat chronically ill families? Are families treated the same based on race, socio-economic class, education level?

4. If Grant were in Mitch's situation, what would have been the outcome?

5. What's a situation where you find yourself helpless or stuck? If you're a parent, how do you teach your children to make difficult decisions?

6. When faced with impossible decisions, what is your first reaction—fight, flight, or fawn? Do you see strength or weakness in that?

7. The relationship between Grant and Kathryn grows bitter, does that seem realistic? Why or why not? Can you identify with either of their views?

8. If you suspected a loved one was hurting another—even if they weren't intending to—how would you address it?

9. Faced with the death of one of their children, Kathryn and Grant search for any answer that would help, no matter how crazy. What would you have done? What should they have done differently?

10. Is it wrong to have a favorite? Or is it a natural inclination to draw closer to those people—children or not—to which you feel a closer bond?

Bio:

Ty Carlson is a sci-fi writer who delights in the unseen strangeness and wonder of "what if." Growing up in the Ozarks of Arkansas gave him and his three siblings plenty of room to play knights and dragons or jungle explorers, igniting his imagination early on. Ty started writing at a very young age and his passion has only grown over time. He loved to read so much that he once was grounded from reading, a fact that his brothers tease him about to this day. He hopes readers discover new ways to see the world through the perspectives offered in the stories he tells.

Some of Ty's favorite reads include the classics from Fitzgerald to Tolkien to Card, and he has fallen in love with a multitude of worlds. When he's not writing, he's playing with his kids or enjoying some time in a video game. On the rare occasion, when he and his wife can get a few minutes to themselves, they enjoy listening to the sounds of the world waking up while enjoying a cup of coffee—with cream of course. His debut book is *The Bench*, which marks his first steps as a Sci-Fi author like so many he's admired (and been grounded from)!

More books from 4 Horsemen Publications

Fantasy, SciFi, & Paranormal Romance

Amanda Fasciano
Waking Up Dead
Dead Vessel

Beau Lake
The Beast Beside Me
The Beast Within Me
Taming the Beast: Novella
The Beast After Me
Charming the Beast: Novella
The Beast Like Me
An Eye for Emeralds
Swimming in Sapphires
Pining for Pearls

Chelsea Burton Dunn
By Moonlight

Danielle Orsino
Locked Out of Heaven
Thine Eyes of Mercy
From the Ashes
Kingdom Come
Fire, Ice, Acid, & Heart
A Fae is Done

J.M. Paquette
Klauden's Ring
Solyn's Body
The Inbetween
Hannah's Heart
Call Me Forth
Invite Me In
Keep Me Close

Jessica Salina
Not My Time

Kait Disney-Leugers
Antique Magic

Lyra R. Saenz
Prelude
Falsetto in the Woods: Novella
Ragtime Swing
Sonata
Song of the Sea
The Devil's Trill
Bercuese
To Heal a Songbird
Ghost March
Nocturne

www.ingramcontent.com/pod-product-compliance
Lightning Source LLC
Chambersburg PA
CBHW020522110726
47899CB00004B/1204